Alan & Jean Northeast

66 US DOLLARS

AUSTIN MACAULEY
PUBLISHERS LTD.

A CIP catalogue record for this title is available from the British Library.

ISBN 978 178455 092 9

www.austinmacauley.com

First Published (2014)
Austin Macauley Publishers Ltd.
25 Canada Square
Canary Wharf
London
E14 5LB

Printed and bound in Great Britain

Chapter One

The damp chill of a mid-December morning penetrated every corner of the drab, old-fashioned courtroom, filling it with an atmosphere of gloomy austerity in which four men sat waiting in uncomfortable silence. Two of them, smartly dressed in business suits, sat together on one side of the chamber, fidgeting impatiently in their anxiety for proceedings to commence. More casually attired in a leather jacket and open-necked shirt was a thin, wiry man sitting impassively by himself on a bench in the middle of the courtroom. His deep-set eyes stared with fixed intensity straight ahead at the unoccupied wooden dais at the head of the courtroom, and his work-calloused fingers slowly stroked the grizzled goatee beard that adorned his gaunt, sallow features. Only the young reporter at the back of the courtroom seemed at ease as he lolled back in his seat and read over some shorthand notes from a dog-eared notepad.

A door behind the dais squeaked open, and in trotted a slight, balding man with a wad of files tucked under his arm. He went over to a small desk at the side of the courtroom and stood behind it.

"All rise!" he called.

A stout, florid man marched in purposefully, followed by a severe looking middle-aged woman, and a bull-necked man with close-cropped hair. They took up their positions on the dais behind a large polished table, with the stout man in the central Chairman's seat.

"The Court is in session!" called the clerk. "The plaintiff before the tribunal in this case is Neil Geddes, a boilermaker, claiming wrongful dismissal by the defendants, Marine & General Engineering Limited on November the eighth, nineteen seventy-seven."

"Is either party legally represented?"

"No, sir."

"Proceed with the evidence, then."

The clerk's thin hand shook as he held up a document and started to read from it.

"The plaintiff claims that on the date in question he needed time off work to accompany his wife on a hospital appointment."

The two businessmen exchanged anxious glances. The younger one raised his eyebrows in an expression of amazement as the clerk continued his recital.

"He went to see Mr. Jack Durham, the yard manager, and made a request for leave of absence which was refused. The plaintiff then advised the yard manager that he still intended to take the time off, which he subsequently did. When he reported for work the next morning he was handed a written notice of dismissal by Mr. Durham, and was told to leave the premises immediately. Here is a copy of the dismissal notice for the court's perusal."

He walked over and handed the document to the woman. She rewarded his obsequious half bow with a chilling little smile of condescension, and he returned to his station. After reading the notice very slowly and carefully she passed it to the Chairman, who took even longer over the brief contents. The third member of the tribunal barely glanced at the letter before handing it back.

The Chairman stared across the courtroom at Neil Geddes who stared back stonily.

"Mr. Geddes, have you anything you wish to add to the evidence you have heard presented by the clerk?"

"No. I have nae."

"Then we shall now hear the evidence on behalf of the defendants. Is Mr. …aah …Durham in court?"

The younger businessman stood up and identified himself. A tall, well-built fellow in his late thirties, Jack Durham spoke up clearly with an air of self-confidence

"And the gentlemen with you?" enquired the Chairman.

"This is Mr. Royston Healey, our Managing Director."

"I see. Mr Durham, have either you or Mr. Healey anything you wish to say to the court?"

Jack Durham looked at his boss who indicated his go-ahead with a brief nod.

"Well," began the manager, taking an upright stance, "the evidence presented so far is not entirely accurate. Neil did ask me for the time off, but he didn't say anything about taking his wife to hospital. He just told me he wanted to take the afternoon off and I said no."

"What reason do *you* say he gave for wishing to take the afternoon off?"

"He said he was fed up with hanging around the yard all day with nothing to do."

"And was there, in fact, nothing for him to do?"

"There's always something to do in a shipyard, but things can sometimes get a bit slow at this time of the year. But that's not the point, anyway. We're on contract to provide a special emergency service repairing road tankers for the refinery. A job can come in at any time of the day, and we have to attend to it immediately."

"Is Mr. Geddes the only member of your workforce who can do this type of work?"

"He was the only one available at the time."

"So you did have other workers with the necessary skills, but were otherwise occupied on that occasion."

"Well, yes, you could say that, but…."

The Chairman leaned across and conferred in whispers with the woman at his side. The bull-necked man sat glaring balefully at the plaintiff, who in turn stared down at the floorboards.

Jack Durham felt a sudden surge of panic rise within him. He was the only person in the room who was standing, and it was making him feel extremely nervous. It had never occurred to him that the case might go against him.

"It's not the way it seems," he suddenly blurted. "He'd been badgering me for weeks to lay him off. This was just his way of getting what he wanted."

The Chairman frowned in puzzlement.

"Why on earth should he want to lose his job?" he asked.

"He said he could get more money on the dole than he was getting for a flat week with us. If he left of his own accord he'd have to wait six weeks before he'd get any unemployment benefit."

Royston Healey's bored expression gave way to a pained wince and he buried his head in his hands. The reporter at the back of the courtroom stopped raking out his ear with the end of his pencil and sat forward attentively.

"I see," said the Chairman gravely, turning his gaze on the plaintiff. "Mr. Geddes, is this the case?"

"I've already said what happened. I had tae tak' ma missus tae hospital."

"Have you any means of substantiating this?"

"Aye. Here's the hospital appointment card."

Taking a small pink card from his pocket he stood up and walked toward the Chairman. He was promptly intercepted by the clerk, relieved of the card, and waved officiously back to his seat. Having satisfied himself as to the document's authenticity, the clerk placed it reverently before the woman. There was a short silence as each member of the tribunal examined the new evidence, followed by another whispered exchange before the Chairman cleared his throat to make an announcement.

"We have examined the evidence placed before us and we shall now retire to consider the verdict. Please remain in the courtroom until we return."

"All stand," called the clerk, and everybody shuffled obediently to their feet as the tribunal members made a slow and dignified exit.

During their absence the clerk busied himself with his papers, oblivious to the continued fidgeting of the two suits across the room. Neil Geddes resumed his stoic contemplation of the wooden dais, and the reporter scratched absentmindedly at the acne on his chin. When the tribunal returned after some fifteen minutes the Chairman was carrying a portable tape recorder, which he placed ceremoniously in the centre the table.

"We have considered all the evidence," he announced, "and have prepared a recorded statement for the court. When you have heard the statement please remember that the decision of this tribunal is final, and no further discussion may take place."

The recorder was switched on, and the Chairman's voice bleated thinly from the small loudspeaker. After a lengthy preamble, the verdict was given in favour of the plaintiff. Neil Geddes was mildly admonished for the disrespect he had shown toward an official of the company that employed him, and the tape hissed on for a few seconds before the Chairman carefully pressed the stop button.

"Do you wish for reinstatement, Mr Geddes?" he asked.

"No. I've already lined up another job. I start in the New Year."

"In that case it remains only to fix the sum for compensation. For how many weeks have you been out of work?"

"It'll be six weeks on Monday."

"And how long were you employed with Marine and General?"

"Since January this year."

Another whispered conference between the Chairman and the bull-necked man followed in which there appeared to be some difference of opinion. The Chairman's face was a deeper shade of red when he turned his attention back to Neil Geddes.

"The sum is fixed as follows," he announced stiffly. "Four hundred and eighty pounds is awarded for loss of earnings, and one hundred and fifty pounds to cover the expense and inconvenience of finding new employment. Are you satisfied with this award?"

"Aye. It'll dae."

Turning to Royston Healey, the Chairman continued.

"You are directed by this Court to pay the sum of six hundred and thirty pounds within ten days. Is this absolutely clear?"

Jack Durham opened his mouth to speak, but his boss beat him to it.

"Yes, your honour."

"Very well. I declare an end to these proceedings."

The Chairman stood up to leave, but was stopped in his tracks by the harsh voice of the bull-necked man.

"Just a minute! I've got something to say, if you don't mind."

For an instant the Chairman was nonplussed by this unexpected public challenge to his authority, but conceded nonetheless.

"By all means," he muttered peevishly, mopping a moist brow as he sat down again.

The bull-necked man glared at Neil Geddes for a while before speaking, slowly and deliberately.

"Have you let your Union membership lapse?"

"I say!" protested the Chairman. "This is hardly the place to..."

"My point is relevant," interrupted his colleague, "and important."

"Well if you insist," blustered the Chairman. "You'd better carry on, I suppose."

Again the bull-necked man glared at Neil Geddes before continuing in the same harsh tone.

"I repeat. Have you let your Union membership lapse?

"Aye."

"And why is that?"

"That's ma ain business."

"Not when it involves the time and expense of a court hearing paid for out of the taxpayers' money. Far too much of the Court's time is wasted these days on fiddling little cases that could easily have been dealt with by a union official. It is precisely this sort of thing that Unions are meant to deal with. Perhaps after this little escapade you'll realise the importance of keeping up your membership. No man is an island, and you never know when you might be needing some support. I expect to see you at the very next meeting, fully reinstated with all arrears paid up."

The stunned silence that followed was eventually broken by the Chairman as he cleared his throat and spoke, somewhat sheepishly.

"Well, then, if you're quite satisfied..."

"I've said my piece," snapped the bull-necked man, standing up. He marched out and the other two tribunal members followed with as much aplomb as they could muster.

"The Court will rise," piped the clerk, despite the fact that everybody had already stood up to go.

* * * * * * * * * *

Silence prevailed as Royston Healey drove out of the city traffic back to the yard. He was normally a most forceful driver, but he seemed in no hurry on this occasion. Jack sat alongside him staring disconsolately out at the factories that lined the broad dual carriageway, his mind churning over the events of the morning. It was not until they had turned off the main road into a pleasant country lane that Jack finally spoke.

"I can't get over that bloke coming out with all that Union stuff. Who the hell was he, anyway?"

"That, my friend, was Jim Bulstrode. He's the Boilermaker's head honcho in the docks. The man has virtual power of life and death."

They drove along in silence for a while until Jack's next thought bubbled to the surface.

"If only Neil had told me he was going to take his wife to hospital, none of this would have happened."

"Oh come on, Jack!" said Royston with a cynical sidelong glance at his passenger. "Get real! Neil Geddes is not the sort of man to get involved with taking wives to hospitals."

"But the appointment card…"

"Pure coincidence. He must have thought it was his birthday when he found out his wife had been to hospital that day. It was the hand of providence, my friend. That verdict had nothing to do with any hospital appointment. Neil won the case because of Bulstrode. They are most probably mates. He used to be very active in the Union when he worked in the refinery."

"So why would he drop out?"

"Ah! That I couldn't say. He's always been a bit of a maverick. But after that little episode today I'd be very much surprised if he don't toe the party line for a while. You can see the way it all works. Bulstrode gets Colonel Blimp and the blue-rinse job in the back room and puts the arm on them. No contest! They know he could bring the whole bloody port to a standstill if he wanted. As for that weird business at the end, he was simply letting Geddes know that it was the Union that won the case, so when he got his compensation he'd damn well better get his tuchus down to Union headquarters with their cut of the winnings."

"Surely he wouldn't go to all that trouble just for one man."

"There is more joy in heaven over one sinner that repenteth…" said Royston, and without warning he turned into the car park of an old, thatched, public house. "I'm famished. You can buy me lunch!"

The pub was full of businessmen, a few of whom exchanged greetings with Royston as he made his way over to the bar followed by Jack. A large fire crackled cosily in the hearth, and Christmas decorations lent an air of festivity to the long, low room. Jack ordered lunch and the two men carried their drinks over to a small table by the fire. Royston was content to sit in silence for a while, looking around to make sure he had not missed anyone he knew, but Jack was anxious to continue their previous conversation.

"I can't say I'm looking forward to your father's reaction when he hears about this morning's turn up."

"He will do his proverbial nut," returned Royston, with a sigh. "I don't have to remind you that we've had a couple of exceptionally slow months. Having to find another six hundred and thirty quid isn't exactly going to help our cash flow. And I wouldn't go telling him that Geddes wanted to be laid off and you refused. He would not understand. In fact I'm not sure that I do."

"I wanted to hang on to him because he's the best welder I've ever known."

"He is good, I'll grant you that, but I warned you he was a handful when you took him on."

"No," said Jack, shaking his head, "everything would have been alright if we didn't have a social security system that pays a man more to stay at home and do nothing than he gets for going to work."

"How would you like to clock on at eight o'clock every morning, all year round, for the sort of money he earns in a flat week? I just don't understand why you didn't let him go, if that's what he wanted."

"I was going to use him on building the new ferry. He'd have been just the man for the job."

"Now you've really lost me!" said Royston, laughing. "If you wanted him for the ferry, what possessed you to sack him?"

Jack coloured up.

"Well you can't have people wandering in and out of the yard whenever the fancy takes them. You'd never know where you were. You have to have some sort of discipline."

"If you keep your workforce busy, and occasionally whisper the magic words 'double time' in their shell-likes, you've got all the discipline you need. What we need is another nice little tickle like those barges. Everyone did well out of that job. Even the Old Man was satisfied."

"Well, with any luck we'll be laying the keel for the ferry immediately after Christmas."

"We certainly need something," said Royston with a sigh. "There's not much going on at the factory just now, and precious little is coming out of the refinery."

A barmaid came over to the table with their lunch, and laid it out for them with an efficient bustle.

"Aha!" said Royston. "Just the job. Bring us another round, my love, and have one for yourself!"

* * * * * * * *

As soon as Royston turned the car into the yard gates both he and Jack knew something was wrong. The car park was nearly empty, and an eerie silence prevailed. Jack tried the big sliding door of the welding shop and found it locked shut. The two men started to walk down the yard to investigate and met up with the yard foreman.

"What's going on, Stan?" asked Jack.

"Oi was 'oping you moit be able to tell me!" replied the foreman, sullenly.

"Tell you? Tell you what?" snapped Royston, impatiently. "Where is everybody?"

"As if you didn't know!" muttered Stan, turning his back to walk away. The gesture of contempt was so blatant that Royston was taken aback.

"For God's sake, Stan, are you going to stop behaving like a tart and tell me what's going on or what?" wailed Royston. The foreman turned back and gave his boss a searching look.

"Well Oi'm buggered! You really don't know, do you?" Stan paused for dramatic effect. "The firm's gooin' bust, thass all."

"What on earth are you talking about?" asked Royston with a nervous laugh. "Where'd you get that from?"

"Roit from the 'orse's maith. The Ol' Man calls us all to a meetin' at dinnertoim and told us there weren't any money to pay our wages. He was rabbittin' on abait the bank and the ooverdraft. We didn't really understand wot he was on abait..."

"Hang on a minute," said Jack. "Are you telling us that the men haven't had their Christmas pay?"

"That's woi they've all garn 'oom. No point 'angin' aroun' here if we'm not getting paid."

"This doesn't make any sense," muttered Royston. "There must be some mistake."

"Well you'd best goo and ask the Ol' Man," suggested Stan. "Thass what he told us."

They found the chairman in the boardroom, shouting down the telephone. His voice rose to a crescendo as he stood up to deliver a parting salvo, followed by a string of terrible oaths before slamming down the receiver. He glared furiously up at his son over the top of his half moon spectacles.

"Fucking Unions!" he snarled. "The cretins just cannot understand that the cupboard is bare. I'm gutted and hung out to dry, yet they're still baying for more blood!" He slumped back into his seat at the head of the table. "What are you two half-wits staring at? Don't you understand? I'm ruined!"

"But why now?" Royston's voice sounded pathetically small.

"The bank refused to meet the wages cheque!" bawled his father.

"What, just like that? No warning?"

"Nope!" huffed the Old Man. "We sent the wages cheque over at ten o'clock and they refused to cash it. Sent back a message for me to contact the manager. What a moron! By the time I'd finished arguing with him it was too late to do anything else. If only there'd been more time."

"So what happens now?" asked Jack, quietly.

"The bank's putting in a receiver. We'll probably have to go into liquidation. Thirty years down the drain because of some gnome in a pinstripe with no more imagination than an amœba. If I'd wanted half a million to open up a poxy discotheque or a unisex hair salon they'd have given it to me in gold bars. But for a nasty, dirty shipyard where we waste time actually making things, no bloody chance!"

In sheer nervous frustration the Chairman sprang out of his seat and went over to the large window overlooking the yard. The sight of the empty, lifeless sheds in the gathering, early winter dusk sent a chill through his heart, and his thin shoulders slowly sagged. With a sigh he turned wearily back from the window.

"Look, Jack, you might as well cut off home now. There's nothing to be done here. Tell Mary I'm really sorry about the way things have turned out. You've done a good job in the yard. It's a shame it all has to end in such a bloody shambles."

"Maybe we're not beat yet," urged Jack. "There's always the ferry contract. They're ready to sign, and I can ask for the down payment for laying the keel. Twenty-five grand. We can pay the wages and still have enough to lay the keel in the New Year."

"Jack, we owe the bank fifty thousand, and private loans another thirty-five. Trade creditors sixty-eight thousand, Inland Revenue fifteen and the Vatman another eighteen. By the time you add the Christmas wages you're talking about the best part of two hundred thousand pounds."

"Jesus Christ!" gasped Jack in amazement.

"Royston's precious new factory!" growled the Old Man, glaring again at his son. "It's been bleeding us dry since the day we took it on. I should never have allowed myself to be talked into it. If we'd just stayed with the yard, none of this would have happened."

The Old Man took off his spectacles and rubbed the narrow bridge of his hooked nose. Placing a hand on Jack's shoulder he said:

"I appreciate your fighting spirit, Jack, but really the situation is hopeless. There's nothing you, or I, or any other bugger can do about it."

The tone of finality in his voice left no room for further discussion. In the ensuing silence, Jack became aware of a compressor clattering away in the engineering shop at the bottom of the yard, automatically pumping air into a cylinder that had started to leak nearly a month ago. He found himself making a mental note to turn it off before he left for home, and suddenly realised that it was no longer any of his business. He was out of a job.

What a way to start the New Year!

Chapter Two

With a smile on her lips, Mary stepped back from the kitchen table to view her handiwork. It was definitely the best Christmas cake she had ever made. True, the marzipan snowman was as tall as the bell tower on the marzipan church, but this added a touch of surrealism that appealed to her innate sense of fun.

The kitchen was small and equipped only with the basic necessities, but it had a warm, cosy atmosphere enhanced by little bunches of holly fastened neatly at regular intervals along the picture rail and over the doorway. There were no curtains at the window, and outside the cold night pressed black against the glass, with an easterly wind that rattled the sash from time to time. Seated at the table gazing at the cake in silent wonder was Mary's three year old daughter, a beautiful child, with expressive, blue eyes, straw blonde hair, and a quiet, old-fashioned air about her. Mary placed two pieces of home-made almond paste onto a strip of greaseproof paper and slid it wordlessly across the table. Whispering her thanks, Wendy slipped down off the chair, popped one of the prized morsels into her mouth, and carried the other off to the adjoining living room for her sister.

Susan was a slender willowy girl in her eleventh year who had also inherited Mary's good looks. She accepted her sister's offering with a loving smile, pausing only for a moment to savour the sweet almond taste before resuming her task of decorating a fine spruce tree that had been spirited out of the nearby forest before dawn that morning. Entranced by the magic of tinsel and glass baubles Wendy stayed to watch, sitting cross-legged on the carpet at a safe distance from the log fire burning steadily in a newly built brick hearth. Susan's nimble fingers worked skilfully through the delicate process, creating a pleasing harmony of light and colour against the deep, lush green of the branches. When Mary came through from the kitchen to switch on the coloured lights they all snuggled up together in the big old fireside chair to enjoy the effect, safe and warm in the security of their mutual love.

Under the hypnotic effect of the flickering firelight Mary's thoughts drifted off to her plans for the New Year, and she did not hear the sound of Jack's key in the latch of the front door, nor the sound of his heavy tread on the bare floorboards in the narrow hallway. Suddenly he was there, in the room, filling it with his hard masculinity. The soft shadows vanished as he switched on the light; it was obvious from the set of his face that his day had not gone well.

"Well, it's alright for some, I must say," he said with a bitter little laugh.

Mary felt a stab of disappointment at the unfairness of this remark, but responded with her usual equanimity.

"We were just taking a moment to admire the tree," she explained. "Susan did the decorations all on her own. It looks really good, doesn't it?"

"I guess so," his reply was abrupt and dismissive. "Listen, I need to talk to you about something important. We'd better go in the kitchen."

He led the way and in the confines of the tiny room his bulk seemed almost menacing when he closed the door behind them. Mary went straight to the stove to check the stew simmering on the hob, and gave it a stir before turning to face him.

"So! What's put you in such a delightful mood?"

He gave a great sigh and murmured:

"Look, I apologise for what I said in there. It was stupid and unfair."

She forgave him instantly and stepped across the room into his arms. After a long, silent embrace he broke away and holding her shoulders at arms' length looked deep into her eyes as he spoke again.

"I'm sorry, my love, but I've got some pretty bad news. The yard's gone bust. I'm afraid I'm out of a job."

Without a word Mary returned to the stove and stirred the stew thoughtfully for several moments before turning to face him again.

"I thought everything was supposed to be going so well," she said quietly. "You've had plenty of work coming in, haven't you?"

"Oh, the yard's been doing okay. That's not the problem. It's the new factory that has dragged us under. Apparently it's been losing money heavily ever since they started up down there. The Old Man's been using the profits from the yard to keep everything afloat, but the factory lost a fortune on that last big job in the refinery, and now the whole lot has gone kaput."

"But what about the new ferry? What's going to happen about that?"

"It'll have to be cancelled. It wouldn't have made any difference anyway. The profit would have been swallowed up by this mountain of debt. The Old Man reckons it runs to nearly two hundred thousand pounds."

Mary gave the stew another stir.

"I suppose we can say goodbye to the Christmas bonus then."

"It's worse than that, my love," replied Jack darkly. "There's no money even to pay the wages. The men have been sent home without pay. I'm afraid we'll have no money until the receiver arrives to sort out the mess."

This gloomy prognosis was received by Mary in complete silence; Jack sat down at the table, watching her small, neat figure as she went on with the preparation of dinner. When she finally spoke it was with a tone of cheerful resignation.

"So that's that, then! Well at least it gave us a start."

"I must say, you're taking it very well," observed Jack.

"Well let's see! I'm thirty-three years old, living in sin with an out of work boat builder, I've two young children to feed and clothe, we're not even half way to doing up this place, we're mortgaged up to our armpits, completely broke, and it's Christmas next week. What is there to worry about?"

Jack sat mumchance, unable to think of any further response. In their three years together she had taken every difficulty in her stride without complaint, and supported him with unquestioning loyalty. Even now, when everything they had achieved was under threat, she faced the situation with far more courage than he had any right to expect.

So," she continued, "now I've got all that off my chest we might as well get on with dinner. I don't know about you, but I'm absolutely famished. What do you think of the Christmas cake, by the way? Do you like my forty foot snowman?"

* * * * * * * * * *

As it turned out Christmas went off very well, thanks to Mary's providence and foresight. Unbeknown to Jack, she had been squirreling provisions away in her store cupboard for months, so the only outstanding item of any importance was the chicken, which had been ordered from a local farm for collection on Christmas Eve. Neatly wrapped packages appeared under the tree as if by magic, and another dawn raid in the forest produced a further abundance of holly to decorate the living room. Mary was up at six o'clock on Christmas morning to light the living room fire and make sure all her arrangements for the day were in order. She was well aware that Jack did not share her enthusiasm for the festive occasion, but was determined to do all she could to ensure he really did take advantage of the opportunity to relax and simply enjoy himself in the bosom of a loving family. As a result he passed the whole day as in a beautiful dream, and even condescended to partake in a marathon session of board games after tea.

On Boxing Day they went for a drive deep into the forest in unlawful search of firewood. The girls assisted with boundless energy and enthusiasm, gleefully carrying everything they found, from twigs no bigger than a pencil to great branches they could barely drag through the thick bed of leaves. By midday the capacious boot of Jack's old Wolseley was full, and with creaking rear springs they headed for home to sort out their ill-gotten gains. The afternoon was spent unloading the wood, cutting it all to the right size, and stacking it up against the back wall of the bungalow. As she busied herself in the kitchen, Mary could see the three of them through the window, Jack sawing and splitting whilst his young helpers bustled about him in the December twilight. It filled her gentle, loving heart with joy to see them working together with such harmony and contentment.

But as if the Gods had granted this serenely happy interlude only to enable Jack and Mary to recover enough for the next onslaught, trouble was quick to return to their abode. During the first week of the New Year Jack answered an unusually aggressive knock at the front door. In the gloom of the late afternoon he found two large men incongruously squashed into the narrow porch.

"Are you Jack Stanley Durham?"

"Yes."

"I have a writ for you, which you are obliged to accept."

Bewildered, Jack obediently took the envelope as the bailiff continued to speak.

"Sign here for my receipt please sir."

Again, Jack found himself complying automatically.

"You'll notice that the hearing date is January 25th, sir. Please get in touch with the Court as soon as possible, either direct or through a solicitor. It is unwise to let the matter drift, so it is in your own interest to act immediately. Goodbye sir."

Jack recovered enough to resist a ridiculous impulse to thank the bailiff. He watched the two men wedge themselves into a small car and drive away before he took the contents out of the envelope he was holding. Making his way slowly back to the kitchen he scanned through the documents with growing disbelief.

"What is it?" asked Mary, seeing the concern on his face.

"It appears that Her Majesty's Commissioners of Customs and Excise intend to petition for a receiving order to be made in respect of my estate. This is a writ from the High Court of Justice in Bankruptcy, no less."

"What on earth for?"

"They claim I owe over nine hundred pounds for V.A.T. in respect of Taskforce."

"Taskforce? What are you talking about?"

"It's a trading name for a business I started with a chap in Bournemouth a few years back. It all fizzled out just before you and I came together."

"What sort of business?"

"A Temp agency."

"I beg your pardon," gasped Mary, hardly able to believe her ears.

"Well, the original idea was for executive placements, specialising in accountancy and finance. Justin was working for one of the big agencies, and reckoned there was a gap in the market which we could exploit."

"And?"

"The whole thing was a complete flop. I thought he'd have a load of contacts to get us started, but he didn't. He wasn't interested in actually doing anything himself, so I ended up doing the lot on my own. Getting brochures printed, sending out direct mail shots, telephoning all round, tramping all over Bournemouth cold selling. Out of all that I finally got one assignment. Re-organising the coding of spares for a big motor dealer. By this time I was so fed up with trying to sell the service that I took the stores job myself. It was a pretty big job, and lasted for several months. I quite enjoyed it, and they offered me more work helping their chief accountant. I was working freelance all this time, and this accountant chap advised me to register for V.A.T., which I did. The biggest mistake I've ever made in my life!"

"But you must have been making good money if it was worth registering for V.A.T. What happened to it all?"

"Well, when it came to drawing up some accounts of my own, I found that what with a massive great printer's bill for the brochures, direct mailing expenses, the cost of running a car and an unbelievable telephone bill, there was very little left. All the time I was trying to get started I had no income, and borrowed from the bank against my insurance policy. They had to be paid back or they'd have cashed in the policy for half its worth."

"What about this partner? Shouldn't he have paid something towards all this?"

Jack sighed again as he was forced to recall his stupidity.

"He'd disappeared."

"Disappeared?" echoed Mary, incredulously.

"Well, yes. We sort of lost contact while I was working at the garage, and when I tried to get in touch with him I found he'd moved on. All I could find out was that he'd met this rich American woman and was living out in California."

Mary sat staring at Jack in silent amazement. Did this sort of thing actually happen in real life?

"Does all this mean we really are in financial trouble?" she asked quietly.

"No! Of course not!"

"Then what's this writ for?"

"It's just the Vat man trying it on. If I owe anything at all, it can't be more than a couple of hundred. I don't know how they've managed to arrive at a figure of nine hundred pounds. It's complete and utter nonsense."

Jack tossed the papers onto the kitchen table dismissively, but Mary saw through his false bravado in an instant. She picked up the writ and started to read it.

"I'm telling you, there's nothing to worry about," continued Jack. "We'll just tell them they've made a mistake and that'll be an end to the matter. I'll take care of it first thing in the morning."

But Jack could not have been more wrong. Having been set in motion, the wheels of justice could not be stopped, so nothing could be done until the court hearing at the end of the month. January was spent in an uneasy atmosphere of suspense, further exacerbated by the onset of freezing weather that made their primitive living conditions almost intolerable. The renovation work they had started with such joyful optimism when they bought the property was well behind schedule, and without any form of heating the two bedrooms were so bitterly cold and damp that the only solution was to move all the beds into the relative warmth and comfort of the living room. Mary and the two girls were quite prepared to make the best of the situation, but Jack found it much harder to accept such a reduction in his circumstances and made little attempt to conceal his distaste for the arrangement.

When the day for his insolvency court hearing arrived Jack tried to put on a bold face, but he did not have a shred of evidence with which to defend the claim being made against him, and his affairs were duly placed in the hands of the Official Receiver. From the very first meeting with the officer in charge of his case he was left in no doubt that he had lost all control over his life, and was henceforth owned by the receiver who would disembowel him with ritual care. Even if he were able to produce the nine hundred pounds claimed by Customs and Excise, the liability could not be discharged. His circumstances had to be painstakingly examined to ensure that he had no other debts, and furthermore he would be charged for the service. When it emerged that the bungalow was heavily mortgaged, that he was paying off a personal loan taken out to fund building renovations, and that he was heavily overdrawn at the bank, there was very little room for him to manoeuvre. Personal papers, details of all financial transactions, tax documents, even his cheque book, all had to be handed over together with an inventory of any valuable possessions. Every detail of his pathetic, bungled life was laid out before him, and he was advised that if he wanted to keep the bungalow he must find employment immediately to provide funds for the receiver. The only alternative was to file for bankruptcy and lose everything.

But finding another job was easier said than done. The demand for boatyard managers proved to be extremely limited, and having telephoned round all his industry contacts with no success, Jack realised that it could be weeks, even months, before a suitable vacancy occurred. Giving way eventually to Mary's gentle but persistent persuasion, he reluctantly agreed to sign on at the employment exchange, but his arrogant attitude at the interview with the executive placements officer did little to improve his chances in that direction. To supplement Jack's meagre unemployment benefit in the meantime, Mary put in for extra shifts at the local sports centre where she worked as a part-time swimming pool attendant. This meant the responsibility for looking after Wendy devolved on Jack, who was by no means happy to accept such a burden, particularly as he was trying to press on with the renovation work. At first his manner towards the child was grudging, sometimes even impatient, but she proved to be so well behaved and such good company that an unexpected bond of friendship started to grow. She was never far from his side, and even when he started on the removal of two unwanted chimneybreasts she insisted on being allowed to help. Undeterred by the flying soot and dust she carried the bricks one at a time out into the garden, stacking them neatly in accordance with Jack's instructions. Mary was deeply concerned when she came home from work that afternoon to find her daughter covered in grime and the skin on her tiny hands worn so smooth that the fingerprints had disappeared. Showing no concern regarding the hazards to which he had submitted his young charge, Jack dismissed Mary's objections with the callous observation that a little hardship helped to build character.

* * * * * * * *

It was towards the end of February that Jack answered the telephone one cold but sunny afternoon to receive news that sent him bursting into the kitchen. Mary had just returned from her morning shift and was seated at the table writing out her time sheet for the week.

"Oh, not in here!" she pleaded, fearing fallout from the cloud of dust that seemed to follow him everywhere.

"That was Stephen," he announced excitedly.

"Stephen?"

"On the 'phone. You know! The chap who did the design work on the ferry."

"Oh, right. What did he want?"

"He's got a client who's building a twenty-four metre tug, and he's asked Stephen if he knows anyone who can run the job. It's right up my street!"

"Jack, that's marvellous!" cried Mary.

"There is just one thing, though."

"And that is?"

"The job's in Cyprus."

Her response was swift.

"If you think you're going to troll off abroad leaving me to cope with all this you've got another think coming!"

"You and the kids go too."

Mary's heart skipped a beat. Words failed her.

"We haven't discussed any details yet," continued Jack, his voice strangled with excitement. "They just want to know at this stage if we would be interested, and of course I said we were. I've arranged for us all to meet tomorrow lunch time when you finish your shift. This is it, my love! Our troubles are over!"

He burst into song with, 'Let the good times roll' and started to prance around the kitchen in a gangling dance of triumph. Mary sat watching the dust fall from his overalls onto her clean floor and just smiled.

* * * * * * * *

The recreation centre where Mary worked typified the latest style of leisure complex, and had a comfortable licensed bar that provided an ideal venue for the meeting. She was still on pool duty when Jack arrived on his own, a little ahead of the appointed time, so he bought himself a pint of Guinness and made his way across the crowded bar to an unoccupied table near the wide, picture window overlooking the main sports hall. Girls from the local sixth form college had just started a game of netball, and his attention was particularly drawn to a leggy blonde who appeared to be one of the team captains. He became so engrossed in watching her that he was startled when a large hand gripped his shoulder, and a familiar, cultured voice whispered in his ear.

"You dirty old man. What would Mary say?"

"Stephen!" Jack's colour rose as he tried in vain to think of a witty response. "I was just…"

"Of course you were. But if you could just tear yourself away from your sporting interests for a minute or two I'd like you to meet my good friend and valued client, Mr Frank Palmer, Chairman of Medmarine Limited."

With a firm handshake, bold eye contact and a waft of expensive cologne, Frank Palmer was an imposing figure of heavy build, just short of six foot in height. In his early forties, he had an easy going, almost negligent air of confidence that bespoke success in life, but it was his unconventional style of dress that made the greatest impression on Jack as he took in the pale blue safari jacket, worn over neatly pressed trousers of light khaki finishing in suede desert boots. The lapels of his open necked silk shirt were turned down neatly outside the jacket, giving him more the appearance of a big game hunter than that of a shipping tycoon.

Having effected the necessary introductions, Stephen went over to the bar, leaving the two men to become acquainted.

"I'm sure we've met before somewhere, haven't we?" asked Jack

"Could be. I meet a lot of people in the course of business." Frank Palmer was quietly spoken, with a friendly, engaging manner. "I bought a ship in Portsmouth last year, so I was in the area quite a bit. Maybe it was then."

"Ah yes, that's it. The 'Seahorse'. She was in Thorney's for a refit, wasn't she? Where is she now?"

"Up in Aberdeen. She's on contract as a supply ship for the oil rigs."

Their conversation was cut short by the arrival of Mary, still dressed in the snugly fitting white polo shirt and short pleated sports skirt she wore for work. The outfit suited her slender figure to perfection, and Jack noticed a light of keen appreciation in Frank Palmer's eyes when he rose to greet her. As Stephen was still standing at the bar waiting to be served, Jack went over to add Mary's drink to the order.

"Fresh orange juice for Mary. No ice."

"Righty-ho!" Stephen turned to give her a wave of greeting. "She certainly seems to be hitting it off with his nibs. That's quite a woman you've got there, Durham. I can't think what she sees in you. Have you any idea how lucky you are?"

"Yeah, she's doing okay." With a satisfied smile, Jack surreptitiously watched her reflection in the mirror behind the bar. "She seems pretty keen on the idea, as it happens."

"Let's hope so, because the job's yours for the taking, Jack. He said as much on the way over. Christ almighty! What does a chap have to do to get a drink in this place?"

As soon as they returned to the table Frank Palmer proceeded straight away to business.

"So, you're interested in this Cyprus caper, huh? How much do you know about the situation out there?"

"Not much, I'm afraid," confessed Jack. "Of course we know about the troubles, and the Turkish invasion, but not a lot about what's happened since then."

"Right, so you know the island is split in two, with the Turks in the North and the Greeks in the South. I'm only interested in the Turkish sector: that's where the real action is. It's still under an international trade embargo, but over the past year or so things have started to pick up a bit, especially with some of the Arab countries like the Lebanon. So anyway, the main Turkish Cypriot port is Famagusta. It's got good berthing facilities but they can't handle heavy tonnage because they haven't got a proper harbour tug. That's where we come in. I've set up a new company that will operate on a joint venture basis with the Famagusta shipyard, and we're going to build a new tug for the port authority. Nothing like it has ever been done in Cyprus before. When the tug's finished we've got another project lined up to build a floating crane for the port of Alexandria. Stephen's already completed the design work, so all we need now is someone to run the show."

Frank Palmer paused to take a sip from his drink and Jack, hoping to sound worldly, asked:

"Isn't it a bit risky getting involved with something like this while the political situation is so dodgy? It occurs to me the Greeks'll want to get their own back some time."

"Of course there are risks. But they're worth taking to get in at the beginning, ahead of the competition. As for the Greeks getting their own back, you can forget it. There's no comparison between the military strength of Turkey and Greece, and you have to remember that Cyprus is only fifty miles from the Turkish mainland, so it's a lot easier for them to land troops. Not only have the Greeks got a smaller army, but they're also hundreds of miles further away."

He paused again and looked across at Mary.

"I hope all this talk of war doesn't put you off, my dear. But I do want to give you a true picture, you know, warts and all."

Mary shrugged her shoulders and replied:

"Politics are unavoidable, I suppose, but I'm more concerned about living conditions. You know, ordinary things like shopping, schools, health care."

With a reassuring smile Frank Palmer leaned forward in his seat and explained that the company would take care of everything. The package included first class family accommodation and private education for the children at the Armed Forces school in Dekelya. A Range Rover would be allocated for their own personal use, and there would be two weeks home leave every six months with expenses paid for the whole family. He went on to promise that on completion of the tug Jack would be offered a directorship and share options. Half his remuneration would be paid in Turkish lira by the Famagusta shipyard, with the remainder to be paid tax-free in Sterling. The family would be able to live in comparative luxury on the Turkish lira, without touching any of the Sterling. Mary realised that their finances could be back on an even keel within a year, perhaps even sooner.

The interview progressed in the same easy, informal atmosphere as Frank Palmer outlined the way he intended to set up the shipyard operation. Half a dozen skilled British craftsmen would be recruited to form the nucleus of the workforce, supported by the existing Cypriot yard hands all under the direction of Jack. Administration would be handled by the Famagusta Navigation Company, which would also take care of any dealings with the Turkish Cypriot government that might arise. Mary listened thoughtfully as the three men chattered on. She could tell that Jack had already made up his mind, but she was yet to be convinced about the wisdom of taking her children off to a foreign land about which she knew absolutely nothing? It was all happening a little too fast for comfort.

Her silence was eventually noticed by Frank Palmer who once again turned to give her his full attention.

"I'm pretty sure that Jack is hot to trot, but how about you, Mary? What do you make of it all?"

"Oh I agree that Jack would be in his element. The job is right up his street. But it's such a huge step to be taking, especially with two young children."

"I can understand your reservations about making this sort of move," replied Frank Palmer. "I'm sure there will be a hundred and one questions you will want answered, so here's what I'm prepared to do. I have to go over to Cyprus during the next week or so, and I suggest you both come with me for a long weekend so you can see everything for yourself. I'll pay all expenses, of course, but it will have to be just the two of you. I take it you can make arrangements for someone to look after the children for a couple of days."

"Yes, of course," replied Mary. "That would be marvellous. Thank you."

"Well, this project is pretty crucial for the Group's activities in the Middle East, so I want to make sure you both know exactly what to expect. I take it your passports are both in order."

"I've never had a passport," replied Mary. "I've never been abroad before."

"Not to worry. You can get a temporary passport at the post office. Give my secretary a ring when you've got it, and she'll sort out the travel arrangements. Now if there's nothing else, I really do have to make tracks. I've got to get back to London for a dinner at the Mansion House. No rest for the wicked, Eh? And don't worry, Mary. You're all going to love it out there, I promise you."

* * * * * * * *

On the appointed day the two girls were dropped off with relatives in Basingstoke en route to Heathrow airport where Frank Palmer met them at the baggage check-in. Again he was most charming, and kept up a steady stream of light-hearted conversation as they took coffee in the departure lounge waiting for the Istanbul flight to be called. They were flying economy class with Turkish airlines, and boarding the aircraft was a frantic scrum amidst hoards of perfumed and perspiring Turks all trying to push their way to the front, but Frank Palmer managed to obtain three seats together, with Mary next to the window and Jack in the middle. Several minor altercations took place between large Turkish ladies competing for locker space in which to stow their great bales of hand luggage, but when order was finally established an eerie silence spread throughout the passenger compartment as anxious fingers worked nervously along strings of prayer beads in a last minute bid to appease the Almighty.

Shortly after take-off a meal was served, and the two men fell to with hearty appetites while Mary pushed the unidentifiable grey lumps around the plastic tray. When everything had been cleared away Frank Palmer took a shipping magazine out of his briefcase and handed it to Jack, directing his attention to a particular photograph inside. It depicted Frank Palmer himself on the deck of a small ship with a group of smiling, bearded men whose nautical appearance identified them as members of the crew.

"Taken on my little survey vessel last year when she was working up in the Baltic."

"Very nice," replied Jack. "Have you owned her long?"

"Oh, it must be four or five years now. Yeah, she joined the fleet in seventy-three. Trouble is, good survey contracts are getting a bit hard to come by these days. Too many ships chasing too little work. I've been tempted to let her go of late, but with an operational base in Cyprus it might pay me to convert her to a passenger vessel and set up a service between Famagusta and the Lebanon, or even Latakia. She could be fitted out with a nice little duty-free shop; the Arabs would go for that in a big way. What do you think?"

"D'you mean you'd want to do the refit in Famagusta?".

"That's the general idea. You could to take care of that, couldn't you?"

"If there's enough skilled labour, yes. But surely we'll have enough on our plate building a tug and a floating crane – to begin with, anyway."

"Oh, I shouldn't worry too much about the labour situation. I can always send men out from the UK. There's plenty who'd jump at the chance."

"We wouldn't have any problem getting work permits then?"

Frank Palmer appeared to be amused by Jack's concern over such a trifle.

"Not if you know the right people, and we've got Osman Toprak on our side."

"I don't think you've mentioned him before. What does he do?"

"It'd be easier to tell you what he doesn't do. He's probably the most successful businessman in Northern Cyprus, and he's got extensive interests in the UK as well. He lives on the island most of the time, but he's also got a flat in Chelsea, overlooking the river. They have a beautiful house not far from Kyrenia, and he runs things from an office in Nicosia. He knows everyone of any importance, right up to President Denktas himself. He's on the board of a dozen companies, including Famagusta Navigation. His wife can trace her ancestry right back to the time of the Crusades, and there's even some sort of connection high up in the Mosque. I've been dealing with him for several years now, and it never ceases to amaze me how much power and influence that man has on the island."

"So how much does he know about ship building?" asked Jack bluntly.

"Fortunately, very little," replied Frank Palmer with a chuckle. "His involvement is strictly arm's length. You won't have much to do with him yourself, but if we do need any wheels oiled, he's the man with the oilcan – metaphorically speaking, that is. Anyway you'll be meeting him yourself soon enough – he'll probably be at the airport when we reach Cyprus."

* * * * * * * *

They arrived at Istanbul airport shortly after seven, local time, but the connecting flight was so badly delayed that it was nearly midnight by the time they disembarked at Ercan airport and made their way on foot across the tarmac to a small, new looking terminal building. Once they were through immigration control Frank Palmer started to look around the hall for Osman Toprak, but it was not until they had collected their luggage that the Cypriot finally appeared. He was a man approaching middle-age, short, stout and balding. His suit was from Saville Row, his monogrammed shirt was beautifully tailored in silk, and his Italian handmade shoes gleamed in the bright fluorescent light of the baggage hall.

"We'll soon have you through customs," he announced, in perfect English. "I have arranged special clearance for you all. Would anyone like something to drink? We can use the VIP lounge."

"I think we'd rather go straight to the hotel, Osman," said Frank Palmer. "It's been a long day, and we're all very tired."

"Of course," replied Osman Toprak, smiling at Mary. "I have a taxi waiting for you. The boy can bring your luggage. This way, everybody."

He snapped his fingers and a porter appeared instantly with a trolley. To Mary's surprise Osman Toprak took hold of her elbow as if they were old friends, and proceeded to steer her towards the exit. Jack followed behind with Frank Palmer.

"So, what do you think of our fine new airport?" asked Osman Toprak as they walked slowly along.

"I'm afraid I am no authority," replied Mary. "This is the first time I've ever flown."

"All this has been a great achievement for us," he continued, proudly sweeping his short arm round in a proprietary gesture. "The main airport for the island is south of Nicosia on the Greek side. We could not hope to survive without good airport facilities, so we decided to go ahead with this fine new building."

Were it not for Frank Palmer's timely intervention, Mary stood in danger of being dragged off for a guided tour of the airport facilities. Despite the lateness of the hour, Osman Toprak seemed reluctant to allow the travellers to be on their way, and even after Jack and Mary had sunk into the luxurious upholstery of a waiting Mercedes limousine, Frank Palmer was kept talking on the pavement outside. Mary watched them both, intrigued by the contrast between the Cypriot's busy, officious manner and the casual, almost languid demeanour of the Englishman. At length he climbed into the front passenger seat of the car and turned round to apologise for Osman Toprak's lack of consideration.

"It's business, business all the time with him. He never stops. He'd keep us up all night if he had his way. He certainly seems to have taken to you, Mary. I should warn you, he can be a bit of a ladies' man, given half a chance. But anyway, we haven't got far to go now. An hour at most."

Very little of the countryside could be made out as they sped through the night along the wide, straight road to Famagusta. After about half an hour they turned off the main road and passed through one or two poor looking villages with small flat-roofed houses built right to the edge of the narrow streets. Snuggled up against Jack in the back seat, Mary felt a thrill of anticipation when Frank Palmer announced that they were just coming up to their final destination, for it was the first time in her life that she had ever stayed in an hotel. The car swept up a long drive lined with palm trees to stop in a discretely lit paved courtyard bounded on two sides by the long, low hotel building. They entered a magnificent, spacious lobby furnished elegantly in colonial style to a standard of luxury that drew instant admiration from both Jack and Mary. Everywhere was ablaze with light, but there was no sign of any staff.

"Not bad, eh?" remarked Frank Palmer with casual pride. "It belongs to Kaplan, a friend of mine. He's a Cypriot by birth, but he's lived most of his life in England. He runs a high-class restaurant in London just across the road from my offices. His sister and her husband keep an eye on things while he's away, but at this time of the year there's not a whole lot for them to do. In fact I wouldn't mind betting we're the only guests here tonight."

So saying, he struck a bell on the reception desk, and called out 'Shop!' This prompted the appearance of a powerful looking man in his mid forties, with close cropped wiry, grey hair. He was casually dressed, with baggy trousers, sandals, and shirtsleeves rolled up over the strong brown arms of a working man.

"Suleyman!" cried Frank Palmer cheerily. "It's good to see you again."

From the surly expression on the Cypriot's weather beaten face he did not appear to share in his guest's delight at meeting again. He rubbed the grey stubble on his chin and said:

"Hello Frank. You are too much late. I get fed up waiting for you."

"Yes, I'm sorry about that, old friend, but it couldn't be helped. We ran into all the usual delays I'm afraid."

"Kaplan not with you?"

"No. I think he's coming over with the family in a week or so. Why, are there any problems?"

"Always problems. I get fed up."

Suleyman made short work of the registration formalities and escorted them up a wide, oak staircase to their rooms on the first floor. The spacious opulence of the accommodation was a source of silent wonder for Mary as she made her tour of inspection, especially when she discovered the French doors behind a pair of heavy brocade curtains, and opened them to hear the sound of waves gently washing a beach somewhere in the darkness below. She stepped out onto a small balcony where she was soon joined by Jack.

"So what do you think of it so far?" he whispered, slipping his arm round her waist.

"I think I know how Alice must have felt in Wonderland."

"What d'you make of Frank Palmer, though?"

"Well, he's certainly not stingy. This room must be costing him a fortune."

"So you're happy for me to take the job then?"

"Oh, give me a chance, Jack. We've only just arrived. Let's just wait and see, shall we?"

"Just as long as you know I really want this job. It's the chance of a lifetime. I know it is."

"We've got to think about what's best for the girls as well as for us, Jack. I don't want Susan's education to suffer."

"I don't understand what you're worried about. They'll have the time of their life out here. Think of the experience they'll be getting. And if the Army school doesn't work out we can always pack 'em off to a boarding school in England. We could afford it, on the money I'll be getting."

"I'm not packing my children off to any boarding schools!" cried Mary. "How could you think I'd do such a thing? I didn't have children just to hand them over for strangers to bring up. I love them and I want them with me all the time. Surely you feel some affection for them, don't you? They both think the world of you. Sometimes I just don't understand you at all."

"Look, I don't want to get into a big debate at this time of night." He took his arm away from her waist and sighed. "It's been a long day, so perhaps we should discuss it all in the morning, when you're not so tired."

"I'm not the least bit tired," she retorted sharply. "I intend to make the most of all this. You go to bed if you want. I'm going to stay out here and listen to the waves."

With another sigh, Jack went back into the bedroom, leaving Mary to commune with the night. Beneath a heavily clouded sky the darkness that enveloped her was filled with the mystical sound and smell of the sea. Far offshore, the lights of a ship pricked a row of tiny holes in the thick blackness, and Mary felt somehow reassured by the sight. Below her, under the balcony, she could hear some small nocturnal animal rustling about in a flowerbed, and again she had a sense of fellowship with the unseen creature sharing her vigil. As she sat huddled up in a wicker chair, she pictured the girls sleeping safely thousands of miles away in England. It was the first time she had ever been apart from them for more than a few hours, and she was already missing their bright laughter and winning ways. She was at a loss to understand why Jack had not come to love them as a father, especially as they both adored him, but his callous remark about sending Susan away to school clearly showed the true state of his feelings towards the child. Turning the problem over and over in her mind but finding no solution, Mary stayed out on the balcony well into the small hours, until the encroaching chill of night drove her inside to seek the warmth of her bed. Even then she lay awake listening to the sound of Jack's heavy breathing as he slept there beside her, so close, and yet so far.

Chapter Three

It was the slow, rhythmic sound of the waves that first coaxed Mary from her deep slumber to find herself quite alone in the bed. The morning light filtered gently through the slatted shutters, suffusing the room with a soft, golden glow of dreamy languor from which she was in no hurry to emerge. Lying there in a blissful state of drowsiness, she listened contentedly to the soothing rhythm of the sea washing over sand, letting the time slip by in a way that would have been unthinkable at home in England. Through half closed eyelids she watched a small green lizard dart out from behind a watercolour of some ancient ruins, pause for a few seconds to flick out its tongue, and continue onwards in a gravity defying dash across the wall to disappear out of the window. Seeing the busy little creature going about its daily business cleared the last remnants of sleep from Mary's mind, but still she lay motionless, drinking in the freedom of this rare and precious moment of self-indulgence. Her gaze travelled slowly around the room, taking in every detail until finally coming to rest on the closed shutters, drawn there by an instinctive curiosity as to what lay out there in the sun. With a sudden burst of energy she sprang from the bed and padded barefoot across the thick Turkish carpet to the window.

Stepping out onto the sun-drenched balcony, Mary stood blinking in wonder at the sight before her. Under the dazzling canopy of a cloudless sky, an endless expanse of sparkling blue sea stretched away to the impenetrable purple horizon. In an atmosphere of complete tranquillity the only sounds to be heard were the rustling of palm leaves caressed by the morning breeze and the gentle surge of the surf on the deserted beach below. Every fibre of her being rejoiced as she filled her lungs with the sweet, pure, morning air. Eyes closed, she lifted her smiling face to the sun in silent rapture, soaking up the warmth cascading down over her body, and surrendering heart and soul to the pleasure of the moment.

Mary dragged herself away from the splendour of the view to luxuriate in the foaming, rose scented waters of her bath, contemplating her life thus far. She recalled the previous week, standing in the freezing rain, 9 o'clock at night, mixing concrete for the garage base. The bungalow and all it's problems now seemed so far away; a different world in fact. But she knew if this new opportunity worked out for Jack all their money problems would be solved.

Whilst drying herself, a new idea flashed into her mind. Quickly wrapping the towel around her she hurried out into the bedroom, sat down at the desk, took out a sheet of notepaper and urgently commenced writing.

Journal Entry
Saturday 15th March 1978

My senses were so overwhelmed by waking up in this haven of loveliness; I must keep this memory alive forever. What an adventure for my first foray into the unknown territory that is abroad! My mission, (as I have chosen to accept it), is to write up a regular journal of the thrills and spills I stumble upon as I journey along this wonderful experience of Mediterranean living.

What a task I have set myself expressing my thoughts through words!

That unreal feeling of waking to the sounds of the sea, the image in my mind's eye of the waves breaking over the sand and dragging back those tiny grains into the ocean as if my time on this earth has been pinpointed by this event. The wonder of where I am – actually on this beautiful island of Cyprus, in a picture book hotel overlooking the beach. Lying there, alone in bed, it was almost as if I was afraid to open the balcony shutters and reveal the view and end that moment of anticipation. No going back to my own images whirling around in my mind's eye, anticipation gone – so be it – I had to see the wonder awaiting me – almost afraid to awaken the senses within me for fear of what I shall unleash. Had I actually arrived in heaven? Then it was done. Bathed in warm, sensuous, sunshine soaking me like a soothing shower, Oh joy of life giving rays as I looked out onto the vast expanse of sparkling blue – no not blue, blue is too ordinary – lapis lazuli ocean, reflecting the infinite azure sky and leaving me breathless. The air so clean and fresh I couldn't seem to breathe enough of it into my lungs,

Revitalised, energised and changed forever. To think, 33 years old, first visit to a foreign land and it could not be more wonderful.

(Just look at me – writing like a schoolgirl on her first date!! Well it is a long way from north London and no mistake!)

But as I stood looking out over the sea, that moment had such a moving effect on me – almost a new me – like being in love for the first time. It's true, you see reality through rose-tinted spectacles and the world looks and feels a finer place. I wonder how long it will last!

* * * * *

Jack's own experience of these beautiful surroundings was somewhat less spiritual. He had risen at dawn to start the day with an early morning swim in the sea, but finding the water rather too cold for his liking he took an early breakfast instead, followed by a walk along the beach. On his return he found Frank Palmer looking down into the vast abyss of an empty swimming pool, which, unlike the rest of the hotel was in a very bad state of repair.

"Morning, Frank. Bit of a mess, isn't it?"

"I'm afraid it is. It hasn't been used since the troubles. Kaplan has asked me if I can get it repaired, and I said I'd see what we can do. Do you know anything about swimming pools, Jack?"

"Afraid not. I wouldn't know where to start."

"It's probably not as bad as it looks. What d'you think? Shall we have a go?"

"Well, I suppose we could," replied Jack tentatively. "Replacing the hand rails and ladders should be straightforward enough."

"I'm sure there's nothing to it," insisted Frank Palmer with breezy optimism. "It's a salt water pool, so I guess you just have to pump the water up from the sea."

"From the look of it I shouldn't think it would hold water. There must be hundreds of tiles missing, and I don't like the look of those cracks up at the shallow end."

"All the same, I think it would be a feather in our cap if we could pull it off. It would be great PR. Let's talk about it over breakfast, and then we'll have to get going. I've laid on a pretty tight schedule for today – there's a lot I want you to see."

"I've already had breakfast. About an hour ago."

"Well, I must have a quick bite before we set off, so if Mary's ready I'll meet you both in the lobby, say in half an hour."

They set off in a taxi for Famagusta just after nine o'clock, by which time the day had already become quite warm. Frank Palmer, sitting in the front passenger seat, skewed round to face Jack and Mary in the back.

"We'll go to the shipyard first, then a quick visit to Famagusta Navigation. After that we're off to Kyrenia for lunch with Osman Toprak on his boat. How's your room, by the way? I trust you both slept well."

"It's a beautiful room," replied Mary. "I loved waking up to the sound of the sea."

"D'you think you'd be okay living there for a while, until we get you all settled into something more permanent?"

"I dare say I could get used to it."

As they approached Famagusta the road ran alongside a massive old city wall, still badly pock-marked from heavy machine gun fire and shell damage. Instead of entering the city through the main gate, the driver followed a road running round the outside of the wall until the harbour suddenly came into view and they pulled up outside a wide pair of iron gates.

"So, this is it," announced Frank Palmer proudly. "The Famagusta shipyard!"

"Oh, this is amazing!" exclaimed Jack, his face aglow with excitement. "What a location! And look at all the room we've got! We can really make something of this."

From the gateway ran a wide concrete service road flanked on one side by a row of well-built brick workshops. Between the service road and the water's edge a vast area of scrubland had already been cleared for development, and over on the far side there was a slipway with a large wooden fishing vessel on the cradle.

"Well it doesn't really look much at the moment," said Frank Palmer. "But it shouldn't be too big a job to smarten it up a bit. It's all British built, of course, and you'll find some of the workshops are still quite well equipped. We'll get Faruk to go round with us. He's a sort of *major domo* installed by Famagusta Navigation to look after the day to day admin; very useful chap. You can use him as a sort of 'gofer'. He knows the ropes here and speaks very good English. I think he was once some sort of minor official in the British Administration."

They entered the yard and made their way across to the main office just inside the gates. An old man sitting on a rickety wooden chair outside the entrance door sprang to his feet and attempted what he believed to be a military salute, but as he possessed only one tooth and sported two days growth of beard the effect was almost comic. Once inside the building they could see very little at first as all the shutters were closed. There was an odour, not altogether unpleasant, in which traces of disinfectant and polish could be detected. They were standing in a long, narrow passage with a polished quarry tile floor and gloss painted brick walls. From a door at the far end emerged a corpulent middle-aged man dressed all in khaki. Gold teeth glinted as he smiled to greet the visitors.

"Good morning, Frank. It is very good to see you again." The man's small, black eyes turned to Jack. "I am Faruk Kurnaz, and am always at your service Mister Durham."

"Please call me Jack. This is my wife, Mary."

"I am most honoured to meet you madam. We do not get visits from many English ladies in our establishment."

"Well, it certainly smells nice and clean."

The gold teeth gleamed again.

"We aim to please, and I am always at your service, madam. Please, allow me to show you the rest of the accommodation."

Faruk ushered them into a large room at the front of the building and opened the wooden shutters to admit a blaze of light. There were two heavy old mahogany desks, each with a comfortable wooden manager's chair, and a row of steel filing cabinets, all left behind by the long departed British administration. Three cheaply upholstered utility armchairs arranged round a low coffee table were a more recent addition. The same smell of polish and disinfectant prevailed, from which it was obvious that some considerable pains had recently been taken in anticipation of their visit.

"This will be your headquarters, Mister Durham – excuse me – Mister Jack. The window looks over the entire yard as you can see. There is also a fine view across the harbour. I am sure you will be most comfortable here."

"I shan't be spending much time inside an office, Faruk," replied Jack. "I shall be out there in the thick of it."

Again the auric smile flashed.

"Ah yes, The British Way. It will be very good, working with the British again. We were all very sorry when you had to leave. Things have never been the same since. But come! Let me order you some refreshments. We can offer tea, soft drinks, or of course, Turkish coffee."

"Thanks, Faruk," replied Frank Palmer, "but I think we'd better see the rest of the yard first. We've a lot to get through today."

"Of course. Business first. The British Way. Very good!"

The tour of the yard consisted of little more than a quick look into each of the workshops and a cursory inspection of the slipway, but it was enough for Jack to satisfy himself that all the necessary facilities were in place before they made their way to the offices of the Famagusta Navigation Company, situated in a large, ugly, flat roofed building about half a mile away. Inside they climbed a broad, marble staircase to the first floor office of Mehmet Boga, the General Manager, and were ushered into the great man's presence by an obsequious clerk. Behind an enormous desk sat a bulky, middle-aged man with no neck and a small Hitlerian moustache. He rose majestically to greet his visitors in turn with a limp, moist handshake that was completely at odds with his severe appearance and loud, resonant voice.

"So, Jack," boomed the General Manager once they were all seated, "you are going to put our little shipyard on the map."

"With your invaluable assistance, I hope." Jack's unpractised attempt at diplomacy sounded somewhat trite, but the Cypriot nevertheless inclined his head in response.

"Our humble resources are entirely at your disposal. Anything you need, you have only to ask."

"That's right," put in Frank Palmer leaning forward in his seat. "Mehmet has kindly agreed to look after you personally. We're really lucky to have him on the team."

"Come, come, Frank! You will embarrass me with such high praise. If I can be of service I shall be the happiest of men. We are most grateful to have the benefit of your technical expertise Jack, and I shall make it my personal responsibility to see that you are not bothered with unimportant administrative matters. You can rely on me and my staff to give you all the support you need. Perhaps you would like to meet some of them now?"

"That'll have to be some other time, Mehmet," replied Frank Palmer. "We can't stop too long today, and I do need to talk to you about those engine spares you asked me to order. I'm afraid we've run into a bit of a problem regarding the bearing sizes."

As the two captains of industry entered into their discussion Jack was drawn in as a matter of course, and once again Mary found herself in the fascinating position of a fly on the wall. As she listened to their conversation it seemed to her that a great deal of time was wasted in male posturing, with each striving for a position of dominance convinced that his own contribution was the most valuable. It was her first insight into the world of office politics, and something deep inside her recoiled instinctively from its destructive power.

It was nearly two o'clock when they left Mehmet Boga's office to rejoin their waiting taxi. The afternoon temperature had risen to such an extent that it was necessary to have all the windows open, and responding enthusiastically to Frank Palmer's request for a speedy journey to Kyrenia, the driver propelled the vehicle westwards flat-out along the wide, straight road, making conversation virtually impossible. Overtaking was carried out with complete disregard for oncoming traffic, putting them all in constant danger of a head on collision.

"I do apologise for this man's driving," shouted Frank Palmer above the wind and engine noise after they had squeezed into a particularly improbable gap between two lorries. "This is the way they all drive out here. You'll soon get used to it."

"I'm quite enjoying it," returned Mary with a smile. "It's like being in some sort of adventure movie. None of it seems real."

"I know what you mean, but the best is yet to come. Wait 'till you see Kyrenia!"

Once through the Beshparmak Mountains the road took on an altogether different character as they drove through pleasant suburbs, where elegant villas stood in spacious, well-maintained gardens exuding an aura of comfort and prosperity. On reaching the town centre the taxi crawled slowly through the busy narrow streets, and Mary had plenty of time to notice all the stylish little boutiques and restaurants. But only when they emerged abruptly onto the wide harbour promenade was the true enchantment of Kyrenia revealed. She gazed in wonder at the elegant sweep of the quayside out towards the harbour entrance where the towering might of the great medieval castle dominated the eastern skyline. Small pleasure craft and brightly painted fishing boats bobbed on their moorings all along the waterfront, from which arose a gentle orchestration of creaking warps and tinkling rigging. A wide road separated the broad, cobbled quayside from a colourful terrace of old harbourside buildings, many of which housed a restaurant or bar on the ground floor. Nimble waiters flitted hazardously across the traffic, bearing trays of food and drink to the crowded tables along the esplanade from which the sound of ice cubes chinking in tall glasses, the clatter of cutlery on plate and the murmur of conversation gave promise of the epicurean delights about to be enjoyed.

"Girne!" shouted the driver, startling Mary out of her trance, "çok, çok güzel!"

"What's that he's saying?" asked Jack.

"I'm afraid I can't help you there," replied Frank Palmer. "Girne is their word for Kyrenia, but as for the rest, I've no idea."

"He's probably saying how beautiful it all is," murmured Mary.

"Evet!" agreed the driver, grinning delightedly over his shoulder at Mary. "Iss beauty, innit?"

On turning his attention back to the road ahead the driver was obliged to brake violently in order to avoid hitting a waiter running across the road with a tray of drinks, whereupon a heated exchange inevitably followed in which each impugned the ancestry of the other. Frank Palmer seemed unaccountably irritated by the incident, and there was an edge to his tone when he urged the driver to find a parking place close to Osman Toprak's mooring. This done, the driver turned again to smile at Mary, whose intuitive grasp of Turkish had marked her for distinction.

"Osman Toprak boat. Iss beauty, innit?"

The craft to which he referred was a smart looking modern motor cruiser moored stern on to the quayside. Osman Toprak trotted busily down the gangplank to greet his visitors, but the expression on his round, glabrous face clearly showed his annoyance.

"I was beginning to think you had forgotten our appointment," he complained. "I have not even had any lunch. I always have a nice lunch on Saturday. It is the only time I ever get to myself. It is too late to eat on the boat, so we will have to make do with Birol's. He is married to my cousin and will do the best he can, I suppose."

Having rapped out some instructions to the taxi driver, Osman Toprak led the party a short walk along the quay to a group of tables opposite one of the better looking restaurants. It was, in fact, his usual Saturday haunt, and the small group of waiters observing their arrival from inside the restaurant held an urgent, whispered debate as to which would have the dubious honour of attending the party. They all knew that only blood, sweat and tears could be expected of any encounter with Osman Toprak, particularly when he was entertaining guests. Finally, the youngest was bullied into submission, and he reluctantly crossed the traffic to face his ordeal.

"My guests are important visitors from England," announced Osman Toprak in English to the hapless waiter. "Tell Birol bey I want nothing but the best! Mary, what would you like to eat?"

"Nothing with more than four legs, if you don't mind. I quite like lamb, if there is any."

"The lamb here is very good, and I can recommend the şaslik. Shish kebab in English. In fact we'll all have şaslik. Is everybody agreed?"

Without waiting for a reply, Osman Toprak turned to the waiter and spoke rapidly in Turkish, emphasising certain commands by stabbing a well manicured forefinger at the young man's notepad. The drinks arrived first, carried by two of the other waiters who had relented in a spirit of solidarity. A fine selection of meze kept them all busy until the arrival of the kebabs, sizzling on the hotplate and smelling most appetising to Mary who had eaten practically nothing since leaving England the day before. As the meal reached its leisurely conclusion over coffee Osman Toprak decided it was time to mount a discreet charm offensive on Mary, whose heart and mind he felt sure was yet to be fully won.

"So Mary, my dear, what did you think of the meal? I trust the lamb was to your liking."

Again he gave no opportunity for a reply before continuing with his solicitations. "You will find the cost of living here in Cyprus extremely reasonable. Less than half the cost in England I should think. And there is a very good market in Magusa where you can buy everything fresh. There's nothing better than getting your fruit and vegetables fresh from a market stall, don't you think?"

"Yes," agreed Mary, wondering with some amusement when Osman Toprak last involved himself with anything so mundane as buying a vegetable. "I always enjoy shopping in a proper market. Is it there every day?"

Not wanting to show his ignorance, Osman Toprak avoided answering the awkward little question by seizing an opportunity to rebuke the young waiter for some trifling offence. Realisation was beginning to dawn on him that this young woman was not going to be so easily finessed; perhaps it would be better to continue in the privacy of the boat.

"Jack," he said, smiling, "I wonder if you would be good enough to take a look at my boat while you are here. I could do with some professional advice on one or two small matters."

"Of course. I'd be delighted. What's the problem?"

"Oh, nothing serious. Perhaps we could all go there now, if that's okay. I'll just sort out the bill and we can take a stroll along the quay."

As they started to walk back to the boat Osman Toprak contrived once more to pair himself off with Mary, and again Jack and Frank Palmer duly followed a few paces behind.

"Is this not truly magnificent?" asked Osman Toprak, gesturing towards the harbour as if he owned it. "Such a climate! Such a healthy, gentle pace of life! There can be no better place on earth to bring up children. I have to spend much of my time in London on various business matters, and usually take my family with me. The children love the excitement of London, but they are always so happy when we return to Cyprus."

"Of course they are," replied Mary. "It's their home. It's where they belong. There's no place like home."

Osman Toprak forced a smile to hide his inward concern at the lack of progress he was making. Bringing children into the conversation should have opened up all sorts of possibilities, but yet again her simple, honest reply had left him with nowhere to go. For the second time he had been stonewalled. Was she genuinely as straightforward as she appeared, or was she playing some sort of clever game?

"Speaking of home," said Osman Toprak, breaking the silence which had followed Mary's last observation, "I would like to invite you all to my house for a little gathering we are holding tonight. Just a few friends, you know. I do hope you can come; you'll meet some very interesting people. My wife is particularly keen to make your acquaintance."

They had reached the motor cruiser, and Mary was courteously handed up the step onto the gangplank as the others caught up. They all waited patiently while their host struggled to open the wide, glazed, sliding door at the entrance to the main saloon.

"This is what I wanted to ask you about, Jack," wheezed the Cypriot, mopping his brow with a silk handkerchief. "This door keeps sticking. It seems to be getting worse."

"I'm not really up on patio doors," was the sniffy reply. "More in the line of a double-glazing fitter. Have you tried lubricating the track?"

"Several times. And it's been to the yard twice. There must be something that can be done. Any suggestions?"

"Well, if you had a proper bulkhead fitted – inch marine ply should do it – with a solid wood wheelhouse door hinged in a proper frame, that should solve the problem."

"That sounds rather drastic; I thought it might be something simple. Some sort of adjustment or other. But here we are, talking shop, when we should be talking about more pleasant things. Frank, I was just telling Mary that you are all invited to my house tonight for a small party we are having. I did mention it to you, did I not?"

"I don't think you did, Osman, but we'd be delighted. What time do you want us?"

"Any time to suit yourselves. We can all go back together if you want. But first, let me pour you all a drink, and see if we can convince this young lady to come and live in Cyprus."

The capacious saloon had a well stocked bar at which Osman Toprak busied himself in the preparation of gin and tonics for his guests and a mineral water for himself. He was wearing a determined expression as he pulled up a small tub chair to be next to Mary.

"Now," he began, "let us tell you everything you wanted to know about Cyprus, and were afraid to ask!"

"I do like Cyprus, what I've seen of it so far. But I suppose I am still a bit worried about schooling for the children, and, of course, where we shall be living. I know I keep harping back to the subject, but we haven't really discussed it properly, have we?"

Osman Toprak was eager to reply.

"I can assure you, dear lady, that you should have no worries on either account. I give you my personal guarantee that you will have everything you need in the way of schooling and accommodation. The English school in the British Sovereign Base at Dekelya is most certainly the best option for your daughter. The officers' children are sent there, and I believe the standards are very high. It is only a mile or so from Mağusa, and there are many other facilities on the base. Shops; a swimming pool; tennis courts. I am sure she will do very well there."

"What about transport?" asked Jack. "How will we get her there?"

"That's all in hand," replied Frank Palmer, quickly. "I've already made arrangements to ship out your Range Rover. You'll have exclusive use of it at all times. It's all in your contract."

"And accommodation? I wouldn't want to be too far from the yard."

"There are two or three options, all quite close to the yard," said Frank Palmer. "But you can all stay at the hotel to begin with. It'll give you an ideal opportunity of sorting out the swimming pool."

To Mary's surprise the conversation switched immediately to the subject of restoring the swimming pool; it appeared the discussion about schooling and accommodation was at an end. While the three men chattered away, Mary sat quietly reflecting on the events of the day, trying to sort out the reality from the fantasy. It did all remind her so much of Alice in Wonderland, especially as she was now sitting at a sort of Mad Hatter's tea party. She studied each of them in turn; the Cypriot, with his beady eyes darting everywhere as he spoke; Frank Palmer with small beads of perspiration on his brow; Jack lolling back in his chair affecting an air of professional detachment.

Osman Toprak, sensing that Mary's thoughts were elsewhere, rose to collect up the glasses and said:

"Look, it's getting late. Let us adjourn to my house. I am sure my wife will be able to put your mind at ease, Mary. My guests will be descending on us in a couple of hours, and I need to get changed first."

"Is it a formal affair?" Mary was wondering if she would be suitably dressed for the occasion.

"Not in the least. The dress you are wearing is quite charming."

"You can get something here in Kyrenia if you like," suggested Frank Palmer. "There are some very good dress shops here."

"That's a good idea," agreed Jack. "What can you recommend, Osman?"

"Tell your driver to take you to Romena's boutique. My wife goes there all the time. They specialise in the smaller sizes and always have the latest fashions. Do feel free to mention my name. But I must leave you to it, I'm afraid. Duty calls."

* * * * * * * *

Osman Toprak's villa was located just to the east of Kyrenia, situated right on the edge of a rocky cliff overlooking the Mediterranean Sea. Access to the house was via a long, straight private road along which the taxi driver raced gleefully at top speed, sending up a cloud of dust behind. As the car drew up outside an impressive portico, Osman Toprak's wife emerged to greet the new arrivals. A slim, elegant woman of good bearing, Julia Toprak spoke excellent English with only the faintest trace of accent. Her fine, pale skin and stylish mode of dress gave her a distinctly European appearance which she always took great pains to maintain. Mary felt an instinctive liking to this charming, well-bred woman, and gladly suffered being led upstairs to one of the many guest bedrooms where she might bathe and change into her new dress. The affinity was mutual, and the two women sat for some time talking quietly together until eventually Osman Toprak's querulous voice was heard calling for his wife's assistance with some awkward new cufflinks.

Now on her own, Mary bathed, arranged her hair almost to her satisfaction and put on her new dress. It was of white muslin so light as to be almost diaphanous, with just a wisp of shoulder strap supporting the décolleté neckline. Her hostess had also provided a pair of red, high-heeled sandals that consisted of no more than a few thin leather strips. As Mary appraised the overall effect in a cheval by one of the windows she wondered at first if it was all a little too daring. No! In for a penny, in for a pound. It was time to make an impression.

Jack was deep in conversation with a young Cypriot couple as she entered the crowded drawing room. He glanced briefly over in response to some automatic sexual radar, did a second take, and then a third, which turned into a stare of amazement as he recognised who it was. Excusing himself to the couple, Jack hastened over to her.

"Jesus Christ, love! You look amazing! Absolutely stunning! I hardly recognised you!"

"Well thank you very much!"

"No, no! That was definitely meant as a compliment."

"And delivered with your usual delicate touch! What a thing to say! "

Her sharp words served to disguise the warm feelings kindled within her by the desire she saw in Jack's eyes, but before she had a chance to bestow her forgiveness Osman Toprak descended on them, accompanied by his wife.

"Mary, my dear, what a beautiful gown! You look delightful, absolutely delightful. But we can't allow Jack to monopolise you all night like this – I know Julia's friends are all most anxious to meet you. In the meantime, if you don't mind, I'll just borrow Jack for half an hour or so – Frank and I need his help on a technical matter. I promise not to keep him too long."

So saying, the wily Cypriot gave his wife a peck on the cheek and led Jack off in the direction of the bar.

"That man!" exclaimed Julia. "He's about as subtle as a bulldozer! I really do apologise for that little performance, Mary. I hope you don't mind."

"That's okay," replied Mary with a chuckle. "I think I can guess what's going on."

"Well I'm glad of that, anyway. I really don't care for all this cloak and dagger nonsense, but they seem to thrive on it."

"Honestly, I don't mind in the least. As long as it keeps everyone happy. In any case, it would nice to meet some of your friends."

"Friends? Oh yes, of course. We'd better start with Yalcin, I suppose. He's a government minister. I don't think he's taken his eyes off you since you walked into the room. Let's go and put the poor man out of his misery."

It was a truly elevated gathering taken largely from the upper echelons of Turkish Cypriot society, but with a smattering of minor players on their way either up or down, depending on their circumstances. Light classical music provided a discreet background to the lively buzz of conversation that filled the long, elegantly furnished room, so the atmosphere was at once pleasantly sophisticated and cosmopolitan. At the far end three young uniformed waiters manned a lavish buffet under the direction of a white clad chef; the other end was dominated by a massive stone hearth surmounted by an oil painting of Osman Toprak. A lustrous wooden parquet floor liberally strewn with thick Turkish carpets completed the effect of baronial splendour that Osman Toprak's English architect had striven so hard to achieve.

The minister turned out to be a rather dull man who hid his lack of personality behind a vague, preoccupied air of self importance, and although making the acquaintance of such an august person was a unique event for Mary, she handled the situation with her customary aplomb. Since early childhood she had always possessed that happy knack of meeting new people on equal terms, regardless of any difference in class or status. But after ten minutes or so of listening to pompous platitudes Julia decided they had spent long enough basking in the minister's radiance, and they moved on to an elderly judge, quickly followed by an Arab sheik, a creepy little Swiss financier, a young Oxford don researching a book on the Ottoman empire, and finally a fierce looking Turkish army general who spoke hardly any English, and communicated his thoughts by staring down at Mary's cleavage.

"Well, I don't think I've missed anybody," said Julia, an hour or so later when they had a chance to sit down together. "I hope you were suitably impressed."

"It was all very…interesting," replied Mary with a smile.

Julia laughed and then whispered: "Come on Mary! What did you really think?"

Mary hesitated before replying. Under normal circumstances she would never dream of confiding in someone she had only just met, but something about Julia's warm vitality struck a chord deep within her. There was a genuine empathy between them that seemed to transcend all the differences that separated their lives; it was as if they had known each other for years. At length she chose to trust her instinct, throw caution to the wind, and give friendship a chance.

"Seriously? I don't know how I managed to keep a straight face."

"Me too!" whispered Julia, responding joyfully to the confidentiality of Mary's tone. "I knew all along that you wouldn't be taken in by it all. I did tell Osman, but he wouldn't listen."

"It was a bit like running the gauntlet, but as it happens it was all for nothing. I'd already made my mind up to come."

"Oh, I'm so glad. What made you decide?"

"It was something you said when we had our first chat upstairs – when you mentioned how excited everyone was about this new tug. I suddenly realised that Jack would have the chance to do something really important, and it got me thinking about what it would all mean for Cyprus instead of just thinking about what it meant to us. That's about it, really."

"Marvellous!" cried Julia. "We're going to have such fun together, you and I."

* * * * *

"Sunday 19th March 1978

A joyous day! Jack and I embark on our own voyage of discovery for the morning (after breakfasting in the hotel's empty restaurant on goat's cheese and tomatoes). It really is a strange sensation staying in this beautiful hotel by ourselves, like our personal Mediterranean mansion – I can but dream! A taxi called for us just after 9.30 to take us into the old town of Famagusta. We were dropped off in the centre of a large square with little cafés arranged around three sides interspersed with all sorts of shops and a cathedral in one corner. After I bought some postcards we walked down one of the roads leading off the square down to the sea. As we followed the boundary wall around the port I was horrified to see so many bullet holes pierced into the brickwork of the wall. The bricks had been painted cream and the stark contrast of the holes, deep and black burned into my mind. How many innocent people died here? Such a lovely sunny day to be clouded by dark thoughts of what had happened on this beautiful island – and not so long ago. The folly of man!

Walking on we reached a pair of huge wooden gates, which took us through to the shipyard once again. All was very still and quiet, and the dishevelled gatekeeper doffed his cap to Jack as we said our hello's. A thought just occurred: will I have to learn Turkish? Oh Dear!

After a quick visit down the quay we made our way back to the square and to our rendezvous with John Palmer at one of the little pavement cafes where I had the most delicious fresh orange juice I have ever tasted.

We had a lovely salad for lunch followed by fruit, and spent the afternoon relaxing on the beach. To think the middle of March stretched out sunbathing – just too decadent for words! Frank was sweating under an umbrella at a table by the empty pool, which hopefully will be brim full of clear, clean water after

Jack has fixed it. I sent a thank you postcard to Julia for last night's party; I look forward to us becoming firm friends.

There was some consternation at the reception desk over our passports this morning – us not being married and sharing a room – we shall have to see!! Home tomorrow – and back to reality.

Chapter Four

The grim reality of their perilous situation awaited Jack and Mary as soon as their aircraft touched down at Heathrow just before eight in the evening. In freezing, torrential rain they made their way to the car park, only to find the car had a flat tyre. The bald surface of the spare served as a mocking reminder that their backs were against the wall, and the enchantment of a Mediterranean island suddenly seemed a distant illusion. Mary insisted on helping to change the wheel, so both were soaked to the skin for the journey to Basingstoke to collect the girls. They arrived so late that Mary's brother would not hear of them continuing their journey home that night, so a bed was made up on the living room sofa where they spent a few cramped, sleepless hours listening to the wind howling down the chimney and the rain lashing against the window.

More grim reality faced Jack at his next visit to the official receiver's office where he found himself dealing with a new case official who was most suspicious of the whole affair. There were so many conditions that had to be met before permission could be granted for what amounted to emigration that Jack was beginning to despair of making his escape. It transpired that the case would have to be processed in London, so another rainy April morning saw Jack, Mary and the two girls on their way to the metropolis in the Wolseley. They parked in Lincolns Inn Fields and trudged in the rain down Serle Street towards the courts. As they turned the next corner Jack suddenly stopped in the middle of the pavement.

"Of course!" he exclaimed with a hollow laugh. "Yet another of my respected father's prophesies is fulfilled. I've finally wound up in Carey Street!"

"What on earth is Carey Street?"

"You're standing on it!" cried Jack. "You could say it's the opposite of Easy Street. It's a place for losers."

"Just think of it as the first step on our journey to Cyprus," suggested Mary. "And for heaven's sake don't start getting stroppy with the officials. You'll only make matters worse. Perhaps we'd better come in with you."

"No, I don't want to put you through all this rubbish. It's my own mess; I have to clear it up myself. I'll see you at four o'clock in the coffee bar as we agreed."

They kissed, and Jack watched wretchedly as his three girls, huddled together under a single umbrella, picked their way through the puddles in the direction of Chancery Lane and thence to Saint Paul's. He threw back his shoulders and marched defiantly into the court building to face his tormentors, but his resolve all but vanished when he entered the dismal reception area to join the host of worn out, dejected humanity waiting to be processed. How had he come to such a pass? He did not belong here amidst these pathetic, hopeless creatures with their tired, desperate faces. For all he knew, these people deserved their miserable fate, but surely he was merely the victim of bad luck; it was intolerable that he should have to suffer the same indignities.

But suffer he must, and for the next five hours he traipsed wearily from one depressing room to another. Documents had to be stamped, and stamped, and stamped again by surly clerks to be found only at the furthest extremities of the building up cheerless cold stone staircases leading to endless cold corridors. Every time a stamp or a seal was reluctantly conceded, there was a payment to be made, which struck Jack as somewhat paradoxical considering the one commodity you would not expect to find about the person of someone in his unfortunate position was money. This view was shared by a tall, thin, dishevelled man just in front of him at the final stamping station, at which a particularly heavy fee had to be paid. The man was obviously at the end of his tether, and his well-educated voice was considerably raised as he addressed an uninterested clerk across a high wooden counter.

"I am Fucking Bankrupt, for Christ's sake! Why do you people keep asking me for money? Surely Bankrupt means you do not have any Fucking Money!" He turned to Jack as if appealing for support.

"Can you believe these people? Where *do* they find them? Is there a special college in some dingy, Dickensian dungeon where they recruit and train these morons in the dark art of Circumlocution? Where does it all end?"

Jack could only shrug his shoulders in reply. Being similarly afflicted he fully understood the man's frustration, but Mary's parting words had stayed with him all through the long ordeal, constantly reminding him why he was there. He must obtain that final stamp even though his tongue might bleed from the biting.

When Jack did eventually emerge from that cruel and dreadful building with his all important release duly signed, sealed and delivered, his initial feeling was one of complete humiliation, as if the document were a decree of banishment rather than a passport to freedom. He trudged along rain swept Carey Street, head down, shoulders hunched, full of anger and resentment. But as he made his way to the coffee bar in Fleet Street the rain stopped, and he started to realise the dark cloud that had blighted their lives since the beginning of the year was passing. They were free to start a new life, putting all this misery and degradation behind them; if everything went according to plan they might even be able to avoid losing the bungalow. His spirits quickly began to rise as the blessed light of optimism drove the demons from his soul, and by the time he joined Mary and the girls in the coffee house his frame of mind was so euphoric that he went so far as to suggest they should all go for a celebratory meal whilst waiting for the rush hour to pass. Mary was greatly relieved to see him in such a positive mood, but she was mindful of both the expense and the need for the children to be in bed at a reasonable hour, so it was agreed to make straight for home, even if it did involve joining the commuters in their daily ordeal.

By the time they cleared London the children were sound asleep in a warm, cosy tangle of limbs under a thick blanket on the back seat. Jack had said nothing so far of the day's events, but Mary was anxious to learn exactly where they now stood.

"So, what's going to happen about the bungalow?" she enquired hopefully.

"Well, my love, it looks like we should be able to hang on to it."

"Oh, I do hope so, Jack."

"The deal is not too bad, really. We have to pay the Receiver three hundred pounds a month. Pretty much all the Sterling part of my salary. Out of this he pays the mortgage, the personal loan, and what we owe the VAT man. Oh, and his own expenses, of course."

"I don't like the sound of that. What expenses?"

"Yes, I know what you mean. But that's the deal. He's got me by the short and curlies."

"How long do you have to pay this three hundred a month? It's such a lot of money, Jack."

"I know. But it's just until we've paid off the personal loan and the Vat man. A year should do it – two at the most. It depends on how much the Receiver wants for his cut."

"And what about the mortgage."

"The building society seems quite happy to go along with the existing arrangement. They've been pretty good, really."

Mary lapsed into silence. The thought of having their hard earned money siphoned off by some unseen parasite was a complete anathema to such a deeply private and provident woman. She loved Jack dearly, and knew he was doing everything he could to bring them all safely through these difficult times, but at every turn he seemed to encounter yet another setback. If only there were more she could do to relieve his burden! Perhaps she would be able to help in some way when he started his new job, even if it was just filing or answering the telephone. In a silent, loving gesture of reassurance, Mary gently placed her hand on Jack's arm, and looked across at the tired, careworn face lit intermittently by the headlights of on-coming traffic. He really did need a good night's sleep, she thought.

* * * * * * * *

Frank Palmer had made arrangements for the family to fly out with him to Cyprus early in April, so there was precious little time to complete all the necessary arrangements. Mary had no idea when they would be able to return, so she was greatly relieved when an old friend of Jack's asked if he could stay at the bungalow whilst they were away. He had just met the woman of his dreams and they needed somewhere to live while they looked around for a home of their own.

The pace of daily activity during those last few days increased significantly for Mary, especially as she could count on little assistance from Jack, who was kept busy by his new employer telephoning every morning with an endless stream of last minute jobs. Nevertheless, she worked tirelessly through everything that had to be done, finishing at midnight on the very eve of their day of departure. Jack's friend was at hand to transport the family and a mountain of luggage to Heathrow in his estate car. Only Mary looked back as the vehicle made its way slowly up the narrow road, but once the house was out of sight she faced forward with a sense of relief. She had brought them all safely to this point in time. Now everything was in the hands of fate.

Mary's deferral to the influence of fate lasted only until they arrived at the airport terminal where the triage of children and luggage demanded her attention. Frank Palmer, affable as ever, was there at the check-in to help with baggage trolleys. He negotiated the staggering excess luggage payment with aplomb, and smiled benignly when little Wendy was sick over his brand new suede desert boots. They were flying with Cyprus-Turkish Airlines again, and apart from the frantic scrum when they transferred at Istanbul airport, the journey passed without incident. It was the first time Susan and Wendy had flown, and both were silently fascinated by everything, especially the sight of so many armed soldiers. On their arrival at Ercan airport Fate once again handed the reins back to Mary for the retrieval of their baggage. Jack and Frank Palmer did all the lifting, but they were both so engrossed in their discussion of weighty matters that their concentration was sadly lacking. Only when she reported that a case was missing did she gain their full attention.

"Osman Toprak was supposed to be here to arrange VIP treatment and avoid all this," said Frank Palmer with some annoyance. "What was in the case, Mary?"

"All our washing stuff."

"Ah! That explains it. They'll kill for English toiletries here. The case is probably hived off somewhere even as we speak. Perhaps Osman will be able to liberate it. We'd better wait here until he arrives."

The sight of five English people loitering around in the baggage retrieval hall was not, however, acceptable to one particular official who came bustling up to Frank Palmer.

"Why you are waiting?"

"One of our cases has not come through yet."

"All baggage has arrived. You must now pass through customs."

"Here we go again," replied Frank Palmer, rolling his eyes heavenward. "We're going nowhere without the missing case, my friend."

"You must all pass through customs now," insisted the official. "You must fill out one forms for lost baggage."

The discussion was interrupted at this point by a *fracas* at the door leading to the VIP lounge. Osman Toprak was hotly debating his right of access with two officials who appeared reluctant to let him through. In the end he simply pushed past them and hurried over to the new arrivals.

"What is going on here?" he demanded.

"You're just in time, Osman. We appear to be a case missing."

"Leave it to me! I'm used to dealing with these people," boasted Osman Toprak as he turned to the official, whose expression had now turned from its usual nonchalance to one of intransigence.

There followed a predictably aggressive exchange between Osman Toprak and the official who, despite starting with a distinct advantage of height, seemed to shrink visibly as his opponent pressed home the advantage of his education and social status. The outcome was inevitable. Osman Toprak's final tirade, ending with the words "Şimdi! Şimdi!" sent the official scurrying off to find the missing case.

"What does 'şimdi' mean?" enquired Frank Palmer, plainly gratified by Osman Toprak's triumph.

"It means 'now – immediately," replied Osman Toprak. "A difficult concept for these people, I'm afraid," he added, as if he were commenting on an entirely alien race, rather than his own. He turned his attention to the two girls, demanding an introduction in his most engaging manner. Despite the lateness of the hour and the effect of a long and wearing journey, Susan responded with the utmost courtesy to his attention, and answered his questions with a poise and dignity well beyond her age.

These pleasantries were now interrupted by the reappearance of the airport official, sheepishly bearing the missing case. Osman Toprak's final triumphant salvo ensured the unfortunate man was left without a shred of dignity, and they all made their way to the customs hall.

Osman Toprak set about immediately to assert himself. To demonstrate the extent of his influence in official circles he undertook to have their luggage through customs without delay. Unfortunately they came up against an official who seemed unwilling to play the subservient role for which he had been cast, and was determined to demonstrate his own sphere of influence by demanding that the toiletries case be opened. Osman Toprak stepped forward and put his hand on the case in a protective gesture.

"No, no! Quite unnecessary," he snapped in English. "This lady is with me. She has nothing to declare. I will take full responsibility."

"Open case please!"

Osman Toprak reddened, and rapped out a dozen words in Turkish. The official also coloured up, and the travellers awaited the outcome with interest.

"Open case please!"

Another volley from Osman Toprak was countered by a torrent from the official, delivered with his nose scarcely an inch from that of his adversary. Turning to Jack, Osman Toprak said:

"Look, stay here while I go and find someone in authority. This imbecile doesn't know who I am. Don't open the case!"

As soon as Osman Toprak was out of sight, Mary stepped forward and wordlessly opened the case in question. The official did not even look down before directing her to close the case. He then marked all their luggage as cleared, so by the time their protector came puffing back, red, out of breath and alone, they had all been waiting for some time.

"No responsible person to be found," wheezed Osman Toprak. "What happened about the case?"

"He changed his mind," said Mary, who was beginning to feel sorry for their self-appointed protector. "He has cleared all our baggage now."

"I should think so too!" declared Osman Toprak. "You have to be firm with these people or they start taking liberties. Now let's get you all to your hotel without further delay."

Jack, Mary and the two girls were shown to a waiting Mercedes taxi and they all settled into the cavernous rear passenger compartment. Again, Mary watched Frank Palmer engaged in earnest conversation with Osman Toprak outside the terminal entrance. It was curious to observe them, as each had the habit of looking all around whilst they were actually speaking, but gazing intently at the other's face when listening. As they parted, Frank Palmer handed a bulky envelope to Osman Toprak, who hastily thrust it into the document case he invariably carried.

It was well past midnight when they arrived at the Plâj Hotel, so they were mercifully spared any offer of food. When the girls were shown their own room, they were awestruck by its opulence. It was three or four times the size of the room they shared at home, and the addition of a balcony overlooking the sea sent Susan into transports of delight and wonder.

Mary stood on the balcony of their own room next door, staring thoughtfully out into the night and listening to the comforting sound of the waves. Jack was soon at her side.

"A penny for them," he murmured.

"I was just thinking about Frank Palmer. Did you notice he had two passports?"

"I don't think so, my love."

"No, I'm sure of it. I saw the other one in his briefcase when we were checking in just now."

"It was probably just his old one. Did it have the top corner cut off?"

"No, it looked brand new to me. In any case, why would he want to carry an old passport around with him?"

"Maybe it was someone else's passport."

"What would he be doing with some else's passport?"

"I've no idea, my love. But I'm sure there will be a perfectly reasonable explanation. Anyway, I've got more important things to worry about than Frank Palmer's passports. I've got a shipyard to run."

* * * * *

"Sunday, April 9th"

The first day of our new life in Cyprus. It's three in the morning and I can't sleep, so I might as well catch up with the diary. Jack was out like a light as soon as his head touched the pillow, poor old chap. I've been in to check on the girls, and they are fast asleep too. They were as good as gold for the whole journey over – you'd never believe it was their first time on an aeroplane. What a boon to have well behaved children!

I feel so much better now that we're actually here. I did have reservations about it all, especially Susan's education, but after talking to Mike and Sandy next door, most of my worries were dispelled somewhat when they pointed out how travel broadens the mind. They should know, travelling all around the world with Sandy and their two children when Mike was in the RAF. I can see now Susan will learn much from this amazing experience, and until we can get her settled in a proper school I'll be able to help her with the three R's, and Wendy come to that. I'm really looking forward to spending more time with them both. I hope I'll have the opportunity to help Jack out at the shipyard too, but I think I'll wait to be asked first – men can be funny about that sort of thing.

So what with setting up a new home as well, I'd better get used to being awake half the night!"

* * * * *

"The first thing we have to do is sort you out with some transport," said Frank Palmer as he and Jack sat eating breakfast early on Monday morning. "I've made arrangements to hire a Ford Escort until your Range Rover arrives from England. We'll go and pick it up as soon as we've finished breakfast. Then I'll get you to run me up to Osman Toprak's place. I'll be there for the rest of today and I'll probably stay overnight. I'm only here for a few days, and I want to make sure that he has made all necessary arrangements. You'll be alright on your own for a couple of days won't you?"

"Of course. I'll make a start on the building pad."

"Well, don't forget the pool," insisted Frank Palmer. "I've set up a quid pro quo with Kaplan. A fully operational swimming pool in exchange for your accommodation. Use whatever labour you need from the yard. This job has priority. It's really important for us to make a good first impression, and this is an ideal way to do it."

Their taxi arrived, driven by the same cheerfully casual young man that had taken them to Kyrenia on their first visit. He recognised Jack, and gleefully shook his hand as if he were a long lost relative.

"Waeef OK?" enquired the driver enthusiastically.

"Evet, teşekkür ederim," replied Jack confidently.

"Whatever that might mean," quipped Frank Palmer. "I can see it won't take you long to settle in."

The driver set off at his usual breakneck speed, covering a few miles of the Nicosia road before swerving suddenly off to race down a long dirt track. Behind them arose the usual great cloud of dust, watched again in the rear view mirror by the driver with obvious satisfaction. The car came to an abrupt halt in some uncultivated scrubland alongside a large corrugated iron building, from which protruded various rusty pipes emitting water vapour. Frank Palmer did not conceal his annoyance as he addressed the driver.

"I don't want a bloody laundry. I want to hire a car."

"Yes! Yes!" replied the driver eagerly though a mouthful of black and gold teeth. "Car hire! Here! My cousin, Haseem. Too many fine cars. Go in, go in!"

"You might as well wait here, Jack," said Frank Palmer wearily. "I'll go and see if I can make any sense out of all this."

After he had been gone for about five minutes, a pair of double doors at the end of the building was opened, to reveal Frank Palmer standing beside a battered red estate car. He was engaged in heated conversation with a small, dark, scruffy-looking man. Jack strolled over with the vague idea of lending moral support.

"But this car is a wreck!" Frank Palmer was protesting.

"The car is old," explained the small dark man with a shrug of his lopsided shoulders.

"But you must have something better than this if you are running a hire business!"

"This all I have. But all cars are same. It is not easy to find one new cars in Cyprus."

"But what you are asking is far too high for such a car!"

"It is best I can do," said the proprietor, who was showing signs of losing interest. "You can try Lefkosa or Girne. Perhaps you can find one cars for hire in such places."

Frank Palmer glared first at the laundryman, then at the taxi driver, who was grinning delightedly at this unexpected diversion.

"Alright!" he conceded. "I suppose I'll have to take it. But it had better not let me down."

He paid off the taxi and then handed over a large wad of notes to the laundryman. As they pulled cautiously away, the Cypriot ran after them, banging his hand on the back of the car. Frank Palmer pulled up as quickly as the worn brakes would permit, and an unshaven face appeared at his open window.

"If any breakdown," wheezed the laundryman, thrusting a dog-eared business card at Frank Palmer. "My cousin – good mechanic."

With these reassuring words in their ears, they squeaked and bumped uneasily back along the dirt track to the junction with the main road. From here, their journey progressed pleasantly enough on the relative smoothness of the main highway, until they reached the outskirts of Nicosia. At this point the eccentricities of the vehicle's steering mechanism were revealed. Whereas on full right hand lock the car would turn almost within its own length, it was able to turn only slightly to the left before the steering wheel would move no further. They had driven nearly twenty-five miles without having to make a left turn, so Frank Palmer had remained blissfully unaware of the problem. As he was unsure of the way he had approached the turn very slowly, which proved to be their salvation. Instead of making the turn, the car slewed across the road into the path of oncoming traffic, setting off an immediate outburst of horns by way of protest. Miraculously there were no collisions, and Frank Palmer recovered his usual aplomb with impressive speed. Ignoring the persistent chorus of car horns he backed across the road, executed a tight spin to the right, and ended up facing the way they had come.

"Never a dull moment, eh Jack?" he remarked, mopping his brow with a large red handkerchief. "Just wait until I get my hands on Osman Toprak! He was supposed to take care of all this for us. It's a good job we weren't on a mountain road. It would have been 'Goodnight Vienna'! What a fiasco!"

Frank Palmer watched the Nicosia traffic resume its usual chaotic bustle with a wistful air. His fertile mind was testing various possibilities, including the odds against reaching his destination using only right hand turns.

"We're never going to make it to Osman Toprak's place in this," said Jack, somehow sensing what was going through his employer's mind.

"No, I suppose you're right. I'll have to get a taxi. Do you think you can get this heap back to the moron who owns it? You can tell him I want my money back or I shall be reporting the matter to the police."

"I should be alright. The road's pretty straight back to Famagusta. The only sharp left turn is the one on to that dirt road up to the laundry."

"Good man! Take it easy, but make sure you get my money back from that crook before he has a chance to spend it!"

Jack anxiously cleared the eastern outskirts of Nicosia, and had just settled down to the drive back to Famagusta when he noticed a small roadside garage with a half-dozen cars on display outside. One in particular attracted his attention. It was a Mini-Moke, painted bright orange. He decided to investigate.

"Günaydin! Good morning and welcome!" said a smart, pleasant-looking young man who came out to greet him.

"How did you know I was English?" asked Jack, shaking the proffered hand.

"You are betrayed by your stature and your purposeful demeanour," replied the young man, delighted to have this opportunity to show off his expensive education. "We do not see many English nowadays, not since the trouble. More's the pity! My name is Alaydin. What can I do you for?"

Jack warmed immediately to this cheerful and engaging character, confided the morning's events to him, and explained his requirement for a reliable car that would not cost too much. Alaydin could not have been more helpful. All his cars were available for hire. All were highly reliable. The Mini Moke was an excellent choice. Most economic, and a great deal of fun for the children. For a modest deposit he would lead Jack back to Famagusta using no left turns, ensure that a full refund was obtained from the laundryman, and introduce him to a fine restaurant of which his uncle happened to be the proprietor.

True to his word, Alaydin delivered Jack safely back to the laundry, dealt severely with the froward laundryman, and stood watching with evident pleasure as the refund was told out slowly and reluctantly over a scruffy, narrow counter. They wasted no time in reaching the uncle's restaurant in Famagusta, located in a delightful square overlooked by St Nicholas' Cathedral, and feasted on kebabs washed down with a robust local red wine. When it was time for Alaydin to return to his place of business, Jack's offer to take him in the Mini-Moke was cheerfully declined. He would take the Itimat Taxi; far more sensible; no trouble at all. At Jack's offer to pay a month's rental in advance there was, however, no demur. The paperwork was speedily completed on the bonnet of the Mini-Moke at the Itimat departure point, pleasantries exchanged, and hands warmly shaken. Jack was feeling very pleased with himself as he waved off the departing taxi and climbed back into the little jeep.

His euphoria was all too short-lived. On his triumphant return to the hotel Mary took one quick look at the Mini-moke, and then a long, hard stare of incredulity at Jack.

"You must be joking!" she cried. "If you think I'd risk the lives of my children in that contraption you must be mad. It doesn't have any sides. They'll fall out as soon as you turn a corner."

Two young faces turned to Jack in mute encouragement. Loyalty to their mother precluded any vocal endorsement of his folly, but at that moment they wanted to ride in that perilous conveyance more than anything else in the world. Everything depended on his powers of persuasion, but they knew from experience the difficulty of the task that faced him. To their immense relief, their hero opened with a defence that was both bold and confident.

"Nonsense! There's plenty for them to hang on to. They're not idiots. They'll be all right, you'll see. You worry far too much."

"If either of them got so much as a scratch, I would never forgive you. I mean it, Jack."

"We'll take a little run out right away, just to set your mind at rest. Not too far, and I promise to take it easy."

Susan and Wendy had already taken up their chosen positions in the rear of the jeep, where they sat wearing demure expressions intended to convey an impression of maturity and self control to their mother. In spite of her deep concern, Mary was finding it very difficult not to smile at the sight of this quaint little tableau.

"What d'you say, my love?" insisted Jack, sensing that Mary was weakening.

"You will drive no more than ten miles an hour!" she replied severely. "At the first sign of any problem we'll be out of that thing and walking home."

The girls started bouncing up and down in sheer delight until a look from their mother froze them to their seats. Mary was already beginning to regret giving way, but she did not want to throw a wet blanket over their excitement

"Where do you want to go?" enquired Jack, eagerly. "We've plenty of time. It's not worth going into the yard now. It's gone half past three."

"Well, there is a spot I'd like to visit just up the coast, on the way to Bogaz. Osman Toprak telephoned and told me about it today."

"Osman Toprak? What time was that?"

"Oh, not long after you'd left. He wanted to speak to you or Frank, but I told him you were already on your way."

"So what's this place at Bogaz?"

"From what I can gather, it's a small group of houses which used to be owned by Greek Cypriots, and they have been empty ever since the troubles. Osman Toprak says the government has plans to move families into the houses, and we might be able to get one. I thought we might as well go and have a look."

They drove out of Famagusta at a very sedate speed, but Mary's heart was in her mouth the whole time due to Wendy's insistence on standing up. It was Susan who eventually solved the problem by sitting in the middle of the rear seat with Wendy standing safely between her legs, thereby ensuring the comparative safety of them both.

Suleyman had sketched a little map of the location, so they had no trouble finding it. Turning off the main coastal road, they followed a narrow lane through the dense pine and maquis vegetation to reach a large clearing in which stood a half dozen stylish modern dwellings varying from a small two bedroomed bungalow to a substantial two-storey family home complete with carved wooden balconies. They were able to wander at will in all the houses, for the locks had all long since been forced. Apart from this, there was a remarkable absence of vandalism. True, nearly all the electrical sockets and light fittings had been removed, but there was little evidence of malicious damage. There was almost a feeling of reverence about the place, as if it were a shrine to the victims of that hateful civil war. What misery to be exiled from your own home, thought Mary, without realising that her own situation was not so very far removed.

The girls' firm favourite was the little bungalow, every corner of which they explored with wonder and excitement. Jack made straight for the largest house, of course, and stood on one of the balconies looking out to the sea just the other side of some pine trees. What a wonderful place to bring up a family, he thought, and only ten miles from the yard. Mary's preference was for a sprawling bungalow built along two sides of a once elegant paved courtyard, now strewn with weeds, and bordered by an encroaching mass of tangled undergrowth. Not without a certain sense of guilt at entering uninvited, Mary wandered slowly from one silent, pitiful room to the next until she reached the master bedroom where, opening one of the fitted wardrobe doors, she came across a dusty, curling photograph. Smiling out at her were the happy faces of a mother and two children posing proudly in a well-tended garden. A faded inscription pencilled in Greek with the date 1973 could just be read on the back. The picture had such an atmosphere of well-being and contentment that Mary felt her heart swell almost to bursting with sympathy as she closed her eyes to control the tears that threatened to follow. Where was this family now? In some pokey little flat in Limassol, or even languishing in a crowded north London tenement? They would surely have the utmost determination to return some day and reclaim what was rightfully theirs. If she herself had been driven out of such a beautiful home, she knew she would not rest until it could be reclaimed, even if it took the rest of her life.

Jack was untroubled by any such moral considerations as he lingered on his balcony, dreaming of the grand life they could all lead in such a fine house only a stone's throw from the beach. It might even be possible to house other British workers here as well, forming a lively ex-patriot community that would ensure a good social infrastructure for the wives and children, with a minibus to provide the necessary link with Famagusta. As far as he could see only minor renovations would be necessary, so the scheme should not prove all that costly, especially when weighed against the longer term benefits for the joint venture. On the journey back to the hotel Jack waxed lyrical as he outlined his vision of the future, completely failing to notice Mary's silence in response. She had decided to keep her misgivings to herself for the time being, feeling the need for some quiet reflection before sharing her thoughts with Jack. The parallel with their own domestic situation at home in England was gradually becoming apparent, and was far too close for comfort.

* * * * *

Monday, 10th April

A Mini moke – I don't know! But I have to admit it is fun. 'When in Rome', as they say. Julia phoned this morning and invited the girls and me to lunch one day this week. I shall ask her advice about the empty houses, but I already know it really doesn't feel right.

Chapter Five

Although Frank Palmer had made it clear that he wanted the reinstatement of the Plâj Hotel swimming pool to have first priority, Jack considered the preparation of the concrete building pad for the tug to be far more important. Stephen Clarkson had already produced a suitable design incorporating three parallel steel girders to be embedded in the concrete, flush with the surface. A centre steel to accommodate the tug's keel would be flanked by the other two girders to which support struts could be welded as the vessel's frames were erected. The only supply source for steels of the correct dimensions was The Government Store, so an appointment was made for Jack to pay a visit to that eminent establishment.

The Government Stores had been set up following the Turkish occupation of Northern Cyprus to ensure proper control of essential industrial supplies. Located in large warehouses on the outskirts of Famagusta and Nicosia, they housed vast quantities of machinery, spare parts, chemicals, timber, building materials, office equipment and even furniture. Presiding over each store was a zealous government official who regarded with the utmost suspicion all attempts by the general public to purchase any of the treasured items entrusted to his care. Success at The Government Store was limited to those who understood the arcane trading rituals that flourished in those difficult times, or, of course, to those with the necessary family connections.

In his quest, Jack was assisted by Onan, a young factotum employed by the Famagusta Navigation Company. Onan was offered on secondment to the shipyard because he was considered by Mehmet Boga to show great promise. He was, moreover, well connected, being second cousin to the wife of a junior minister in the department responsible for the administration of The Government Stores. To top these invaluable credentials, Onan spoke excellent English, was always well dressed, and possessed a boyish charm that had always eased his passage through life

Onan called for Jack in a big, battered, black Toyota that belonged to the Famagusta Navigation Company and was grudgingly let out by Mehmet bey to the shipyard on an *ad hoc* basis. When they reached the Government Store Onan dashed round the front of the car to open the passenger door for Jack.

"You don't have to do that, Onan. I'm not Royalty, you know," said Jack.

"You could not have opened the door from the inside in any case," replied Onan. "The lock is broken, and the door must open from the outside only."

The hint of condescension in the young man's tone appeared to be lost on Jack, who was already gazing in rapture at the piles of rusty steel littering the weed infested dust of an area in front of the warehouse.

"I think I can see just the length we need for the keel support. Come and give me a hand measuring it, Onan."

"We should go first to see the official in charge, in any case," Onan advised.

"We'll be Okay. We could hardly be suspected of running off with two ton of steel, especially if our only means of transport is that old banger."

The young man was appalled by this request; clambering about a dirty steel yard was not his idea of career advancement. Not only would it endanger his beautiful new shoes, polished that very morning by his doting mother, but devotion to duty of this magnitude should be undertaken only when it would be witnessed by Mehmet Boga. Neither could he understand why someone in Jack's exalted position should be prepared to soil his own hands in such a lowly pursuit. It was with scant enthusiasm that he joined the Englishman in the ill-conceived plan, so he was much relieved when, as they were measuring a particularly rusty length of steel, a short, stocky man behind a furious looking moustache emerged from the warehouse and came hurrying over. His opening salvo was aimed at Onan with a degree of aggressive indignation out of all proportion to the triviality of the offence, but Onan appeared to be unmoved by the impassioned rebuke. Comfortably aware of his own superior position in the hierarchy of Cypriot commercial life, his reply was delivered with such casual arrogance that he gained immediate ascendancy in the exchange.

"I have told to this bloke that we are here on official business, in any case," he explained to Jack. "He wants to see our official purchase order."

"Do you speak English?" Jack asked the official, who merely shrugged his shoulders in reply.

"Tell him we're just looking, Onan, and ask him if he keeps any stock lists of all this stuff. We shall be here all day at this rate."

With lofty indifference Onan once more addressed the official, whose tone was noticeably less belligerent in the conversation that followed. He knew his duty, however, and held his ground with dogged determination. Onan summarised the outcome for Jack.

"He says the records are available only to Government officials, in any case. He says we cannot measure the steel without an official order."

"Oh, for Christ's sake!" exclaimed Jack. "How the hell are we supposed to give him an order if we don't know what's here? Tell him we're working for the bloody Government! Tell him we want to talk to his boss or something!"

The debate continued, but Onan was clearly making little headway. In the end he decided to deploy his big guns, and Jack heard the name of Mehmet Boga mentioned. This appeared to have the desired effect, and Onan reported his success with some satisfaction.

"He has agreed to speak with Mehmet bey on the telephone, but we have to stop measuring the steel, in any case. We can go with him to his office."

Once inside the warehouse Jack stood rooted in wonder as he stared round the treasure trove. The vast space was filled with every kind of industrial equipment imaginable, laid out on the concrete floor in close ranks that stretched to the far end of the long single storey building. Electric motors, engine spares, pumps, valves, cable drums, transformers, gear boxes, bench tools, machine tools, boxes of hand tools, boxes of fastenings, cans of paint, oil drums, gas cylinders, steel water tanks, coils of steel wire rope, all crammed randomly together in a bewildering, anonymous jumble. The guardian of this sanctuary led them into a cluttered wire cage serving as an office, where Onan dialled his boss on the antique black telephone. After a brief conversation he handed the receiver to the keeper who promptly stood to attention whilst addressing the great man. His tone was at first polite and conciliatory, but gradually rose to a pathetic whine as he inevitably lost ground in the face of a far superior adversary. Both Jack and Onan could hear the crash of Mehmet Boga's receiver being slammed down to punctuate his final word, and fully expected the keeper to admit defeat. They could not have been more mistaken; the hint of triumph in the keeper's tone as he told Onan the outcome of the telephone conversation was unmistakable.

"We have to go back and get a purchase order from Mehmet bey," reported Onan, whose interest in the proceedings was quickly evaporating. "If you write down what you need, the steel will be supplied to the nearest available size, in any case."

"Can we at least have a look round to see what's here? I don't want a completely wasted journey."

It was now Onan's turn to moderate his tone, which had previously been somewhat bored and distant, but the keeper's unexpected victory had altered the balance of power, and no understanding of Turkish was necessary to know that this particular battle was lost. Jack's next proposal horrified his dapper lieutenant.

"We'll go back now and get his precious purchase order, borrow a truck and come straight back for the steel."

"But we cannot," protested Onan. "Mehmet bey only signs documents at the end of the day. We have no truck, and it will soon be lunchtime in any case."

"I want to get this sorted today," insisted Jack. "I'll sign the order myself if need be. There are several lorries standing idle at FNC, and we certainly don't have to bother about lunch. So let's get cracking. Back to the office."

Mehmet bey was plainly irritated at having the calm waters of his morning routine disturbed by Jack's unscheduled visit.

"What is the urgency of this matter?" he demanded in his Olympian tone. "Surely it can wait until tomorrow."

"We have to start laying the base right away to enable building work on the tug to start as soon as the steel arrives from England," explained Jack, patiently. "Every day lost at the beginning of a project will delay completion by a week in the long run. Wouldn't it be best for us to have our own order pad at the shipyard to that we don't have to keep running to you for every nut and bolt?"

"You cannot issue purchase orders yourself," stated the manager, shocked at the idea. "You do not have the authority."

"We'll see about that," replied Jack. "Let's get Osman Toprak on the 'phone."

Mehmet Boga eased his bulk back into his chair and studied Jack briefly before replying.

"Osman Toprak is a very busy man. There is no need to bother him with such a small matter. I will issue instructions to raise the order today."

"I'll need it straight away," insisted Jack. "I want to borrow one of your trucks and pick the steel up this afternoon."

"Out of the question. It is not possible to release a truck at such short notice. Perhaps tomorrow we can…"

Jack had stood up and was walking round the desk to the window behind Mehmet Boga. This alarmed the great man who, for a fleeting second, feared for his personal safety.

"I can see three trucks standing idle in the yard," announced Jack. "You're not going to tell me they are all spoken for. We'll only need one for a couple of hours, anyway."

"It is still out of the question. I do not have a driver available."

"No problem! I'll drive it myself," replied Jack, returning to his seat opposite the manager.

"You are not authorised to drive our company vehicles," countered Mehmet bey intractably. "You are not covered by our insurance."

It was now Jack's turn to study the other man's face. He stared at his adversary for several seconds before slowly and deliberately dropping his gaze to the telephone on the desk. Check mate!

"I can let you have a truck for two hours," proclaimed the manager imperiously. "Onan will drive."

Onan had witnessed these proceedings from a seat against the wall behind Jack, unable to observe how Jack had managed this *coup de grâce*. He could not understand why Mehmet bey had caved in so unexpectedly. Perhaps he could come to his mentor's rescue by pointing out that he had never driven a lorry in his young life. On further consideration, however, he realised that such a confession might somehow harm his career and decided to remain silent.

The truck allocated to Jack was, of course, the worst that could be found. It was, in fact, a sulky old British Army Bedford lorry, which showed no enthusiasm for joining the quest in hand. It was skilfully coaxed into life by a grinning mechanic, who promptly disappeared once the reluctant engine was ticking over. When Onan tried to engage first gear there was a most distressing grinding sound, reminding Jack that the gear box on this ancient vehicle was without the benefit of synchromesh, and obliging him to spend a considerable amount of precious time explaining the intricacies of double-declutching to an incredulous Onan.

With a great deal of bumping and grinding the ancient Bedford slowly transported the two men back to The Government Store. Onan did the best he could with the gear stick, but by the time they reached their destination, Jack's ears were ringing with the sickening noise of missed gear changes that had accompanied every mile of the journey.

"Leave the engine running, and come with me!" ordered Jack.

"Can we not rest for a moment?" pleaded Onan, who was perspiring heavily.

"No. I want to get the steel back to the yard and in position today. On second thoughts, I'll look for the lengths we need myself. You take the order into the office and ask his nibs to get the crane organised."

Jack spent the next half hour scrambling about in the piles of rusty steel, marking up suitable lengths with a chalk stick. It was not until he had located everything he needed that he realised that Onan had not yet returned with the crane, so he marched briskly over to the warehouse building. The temperature had risen steadily throughout the morning, and Jack was covered in perspiration, which provided a most effective adhesive for the layer of dirt and rust that covered his face. Finding the door firmly locked and bolted, Jack pounded at it angrily with his fist.

"Kapalı!" announced a truculent voice from behind the door.

"Where's Onan?" roared Jack.

There was a pause before he heard the reassuring sound of bolts being drawn and keys jangling. The door cracked open to reveal the keeper's frowning face. On identifying Jack he reluctantly opened the door fully to admit him.

"Gel!" was the peremptory invitation.

Jack followed the squat figure back to the wire cage where he found Onan casually sipping Turkish coffee.

"Shall I ask him to pour you a cup, Jack bey?" enquired the young absconder politely.

"What's happening about the crane, Onan? No, I don't want any coffee."

"We are too late today, in any case. The crane driver has gone home."

"What, at this hour?" exclaimed Jack, glancing at the dusty clock hanging awry on the wire mesh.

"It is past two o'clock. The store closes at two o'clock."

"When does it open up again?"

"At eight o'clock," said Onan, and with quiet complacency added "Tomorrow."

A sense of rage and frustration rose from the pit of Jack's stomach like the escape of a deadly gas, but he held his tongue while his mind raced. Drive the crane himself? No, he wouldn't know where to start. Bring the crane driver from the shipyard? Not remotely practical, even if it were sanctioned. Offer a bribe? Never! Therein lay the path to ruin. By the time he had considered all the options he had calmed down sufficiently to address Onan.

"Well, that's that then. We'd better make our way back to the yard. Tell him we'll be back tomorrow morning sharp at eight," said Jack, pointing at the clock. "It shouldn't take more than six hours to load six lengths of steel," he added, with sarcastic emphasis.

Having been left to its own devices, the old Bedford engine had long since overheated and stalled. Nothing could revive the sullen brute, despite the frantic efforts of Jack, and the somewhat less energetic efforts of Onan with the starter handle. Only when he was drenched in sweat and reduced to a state of de-hydrated exhaustion did Jack finally admit defeat, and tell Onan to telephone for a taxi. Even this was not possible as the warehouse keeper had locked up and left for home and there were no public telephones nearby. Their only course of action was to start walking back along the long, dusty road to Famagusta under the blazing afternoon sun until they reached one of the little roadside coffee shops along the way. Onan made his telephone call, and they sat in the shade of an awning where Jack was introduced to ayran, a thick, viscous, mint flavoured yoghurt drink which he found surprisingly refreshing. By the time the taxi did eventually materialise it was so late that Jack had already decided to call it a day.

On arrival back at the hotel, Jack went straight away in search of Mary, whom he found sitting under one of the huge parasols on an otherwise deserted beach, reading a guide to Northern Cyprus. The two girls were sporting happily in the sea.

"You look a bit frazzled," observed Mary as Jack lowered himself onto the vacant beach lounger next to her. "And you appear to be going rusty."

"Oh, you wouldn't believe."

"Shall we all go inside for some tea?" suggested Mary.

"In a minute, maybe. I need to speak to Frank, urgently."

"What do you mean?" she asked, looking puzzled.

"Just what I say," replied Jack, somewhat impatiently. "I don't suppose he's back yet, is he?"

"Frank flew back to England today. Didn't you know?"

"He's done what?" cried Jack, in disbelief.

"I thought you'd have known. I can't believe he didn't tell you."

"He said he'd be here for a couple of days. There's a whole load of stuff we've go to sort out. This is unbelievable!"

Jack leaped up and stormed off to reception. Perhaps Frank Palmer had left him a note. Some sort of explanation, surely.

A letter there was. A page of Frank Palmer's bold scrawl.

"Jack,

I know I said I would be around until the end of the week, but something has come up that needs my immediate attention back in the UK. I tried to call you at the yard, but Faruk said you had gone out. Sorry to throw you in at the deep end like this, but I am sure you can cope.

I shall be back in Cyprus in a couple of weeks, and will sort out your accommodation then. In the meantime Kaplan is happy for you all to stay at the hotel on a full board basis. As you know, I have promised him you will sort out the swimming pool in return. There will not be much you can do at the yard until the steel arrives, so I want you to concentrate on the pool for the time being. I have not had time to sort out the car, but I have arranged with Suleyman for you to be picked up from the hotel in the morning and dropped back again at the end of the day. Your Range Rover is already on its way out to you. I hope you managed to get my money back from that chap at the laundry.

See you in a couple of weeks

Frank"

Jack was still standing in the lobby brooding over Frank Palmer's note when Mary and the girls came in from the beach. They all went into the lounge, a spacious, airy, well-furnished room that they had to themselves, and the girls went off to explore the contents of a bookcase in one corner whilst Mary ordered tea and biscuits. Jack handed Frank Palmer's note to her.

"How strange," she remarked, handing the note back to Jack. "But at least it shows he trusts you to get on with it all."

"I suppose so," he replied, carefully pocketing the letter. "There's plenty to do at the yard, and I suppose I'd better have a look at the pool or I'll never hear the last of it. It's a good job I sorted out the hire car myself, or we'd be right up the creek. I'll try sending Frank a telex in the morning."

The tea was served with much ceremony by a beautiful young waiter with a mop of glossy black curls and the face of an angel that broke into a radiant smile when Jack enquired if he spoke English.

"Nein. Ich spreche aber Deutsch."

"Ausgezeichnet! Wie heissen Sie?" enquired Jack.

The young man's name was Erol, who hailed from Turkey, and had worked for two years in Germany. He was particularly attentive to Susan, who was pretending to be so engrossed in her book that she had not noticed him. Erol saw through this dissemblance immediately, and offered her a plate of biscuits in such a charming and courtly manner that she blushed from head to toe. That young lady is growing up fast, thought Mary.

"Do these biscuits taste funny to you?" asked Jack. "Sort of…scented?"

"They do taste funny, Mum," agreed Susan. "Try one!"

"Let me try!" piped up Wendy.

They all munched away at the biscuits thoughtfully, with Wendy wearing an expression of intense concentration.

"They certainly do taste different," decreed Mary finally, giving Susan and Wendy an ideal excuse to pull wry faces and discard their fifth biscuit, half eaten. "A bit like Turkish Delight. They're probably from Turkey."

After tea Jack decided he would like to go for a swim to cleanse himself of the day's toil and trouble, so they all returned to the beach, which they still had to themselves. As was his custom when sea bathing, Jack swam out to deep water where he lay floating on his back gazing up at the sky. Mary remained in the shallows with the girls, where they were soon joined by the young Adonis who had served them tea, and was now off duty for an hour or so. He had brought with him a small inflatable dinghy that he handled with great skill as he rowed about in the calm, still water. This was all a source of great fascination for Wendy who, with the directness of her tender years, wasted no time inviting herself for a ride. At first, Susan remained aloof, as befitted a young lady of good breeding, but emboldened by his alliance with the younger sister, Erol persevered with his good-natured insistence that there was room for three. Taking her cue from Mary's smile of approval Susan joined in the fun, which before long developed into a riotous contest to see how quickly they could tip each other out of the dinghy. The sound of their laughter eventually attracted Jack back from the deep to lie contentedly with Mary in the warmth of the clear, shallow water as the surf rippled lethargically over their bodies.

When Erol had to go back on duty for the evening shift they all went up to the hotel together, the girls insisting on lending their quite unnecessary assistance to carry the dinghy. Wendy was by this time on the brink of exhaustion after the excitement of the afternoon, so Susan took her up to their room for a little rest before dinner whilst Mary stayed with Jack on the terrace to enjoy a few moments alone together. They had been sitting for some time quietly talking about the day's events when their attention was drawn to an outbreak of excited voices in the adjoining lobby where, on investigation, they found Suleyman at odds with the hotel maintenance man in front of the lift doors. Intrigued, Jack enquired as to the cause of all the fuss and bother.

"The lift. He is broke! Three times this week!"

"Oh dear!" commiserated Jack, concealing his amusement. "Anyone inside?"

"Yes. Suzie and Vendee. They are inside."

* * * * *

"Tuesday, 11th April

Had a great day today with Susan and Wendy – we spent a good part of the day at the beach. <u>Must</u> get down to some lessons for the pair of them. Suleyman has offered to give Susan Turkish lessons, which I think she will enjoy. A bit of a do tonight with Wendy and Susan stuck in the lift for about an hour – they thought it was great fun! To lunch with Julia on Thursday, she is coming over to pick us up.

Chapter Six

Life for Mary and her two girls quickly settled into a comfortable routine, despite their unusual environment. Jack left for the shipyard at half past seven each day, so they all rose early to have breakfast together before waving him off to work. A half hour tidying up their rooms was followed by two or three hours in the hotel lounge where Mary had set up a makeshift schoolroom over by the bookcase. She was keen to provide what continuity she could for Susan's education until permanent arrangements could be made at a proper school. Lessons would usually last until lunchtime, when they took a light meal of toast and fruit before heading for the beach. They were sometimes joined by Suleyman, whose little daughter Rabia had become firm friends with Wendy. They were of the same age, and despite understanding not a word of each other's language, managed to chatter away non-stop as they built sand castles or bathed in the warm shallows of the sea under Mary's ever watchful gaze. Before long, each child managed to pick up one or two words of the other's mother tongue, and it amused Mary to hear Wendy call out 'Gel, Rabia!' whilst her little friend would always call 'Come on, Vendee!'

Occasionally Mary took the girls for long afternoon walks along the beach, which stretched for miles in either direction. On one such excursion they came upon the ancient ruins of a huge Roman amphitheatre next to a spectacular basilica, all spread out on a hillside overlooking the sea. They had the whole site to themselves, so the girls were able to clamber freely about the great blocks of stone, their innocent cries of pleasure echoing off the steep slope of timeless rock as they played. Preserved miraculously over the centuries, the beautifully painted ceiling of the basilica enchanted Mary with its seductive portrayal of doe-eyed maidens smiling at heroically proportioned warriors. It all made her realise, quite suddenly, how much she had become a slave to necessity back in England, with every moment of her time being taken up either by a job, domestic duties, caring for her children or helping to renovate the bungalow. How glorious to be a lady of leisure, with the freedom to explore fully each serendipitous discovery that chanced along, like those indomitable English ladies in Victorian times roaming the sands of Arabia on snarling camels, whilst recording their adventures for the benefit of polite society at home. But even here, surrounded by the mysticism of a bygone civilization, necessity would compel her before long to round up the children and return to the hotel in time to serve Jack with his tea and scented biscuits.

Tea and scented biscuits! How readily we seek the comfort of these little rituals, thought Mary as they made their unhurried way back along the beach. It was already their daily custom to take tea in the lounge, occupying the same armchairs around the same low table as they listened to Jack's account of progress at the yard. So far his reports had rarely been encouraging, and today was no exception

"Don't ever try to buy string on this bloody island!" warned Jack, slumping down into his usual chair.

"I'll try to resist that temptation," she replied.

"It's not funny, you know," he growled, cramming two finger biscuits into his mouth and chewing on them pugnaciously

"I'm sorry. I just wasn't expecting you to start talking about string. I'm so used to hearing about steel and welding and three phases, whatever they are. Are you going to tie the tug together with string? "

Jack quelled Susan's giggle with a frown. Then, despite himself, he broke into a smile.

"I suppose it does sound a bit bizarre. I was using my string line to check the shuttering for the concrete base, and the bloody thing broke?"

"What, the string line or the concrete base?"

Another giggle from Susan.

"Do you want to hear this story or not?"

Mary smiled in Susan's direction. "Only if it has a happy ending."

"Fat chance of that!" replied Jack. "I had to spend all morning trying to buy a bit of string. We went all over Famagusta and came away empty handed. They've never heard of a string line here. One shop offered us some rubbish you could pull apart with your bare hands. Another idiot offered some knitting wool. We were shown cotton, sisal chord, some sort of plastic baling twine, but not a sniff of anything I could use. Sicim yokdur!"

"I don't want these two picking up that sort of language," whispered Mary, urgently. "Save it for the shipyard, if you don't mind."

"It means 'there is no string'," said Jack with a chuckle.

"Will you be able to manage without it?" asked Mary, not sure that she believed his translation. It had certainly sounded like swearing to her.

"Well I've tied the two pieces of my old line together, of course, but it means you can't wind it back into its case, and it's bound to get all tangled up. And I don't want to use a knotted string line when I start work on the scrieve board."

"Scrieve board?" echoed Mary.

"It's just a massive drawing board really, about eight meters by seven in this case. I'm going to make it by joining up about twenty sheets of chipboard laid out on the floor of that big empty shed next to the machine shop. Slap on a few coats of white emulsion and Bob's your uncle."

"And what's it for? If that's not a silly question."

"It's for drawing out the sections of the tug's framework to full size so we can check all the measurements. Once we know we've got the exact shape of each section we can take off the wooden templates that are used to fabricate the actual steel frames. The process is called lofting, from the olden days when it was all done in what they called a mould loft. They used to…"

An image of doe-eyed maidens and heroically proportioned warriors surged into Mary's mind at this point, and Jack's voice faded into the background as he rumbled on about the intricacies of the mould loft. It was a pity he could not have been with them at the ruins this afternoon, she thought; there was so much inspiration to be drawn from the achievements of the ancients. They had laboured with the simplest of tools in conditions that would be considered impossible in modern times, yet their faith and perseverance had enabled them to produce work of such quality that it had survived for two thousand years. Jack would be sure to appreciate the skill of the stone carving, the faded elegance of the ruined buildings, and the calm, spiritual atmosphere of that enchanted place.

".... Which means the gain on the deadrise and run of the lower chine bar will always be spot on as long as the datum marks all line up. It's as simple as that!"

Mary gave what she hoped was an attentive nod, but she was longing to tell Jack about discovering the ruins and take him along the beach to see them

"Guess what we found this afternoon!"

"A very pretty sea shell?" he ventured, not without condescension.

"Some ancient ruins," she replied, ignoring his sarcasm. "Not far. Just along the beach. We could take a walk back there now, if you like. You'll love it there. It's so peaceful. Sort of spiritual. It might put you in a better frame of mind."

"There's nothing wrong with my state of mind," he protested. "You can't very well run a shipyard being peaceful and spiritual. Especially when you can't even get a decent bit of string."

"That's what I mean," insisted Mary. "You're not in the shipyard now. You're at home with your family. It's time to relax, and forget all about string."

She could tell from the look on his face that he was in no mood for archaeological discovery. He had probably missed lunch and needed feeding.

"Maybe it would be better to go on Sunday," admitted Mary. "Let's just go for a quick swim now, and have an early dinner."

"Now you're talking," agreed Jack, springing to his feet. "Where's Wendy got to?"

Wendy had slipped away during Jack's shipbuilding lecture to find her new friend, Rabia, who was usually in the kitchen with her mother. On hearing Jack calling her name, Wendy took Rabia's little hand in her own and the two of them marched solemnly up to him.

"Sicim yokdur!" they chanted in unison, and ran off back to the kitchen, shrieking with laughter.

* * * * * * * *

The preparation of the building pad continued to occupy much of Jack's time at the yard, and brought him into close contact with the men. They seemed to take inspiration from his involvement, especially as he was prepared to roll up his sleeves and share in the work. He helped with the unloading of the steel beams when they did eventually arrive, a job that had to be done manually as there was as yet no crane in the yard; he assisted in the task of cleaning off all the rust, which had to be done with chipping hammers and wire brushes as there was no sandblasting equipment available; he even took a turn breaking up hardcore with a sledgehammer, much to the amazement of the yard hands. To them, the sight of a manager engaged in hard, physical work was tantamount to a miracle, and earned Jack the sort of respect usually reserved for a holy man.

Another important benefit Jack derived from this unorthodox approach was the opportunity it presented to assess the individual character and ability of the men, particularly that of Adem Birand, the *de facto* yard foreman. A quiet, unassuming man of about thirty years, Adem Birand had worked in and around the port ever since he left school at the age of fifteen, during which time he had gained a wealth of knowledge and experience to which his workmates instinctively deferred, young and old alike. His short, stocky figure was always to be seen in the thick of any action, whilst his tireless energy and constant good humour ensured he was well liked and deeply respected by the men. Nothing was ever too much trouble for Adem Birand, and he was always prepared to go that extra distance to ensure the best results, regardless of any personal inconvenience. These excellent qualities had earned him the honoured title of 'Usta', which translated in Jack's pocket dictionary as 'master, or highly skilled'.

Once the steel beams were in place Jack decided he could safely leave the rest of the groundwork to the capable supervision of Adem 'Usta', and turned his attention to setting up the mould loft. In this he was eagerly assisted by Emir and Halil, the two carpenters with whom he had already worked on the shuttering. Although neither of them knew more than a word or two of English they did understand Jack's carefully detailed drawing, and set to work building the scrieve board with such purpose and energy that the job was finished well inside the estimated time. Not only had they been fast, but the quality of their workmanship was quite remarkable, considering the limitations of their tool bags. The edge capping was neatly mitred at all four corners; every screw hole had been filled and rubbed down; even the three coats of white emulsion had been applied with special care using brushes rather than rollers to ensure a smooth, even surface.

As he drove back to the hotel on Friday evening at the end of his second week in office Jack felt he had every reason to be pleased with himself. With the construction of the scrieve board successfully completed and the preparation work for the building pad well advanced, he had made a useful start in his new job. The future was looking bright, he had the love of a good woman, and the weekend lay ahead. Perhaps it was time to relax and enjoy life again.

On reaching the hotel he bounded up the entrance steps, charged into the lounge and swept Mary off her feet in a great bear hug.

"My word!" she gasped. "Somebody is in a good mood."

"We're all going out to celebrate," he declared, lowering her gently to the floor. "I'll get cleaned up while you round up the girls. Where are they, by the way?

"Down in the games room playing table tennis with Erol. I think Susan's getting quite good at it."

Jack frowned; Susan's friendship with Erol did not altogether meet with his approval.

"We need to get her into a school as soon as we can. She can't spend her life playing ping pong with waiters."

"Don't be such an old spoil-sport! Susan's just having a bit of fun, soon she'll be up to her ears in school work with all the catching up she'll have to do, anyway this is a wonderful experience for a girl of her age."

"You're right, of course," replied Jack with reluctance, "I think we should pay Osman Toprak a visit to see if we can get the ball rolling with the Army school in Dhekelya. And I want to ask him about those houses up at Bogaz. We need to get the essentials sorted out as soon as we can."

"I've been meaning to talk to you about that," said Mary, seriously. "I'm not sure it would be such a good idea to move into one of those places."

"Why ever not?" cried Jack in astonishment, the last traces of his good mood evaporating completely. "It's like paradise up there."

"Yes, but, it's very remote. I'm not sure I'd want to be stuck out there for hours on end every day."

"No problem," replied Jack, brusquely. "You can come in to Famagusta with me each day. The girls too, of course."

Mary fell silent for a few moments, wondering if she should voice her real objection. Jack really did seem so keen on the idea.

"There is something else," she ventured at last. "I hate the thought of stealing somebody else's home."

"Oh, what rubbish!" scoffed Jack. "Those houses have stood empty for the last four years. The previous occupants have probably forgotten all about them."

"Could you forget you once lived in such a beautiful place, Jack? What would you feel if we went back to England and found the receiver, or whatever the awful man is called, had sold our bungalow to somebody else behind our backs?"

"That's completely different. The Cyprus problem won't be settled for decades, if ever. We'll be finished here and back in England long before then. It's only temporary; just as long as the job lasts."

"That's not the point. It wouldn't feel right. In any case, I don't see how the Government can give away something they don't legally own. Some day the rightful owners are going to want their property back. What happens then?"

It was Jack's turn to fall silent as he considered Mary's point. She was, of course, quite right. The question of ownership had to be relevant, as he well knew. The possibility of an early settlement to the Cyprus problem had to be acknowledged, however remote it seemed at the present time. Deals were done between nations for any number of reasons. What if Turkey had to appease the United States for some obscure diplomatic purpose? How much importance would be attached to Denktas and a handful of Turkish Cypriots then?

"You know I'm right, don't you?" said Mary softly.

"No," replied Jack flatly, unwilling to concede the point. "It's just a typical female emotional response to a perfectly practical situation. But if you're not happy with the idea, I suppose we'll have to kick it into touch. All I wanted to do was get settled as soon as possible."

"I know. And we might have found just the right thing here, under our noses."

"What do you mean?" asked Jack, somewhat impatiently.

"I've been talking to Suleyman, and he says he has a flat in Famagusta which would be just right for us. It's on the ground floor, and Suleyman's family have the flat above. There are two bedrooms and a small garden, and it's close to the shops."

"Sounds okay," muttered Jack. "Won't hurt to take a look, I suppose."

"We can't see inside until next week, when it becomes empty, but Suleyman has invited us round to tea with his family. We can see what his flat is like and have a look around the area. You'll like Nihan."

"Nihan?"

"Suleyman's wife. She's very nice. Did you know they lived in North London for a time? Back in the sixties, she said."

"Yes, I think Suleyman did mention it. When's this tea party going to take place?"

"Any time you like," replied Mary. "It's an open invitation. We can go now, if you like."

"OK. We might as well get it over and done with. You check with Suleyman. I'll go and get cleaned up."

Their destination was outside the old walled city, in the residential district of Baykal. They pulled up in a pleasant, wide, suburban street of relatively modern, well-built properties. Children of all ages were playing happily on the broad pavements, and even in the road itself, putting Mary in mind of her own childhood in London during the fifties when street cricket occupied the long summer evenings. Every front door stood open, with chairs placed outside to accommodate small covens of female elders whose job it was to watch over the younger members of their respective tribes. Some of these groups even had the additional benefit of television, where the family set had already been carried outside in preparation for the evening's *al fresco* viewing. Swallows and house martins wheeled and swooped overhead, their calls mingling with the sound of children's laughter and the strains of music from the television sets.

The Mini-Moke was instantly surrounded by small, dark faces, staring in wonder at Wendy's blonde hair, already bleached nearly white by the sun. One bold little boy, in his folly, reached over and grabbed Wendy's long plait, but he soon let go when she turned and soundly slapped his face. The boy immediately burst into tears, and went running off to report the assault to his mother, just across the road. She listened patiently to her son's whinging voice for a few seconds before seizing his ear in one hand, and spanking his backside so vigorously with the other that the dust flew from his trousers.

Nihan appeared at her front door with little Rabia, who lost no time in rescuing her golden-haired friend from the unwanted attentions of the other children. She boldly shooed them away, and put her arm around Wendy's shoulder in a loving and protective gesture, much to the smiling approval of both mothers. Suleyman read the riot act to the assembled group of children, and reminded them that he could see them all from his living room window, and woe betide any child he saw anywhere near the Mini-Moke. They had all seen what had just happened to that rascal Aziz following his unwise attempt to make free with Wendy's hair, and a similar fate would befall any other child caught in the act of unauthorised touching.

Suleyman's flat was a gratifyingly cool, spacious and orderly haven of highly polished wood, gleaming silver and sparkling glass, abounding with family photographs that covered the walls and adorned every shelf. As soon as the visitors were seated, Petek, the eldest daughter came to each in turn with a bottle of lemon fragrance, a little of which was poured over their hands as refreshment. Nihan brought in the tea on a large silver tray, and Shirina, the second daughter followed bearing another silver tray laden with Turkish sweetmeats. Both girls were a little awed by the prospect of having an English family move into the flat below but their initial shyness soon disappeared when Mary opened up a quiet, easy conversation with them.

"I am building this houses myself," announced Suleyman proudly to Jack. "First I build the top, for my family, then downstairs for my children if they need when they will grow up."

"When was this?" inquired Jack.

"Downstairs is finish only last year. I rent out until my children need."

"Why didn't you take the downstairs flat for your own use?"

"No, no. In Cyprus we build on top first. Then you can live upstairs while you finish downstairs. If you make downstairs first everything gets too much dirty when you make upstairs. Every mess coming down on top of the family. Not good."

"Is the finish downstairs as good as it is up here?"

"Is very good house downstairs. Very good. Two big bedrooms. One rooms to sit, like this rooms. One rooms to eat. Very big kitchen. One bathrooms. When he goes, this one downstairs now, I make everything clean, everywhere new paint. It will be very good for you and Mary and your children."

He paused to look out of the window to the street below, and was not pleased with what he saw. The window flew open, and he roared his protest at such a volume that both Mary and Nihan put their fingers in their ears, at which every female in the room burst into laughter.

"They are not really bad children," explained Suleyman as he closed the window, "but their mothers are too soft. They do not beat them enough."

This from a man who had never laid a finger on his own children.

Mary smiled across the room at Jack, and he smiled back. They had found their new home.

* * * * * * * *

The nerve centre of Osman Toprak's business empire was located in Ataturk Square at the heart of Nicosia's bustling business sector, close to the government buildings. To this eminent seat of power Jack and Mary directed their steps the following Monday morning for an audience with the great man himself to discuss the education needs of their daughter. Jack squeezed the Mini-Moke into an improbably small parking space, and they joined the noisy, jostling throng of pedestrians.

Everybody knows where my office is situated, Osman Toprak had boasted, but they had to ask several people along the teeming pavement before they found one who was actually in possession of this universal knowledge, and that was only because his fruit stall was right outside their destination. Why they had expected something on a grander scale neither of them knew, but they were not expecting a low, old-fashioned shop front with a cracked window and flaking paintwork. A small brass plate beside the door confirmed that they were at the right address, so Jack pushed the door open to the ridiculous jingling of a shop bell bouncing about on a rusty metal spring, and very nearly fell down three steep steps into a cramped, dingy reception area.

The room was barely three metres wide, with a high, narrow counter running down the middle. So low was the ceiling that Jack almost felt as if he had to stoop for fear of brushing the brown, smoke-stained paper with his hair. Behind the counter sat two elderly clerks pretending to be so busy that they had not noticed a large Englishman tumbling into their secluded world. Stacked all around them were stout, cardboard packing cases, and above their heads a rickety shelf precariously supported a row of alphabetically indexed lever arch files. At the far end of this dismal cell, almost invisible in the gloom, was another door, ill fitting in a distorted frame.

"Burun oturun!" said one of the clerks without looking up.

"I beg your pardon!" barked Jack, glaring at the man.

"Pliss to take a seat!" replied the clerk, pointing with his pen to the wall opposite, still without looking up.

Jack looked behind him at a row of old cinema seats, all folded in the upright position, and showing distinct signs of wear and tear. He pushed one of the seats down to reveal the grubby, stained upholstery, and let it spring up again with a clatter.

"We do not require a seat," said Jack, stiffly. "We are here to see Osman Toprak. Our appointment is for ten o'clock, so I should be grateful if you would let him know we are here. Şimdi!"

The edge in Jack's tone obliged the clerk to look up. So this was the reason for Osman Bey's unscheduled Monday morning appearance. Another English who thought he was Allah's gift to Cyprus. The other one, Frank Palmer, was just the same. Always making demands. It was bad enough working for that skinflint Toprak, without being persecuted by foreign infidels into the bargain. With a deep sigh of resignation, the clerk rose, squeezed past a stack of boxes and disappeared into the back room.

"Well show them in, man!" Osman Toprak could be heard to command, in English for full effect.

Here again, the room was far from any expectation held by either Jack or Mary. It was larger, perhaps better furnished than the outer office, but hardly any cleaner, and more cardboard boxes competed for space with ancient lever arch files and dusty ledgers on every horizontal surface, including the floor. A fusty, claustrophobic atmosphere prevailed, despite the open window through which poured a steady torrent of sound from the square outside. The contrast between what could only be called the squalor of his office and the ordered elegance of his home was a source of wonder to Mary, to whom the now familiar sense of being in wonderland was returning.

"So, Mary, where are your delightful children?" enquired Osman Toprak, with his trademark smile of benign condescension

"They're back at the hotel with Nihan."

"Nihan?"

"Suleyman's wife."

Osman Toprak placed the tips of his fingers together, and put the forefingers to his lips; a pensive look crossed his sallow features as he appeared to search his memory.

"Ah yes. I remember her now. A good woman. Your girls will be safe with her."

This is a performance, thought Mary, who was quite sure that Osman Toprak knew all of Suleyman's family. Why was he putting on this act? She really was finding it most difficult not to dislike this little man.

"Yes, all the children get on very well together. Wendy is already great chums with Rabia, and Susan is a firm favourite with the older girls."

"Ah yes! Susan! Such a beautiful girl. How old is she now?"

"She is ten years old," replied Mary sharply; there was something in the Cypriot's unctuous tone that was making her flesh creep.

"You'll appreciate how important it is to find her a good school," interposed Jack, who was aware that Mary's hackles were on the rise

"Of course, of course," agreed Osman Toprak, wondering yet again why this woman was so impervious to his charm. "I am happy to assist you in any way I can, but you must understand that there are procedures to follow. I have made enquiries with an old friend, a retired headmaster now living in Nicosia. Perhaps you would like to read this note he sent me."

Jack accepted the small, single sheet of paper and leaned towards Mary so that they could both read its neat, handwritten contents together.

Nicosia
14 April 1978.

Dear Mr Toprak

I have asked our Consular Officer about the possibility of Mr. Jack Durham's daughter attending a school in the E S B A. He suggests that if Mr. Durham would like to write to him (Mr. N Marsden) at the British High Commission, he will consult the SBA immigration authorities.

Yours sincerely
N. Roper "

"What does this mean?" asked Jack. "Why do we have to write? Why can't we just make an appointment to go and see him?"

The benign smile returned to Osman Toprak's features, and he indulged himself in a knowing chuckle.

"That will not be possible, I'm afraid. The British High Commission is situated in the Greek sector. You do not have access to the Greek sector."

"But surely they're in touch with the Consul in the Turkish sector. Why can't we go and see him?"

"There is no British Consul in the Turkish sector. There are no diplomatic relations between the British Government and that of Northern Cyprus; it is because of the troubles, you understand."

Noticing the look of concern on Mary's face, Osman Toprak adopted a more conciliatory tone as he continued.

"There is no need to worry, my dear. Life is a little more difficult in Cyprus these days, but everything is still possible. It simply takes a little more time, that's all. Let me have your letter when you have written it, and I shall make sure it reaches the British High Commission without delay."

"If you'll let me have a pen and some paper, I'll do it straight away," said Jack, making no attempt to hide the frustration he was feeling.

"Always in such a hurry! Tomorrow will do just as well."

"And then we'll lose another two days, which will inevitably turn into a week. This is really important to us, Osman. We thought all this would have been sorted before we came out here."

Osman Toprak provided the paper, and offered Jack his own fine gold fountain pen.

"No, I'd rather use a biro, thank you Osman. And I'll need a sheet of carbon paper. I want to make a copy."

Osman Toprak attempted to engage Mary in conversation as Jack wrote out the letter using a corner of the cluttered desk, but finding her unresponsive to his blandishments he eventually fell silent. When Jack handed the finished article back across the desk, Osman Toprak read over the contents, nodded, and tucked the note into an envelope.

"This will be on his desk first thing tomorrow morning," he assured his guests. "Now let us move on to your accommodation needs. Did you visit the houses in Bogaz yet?"

"We did," replied Mary. "They're very nice, of course, but they're not quite suitable for us. A bit too remote, we thought. We've been talking to Suleyman about taking the other flat where he lives."

"You would rather live in Baykal than Bogaz?" cried Osman Toprak in astonishment. "In Gazi Magusa?"

"I want to be as close to the yard as possible," explained Jack, hoping to head Mary off before she had an opportunity to voice her real objection. "It will be better for the shops and the schools as well. We've had a look at the place, and it seems to be just right for us."

"Frank told me you have a nice house in the New Forest back in England. Are you sure you will be comfortable living so close to the city?"

"We were both born and raised in London," said Mary, with some degree of indignation. Jack could see that Osman Toprak was heading for trouble again and interceded with a self-deprecating chuckle.

"Just two kids from the smoke," he quipped. "We'll all be just fine in Baykal."

"Well, if you're quite sure," conceded Osman Toprak with a frown. He was annoyed that his idea of settling them in Bogaz was not destined to bear fruit, for as in most of his dealings, there had been an ulterior motive. Several of his relatives had been pestering him to use his influence regarding the Bogaz settlement, and housing the family of a British shipbuilding engineer engaged in essential work would have paved the way quite nicely for any further suggestions he might put before the Government

"We are," confirmed Jack, "but we are really grateful for all the trouble you have taken, Osman. Perhaps you would like to join us for lunch, so we can show our appreciation."

"That is most kind, but I am afraid I have to be in Kyrenia for an important meeting. If you plan to have lunch in Nicosia you should try the Saray at the bottom of the Square. The food is very good there. Mention my name and they will be sure to look after you."

Chapter Seven

During his eventful career Jack had been involved on several occasions with projects featuring the use of concrete. It was a subject he knew well, so it was understandable that he should consider the building of a simple concrete base to be completely straightforward; but this was not to be. The first sign of trouble came when the cement mixer offered by Famagusta Navigation for the job turned out to be nowhere near the required capacity. After a frantic two day search of the entire Turkish sector the only alternative that could be found was a choice between two battered, old machines rusting away at the back of The Government Store. Jack purchased them both, for a sum well in excess of their worth, even though they needed to be stripped down for a thorough overhaul before they could be used. Further chaos followed when a convoy of lorries thundered into the yard carrying the wrong grade of ballast, all of which had to be sent back. There was even a problem with the supply of cement powder, due to delays in a shipment from mainland Turkey that had resulted in a national shortage. By the time everything was safely to hand, so much time had been lost, that Jack was obliged to tear up the carefully planned work schedule he had prepared and start all over again.

At an earnest council of war with Faruk and Adem Usta, Jack announced his plan to employ the entire yard's labour force using both concrete mixers in a bid to complete the whole area of the building pad in a single day, starting at dawn and working on for as long as it took to finish. It was a bold idea, but it seemed to fire the imagination of everyone concerned, especially when they learned there would be a substantial bonus in their wage packets at the end of the week. There was a definite atmosphere of excitement when they all assembled at day break for assignment to their various tasks, and the men pitched in with a will as the sun rose clear of the eastern horizon. Operating in shifts through the meal breaks to ensure continuity, they toiled on for hour after hour, heedless of the midday heat and the ache in their limbs. Not until the sun was low in the western sky did the relentless clatter of the mixers cease, signalling the end of a successful day. To mark the occasion Jack invited each man to inscribe his initials in the concrete for the benefit of posterity, which they all did with a shared sense of communal pride.

With this important task out of the way at last, Jack lost no time moving onto his next project, which was to undertake a thorough appraisal of the yard equipment. He decided to start with the fabrication shop, and asked Faruk to show him where the oxygen and acetylene tubes were stored. As they made their way across the yard Faruk invited Adem Usta to join them in case any technical issues should arise from the inspection. The ever obliging foreman led them over to a small shed behind the fabrication shop on the far side of the yard, and slid back the rusty corrugated steel door to reveal just one solitary oxygen bottle.

"Is this all the oxygen you have?" enquired Jack.

"We can get more at one hour's notice," replied Faruk loftily.

"And where's the acetylene?"

"Nerede asetilen?" echoed Faruk.

Adem Usta's grin broadened as he beckoned them to follow him round to the fabrication shop, an untidy, cluttered hell hole littered with carelessly discarded stubs of spent welding rods and grimy lumps of steel.

"Burada," explained Adem Usta, lifting the lid off a large iron pot, the like of which Jack had never seen before. "Water inside – then stones – make asetilen."

Next to the pot was an old dustbin containing an assortment of dark grey rocks. Adem Usta picked one up and handed it to the mystified Englishman.

"Make asetilen," he said, with the greatest of pride.

"This I must see!" exclaimed Jack. "Tell him to set up a demonstration, Faruk!"

Hasan the welder was summoned. As the nature of the task before him was explained, a knowing grin stole across his sly features. The acetylene generator was duly set up, and Jack clamped a scrap of half inch steel plate into the bench vice. He marked up a curved line with a piece of chalk, and stood back to watch the demonstration. After a great deal of fiddling with the gas adjustment controls, Hasan eventually commenced cutting, whereupon a great deal of wheezing, spluttering and popping ensued, with frequent long intervals when the flame died and had to be reignited. Jack observed these proceedings with rapidly increasing despondency, and impatiently called a halt to the fiasco.

"This is no good at all, Faruk," he complained. "The gas has far too many impurities. At this rate it would take six years to build the tug rather than six months. We'll have to find a proper supplier and use bottled gas."

At this point Adem Usta spoke sharply to Hasan, and the inevitable argument broke out with Faruk eventually joining in. The foreman had accused the welder of incompetence, which had been hotly denied. It was the gas that was to blame. He had received no complaints when he worked at the big yards in Izmir. It was impossible to obtain good results working in these primitive conditions

"Hasan says that you cannot find acetylene in bottles anywhere on this side of the line," explained Faruk to Jack. "He says his union has been campaigning since two years for the Government to set up a proper plant."

"His union?" cried Jack. "How many of these men are union members?"

"Hasan is the only one."

"Soon make all Union," declaimed Hasan with a sweep of his short powerful arm in the direction of the yard.

Jack could not make up his mind what worried him more, the absence of acetylene or the presence of a union. These twin spectres continued to dog his thoughts as he trudged around the yard with his clipboard, poking about in the cobwebs of neglect and decay. By the end of his inspection the list of items ran into three depressing pages, and Jack was beginning to realise the true extent of the problems that faced him.

At the end of the third week an opportunity arose to learn a little more about the Union situation from Faruk. All the yard hands had gone home for the weekend when Faruk looked into Jack's room to take his leave before making his own way home. Jack was checking the men's time sheets, and was just in the process of reviewing Hasan's claim for some overtime.

"Tell me, Faruk, why is Hasan so unpopular with the others?" he enquired.

"They think he is lazy. Some even think he is dishonest. And he always pesters them to join the union."

"And they're not interested?"

"There are some who feel it is not the right time to be thinking of such things. We must first build up our country again. Many of us lost everything during the troubles."

"Does that include you? Forgive me for asking."

"I once held a senior position with the Government of Cyprus, and had a fine house near Larnaca. Now I work as a humble clerk and live with my family in rented accommodation that I can never hope to own," replied Faruk with chilling frankness

"Do you ever think about returning to your own home in Larnaca?"

"It is useless to have such thoughts. The situation is out of our hands. My wife and my daughters wept for weeks when we were evacuated to this place. But life goes on."

"But surely you expect your property to be returned to you some time in the future. You are still the legal owner."

"It is true that I have the property deeds, but that does not stop a Greek Cypriot family living in my house. Possession is nine tenths of the law, as I believe you say in England. It is not so surprising that there is little interest in joining a union. What can the union do to give us back our homes?"

These observations made Jack feel uncomfortable, just as Faruk had intended. With so many unfortunates in the same position there was little opportunity for anyone to voice his own individual grievances. The suffering and resentment went deep, to the bottom of the soul, and the passing interest and brief show of concern from an outsider was of no value at all.

"I admire your fortitude," said Jack for want of a better reply. "Never give up hope, eh?"

"We live in hope, but die in despair," returned Faruk with gloomy dignity, "and if that is all for the time being, I bid you good day."

Jack considered the conversation on his journey home, wondering how people like Faruk and his family found the heart to carry on after losing everything. Compared to their sufferings, his own recent difficulties were insignificant, especially as he still had ample opportunity to turn the situation round and make good the damage. He had been given the chance to make a difference, not only in his own life, but also in the lives of his fellow shipyard workers; even in the economic recovery of Northern Cyprus itself, so he must not allow a few minor setbacks to hinder him. What he needed was a really good personal assistant, one who would relieve him of all the petty, time-consuming annoyances that plagued him every day, and allow him to concentrate on the really important issues. But how to find someone reliable? That would be a major task in itself.

The answer was, of course, quite obvious, but did not occur to him until he had reached the hotel and entered the lounge where Mary was waiting for him to join her for tea. He sat for some time silently watching the movement of her hands.

"You're very quiet today," she observed with a smile. "Something on your mind?"

"I was just wondering if you would fancy giving me a hand at the yard."

"As a welder or as a marine engineer?" she rejoined brightly. "I am equally skilled in both trades."

"No, in the office," he explained, with a chuckle. "I need to get something typed up. It's a confidential report for Frank Palmer on the state of things at the yard. It'll make pretty depressing reading, and I don't want anything getting back to Mehmet Boga before I have had a chance to talk it over with Frank, so I can't involve Faruk or any of the girls at FNC."

"Does that old machine in your office actually work? From what I remember it was an antique, and you need the strength of a navvy to press the keys down."

"You're English, aren't you? You'll cope."

Mary smiled; a little secret smile of satisfaction. At last her heart's desire was to be fulfilled. It was all she had ever wanted, just to be at his side in their journey along life's uncertain highway. Now she would be able to look after his every need, both at work and at home, sharing his burden, clearing his path to success. Nothing would be impossible once they were working together.

Nihan had already offered to look after the children whenever the need arose, and on Monday morning, just as they were all finishing their breakfast, Nihan came in from the kitchen to claim Susan and Wendy for the day. She teased them, much to Mary's amusement, by telling them they would be working as chambermaids, but the joke backfired when the girls both expressed unfeigned delight at the prospect. Instead, Suleyman agreed to start Susan's Turkish lessons straight away, whilst Wendy would join Nihan and Rabia in the kitchen.

Mary's worst fears concerning the office typewriter were confirmed as soon as her fingers touched the keys. A brand new ribbon had been installed in her honour, but the reel advance was not properly synchronised, and bunches of ribbon kept building up if she made any attempt to work at speed. Even so, in less than an hour the list was typed up, in triplicate, and Mary had returned from washing the ink from her fingers.

"Is it really as bad as it seems?" she asked, as she handed the finished document over to Jack.

"This is only the beginning," he replied, darkly. "I haven't even touched on problems such as certifying the steel, classification, surveying and the like. We're in for a long, hard slog I'm afraid."

"Surely most of these items are down to Famagusta Navigation and Osman Toprak. Shouldn't you be tackling them on the subject? There's not a lot Frank Palmer can do about it in London."

"I don't want to go head to head with Mehmet Boga just yet. I don't really know much about the set-up between Famagusta Navigation and Frank Palmer's company, so I don't know what he is responsible for, and what they are responsible for. My contract is with Frank Palmer. I don't want to get involved with local politics."

"So you can't really do a lot until he comes over again?"

"Oh, there's plenty of work for me to do on the scrieve board, don't you worry. And as soon as we've finished laying the concrete for the building pad I'm going to have a massive clear up of the whole yard. The place is like a tip."

"I was only thinking you could make a start on the pool. I think Frank is counting on you to fix it up."

"I'm here to build a tug, not ponce about with bloody swimming pools. I may get round to it in time."

"You did say that your contract is with Frank. Perhaps you should be doing what *he* wants."

"What is this?" cried Jack. "You've not been here five minutes and you're trying to tell me how to do my job."

"I was only saying…."

"Well don't," snapped Jack. "I don't suppose it has occurred to you that I might know what I am doing."

"You're the boss," observed Mary quietly. "You obviously don't need me here, so I'll get back to the hotel and see if I can make myself useful there. Where do I catch the bus, do you know?"

"Oh for heaven's sake, woman! Sit down! There's no end of stuff for you to do here. I told you, I'll get round to the pool when I'm good and ready."

"Like I said, you're the boss."

"And don't you forget it!" returned Jack, slapping her soundly on the buttocks. "Now I'll introduce you to the joy of checking time sheets."

* * * * * * *

Later that day, when Jack was out in the yard, Mary took a telephone call from Suleyman to say his downstairs tenant had gone, so they could go round and see the flat anytime they wanted. They would find a key under the geranium plant pot in the porch. In her excitement Mary forgot all about the argument with Jack, and went out into the yard to look for him. Her presence astonished the yard hands, for whom the sight of the small, dainty figure of a woman making her way across a shipyard on her own was scarce to be believed. She found her man down the bottom of the slipway engaged in a laboured conference with Adem Usta, earnestly thumbing through the pages of his pocket dictionary.

"Suleyman's just been on the 'phone," said Mary, smiling in response to Adem Usta's deep bow. "He says we can go and see the flat whenever we want. Can we call in at Baykal on the way back to the hotel?"

"Baykal – very good! Good people!" proclaimed Adem Usta, smiling broadly.

"Okay," agreed Jack, pocketing the dictionary with relief. "But what about the kids? They'll want to see it too."

"I thought it might be nice to see it first; you know, just the two of us."

"So, we might as well go now. The men are about to break for their dinner anyway. Gule gule, Adem Usta."

When they pulled up outside the flat, the usual group of children came swarming round, all chattering incomprehensibly to the new arrivals. News that an English family was coming to live in the street had already spread through the neighbourhood, and everyone was consumed with curiosity. A very large woman from the house next door came to their rescue, eager to establish an early acquaintance with this celebrated addition to the community.

"Too much children," she cried, and scattered them with a few well-chosen threats. "You come see Suleyman his house? Key under flower. I bring."

Before they could prevent her, the amiable woman lifted the heavy plant pot as if it were a cup and retrieved the front door key, which Jack accepted with a great show of politeness. He opened the wide door, and proceeded to astonish the onlookers by sweeping Mary up in his arms to carry her over the threshold. These English certainly had strange ways thought the large neighbour, and wistfully speculated on how her own diminutive, emaciated husband might manage such a feat with her ample proportions should the occasion ever arise.

Once inside with the door closed behind them, Jack and Mary hugged each other in delight, and gave a blessing to Suleyman. The apartment was perfect in every way, with a spacious living room extending into a light and airy dining area, a vast fitted kitchen, and two large bedrooms, one of which had French doors leading out through a veranda into the small secluded back garden. Although the bathroom was rather small and had no window, it was beautifully tiled from floor to ceiling and had been kept spotlessly clean. Jack followed Mary from room to room, smiling in detached amusement at her delight at every new discovery. How they would find enough furniture to fill such a large apartment heaven only knew, but he was not about to ruin her moment of pleasure with such mundane considerations. They had at least taken another small step in the right direction, and even if they did have to make do at first with furniture from The Government Store, it could always be replaced at a later stage once the company started to make money.

But if Jack had thought his negotiations for such items as steel, cement mixers and pumps were difficult, this was as nothing compared to the tenacity with which domestic goods were guarded. The chary storekeeper had already marked Jack's card as a troublemaker, and appeared to be outraged at this English madman's new expectations regarding his precious stock of furniture. Without a written authorisation signed by the District Commissioner for Finance, none of Jack's preposterous demands for beds, tables and chairs would receive any consideration.

"At least you've been able to see first-hand what I'm up against," Jack grumbled as he drove Mary back to the hotel after their first unsuccessful foray. "I don't think you really believed me when I was telling you about the song and dance with those lengths of scrap steel."

"I don't know why you have to get so uptight about everything. The poor chap was only doing his job. Not that the stuff we saw was up to much, anyway."

"I know," murmured Jack peevishly. "I suppose anything worth having was whisked off years ago. It's all most likely sitting in the homes of various bigwigs and government officials. No wonder the District Commissioner didn't want to see me."

"You're seeing him next week, Jack. You'll just have to be a bit more patient, that's all. It's not as if we're desperate, is it? I'm sure something will turn up."

Jack maintained a strategic silence for the remainder of their journey; there were times when he found Mary's relentless optimism completely misplaced. On many occasions a good old-fashioned dose of gloom was far more appropriate, and this was surely one of them. By the time they reached the hotel Jack had managed to work himself into a thoroughly bad mood, which was not improved when he was informed by Sunara that there were no waiters available to take his order for tea, all being at an important training session. Mary was on the point of going into the kitchen to make the tea herself when a torrent of angry shouting from the restaurant stopped her in her tracks. The voice was unfamiliar, and extremely loud. As the restaurant was separated from the lobby only by a row of glazed panels, Jack wandered casually across to gain a better view. With a sideways gesture of his head, he invited Mary to join him and they both stood intrigued by the little scene before them.

A row of five waiters stood to attention in the middle of the restaurant. Facing them, and with his back to Jack and Mary, was a squat, powerful figure in shirtsleeves with his arms akimbo and feet planted firmly apart. He was leaning forward from the waist in a singularly aggressive attitude, as he directed another furious tirade at the unfortunate young men. This was clearly in the form of an enquiry, as the interrogator's voice rose at the end to a strangled shriek that reverberated round the room.

"Kaplan is back," came the whispered voice of Suleyman, who had stolen up behind them to witness the condign retribution falling on the waiters. "He is training the waiters. He gets too much upset at them, because they are too lazy and stupid. Look now at Ismail; he tries to lay the table. All wrong, all wrong. I show him too many times, still he does not understand."

Suleyman's analysis of Ismail's poor performance was promptly endorsed when a furious Kaplan swept his forearm across the table that had just been so fastidiously laid, sending a shower of cutlery and plates crashing to the polished marble floor. Ismail stooped to pick up the only whole plate left as it span mockingly on its edge, but Kaplan sent it flying with a well aimed kick before the waiter could reach it. More shouting followed, and the miscreants fell on their knees to retrieve whatever was within their reach. As each stood up in turn the cutlery was snatched angrily from their trembling hands by Kaplan himself who proceeded with a demonstration of how the job should be done, barking out a staccato commentary the whole while.

As he worked round the table his features were revealed to the three unseen spectators watching in fascination from the lobby. A good face, Mary thought; square, strong, almost handsome with its intense look of concentration on the work in hand. His abundant hair was rather too long, and an unruly forelock kept falling down over his eyes, necessitating constant correction with a rapid, unconscious backward sweep of the wrist over his forehead.

"Is he back with his family?" enquired Mary.

78

"No," replied Suleyman, his voice having resumed its usual booming volume. "They only come to Cyprus in August when the children are on holiday from school. They are liking London too much."

On hearing Suleyman's voice Kaplan looked up, and noticed the onlookers for the first time. It was Mary that held his interest, and his face became instantly illuminated with a smile of welcome. He rapped out a string of commands to the waiters and marched out of the restaurant, much to the poor men's relief as they realised their ordeal was over, for the time being at least.

"You must excuse all that," said Kaplan as he approached. "These waiters make me crazy. A hundred times I tell them, but they are too lazy or too stupid to understand."

"Or, perhaps, too frightened?" ventured Mary, with a mischievous little smile.

"Ah! Yes! Of course! Mary!" returned Kaplan, also smiling. "Osman Toprak has warned me about you."

"I'm flattered, I'm sure," she rejoined. It was as if they had been sparring partners for years.

"And Jack! What do you think of my little hotel?"

"We're enjoying our stay here very much indeed," said Jack, warmly shaking Kaplan's outstretched hand. "And it's good to see there is somebody who is still prepared to maintain some sort of discipline."

"Don't let me start on that!" warned Kaplan. "Every time I come back it's the same. Everything goes to pieces while I am away. I have to start from scratch every time I come back. Suleyman does his best, don't you brother? But he's too easy on them, and they are taking liberties. Especially those animals from Turkey. All they understand is stick. Stick. Stick."

"Have you ever *tried* a carrot?"

"My dear Mary, there are not enough carrots in all of Cyprus enough to make a difference. You will see. You will see. And as for building a ship over here! Well I hope you know what you have let yourself in for, Jack. You will need the patience of a saint."

"I don't scare easily, Kaplan. You might be in for a bit of a surprise."

"I hope so, my friend. I really hope so. But we'll talk more of this at dinner. Are you free for dinner tonight? As my guests, of course."

"We shall look forward to that," replied Mary, with all sincerity.

Chapter Eight

It was with particular care that Mary completed her toilette in preparation for the dinner engagement with Kaplan that evening. Placing little reliance on make-up, she was accustomed to using only a very light eye-shadow, and the merest suggestion of pale peach lip-stick, worn more as a protection against sun and wind than for any cosmetic consideration. Blessed with a really fine complexion, Mary took care to avoid direct exposure to the sun. She habitually sought the shade of her favourite parasol on her daily visits to the beach with the children, and was never without her wide-brimmed straw hat. Nevertheless, in the short time since their arrival she had managed to acquire a beautiful light, golden tan.

She decided to wear the same dress that she had worn to Osman Toprak's party; the choice was not difficult as it was by far the best gown in her sparse wardrobe, and she felt it was somehow important to make a good impression on Kaplan. It really is beautifully made, she thought as she studied her reflection in the full-length mirror. Standing sideways on, she smoothed the light fabric down over her flat stomach and allowed herself one of her little smiles of secret satisfaction. She still had the figure of a teenager, despite the ravages of childbirth and nursing hungry infants.

Jack entered the room in his usual boisterous manner; he was about to speak but stopped short at the sight of Mary as she turned to him.

"Come here!" he growled, pouncing on her.

"Oh no you don't!" she cried, ducking away from him.

"Oh come on," he pleaded. "Just a quickie!"

"I know you and your quickies," she returned, gracefully avoiding another lunge. "We'd still be at it two hours later. Besides, it's nearly time to meet Kaplan, and you still have to get ready."

"What do you mean get ready? I *am* ready."

"Oh Jack, look at the state of those trousers! And surely you're going to have a shower."

"Good idea! We'll take a shower. Together."

"I've just told you, there's no time for any of that. Just make yourself presentable, and I'll wait for you down in the lobby. A shave wouldn't go amiss," she added, running her fingers lightly over his five o'clock shadow on her way to the door.

Down in the lobby, Kaplan was talking and laughing with Sunara at the reception desk. He turned and smiled as Mary approached.

"My dear girl, you look stunning," he declared, lightly kissing her hand.

"That is a beautiful dress," added Sunara. "Did you bring it with you from England?"

"No, I bought it in Kyrenia."

"It really suits you."

"Thank you."

"We were just talking about you," declared Kaplan, reluctantly releasing Mary's hand. "Sunara is an expert in astrology, and we were trying to guess the star signs for you and Jack."

"You have to be Cancer, am I right?" asked Sunara.

"Never!" protested Kaplan. "Cancer is the crab, isn't it? Look at her! You couldn't imagine anything less like a crab. She has to be Virgo!"

"How did you know I was Cancer?" asked Mary.

"I have noticed you are a very private person, and you are very protective with your children. Also you swim so well. It is easy to see that you love the water, so you have to be a water sign."

"I'm sorry to say I've never really thought there was anything in star signs," confessed Mary. "I've always thought of it as just a bit of fun."

"Oh no! There is a lot more to it than just fun. There is one particular book you should read. I can lend it to you if you like."

"Thank you, Sunara. I should like that. But tell me, what do you think Jack's star sign is?"

"That is more difficult," admitted Sunara. "We do not see so much of Mr. Jack. He seems to be very hard-working, and he is always well organised. Maybe Capricorn?"

"Ah, that would be telling," teased Mary

"Speaking of which," remarked Kaplan, "where is this hard-working, well organised man now? We shall have to be going if we want a good table, and it will take twenty minutes to get there. You will need a shawl or something, Mary. The evenings can still be a little chilly at this time of the year."

"Oh, I thought we'd be eating here. I didn't expect to be going out."

"No, I do not want to eat here. Watching those waiters fumbling about, it will ruin my appetite. I'm taking you to a very good fish restaurant up the coast near Bogaz. You do like fish, Mary?"

"Oh yes, we love it. I'll just pop up to get a shawl, and see what's happened to Jack."

Watching Mary's light step as she walked quickly back across the lobby and appeared to float up the staircase, Kaplan gave a deep sigh of appreciation.

"What a delightful woman!" he murmured, and wondered to himself why Osman Toprak should consider her difficult.

"Cancerians do have a dark side as well, you know," said Sunara, who seemed to have read his thoughts. "They are moody, jealous, sometimes possessive, and very quick to take offence."

"I cannot believe she would be moody. I can see she might be sensitive. And in my experience, all women are possessive; and as to jealousy, I should think it would be Jack who would be jealous of any man coming anywhere near Mary."

They were still laughing and chatting away when Mary reappeared and made her elegant descent of the staircase with Jack clumping down alongside her, looking uncomfortably well groomed

"There you are, Jack!" cried Kaplan, smiling broadly. "I've just been learning all about your character from Sunara. Apparently you are hard-working and well-organised."

"With a good sense of humour," added Sunara, brightly.

"This all sounds suspiciously like the dreaded Astrology," rejoined Jack, pretending to frown.

"But you are Capricorn, aren't you?" enquired the receptionist.

"I have absolutely no idea," lied Jack. "It's all a load of superstitious nonsense as far as I'm concerned. It is all blown out of the water if you take the precession of the equinoxes into account."

A complete silence followed. It was the silence of incomprehension.

"You've no idea what I am talking about, have you?" he asked triumphantly.

"But we're sure you're going to tell us," returned Kaplan.

"The precession of the equinoxes," explained Jack, adopting a didactic style of address, "has resulted in all the constellations moving roughly thirty degrees away from the *astronomical* position they occupied in relation to the sun when all this rubbish was dreamed up by the ancients. The so called science of *astrology* conveniently ignores all this, despite the fact that it makes a complete mockery of all your silly horoscopes."

"I'm quite sure of it now," said Sunara with a smile. "You are definitely a Capricorn."

"Just a lucky guess," insisted Jack, but with good humour. "Not bad, though, with the odds eleven to one against."

"Which are about the same odds as us getting a decent table if we don't go right now," observed Kaplan, taking Mary's elbow and leading her off to the hotel entrance.

* * * * * * * *

The headlights of Kaplan's Mercedes swept across the straggling maquis as he pulled off the main coast road at a large sign bearing a crude representation of a fish, on which the single word 'BALIK' was superimposed in large luminescent letters. The car rocked slowly along a narrow uneven cart track between the dense vegetation on either side, and a frown spread across the driver's face.

"I wonder why the sign is not switched on," he muttered as he turned into a wide gravel car park. "And where are all the cars?" he added as the headlights lit up the empty space. "They cannot be closed. Mustapha never closes. This is most odd."

He switched off the engine and wound down his window. The eerie atmosphere that surrounded the car now crept inside, so that Mary involuntarily wrapped her shawl more closely around her bare shoulders. She could hear the sound of the sea close by, but the waves had a harsher, more aggressive sound than usual

"You'd better stay here with Mary," suggested Kaplan. "I'll see what is going on."

He walked over to a large three storey stone building looming up into the darkness, and crossed a paved courtyard set out with a number of tables under an awning flapping noisily in the strong night breeze. After trying the door and attempting unsuccessfully to peer in through the shuttered windows, he stepped back to look up at the first floor windows, and called at the top of his voice.

"Mustapha!"

There was no reply. Kaplan stared hopefully up at the windows, and they stared back in stony silence.

"Mustapha!"

Still no response. Kaplan strode back to the entrance door and pounded it angrily with his fist.

"Mustapha!"

This time one of the small first floor shutters flew open to reveal Mustapha's lean silhouette against the background light.

"Balık yok!" he cried.

"This does not look good," murmured Jack, turning to Mary in the back seat. "Perhaps they've gone bust. The place looks absolutely deserted. Listen to Kaplan! He's having a right go!"

An altercation had broken out between the two Cypriots, and once again, no translation was necessary to understand that Kaplan was not being complimentary. After a particularly ferocious outburst from Kaplan the mysterious words 'Balık yok' were repeated by Mustapha with emphatic finality, and the shutter was abruptly closed.

Kaplan climbed back into the driver's seat with a face of thunder.

"How do they ever think they can get this country going again with this sort of carry on?" he growled angrily. "He says he has no fish, the stupid bastard – 'scuse me Mary. He says there has been too much wind, and the boats have been returning with empty nets. I ask you, a fish restaurant with no fish! What next?"

"Well at least he has a good excuse for having no fish," suggested Mary, barely able to contain her mirth. "In his fish restaurant," she added, bursting into laughter. In an instant Kaplan was laughing too, mostly out of his own sense of the ridiculous, but also out of relief at her light-hearted reaction to the situation.

"Why don't we try the Plâj Hotel?" asked Mary with deliberate insouciance. "I hear the waiter service there is really excellent."

Kaplan roared with laughter, turned to Jack and said:

"You've got a real handful there, my friend. I'm bloody glad she's on our side!"

Back at the Plâj Hotel, the restaurant was completely empty, and those waiters not living in were daring to hope that they would be safely off the premises out of harm's way before their employer's return. At the sound of their master's voice in the adjoining lobby their hearts sank, but on this occasion their fear was completely misplaced; his mood was cheerful and expansive. He was much taken with Mary, and even found Jack interesting, if somewhat heavy going at times. The prospect of dinner in good company was immensely preferable to the hopeless task of training staff that had very little aptitude for hotel work, and even less motivation. Mary skilfully ensured they ended up at her favourite table next to a window with a clear view of the floodlit courtyard, and listened to Jack explaining astro-navigation to Kaplan. She noticed the glaze creeping over her host's eyes and came promptly to his rescue.

"I'm absolutely starving. I could eat a......."

"Nice piece of fish?" Jack chimed in, drawing a polite chuckle from Kaplan.

"That's very quick for you," remarked Mary.

"I have my moments, don't you worry," returned Jack. "You witty ones can't have it all your own way."

"My wife's the same," said Kaplan. "She cannot take anything seriously. It must be something peculiar to English women."

"Your wife is English?" asked Mary in surprise.

"Very much so. Here's a picture of her with our two girls. You have two girls too, don't you? Do they like it here?"

"Loving every minute. They think they're in heaven."

"What about schooling?"

"Osman Toprak is helping us out with that," replied Jack. "We're hoping to get Susan into the Army school at Dekelya."

"And I hear you are taking Suleyman's flat in Baykal. When do you move in?"

"As soon as we can lay our hands on some furniture," said Mary, with a sigh. "We've been down at The Government Store most of today, trying to sort something out. What an experience that was!"

Kaplan looked thoughtfully at her for a few moments before speaking again.

"You are wasting your time with those people. All the good stuff was taken a long time ago. But I might be able to help you out on that one. Let's get the meal ordered first. It always takes them forever to bring the food. While we are waiting I have something to show you both."

He gave some instructions to a deeply subservient head waiter and watched him disappear off to the kitchen before leading his guests out of the restaurant, behind the main staircase, along a short narrow corridor and down a flight of stone steps to a warren of store rooms in the hotel basement. They followed him into a cavernous chamber that Jack judged to be under the lobby, and both gasped in amazement when Kaplan switched on the lights. The whole area was filled with furniture of every variety, stacked up to the ceiling. There were beds, wardrobes, tables, armchairs, settees, television sets, even carpets and rugs.

"I cannot help you much with bed linen, cutlery or crockery," said Kaplan, "but you are welcome to anything in here."

"We can't thank you enough," replied Jack. "What can I say?"

"Do not give it another thought," said Kaplan. "But there is one small favour I would ask in return."

"Anything," chorused Jack and Mary together.

"That is very trusting of you both," observed Kaplan, looking deep into Mary's eyes with a predatory intensity that heightened the colour in her cheeks. "You don't know what I have in my mind."

"Whatever it is, I am sure it can be accommodated," replied Jack. In his rapture at the sight of so much furniture he was oblivious to Kaplan's innuendo.

"Can you please, please sort out that bloody swimming pool? It drives me mad every time I see it."

"Consider it done! I'll start on it first thing in the morning."

"How long is it going to take?"

"I can't really say, Kaplan. It'll depend on whether we can get spares.

"What sort of spares?"

"Well, we shall definitely be needing a new three phase pump motor, and most of the valves will need replacing. The ones you have now are all seized up solid."

"No problem. That's the sort of stuff you *can* get from The Government Store."

"Well, I hope you have some pull with the District Commissioner for Finance. I've been trying to buy stuff for the yard, and it's like getting blood out of a stone."

"Just give me a list. I'll get you whatever we need."

"It'll also depend on the number of leaks we find," continued Jack. "There are some pretty ugly looking cracks in the sides, especially at the shallow end."

"Don't I know it!" said Kaplan, darkly. "Last year we got the Fire Service to bring down one of their big pumps to fill the pool, but the water just kept disappearing. They kept pumping and pumping, but the level in the pool would not come up. It was all coming into the basement down here instead. The water didn't reach as far as this room, but it was waist high down the far end in the dry goods store. You might as well have a look while you are down here."

They followed him again along another corridor and down a further small flight of steps. Jack smiled as Mary wrinkled her nose and shuddered at the dank atmosphere while they waited for Kaplan to unlock the door.

"It was worse down this end because it is lower," continued Kaplan as he switched on the lights and fluorescent brightness flickered on over another large room. "You can see where the water came in from the tide mark. We had to move everything up on the top shelves."

He pointed to the untidy jumble of cardboard containers stacked on the top shelves opposite.

"I told them to get this all tidied up months ago," complained Kaplan, marching across to the shelves. "Look at the state of it all!"

In his indignation he turned as if to appeal to his audience for sympathy. Jack wore an expression of due concern, but Mary was showing obvious signs of amusement. The thunder cleared instantly from Kaplan's features as they relaxed into a bemused frown.

"And what do you find so funny, young lady?" he enquired.

"I'm sorry, Kaplan. It's just…" and her voice gave way to a throaty chuckle that had both men smiling without any idea why.

"The biscuits!" she cried, pointing to one of the boxes. "The scented biscuits!"

The two men exchanged a puzzled glance.

"Perhaps she's had too much sun," ventured Jack.

"Maybe it is hunger," rejoined Kaplan. "It can do strange things to the mind, hunger."

Still laughing, Mary walked across to the shelves, and stretched up to take down a carton of biscuits. She had to stand on tiptoe to reach, and the pulse of both men quickened in appreciation of her slender grace

"Are these what you serve up with tea?" she asked, turning to look straight into Kaplan's eyes with a mocking glint of challenge.

"I suppose so."

"We've been served with these every day at tea-time, and we all wondered about their special flavour. Sort of scented. Now we know why. You've been storing them on top of all those boxes of soap powder. No wonder they have such an unusual taste!"

"The idiots!" cried Kaplan. "They will ruin me if they do not first drive me mad! Twenty boxes of biscuits, only fit for the dogs!"

"Not to worry, Kaplan," said Mary, chuckling again. "We'll eat them, won't we Jack. We've grown quite used to the flavour."

Kaplan, however, seemed inconsolable. He started pulling out boxes with a furious energy, muttering to himself angrily in Turkish. Jack was about to join him when Mary, fearing that the meal they had ordered would be growing cold, suggested an alternative plan.

"Why don't we go up and have some dinner. Leave all that. I'll sort it out in the morning. Another night isn't going to make any difference."

"Mary, please forgive me!" exclaimed Kaplan, letting the box he was holding fall unceremoniously to the concrete floor. "You said you were hungry an hour ago!"

They regained their table to find no less than four waiters rooted in terror around the trolley on which their first course was waiting to be served. At the sudden, unexplained disappearance of the three diners, a frantic, whispered court of enquiry had been convened by the head waiter, who accused the others of driving the guests away with their incompetence. Great was their relief when Kaplan calmly took his place at the table without comment. The meal was served with some trepidation at first, with the three waiters nervously darting in and out like little mice, but as it gradually became evident that there were to be no repercussions, the usual swagger returned to their bustling activity and the main course of roast chicken followed with greater panache.

"So, Mary, did you really mean it when you offered to sort out the dry store tomorrow?" asked Kaplan. "You're sure you don't mind?"

"Of course I meant it. It will give me something to do. You can't just lie in the sun all day, can you?"

"Maybe not you, but I bet it is the dream of every one of these waiters. I've never known such an idle bunch."

"How long have you owned the hotel?" enquired Jack.

"I do not actually own it as such. It is owned by the Government. I got dragged into it, kicking and screaming. You see, when the troubles all came to a head in seventy-four, all the Turkish Cypriots living overseas volunteered to come back and fight. But they only wanted the young ones for soldiers. They told us we were too old to fight, but we could do our bit in other ways when the war was over. Then we would be needed to build the country up again. So after they made the green line, then they call us back to get everything going again. I used to run a hotel in the Midlands before I got the restaurant in London, so they gave me this place to run. What a nightmare! The war was all over in a few weeks. Me, I could be stuck with this place until I die!"

"Does it mean you'll have to pack up your business in England?"

"No, that is out of the question. I have a family to support, and they are all used to having the best of everything. I could not do it on what this place makes.

I am entitled to a half share in the profits, but that is just a joke. I'll be in my grave before this place shows a profit!"

"So you're left dashing about between two businesses in two different countries."

"You've got it. Like I said, it's a nightmare. It would not be so bad if I could find a good manager. Suleyman, well he is okay, as far as it goes, but his heart is not really in it. He only does it as a favour because he is married to my sister. No, what I need is a good manager, preferably English. How about it, Mary?"

"How about what?"

"How would you like to run this place for me, as manager?"

"You can't be serious!"

"I have never been more serious."

"Hang on a minute, Kaplan!" interjected Jack. "This is all very well, but Mary already has a job, helping me at the yard."

"I can believe you are a woman of many talents, Mary, but I am surprised that shipbuilding is one of them," said Kaplan with a wry little smile.

"I just help out in the office," explained Mary, "and that's quite enough for me, especially with a new home to set up. Besides, I don't know anything about running a hotel."

"You would pick it up in no time. You would be a natural. But I will not press you. Any time you get tired of playing with boats, you know where to come."

Jack was completely nonplussed by this unexpected offer to Mary, especially when he realised it had been made in full earnest. In his own mind he regarded her just as an extension of his own persona, so it came as a shock that an experienced businessman like Kaplan should consider her as a player in her own right. Of course, the whole idea was absurd, but the seed had been sowed; what if it took root in her mind?

"Did you see anything of the fighting yourself when the Turks finally invaded?" asked Jack, anxious to change the subject.

"We don't like to use the word 'invaded'. We prefer 'intervened'. But to answer your question, no, we didn't. Like I said, I volunteered for the Army but they turned me down. I tried to get back to make sure my mother and my sisters were okay, but it was impossible. We were very worried because Famagusta was put under siege by the Greek terrorists, who surrounded the old city. All our people are running inside for safety. The food ran out and people were eating rats and dogs – 'scuse me Mary – but still nobody wanted to go outside the walls with the Greeks waiting to rape the women – 'scuse me Mary – and murder the men. The Greeks, they bring bowsers next to the city wall – they are going to pump thousands of gallons of petrol over the wall and burn everything – people, animals, houses – everything…."

Overcome with emotion as he recalled the sheer horror of the situation, Kaplan tossed his knife and fork down on his half empty plate and groped in his pocket for a handkerchief.

"You never get the full story from the newspapers," remarked Jack, more to fill the silence than anything else. "We didn't read about any of this. All we heard about were the atrocities committed by the invading Turks…."

He was desperately searching in his mind for a way to correct his repeated reference to an invasion when a sharp kick from Mary under the table reminded him that silence would be far more appropriate.

"There were terrible, terrible things on both sides," admitted Kaplan. "There was no need for the Turkish army to use napalm, but when they did, the Greeks became like – like – animals. Killing and torturing everywhere. Afterwards, in the mountains, our troops kept finding the bodies of Turkish Cypriot boys hanging from trees with their – their – you know – penis – 'scuse me Mary – cut and stuffed in the mouth. Then our boys do the same to their boys. How can you expect peace after all that? People do not forget that sort of thing. Nothing but trouble for thousands of years."

"Yes. The son of Priam certainly opened a whole can of worms when he tried to make off with another chap's wife," observed Jack, trying somewhat lamely to bring the conversation onto a more favourable tack.

"That is just what I mean," persisted Kaplan, determined to continue on his original course. "It is the damned rulers and politicians that make all the trouble, and the ordinary man in the street who pays the price. How many presidents and princes do you find in the front line getting shot at? When war comes, especially civil war, men raise their hands against their friends, even their families. Until the troubles here in seventy-four we all lived in peace as Cypriots. We all speak both languages. The children grew up with both languages. Now our children learn only Turkish. The next generation will not even be able to talk to each other even if peace and unity does return to Cyprus."

"I didn't realise that you all spoke both languages," said Mary.

"Of course we do," returned Kaplan, regaining his composure. "Cypriot life is based on village communities. Every village had Muslims and Christians, but nobody worried about these things. In the heart they were all Cypriots, first and last. In the village where I grew up I speak Greek as much as I speak Turkish. I love the Greek language. You can even say many Turkish words come from the Greek."

"Such as?"

"Mostly words to do with entertainment or pleasure. Like 'portakal ' for example – that fruit you are peeling so badly, my dear."

Mary had selected an orange for dessert, and was indeed making a poor fist of removing the peel.

"Allow me, madam," insisted Kaplan, gently removing the knife and the orange from her juice-covered fingers. "I think we shall have to give up on this poor thing," he continued, handing the battered fruit disdainfully to a hovering waiter with an instruction to bring a finger bowl. He carefully selected another orange, and sliced a neat disk of peel off the top with such accuracy that the tips of the segments were revealed, yet remained untouched by the blade. Working with practised skill he then made four longitudinal incisions to the exact depth of the peel, thus dividing it into four equal parts. With deft movements of his thumb he removed the quartered peel revealing the tender fruit, exposed to perfection. Cupping his fingers, he perched his masterpiece on the very tips and handed it to Mary.

"I have never known a woman who was any good with a knife," he declared. "You either injure yourselves, or make a terrible mess of whatever you are trying to cut. When you have had enough of your husband's boring old shipyard, Mary, and come to work for me, it will be written into your contract that you have nothing to do with knives."

"I can live with that," she replied, through a mouth full of orange.

* * * * *

"Thursday 4th May

What a great day! I do like Kaplan and enjoy his company very much; he's certainly very knowledgeable and great fun; AND the offer of a job too – all very interesting!

I couldn't make out what Sunara was up to tonight. Of course she would know our birth dates, they are in our passports, which she saw when we registered! Perhaps she was showing off to Kaplan, although I should think he's much too wise to fall for any of her machinations. Or is it Jack she was making up to?

Chapter Nine

A few minutes short of eight o'clock the next morning Kaplan sauntered into the hotel kitchen to consult with his sister. He wanted to ensure that the breakfast menu had at least one item suitable for an English family, and was amazed to learn that Jack, Mary and the two girls had breakfasted at seven. He was even more amazed to learn that Mary was already down in the basement sorting out the dry goods store, and made his way moodily out of the kitchen, greatly annoyed with himself for not rising earlier.

At the sight of Mary, however, his mood improved instantly. She had enlisted the help of both her daughters; equipped with a clipboard and pencil, Susan was listing each box as it was sorted; Wendy was in charge of hunting down cockroaches which she did mercilessly, using the back of a wooden hand brush to dispatch them. It was a scene of the most intense activity and enthusiasm that gladdened Kaplan's heart profoundly. The rapid, hammering of wood against concrete signalled the demise of another unfortunate cockroach.

"That's nine!" cried Wendy in triumph as she swept the crushed insect into the mass grave at the bottom of a large dustpan. Susan peered tentatively over her sister's shoulder at the carnage and shuddered.

"You're weird, you are!" she remarked, and quivered again.

"Good morning, ladies!" said Kaplan, whose appearance at the door had gone unnoticed. "What do we have here, then?"

"Good morning," returned Mary, smiling as she straightened up. "Susan, Wendy, I want you to meet Mister...do you know, I have no idea of your surname."

"Kaplan is my surname. Everybody calls me Kaplan. Even my children... even my Wife, unless she is angry with me, of course. Then the names become more...colourful."

"Mister Kaplan," continued Mary. "He is Rabia's uncle."

Wendy put down the dustpan, and transferred her weapon to her left hand, leaving a somewhat grubby right hand to be offered with every show of politeness to Kaplan.

"Are you the boss of this hel-tel?" she enquired, staring intently up at his smiling face.

"Yes, I am," he admitted, taking the proffered hand.

"There are too many cockroaches in this hel-tel."

"Then you can be my pest control officer. You look as if you can handle the job."

"I'm too small to have a job. But I will kill a few more, if you like."

"And what about you, young lady?" asked Kaplan, turning to Susan. "Are you also too small to have a job? And where on earth did you find a clipboard? It must be the only one on the island."

"It's mine," she replied shyly. "I brought it with me from home."

"Susan loves making lists," explained Mary. "She goes nowhere without her clipboard. If I remember rightly, she came from the womb clutching a clipboard."

"Mum!" protested Susan.

To relieve her embarrassment, Kaplan held out his hand for the clipboard, scanned the neatly written columns, raised his eyebrows and vented a low whistle.

"This must be my lucky day," he declared. "A manageress, a pest control officer and a stock-taker all found in the same day. I can go home to England and leave you all to it."

"Will I get my own room, like Sunara?" asked Susan eagerly.

"I do think Mr. Kaplan was joking, Susan," said Mary gently.

"I know that," replied the poor girl, colouring up with confusion. The prospect of a job where she would actually be paid to make lists and have a room to herself had presented a brief glimpse of heaven. She loved her little sister dearly, and was really quite happy to share a room; but those little fingers did find their way into everything. If they were a family of gangsters, she had often thought, Wendy would definitely be nicknamed "Fingers".

"I was hoping to have breakfast with you all," declared Kaplan, handing the clipboard back to Susan with a grin and a wink. "I suppose Jack has escaped to his precious shipyard without a second thought to my swimming pool."

"He's just gone in to get things started," replied Mary. "He said he'd be back at about ten with a couple of yard hands and some tools. They're definitely going to start on the pool today."

"Praise be to Allah. And it will leave me with plenty of time to shake up the waiters and have some breakfast."

True to his word, Jack arrived back just before ten in a small pick-up with three men from the yard, and an impressive array of equipment. As they carried the tools round to the pool area Kaplan buttonholed Jack and dragged him off to the hotel lobby for a briefing over aggressively strong Turkish coffee.

"In layman's terms, Jack, can you tell me roughly what you are planning to do?"

"Salahi is going to strip down the old pump motor, just in case it can be repaired. Ibrahim will be trying to free off all the corroded valves, but I don't hold out much hope for any of those. Ahmed will be working inside the pool prepping all the fissures. I shall be measuring up all the new pipework. The whole lot is rotten and will have to be replaced."

"Prepping the…what….the fishes?"

"Preparing the fissures…the cracks in the concrete pool lining. They all need to be ground out with a disc grinder to make sure we get back to clean, sound material. He'll probably have to knock out quite a bit of tiling as well to make sure we get to everything."

"What can I do to help?"

"Oh, you don't want to get involved in this job, Kaplan. There will be blood and snot flying in all directions."

"A bit of blood and snot does not worry me Jack. I've done my share of dirty work, believe you me. I can certainly knock off a few tiles, if nothing else.

You don't need a degree in engineering to do that. I've heard you like to lead from the front. Well so do I."

By noon Jack had finished taking all the pipework measurements, and he climbed down one of the rusty ladders into the vast, empty pool to assess progress. The sight of Kaplan's somewhat portly figure clad only in a pair of old khaki shorts, and covered from head to toe with concrete dust from Ahmed's disc grinder would have been comic were it not for all his coughing and wheezing.

"You should be wearing a face mask, Kaplan," said Jack sternly.

Mary appeared at the edge of the pool and looked down at them.

"I've already told him that," she called.

"Ahmed should have given you one when you started," added Jack.

"He did, but I couldn't get on with it."

"Well you should at least be covered up," said Jack. "You'll fry down here. It's like a sun trap."

"I've told him that too," called Mary. "He just won't listen."

"This dust will keep the sun off," argued Kaplan. "Besides, I am used to it. We thrive on the sun in Cyprus."

"Well it's time for lunch, anyway. You look as if you could do with a break," observed Jack.

"No, I don't want to stop," returned Kaplan. "I want to get this pool finished. Perhaps Mary would kindly ask Nihan to bring out some sandwiches and beer? That should keep us going, değil mi Ahmed?"

"Evet, Kaplan bey," agreed Ahmed, grinning broadly.

"If you're going to press on I might as well join you," said Jack. "I'll start at the other end."

The three men made a good team as they toiled away under the relentless afternoon sun, in the suffocating clouds of dust swirling through that sweltering crucible. Fortunately there was an offshore breeze, so most of the dust was blown straight out to sea, but even so, Mary had to go inside for the protection of her throat and lungs. At regular intervals throughout the afternoon she emerged with jugs of water or orange juice, until finally at six o'clock she called down to tell Jack that the early evening breeze was turning onshore, and they would soon be smothering the hotel with concrete dust.

"She's one of a kind, your missus," observed Kaplan, as they carried the tools down to the pump room for overnight storage. "She does not miss a thing, does she?"

"I know," replied Jack, with a rueful grin. "Although it can be a bit wearing at times."

"You want to thank your lucky stars!" returned Kaplan, sharply. "A woman like that…?"

"You just want her running your bloody hotel."

"She would be ideal."

"Sorry, Kaplan, not a chance. I don't want her taking on that kind of commitment."

"Well, you can't blame me for trying. But anyway, thanks for making a start on the pool, Jack. I really do appreciate it."

"My pleasure. The preparation work should be finished in a couple of days, and there won't be great deal more we can do down in the pool itself until the caulking compound arrives. Frank will be bringing it with him from England when he returns, but I've no idea when that will be. In the meantime I suppose we could make up some new pool ladders. These have just about had it. And Mary says you really should have a new hand rail round the sides."

"She's an expert in pool design as well, is she?"

"Not exactly," replied Jack with a chuckle. "She was a swimming instructor back in England, and a lifeguard as well. She is very safety conscious where the water is concerned."

"My God!" cried Kaplan. "Is there no end to that woman's talents? You do realise that she is far too good for you?"

"I'll drink to that. Let's go and get a beer."

Still covered in dust, the two men selected a cool, shady spot on the terrace where Kaplan, ignoring the astonishment of the waiter at the extraordinary spectacle his boss presented in baggy shorts and tattered plimsolls, ordered two large beers.

"So what happens next?" he asked, using the back of his hand to wipe the muddy mixture of beer foam and concrete dust from his top lip.

"A visit to The Government Stores, I should think. We need steel tube, flanges, valves and a new pump. I'll see if I can scrounge the loan of a lorry, just in case that bloody-minded storekeeper actually allows us to buy anything."

"Right. First thing in the morning then. And don't worry about the storekeeper. Just leave him to me!"

It was indeed first thing in the morning when they arrived at The Government Store in a lorry borrowed from FNC with the sanction of none other than Mehmet Boga, who had suddenly become uncharacteristically magnanimous at the mention of Kaplan's name. Seizing the initiative right from the outset, Kaplan soon proved to be more than a match for the storekeeper. Jack stood by in silent admiration as the hotelier cajoled, wheedled, charmed, bullied and threatened his way down the shopping list with relentless concentration, homing in with uncanny percipience on every secret hiding place, wearing down any opposition with sheer force of personality. By ten o'clock everything they needed had been loaded on to the lorry for transportation back to the shipyard in triumph.

Although Jack had initially been reluctant to commit yard resources to anything so frivolous as swimming pool repairs, he now realised that apart from honouring a personal commitment to Kaplan, the job presented an ideal opportunity for assessing the ability of Hasan's steel fabrication team to work from a drawing without the need for constant close supervision. Using Kaplan to interpret, Jack carefully explained the drawings to Hasan, who promised them that by the end of the week the Plâj Hotel would have the finest swimming pool ladders in all Cyprus. Apparently satisfied with these assurances, Kaplan invited Jack to join him for lunch back at the hotel to celebrate the success of their raid on The Government Store. Not until he found himself back in the hellish crucible, wielding a heavy disc grinder did Jack remember the old saying that there was no such thing as a free lunch. Kaplan was obviously a man who operated in many subtle and varied ways.

The natural, spontaneous friendship they had formed with Kaplan meant a great deal to both Jack and Mary. Having such a man as an ally made them feel less isolated, less vulnerable; it gave them a greater sense of belonging to the community. He was, moreover, such a generous and attentive host; both the breakfast and the dinner menus were changed to include the children's favourites; flowers materialised in both bedrooms; cool drinks appeared as if by magic whenever Mary was on the beach; a much better brand of tea was served in the afternoons, and the biscuits no longer tasted of soap.

Every evening that week the trio dined together, putting the world to rights over improbable quantities of coffee and French brandy. No aspect of philosophy, religion, history, anthropology or politics escaped their light-hearted exploration. Their debates were never too serious, seldom very well informed, but always highly entertaining. For a man who professed only a casual adherence to Islam, Kaplan was extremely well versed in its history, much to the fascination of his guests. His political views were even more interesting, for he firmly maintained that the period during which Cyprus was under British administration was the best time in the island's history; and he knew many Turkish Cypriots who felt the same.

Towards the end of the week Kaplan called in at the yard to see what progress had been made on the new ladders for the pool. He was by no means expecting the job to be finished, but he was certainly not prepared for the disappointment of finding only one ladder was anywhere near completion. Jack was deeply apologetic as he tried to explain.

"I really am sorry, Kaplan, but I had no idea they would be so slow."

"You've got a lot to learn, Jack. It's a different world out here. Time has no meaning for these people. I did warn you, if you remember."

"I know you did. And I've got to admit I'm getting pretty worried about the situation. Hasan is supposed to be one of the best welders around."

"In that case, God help us all! I don't know why you don't fire the lot of them and bring some proper workers over from the UK. It's the only way you'll get anything done."

"I don't think sacking people is the right thing to do," said Jack thoughtfully, "but I do know that Frank is recruiting British tradesmen."

"You'll be lucky!" exclaimed Kaplan. "For one thing he hasn't got the time, and for another he wouldn't know where to start. You'd be much better off going back to England and doing it yourself. You must know loads of good men from your old yard."

The suggestion stayed in Jack's mind for the rest of the day; as the idea gradually took shape it began to dominate his thoughts. Kaplan was absolutely right, of course; two or three skilled British tradesmen would make all the difference in the world, men like Neil Geddes for example. Not for the first time Jack found himself thinking back to that disastrous industrial tribunal, and wondered how that dour, difficult Scot was faring. How would he react to the offer of a job in Cyprus? The idea was almost unthinkable, and yet...

As he drove over to Baykal to pick Mary up from the flat at the end of the day Jack started to think of other names that sounded a positive note in his recollection. There was much to be said in favour of dealing with people he already knew; shipwrights, marine engineers, boilermakers, pipe fitters. It all made so much sense that Frank Palmer would probably be only too pleased to hand over the responsibility, and the idea of a short trip back to England was bound to meet with Mary's approval. It would probably be wiser not to mention it to her yet, however; not until it had been discussed with Frank Palmer.

Jack pulled up outside their new home to the usual reception of curious children, and made his way through the open street door, to find Mary on her hands and knees, backing out of the kitchen which she had just finished scrubbing. She was unaware of his entry, so he crept up behind her and slapped her roundly on the buttocks. Her response was a wet floor cloth full in his face, delivered at such speed that it took his breath away.

"Is this any way to greet your Lord and Master?" he protested, ruefully wiping the water from his chin.

"We've finished the redecorating, and I've cleaned this place from top to bottom," she declared, ignoring his discomfort. "It's all ready to move in. All we need now is the lorry. We can load it up tonight and move in tomorrow."

"It just so happens there's a lorry at the yard. I was hoping to deliver the ladders for the pool this afternoon, but they're still not ready. Are you sure you want to do any more today? You look just about all in."

"That's just the heat. I'll be fine once I've had a cup of tea and put my feet up for ten minutes. Let's go and get that lorry! The sooner we make a start the sooner it'll be done."

It took Jack, Kaplan, Mary and the girls no more than a couple of hours to load the furniture onto the lorry that evening. Under Mary's expert supervision the raid was executed with military precision. Jack and Kaplan handled the heavy objects, Mary and Susan teamed up for items such as beds, tables and chairs, whilst Wendy and Rabia took care of such sundries as table lamps, mirrors and rugs, chattering away the whole time in their own strange mixture of English and Turkish as they trotted back and forth.

At six o'clock the next morning a somewhat bleary eyed Kaplan joined the removal team to be crammed into the ancient Bedford's smelly cab for the journey back to Baykal. Half asleep, he suffered the bumpy, jerky ride with Wendy on his lap, and his head lolling against the window as they made their way slowly through the deserted streets. Mary had insisted on making an early start in the hope of avoiding unwanted attention from the neighbours, so it came as quite a surprise when they arrived to find the street was already bustling with activity. Kaplan soon came to life as they started carrying the furniture into the flat, especially when he noticed his brother-in-law smiling down at them from the first floor window.

"You've made a good job of the painting," observed Kaplan, strolling around the kitchen after they had finished. "You'll be very comfortable here. Pity there are no pots and pans. I could murder some bacon and eggs."

"Bacon and eggs?" echoed Jack in surprise. "What about Sharia?"

"I take about as much notice of the Koran as you probably do of the Bible. How are we ever going to rebuild our tourist trade if we do not serve bacon for breakfast? I tell you what, why don't we all drive back to the hotel for some right now? I've got some bacon hidden away in the cold room. Who wants egg and bacon?"

Four voices having chorused assent, they all piled back into the lorry eagerly anticipating the illicit treat in store. As the duty chef refused point blank to soil his hands with the unclean flesh of a dead pig, Kaplan rolled up his sleeves and wielded the frying pan himself. It took him no time at all to prepare a huge dish of fried eggs, and another of crisp, succulent bacon, all of which he served personally to his waiting guests with a great show of swank and swagger before sitting down with them to devour his own share.

"Eggerny bacon!" declared Wendy gleefully, and fell to, followed closely by the rest.

* * * * *

"Saturday, 6th May

Jack has been working with Kaplan on the pool all weekend, so the girls and I took a taxi into Famagusta after breakfast. All the furniture at the flat needs a good clean, and I wanted to have a look around to see what shops there are, and if there is a library of any sort. We found a huge indoor food market just off the square– there must have been more than fifty stalls. The fruit and vegetables looked good and fresh, but the butchers' stalls were a touch gory. They just hang the carcass up and hack lumps off on demand. Wendy was fascinated – she really is a bloodthirsty little madam. It seems it's mostly the men who do the shopping here, trundling around on their bikes with panniers for the groceries – when they are not sitting around in cafes drinking that dreadful sludge they call coffee and playing backgammon, that is.

I collected the photographs from the chemist – some taken of the girls at the Roman ruins and others taken at the beach. They have come out very well indeed; this is such a beautiful island and I mean to make the most of our sojourn here. We really are so very lucky to have this opportunity.

We found a library – only a small one, it was attached to a lovely little bar tucked into a big tower at the end of the old city wall. I bought some soft drinks and the young man who served us was most attentive to Susan – he couldn't take his eyes off her. I wish we didn't attract so much attention – people do seem to stop and stare wherever we go – not just the men, but the women as well. I suppose it's because we are English and the Turkish Cypriots are not used to fair people being here now. The library really is very good. Most of the books are English, and many of the classics are here – even Emile Zola and Tolstoy. The young chap at the bar told us the library was set up by the British back in the fifties for the soldiers stationed here. I had to fill in a registration form to join and it was still the old British stationery – nearly twenty years old!! We've taken out three books – Hornblower for Jack, Silas Marner for me, Pride and Prejudice for Susan. There wasn't anything really suitable for Wendy, but I'll buy her something next time we go to Nicosia. I hope Jack will like his book – I want to encourage him to take some time off this afternoon, even if it's only a couple of hours. He's working 'too much hard', as Suleyman would say, and it's making him just the teensiest bit grumpy."

* * * * *

Mary's plan was not, however, destined to meet with much success. At seven that evening Jack was still sweating away alone in the subterranean pump room, wrestling stubbornly with the steel and cast iron chimera that lurked there. Even then, she was able to drag him away only by telling him that Osman Toprak had arrived unexpectedly for dinner, and was asking for him. As he showered, Mary laid out his clean clothes, and once she was satisfied that he was presentable, they went together down to the restaurant where Osman Toprak and Kaplan were already seated at the usual window table, chatting over their gin and tonics.

"At last!" wailed Osman Toprak, looking at his wristwatch. "We've been sitting here waiting for over an hour. My stomach thinks my throat is cut!"

"Let him be!" said Kaplan, rising to greet Mary. "The man is a hero. He's a better man than me, anyway. I had to leave him to it. I couldn't stand it down there any longer."

"So what's the problem?" asked Osman Toprak in a tone completely devoid of interest. He attracted the attention of the head waiter with a snap of his fingers and beckoned him over with an imperious wave of the hand.

"No maintenance for at least a decade, that's the problem," returned Jack with a scowl. "Now the whole system needs replacing because it's only the rust and corrosion holding it together. I hope you'll take better care of your tug when you get it."

"Well we did have a war on our hands you know," said Osman Toprak, bristling up. "We had a bit more to worry about than swimming pools."

"Never mind, Jack! I think you're doing a great job," declared Kaplan. Having seen the problems in the pump room at first hand he could sympathise with Jack's frustration, and he knew only too well that Osman Toprak's tendency to arrogance could be infuriating. Nothing would be gained if these two were to fall out.

"Quite so! Hear, hear!" added Osman Toprak, deeming it expedient to bring the subject to a close. He was far from happy with Jack's familiarity of tone, but this was neither the time nor the place to bring him to heel.

Once they had all settled down after ordering their meal, Osman Toprak tipped back in his chair and beamed congenially round at his companions. His smile came to rest on Jack.

"So, tell me Jack, how are things coming along at the yard?"

"Good. Yes, good. The concrete is curing nicely, and the scrieve board is beginning to take shape. The yard in general is still a bit of a tip, but nothing we can't put right with a good old bull session."

"Bull session?"

"Yes, it's an army expression. Like spit and polish."

"You were in the Army?"

"I did my two years National Service. Mostly in Germany."

"You were not posted to Cyprus, then?"

"No. I was spared that dubious pleasure. I gather things got a bit uncomfortable back in the fifties."

"Indeed they did. Especially when the British decided to pull out and leave us their mess to sort out."

"Oh come on Osman!" protested Kaplan. "It was the Greeks who were responsible for the mess, not the British."

"Perhaps we should avoid discussing politics," suggested Jack after an awkward little silence. "I'd much rather talk about something more interesting. Like how we are going to finish furnishing our flat, for example. Mary bought a kettle and a teapot today...."

"Plus four pillowcases and some hand towels," added Mary.

"We've kept the receipts," continued Jack. "Do we give them to you or to Mehmet?"

"But I thought my good friend Kaplan had provided everything you need," protested Osman Toprak, plainly unhappy at being accosted with talk of teapots and pillowcases.

"I've given them some furniture, but they still need a washing machine, linen, cutlery, crockery: everything that goes to make up a home. I'm afraid I can't help with any of that."

"These are all items of a personal nature which you would normally buy yourselves," replied Osman Toprak, looking down as he fiddled uncomfortably with his table napkin.

"No, Osman," said Jack quietly, shaking his head, "we were promised a fully furnished flat as part of my contract."

"But your contract is with Frank Palmer, not with Famagusta Navigation. You will have to take it up with him. I will take another look at the joint venture agreement, but I am quite sure that the responsibility of housing British personnel is with Frank's company, not with us. In any case, I understand you turned down perfectly good penthouse accommodation offered to you by Mehmet. I believe that is already fully equipped."

"If you're talking about the flat on top of the FNC offices I don't know whether to laugh or be insulted. It's nothing but a garret, and it's infested with cockroaches. You can't expect us to live in that. Apart from the fact that you can only get to it up a rickety old fire escape, it's far too small, and it's miles from the shops."

"You are certainly a difficult man to please," muttered Osman Toprak peevishly. It still rankled that his little scheme for settling Jack and Mary in the vacant hamlet at Bogaz had foundered. He also felt slighted by their apparent reluctance to recognise his importance in the community. The British no longer ruled Cyprus, and they no longer had any right to come lording it over everyone. It would be better for people like Jack to show a little more respect, and not go around telling important businessmen to take care of tugs.

Fortunately, the food arrived at this juncture, and conversation proceeded with greater equanimity whilst they ate. Coffee was served in a snug little basement bar that was a particular favourite of Osman Toprak, who seemed in no hurry to leave. Save for a young barman the room was empty, and had the comfortable atmosphere of a private sitting room with its deep leather armchairs grouped around circular tables. At first they just talked about their respective families, but it was not long before Osman Toprak found an opportunity of returning to politics with another pejorative reference to British foreign policy. Jack was too weary to respond, but Mary astonished everybody by launching into a vigorous defence of the British Empire. Kaplan lost no time in joining the debate on Mary's side, delighted at the opportunity of airing his pro-British views, whilst Jack simply sat listening with a vaguely amused expression on his face, nodding wisely whenever it was appropriate. With so much to think about he saw little sense in wasting valuable mental energy arguing about matters over which he had no control or events that were long past. He looked across at Mary, sitting bolt upright on the edge of her seat, stabbing the air with her finger to emphasise the point she was making with such lively eloquence, sublimely unconscious of her own beauty and its impact on her listeners as she expatiated upon the benefits of British rule. Realising that he had met his match, Osman Toprak lapsed into silence, fearing the possibility that Mary's disquisition would somehow lead round to the tricky subject of Susan's education, about which he had done nothing. He made a firm resolution to be far more circumspect in future regarding his choice of conversational matter in the presence of this formidable Englishwoman.

It was nearly midnight when the party dispersed, by which time Jack was in a state close to exhaustion. He fell into bed and was sound asleep within thirty seconds, but Mary lay there beside him in the darkness, thinking about the evening and Osman Toprak in particular. Try as she might to like him, she was finding it harder every time they met. There was just something about the man – something reptilian? He put her in mind of Mr. Toad. Vain and self absorbed. Just like pompous old Mr Toad......

* * * * *

Saturday 6th May/cont!

How on earth does Julia put up with that man, in fact <u>why</u> does she? When I think about it, it seems a very strange arrangement, she is so lovely, and he just grim and unpleasant. Still it was good to let off a bit of steam tonight, and who better to feel the heat than Mr Toad.

Chapter Ten

Jack was on his hands and knees completely absorbed in marking out sections on the scrieve board when a polite cough from Faruk standing in the shed doorway interrupted his deep concentration.

"Please excuse the intrusion, Jack bey, but there is a gentleman here to see you from the Port Authority. I can see you are occupied. Shall I tell him to make an appointment?"

"What does he want, Faruk? It may be important."

"He is a minor official, of little importance I think. He just wanted to meet you and introduce himself."

"I was hoping to crack on with laying off these sections this morning. If he doesn't mind getting a bit dusty you can bring him in here for a quick chat."

Faruk inclined his head in acknowledgement, and silently disappeared. He returned almost immediately accompanied by a short, rather rotund, jolly looking man in his late thirties, dressed in the smart but casual manner much favoured by middle-ranking government officials. The knife edged creases in his well-tailored trousers were newly pressed, the short sleeved, khaki shirt looked as crisp as any sergeant major's on morning parade, and he exuded an aura of cheerful efficiency.

"Mr Kemal Aydin!" announced Faruk with rather more formality than the occasion demanded.

"Allow me to present my credentials!" said the visitor, marching briskly up to the edge of the scrieve board, so that his highly polished brown Oxfords ended up barely a centimetre from the capping. There he stood, pretty much to attention, looking reverently at the intricate pattern of lines and curves covering the wide expanse of white painted chipboard. Jack stood up and stepped cautiously across his work, smiling involuntarily in response to the obvious delight beaming from the diminutive Cypriot's eager face. The two men shook hands and Mr Kemal Aydin presented his card, identifying him as the Port Marine Superintendent, and a qualified Lloyds surveyor.

"It is already too hot, and it's only the beginning of May," observed the surveyor, mopping his glabrous dome with a snowy white handkerchief. "You must find it a lot different to working in England. I myself prefer the English climate. I used to love going to work with a bit of a nip in the air."

"Oh, it's not too bad if you're out of the sun," replied Jack, stepping off the scrieve board to reduce the amount by which he towered above his visitor. "But I'm not so sure how I shall get on when we're working outside, especially in July and August. We'll have to rig up some sort of awning, I suppose. So when were you in England, Mr Aydin?"

"I was trained in England," declared the surveyor with obvious pride. "But please, Mr Durham, everybody knows me just as Kemal."

"Okay, Kemal. As long as you call me Jack in return."

"I should be honoured, Mr. Jack."

"I meant just Jack. Not Mr Jack."

"It will be my pleasure, Jack..."

Kemal just managed to stop himself adding 'bey' to Jack's name before continuing with his account of the time he spent in England.

"I was based in London, but I travelled to shipyards all over the country – Plymouth, Harwich, Southampton, Liverpool, and even up to the Clyde."

"Hull or engine room?"

"Both, actually. I was lucky enough to qualify in both. Most of my experience has been in the engine room, but my knowledge of hull construction has earned me the appointment of Government surveyor on the tug you are building. It is a responsibility I was delighted to accept; I look forward to working with you more than I can say, and the facilities of my department, such as they are, will be entirely at your disposal. You can count on my full co-operation, Jack..."

Again the unspoken 'bey' hung in the air. The little speech had been delivered with a quaint mixture of courtesy, goodwill and authority. Jack had naturally expected the port authority to appoint a surveyor, but his dealings with officialdom so far had left him with a certain sense of unease at the prospect. Kemal Aydin, however, appeared to be a man with whom he could do business.

"I am delighted to welcome you to the project," replied Jack, feeling that some sort of formal acknowledgement of the surveyor's overture would be appropriate. "It will be a pleasure working with such a well qualified professional. I am sure that your contribution to the venture will be invaluable."

"Well I don't know if I can be much help at this stage, Jack..." confessed the surveyor. "I have been a marine surveyor for nearly twenty years, but not once have I actually seen the lines of a ship laid off. I have been reading up a bit on the subject; I believe this is called the scrieve board?"

"Marvellous! Now there are two people in Famagusta who know what it is for."

"Let me see if I understand correctly," continued Kemal, moving round to the base of the board. "The horizontal lines represent the water lines, and the vertical lines represent the buttocks. Using this grid, you can plot the co-ordinates of the ships profile at each frame and build up the shape in three dimensions."

"Exactly."

"And what do you use as your datum line when you actually set up the frames?"

"The load water line. The one drawn in red."

"What materials will you use to make up the templates?"

"Two and a half inch battens and quarter inch hardboard screwed and glued."

"And that will be strong enough to guarantee accuracy? Forgive my curiosity, Jack, but I really am fascinated by what you are doing here. This sort of technology here in Magusa is almost unbelievable."

"I am only too happy to answer your questions, Kemal. You are the first official to take the least bit of interest in what we are doing. As to the frame templates I can safely say that they will be sufficiently robust to cope with rough handling. The lines have been drawn using conic and cylindrical development, so there are no difficult curves to replicate."

"I'm afraid you are now way over my head, Jack Bey," admitted the surveyor with an apologetic smile. "But I'm surprised to hear I'm the first to show an interest. I know for a fact that the Harbourmaster is most anxious to meet you; we were talking about the new tug only yesterday."

"You mean Selim Captain?"

"That's right. He's been involved with the project since the beginning, of course, but none of us thought it would really happen. The idea of building a tug here in Magusa seemed laughable; but having seen this I can dare to hope that one day we might actually see it being launched."

"Well I'd certainly like to meet him," replied Jack eagerly. "I need to find out what cranes will be available when we start laying the keel."

"I can assure you of his complete co-operation. Selim Captain is a very good man, and most professional."

Leaving the cool interior of the shed, the two men stood squinting and blinking as their eyes adjusted to the aggressive glare of the morning sun. The heat of the day was already sufficient to wilt the limbs and shorten the breath. Kemal pointed across to the great dilapidated wooden fishing boat hulk on the slipway. Some of her timbers could be seen where planking had been removed from her topsides in a half-hearted attempt at repair work, and what was left of her green paintwork was blistered and peeling.

"I see somebody's been trying to patch up that old wreck," he observed with a grimace. "A complete waste of time. What it really needs is a chain saw and a box of matches."

Jack had to smile; Kemal Aydin was obviously not a man to mince his words.

"I couldn't agree more. I have refused to have anything to do with it"

"I am most relieved to hear you say so. It must have been there for well over a year, and all they've done is remove a few bits of planking. You won't be able to launch the tug until it's gone, will you?"

"No. I've written to the owners; some sort of syndicate, Faruk says. They don't have any money; so they're attempting the repair work themselves. Obviously without much success. I want the wretched thing off the slipway so we can take on some proper paying jobs."

"Well I wish you luck getting any reply. I know for a fact they haven't paid the yard a penny towards the slipping charge. I'm afraid you are up against the Magusa secret society."

"The what?"

"Oh, they're all in on it, including most of the men in your yard. Everyone is someone's uncle, or cousin, or brother-in-law. Any sort of family connection, no matter how small, gives certain rights: you know, to favours, special treatment, information."

Jack pursed his lips and nodded slowly in understanding. This certainly explained a great deal. It explained the complete absence of discipline in the yard, and went a long way to revealing why it had never made a profit. Frank Palmer had already explained that Famagusta Navigation was effectively funded by the Cyprus Turkish government, somewhat on the lines of a Quango. Now he was learning of a parallel cabal run by the workers, just as powerful, with tentacles just as far-reaching. It also explained why the men were not rushing to join Hasan in the union. As far as they were concerned the union represented just another source of interference, and an unnecessary additional drain on their meagre income. There were quite enough snouts in the trough already.

"I'll just have to send them an ultimatum telling them the slipway is needed for essential repair work on Government vessels," said Jack

"That might work," replied Kemal, raising his eyebrows to hint at his own doubt in the matter. "But I'd do it sooner rather than later. Things have a way of moving slowly since the troubles. I have to admit that Johnny Greek had a much tighter grip on things than we have managed."

"You speak as if the Greeks ran things on their own. Surely there were Turkish Cypriot officials as well?"

"Of course, but we were never in the top jobs. The harbour master would be a Greek Cypriot, and his assistant would be a Turkish Cypriot. The Port Director was Greek, his deputy was Turkish. Until 1974 I was just a marine superintendent, working for a Greek Cypriot boss, the port surveyor. A very good boss he was too. I learned a lot from him. I should think he's in charge over at Limassol now. Our loss is their gain."

Kemal Aydin shrugged his shoulders and smiled philosophically, consulted his wristwatch and said:

"But I must be off. When do you want to meet the harbour master?"

"I was hoping to get all the lofting done before I officially invited anyone. There's not much for him to see at the moment, and the yard still looks like a tip."

"Nonsense! He'll be amazed at what you've accomplished in – what – only a month? I don't think you can appreciate the effect of what you are doing here. It's like a bloody miracle. It is giving us all hope that things might be on the way up again. It has been a long, hard struggle to get the port running properly again, and this tug will make all the difference in the world."

"You're very kind, Kemal, but all the same, I'd like to get the place tidied up a bit at least before I have any official visits. You're always welcome, of course, but…well you know how it is."

"I understand completely, Jack…." returned the surveyor, delighted to be taken into the Englishman's confidence on such short acquaintance. "But I cannot guarantee to hold my tongue for too long. I am dying to spread the good news."

"Just give me a couple of days. And don't be a stranger."

Kemal Aydin's visit left Jack feeling much less isolated in the yard. He did derive a great deal of moral support from Mary's daily presence, but this enthusiastic endorsement from a fellow professional was just what he needed at that particular time. He immediately ordered a thorough clean-up of the entire yard, including the removal of all the clutter outside the yard gates. Notices in Turkish were attached to a couple of rotting plywood launches which had long since been abandoned on the weed-strewn, dusty area of wasteland just outside the gates, announcing that the boats would be burned if they were not removed straight away. Faruk was instructed to ensure the owners were made aware of the situation using whatever underground means of communication were available, and the wrecks miraculously disappeared overnight. He was also instructed to find a scrap dealer to take away all the rusty cast iron debris that had littered the yard and its approaches for years beyond memory. An extremely dirty and disreputable character turned up in the inevitable ex-army lorry, itself in an unspeakable condition. Using Faruk as interpreter, the dealer opened negotiations by telling Jack the payment he expected for undertaking the clearance. Much to the rogue's dismay, Jack countered by telling him the exact value of scrap iron in Turkey, and threatening to ship it all to Mersin himself. The dealer knew this was no idle threat because that was exactly what he would be doing. He also knew that he would have to use one of Famagusta Navigation's ships, who would undoubtedly give their own yard a better shipping rate than they would offer to him. A haggling match ensued, much to the embarrassment of a somewhat squeamish Faruk, who was extremely relieved when the ordeal finally ended. Jack accepted the filthy paw offered by the dealer at the conclusion of the negotiations, but Faruk scurried away before he was invited to touch the offensive creature himself. It was not until he had scrubbed his hands several times that that Jack felt free of the grime inflicted by that limp, sweaty handshake

For two days the men toiled under Jack's relentless direction. He seemed to be everywhere at once; just when you thought he was safely tucked up in the lofting shed engrossed in his precious scrieve board he would appear from behind the sycamore fig tree, or at any one of the many bolt-holes. Not one of them offered reliable sanctuary; he seemed to know them all. Why did the English have this obsession with tidiness anyway? What did it actually achieve? It would all be a mess again in a week's time. Then you had to start all over again. Surely all this energy would be better saved for building the tug.

When the big new hoarding arrived at the end of the week, however, a great surge of pride arose in the yard. With its light blue background and dark blue border, the sign made an impressive sight as it announced the presence of 'Medmarine Services Limited' in letters a foot high. A list of the services available, the address of Frank Palmer's London office and that of the yard were added in smaller lettering below, and an enlarged replica of the company's logo (the letters MSL superimposed on the stylised likeness of an oil rig) completed the message. There was no shortage of willing hands to erect the sign alongside the gate, and after a short interval allowing the men to admire this declaration of their new identity, they returned to their fatigues with a far better will. They no longer worked in a scruffy little shipyard at the end of the harbour; they worked for an international company that undertook 'All types of Steel and Glass-fibre Fabrication', offered 'A complete service to the Offshore Oil Industry' and boasted 'Slipways to 1,000 Tons D.W.T'. Many a backward glance was stolen as the yard hands left for home at the end of the day, resolving to return during the weekend with their families and a camera.

Kemal Aydin drove by in his cherished Morris Minor just as Jack was leaving at the end of that week, and stopped to admire the new sign fronting an immaculate yard. Even the weeds had been cleared away, and the whole area was hardly recognisable.

"So! Another miracle, Jack...." cried the surveyor, climbing out of his car to take a closer look. "I would never have thought it possible. The whole yard is spotless! Absolutely spotless! Now can I bring Selim Captain to see what you have done to the place? I really am amazed!"

"Okay, Kemal. Let's make it Monday afternoon. We've finished laying off another six frames; we're nearly halfway down the table now."

"Well I take my hat off to you. At least you can take a breather over the weekend. You're out at the Plâj Hotel aren't you? It's very nice out there. Give my regards to Kaplan. I might even take the missus for a spin out there myself. Perhaps we could have a little lunch together."

"Any other time I'd be delighted," replied Jack with a rueful smile, "but I'm helping Kaplan to fix up the pool. We'll be hard at it most of the time. We could meet for dinner, though."

"No. We're visiting the wife's mother in the evening. A fate worse than death. But what about you? Don't you ever stop? You'll kill yourself at this rate."

"Well, you know the old song," replied Jack, and sang the first line of 'Mad Dogs and Englishmen'.

"I'll see you on Monday," said Kemal, grinning and shaking his head as he climbed back into his gleaming car.

* * * * *

"Sunday, 14th May

An eventful and good day today. With Kaplan's help I persuaded Jack to take the day off and go exploring. We decided to take a trip up the Karpaz peninsular to Cape Andreas. Not that we managed to get very far though – we were turned back just a few miles past Bogaz. A sort of checkpoint was set up across the road by the Turkish army, and two armed soldiers waved us down. They didn't speak any English, and kept shouting 'pasaport, pasaport.' When they made signs for Jack to get out of the Mini-Moke I really thought we were in for trouble, but he seemed to make himself understood and they let us go.

"We drove back to Bogaz, found another road and decided to give that one a try. It was very narrow, but as there was absolutely no other traffic we bowled along nicely. We did meet a tractor coming the other way, with people of all ages hanging on to the sides and the back – there must have been at least ten of them! It took the driver ages to squeeze past us, and of course they were all staring at us as if we were aliens. Nobody said anything – they just stared in silence. It was like something out of 'Village of the Damned'. There was one little girl who waved to Wendy, and she waved back. They were still waving to each other as the tractor disappeared round a bend in the road.

"We saw no sign of life in any of the villages we drove through – clusters of mud huts, Jack called them. They could have been abandoned for all we knew,

but passing through you felt as if you were being watched. A bit spooky, really. These people must live dreadfully hard lives out here.

"At one place the coast road became really narrow where it followed round a deep, thickly wooded inlet. There were hundreds of trees, and there must have been a thousand Cicadas in every one, judging from the noise they were making. Jack stopped on the hairpin bend at the head of the inlet and switched off the engine. The sound of the Cicadas was almost deafening – like an unearthly scream that went on forever.

"We reached the main road eventually and drove along it to Kyrenia. Stunning scenery – and more deserted-looking villages. Late lunch at Birol's place – the one Osman Toprak took us to when we came over the first time. Was that really only two months ago? We didn't stay too long – I was a bit worried that Osman Toprak might be on his boat and we would bump into him. He and Jack very nearly had words at dinner last weekend, and it might be as well if they don't see each other again for a while."

* * * * *

It was Jack's custom to keep the shutters of his office window closed against the relentless glare of the morning sun until at least an hour past the zenith. As he was absently engaged in opening them, perhaps a little earlier than usual in preparation for the Harbourmaster's visit, he descried the portly figure of Osman Toprak alighting from a taxi that had just pulled, into the yard. He summoned up all the goodwill he could muster and sallied forth to greet the visitor.

"Good afternoon, Osman. This is an unexpected honour. To what do we owe the pleasure?"

"Hello Jack. I was in Magusa on business, so I thought I'd just call in and give you some moral support. These official visits can be a bit tricky you know."

"Delighted to have you aboard," declared Jack, not altogether truthfully. "Presenting a united front, eh? Jolly good idea! How did you know about the visit, by the way?"

"I think Faruk must have mentioned it," replied Osman Toprak casually as he stood looking around the yard. "But I must say, your bull session has certainly paid dividends. You've really improved the look of the place. I congratulate you. The new sign looks very good, too. What does D.W.T stand for?"

"D.W.T? Oh, on the sign, you mean. A little misunderstanding on the part of the signwriter, I'm afraid. It's not supposed to be in all in capitals, or have all those full stops. It's supposed to be an abbreviation for the word 'deadweight'. I'm not really worried about it. The sign is perfect otherwise."

Both men wanted to bury their differences. Jack's initial dismay at the unscheduled visit receded as he mentally acknowledged the value of some heavyweight support on this important occasion. For his part, Osman Toprak was genuinely impressed by the professional appearance of the yard, and his praise had been well intentioned.

"Do you think we could get out of this sun?" pleaded the visitor, passing a hand over his moist brow. "Perhaps we could wait in your office until they arrive."

"By all means. Cold drink or coffee?"

"A coke, if you have one."

They did not have long to wait. On the dot of the appointed hour, Kemal Aydin appeared at the yard gates with Selim Captain, a dark, personable man in his early thirties, well built and above average height for a Cypriot. His handshake was firm, his English excellent and his quiet, professional manner reassuring. Introductions over, they adjourned to Jack's office for the mandatory cup of scalding black caffeic sludge, before commencing their tour of inspection

Walking from the office to the lofting shed, Kemal Aydin skilfully ensured that Jack paired off with the Harbourmaster by engaging Osman Toprak in a discussion of matters relating to Famagusta Navigation. Selim Captain's technical English vocabulary was very good, easily equal to understanding Jack's explanation of the way the tug was to be built. He was most impressed by the scrieve board, and Jack was only too happy to answer the steady stream of intelligent questions put to him. From the outset a mutual professional regard was more or less taken for granted, but it quickly developed into a more subtle appreciation of each other's personal qualities. For nearly an hour the discussion flowed between shipbuilder, harbourmaster and surveyor. Osman Toprak, feeling left out, strutted about the shed on his own little tour of inspection. He stepped onto the scrieve board and bounced surreptitiously on the balls of his feet two or three times, as if to test its strength, then stood with his small feet planted either side of the centre line and his hands clasped behind his back, looking proprietorial. When the group moved out onto the building pad Osman Toprak stayed just inside the door of the lofting shed to shelter his bald head from the sun, frequently consulting his wristwatch whilst wondering what the other three could find of interest in a few steel beams embedded in concrete.

Back in the cooler atmosphere of Jack's office Osman Toprak was more in his element, needing no invitation to assume the role of chairman, as he ensconced himself at Jack's desk for the purpose. Jack removed the antique typewriter from the other desk and perched on the typing chair, leaving the two comfortable seats at the little coffee table for the visitors.

"So," commenced Osman Toprak, once they had all taken a draught of their cold drinks, "you like what you have seen so far, Selim Captain?"

"Yes, Osman bey. As you know, I was not sure that your plan to build a tug here in Famagusta could succeed, but what I have seen here today gives me much hope. I must offer you my congratulations, and to Jack bey as well."

Osman Toprak inclined his head in acknowledgement.

"But I can still see one big problem," continued the harbourmaster quietly. "Where will you find platers and welders?"

"Yes," agreed Kemal Aydin. "This problem is one that concerns my department as well. We are all a bit worried about the length of time it will take to complete the work of building the tug. You cannot hope to do it all on your own, Jack, and I cannot see how you can train local workers up to the required standard quickly enough. Both Selim Captain and myself have been disappointed at the standard of welding in this yard in the past, and…"

"Say no more, Kemal!" said Jack. "I agree with you both entirely. Fortunately the answer to this particular problem is simple. We can bring tradesmen over from the UK."

"British workers? This is very good!" declared the harbourmaster.

"Yes," confirmed Osman Toprak, sensing a propitious moment to remind everybody of his importance. "The matter has already been discussed with our associates in London. They will be providing the necessary skilled labour."

"Then it would seem you have thought of everything," concluded Kemal Aydin. "We can safely leave the matter in your capable hands."

Selim Captain stood up and stretched.

"I must go," he announced. "I have a ship due in any time now."

"I'll walk you to the gate," said Jack, also rising. "Thanks for coming, Osman. You too, Kemal."

As the two men sauntered slowly over to the yard gate, Jack took the opportunity to broach the subject of a crane for the yard. The harbourmaster agreed to do whatever he could, but with so many of the port's cranes out of action for want of spares, he could make no firm promises.

"What if we take one of the unserviceable cranes and put it back into working order ourselves?" asked Jack.

"That would be up to the Port Director, but I am sure he would agree. I will ask him at our next meeting. Have you seen anything you can use?"

"There's an old Jones near the Cambulat Gate that doesn't look too bad."

"I know the one you mean. Yes, the clutch mechanism is broken on that one. I'll see what can be done."

The harbourmaster started off in the direction of his office, but turned and retraced his steps.

"You are here with your wife and family, aren't you Jack?" he enquired, almost shyly.

"That's right."

"I would like to invite you all to my house for a meal one evening. My wife, she is a very good cook. I know she would like to meet you and your family"

* * * * *

"Friday, 19th May

We all went to the harbourmaster's house for dinner tonight; it was really lovely. Selim Captain's wife is very pretty, and quite a bit younger than he is. She is an amazing cook – the lamb she served was so tender you could have eaten it straight off the bone with a spoon. We had a good long chat in the kitchen after dinner while the others sat playing backgammon out on the veranda. From what I gathered later on, Susan gave Selim a bit of a run for his money – That's my Girl!

"Their house is very comfortable, and everything is brand new. They were married only last year, and I get the impression they are not in any hurry to

start a family. It must be strange being married to a man who has spent all those years at sea, but they're obviously very happy together.

"It was good to see Jack relaxing for a couple of hours – (it's amazing the effect a pretty young face can have on a man!) – we haven't seen him in such a good mood for months. He's been working flat out from dawn to dusk every day – in fact it was midnight when he came back to the hotel last night. He's been skipping meals, and I'm sure he's lost weight. Selim told him he was working far too hard, and offered us the use of his sailing boat as a way of unwinding. Jack seemed quite keen on the idea, and I must admit it sounds quite appealing if a bit scary, you never know what sea monsters swim in these warm waters, I don't fancy meeting any large sharks while we are bobbing about on a skimpy piece of wood!!

"It was lovely spending the evening in the comfortable home of Selim Captain, but it made me realise how much I missed having one of our own. Living in a hotel is all very well for a week or two, but you miss the privacy being within your own four walls. The flat is about ready, but Jack doesn't want to move in until Frank has signed the lease, so I'll just have to be patient. Why do men have to make everything so complicated all the time?"

Chapter Eleven

The scheduled Sunday flight from Istanbul arrived late at Ercan airport, so it was nearly midnight before Frank Palmer cleared customs. He was accompanied by two young men aged about twenty, and Stephen Clarkson, the naval architect. Jack and Mary were there to meet them, but as they had room for only two passengers on the return journey to Famagusta, the party had to divide. Stephen went with Frank Palmer in a taxi, which left the two young men to ride in the back of the Mini-moke. They were introduced as Peter and Christopher, who would be joining the workforce as welders. As they all bumped along the open road in the moonlight Jack conducted a sort of informal interview to learn more about their background. He learned they were from Devon, had answered an advertisement in their local newspaper, and had been interviewed by Frank Palmer over the telephone. It was disappointing to hear that they had no previous shipyard experience, and had acquired their training through various government initiatives set up to reduce rural unemployment. Peter was perhaps the elder, and did most of the talking; Christopher's main contribution to the proceedings was a sudden bout of vomiting, a delayed reaction to flying for the first time in his young life.

When they all met up again back at the hotel everyone was too tired for the usual small talk, with the exception of Frank Palmer who buttonholed Jack just as the group was dispersing.

"Sorry I haven't been able to get over before, Jack. I've been literally chained to my desk the whole time since I last saw you. The shipping division has gone absolutely bonkers. We've never known anything like it. Still, you can't grumble, can you?"

"Well, we haven't been doing too badly over here."

"So I gather. Osman Toprak says you have the natives eating out of your hands. Well done!"

"I wouldn't go so far as to say that, but we have made a pretty good start. Laying off is finished, all ready for Stephen to check. He should be able to take the returned offsets back with him."

"That's great news. What about the pool?"

"Nightmare! The pipework down in the pump room is all corroded solid. We're having to dig it out piece by piece. The pool itself hasn't been so bad, and we've finished prepping. Did you manage to bring the caulking compound and the primer?"

"You bet! The lads brought it over as baggage."

"Yes, I wanted to ask you about them. They seem to think they're signed on as welders."

"That's right."

"They're a bit short on experience, don't you think? They've never worked in a shipyard before."

"They told me they were fully certificated welders," replied Frank Palmer, allowing a trace of impatience to creep into his tone. "If they were lying I can always ship 'em back home again."

"We'll soon see tomorrow. I'll run a welding test for them at the yard. I've tested the three local welders already. It's all in my report."

"Your report?"

"Yes, I've written you a full report detailing the problems we're facing. I've got it up in our room. Would you like to have a look at it now?"

"No, you can give it to me in the morning. The next thing I need to do is sleep."

Frank Palmer certainly did look very tired. There was a shadow about his eyes, and heaviness in his step as he made his way up to bed. After fumbling wearily for the light switch he swung his big suitcase up onto one of the twin beds, and flopped back onto the other, letting out a huge sigh. As he gazed up at nothing in particular a small, tired smile stole across his features.

"A report!" he murmured to the ceiling. "A bloody report!"

* * * * *

It was, however, a much brighter Frank Palmer who sat down to an early breakfast with Jack the next morning.

"Is that the report?" he asked, nodding to a folder on the seat next to his manager. "Better let me have a look at it."

He flipped quickly through the pages as he ate; the document went into a great deal of detail, and seeing it all written down in black and white was most disconcerting.

"Has anyone else seen this?" he enquired cautiously.

"Like who?"

"Like Osman Toprak, for instance."

"No, of course not. It's for your eyes only. Mary typed it out, but she's the only one who knows what's in it. Why do you ask?"

"I'm not sure it was wise to put it all down in writing this way. Stuff like this is best just handled verbally."

"But surely it's best to get everything out in the open."

"Between you and me, yes. But not in writing. If this fell into the wrong hands it could make things even more difficult. You have to think about the political implications. We don't want to be reading about our problems in some opposition newspaper, do we? You're not in England now, Jack, so you'll have to get used to the way things are done out here. A word in the right ear will do far more than any report. Don't worry – you'll soon learn."

Jack was deeply disappointed at his employer's reaction, but could see nothing would be gained by labouring the matter at that time. He polished off the remainder of his hopelessly over boiled egg before clearing his throat to speak again.

"There was another matter we need to discuss. We'd like to move into the flat as soon as we can."

"As you wish, but why the rush? You're all okay here, aren't you? Some people would give their eye teeth to be living like this."

"Oh, I don't mind it myself, but Mary misses her privacy, and she wants to get the girls settled into a proper family environment again. We've sorted out the furniture, with Kaplan's help, and Suleyman says we can move in as soon as you've signed the lease. Then all we need is bed linen, cutlery, crockery and some kitchen utensils. I did mention it to Osman Toprak, but he told me I'd have to talk to you about it."

"How much does it all come to?"

"Five hundred should do it."

"Five hundred Turkish Lira? Yes, I think we could stretch to that."

"No, five hundred Sterling!" cried Jack in alarm.

"Relax Jack! I was joking. Don't take everything so seriously! Five hundred Sterling is fine. Cheap at half the price!"

"We shall need a washing machine at some point, but Mary says she can make do for now."

"No need to wait," said Frank Palmer liberally. "You should be able to find a decent second- hand machine for about a hundred. You'll want it in Sterling, I suppose."

"Yes. It'll go a lot further than Turkish Lira."

"Right. We'll open an external currency account in your name, and I'll deposit six hundred straight away. Will that do you? Now, we had better be making a move. I've a million and one things to do today, and it's nearly eight o'clock already."

Stephen joined them for the drive into Famagusta, and they left him at the yard before going on to the bank. The formalities for opening an external currency account seemed to go on forever, but eventually Jack saw twelve crisp new fifty pound notes counted out to finalise the transaction. Back at the yard they found a perspiring but extremely happy Stephen in the lofting shed.

"I have to say, Jack, you've made a great job of lofting these sections. I had a good feeling about the lines even as I was drawing them. You've done a hell of a lot in a month."

"I was only working to your offsets, Stephen; it's a really good design. The harbourmaster is most impressed."

"What is this, a mutual admiration society?" chafed Frank Palmer, grinning broadly. "I think I'd better leave you two ladies to it and keep my appointment with Osman Toprak for lunch. I'll take the Moke, Jack, if you're sure it will get me to Nicosia and back. See you both back at the ranch!"

Soon after he left, the two young English welders arrived in a taxi. Jack showed them round the yard, and waited for the local hands to break for lunch before setting up the welding test. His suspicions were quickly confirmed; Peter's piece was passable, but Christopher's effort was a disaster. On investigation it emerged that their certification had resulted from a six month government sponsored training course, and certainly had nothing to do with any of the recognised classification societies. Matters were made worse when Christopher tearfully confessed that he was already feeling homesick and was missing his girl friend. The lad had never been away from home before and had no idea what would be involved when he answered the newspaper advertisement. Peter's reaction was completely the reverse; he really wanted the job. With a wife and young family to support, and the scarcity of gainful employment back home, he had seen the advertisement as the opportunity of a lifetime. Jack found himself warming to this intense, sincere youngster, and gave him a second welding test. This time his work showed more promise; perhaps there could be a job for him, even if it was just as a tacker.

Jack's next duty was to take the lads round to their accommodation. They were to be billeted for the time being in the little flat at the top of Famagusta Navigation Company's offices. It presented rather a grim picture after the luxury they had enjoyed the previous night at the hotel, and the disappointment in their eyes was plain to see. Peter immediately set about trying to coax the air conditioning into to life, while Christopher moped about in the tiny kitchen with a forlorn expression, opening cupboard doors and peering disconsolately into the filthy oven.

Feeling a little guilty, Jack left the two lads to make the best of it and walked back round to the yard where he joined Stephen in the intricate task of checking the offsets. They became so engrossed that neither of them noticed the passage of time until about eight o'clock, when they called up a taxi to take them back to the hotel for a late dinner with Mary and Frank Palmer.

"How did the lads get on with their welding test?" asked Frank Palmer as they all settled down for an after dinner drink.

"Rather disappointing, I'm afraid. Chris is useless, and he wants to go home anyway – says he's missing his girl friend. Peter's a good lad, and he might make a half decent welder some day with a bit of training. But he's not up to the standard we need for the tug."

"Will he be alright as a goafer? I hate to think I've wasted my time with both of them."

"He could be useful. He certainly has the right attitude. But it's not goafers we need. We have enough of them already. What we need are proper certificated welders."

"He's right, you know," agreed Stephen "Don't forget the tug is going to be classified. The welding really will have to be spot on."

"Well, it's early days yet. I'll run some more ads when I get back to London and see what turns up. In the meantime we can give Peter a try out, and I'll take Chris back with me next week. You've settled them into the FNC flat have you?"

"Yes, but it's a bit of a rat hole, isn't it? I think we'll have to do better than that if we want people to stay with the project for any length of time. We'll have to make them comfortable."

"It just so happens that the solution is literally only just round the corner. The big house just across the road from FNC. You must have seen it. A two storey building with a balcony all round. I think it was originally built for the British High Commissioner back in the glory days."

"Do you mean the one with all the bomb damage?" asked Mary quietly.

"Oh, that's nothing to worry about. It was a stray mortar shell, I am told. It only knocked one corner off, and that can soon be repaired. The building is ideal for our purposes. It has umpteen rooms upstairs, and a couple of the rooms downstairs are huge – just right for a dining hall and a lounge. Actually, I thought you might like to manage the job of fixing it up, Mary; it would be right up your street."

"I'd better look out my overalls and get the cement mixer going then. But you do realise I know nothing about restoring bomb damage property."

"No, no, no. Forget about the bomb damage; I'll get a builder in to do that. I'm talking about organising a team to clean the place up, get it decorated and then furnish it."

"Ah, that's different," replied Mary. "I wouldn't mind having a go at that."

"We'll call it Medmarine House," continued Frank Palmer enthusiastically. "We should be able to accommodate at least a dozen ex-pats – perhaps more. I had it in mind for you to run the place, Mary. You know, organise the kitchen and cleaning staff, keep the lads in order – like a sort of house mother."

"Why does everybody seem to thing I am in need of a job? I'd be quite happy as a lady of leisure."

"No you wouldn't," said Jack. "You'd be bored stiff. I think it's a great idea."

"That's settled then," concluded Frank Palmer. "As soon as I get the go ahead from the Government you can make a start. We can discuss salary nearer the time. We'll go round and have a look at the place first thing tomorrow."

Stephen stood up, yawning noisily, and announced he was going to bed. It was not long before Mary declared a similar intention, leaving Jack and Frank Palmer to continue their plotting and planning.

"You mentioned a dozen ex-pat workers, Frank. I don't think we're going to need quite that many. Six at the most, I was thinking."

"Yes, I know, but I'm looking a bit farther ahead. Once we've launched the tug, orders will come flooding in, especially from the Middle East. Stephen and I are already looking at the possibility of building a floating crane for the port of Alexandria. We're in the ideal geographical location here, and all the Arab countries are keen to support Northern Cyprus. A successful shipyard in Famagusta? It's like having a licence to print money."

"But that still leaves us with the skill shortage problem," returned Jack.

"As I said, I'll run some more adverts when I get back to London. Unless you have any better ideas."

"Well some of the guys from my old outfit, Marine & General, might be interested. Platers, welders, and there's a really good marine engineer who'd be ideal when we come to fit the engines. He's worked with Cats before. And I can think of a first class shipwright as well."

"You think they'd be interested in coming out here, away from their families?"

"I don't know, but it's worth a try. I could do with organising some equipment with British suppliers as well. There's a whole load of kit that we need more or less right away. I'd only need about a week."

Frank Palmer took out one of his little cheroots and lit it slowly, giving himself time to think. Jack took a long draught of his beer and waited in tense silence for his employer's reaction.

"What about Mary and the girls?" asked Frank Palmer evenly.

"They'll need to go with me, of course. We already have our return tickets, and they run out in two weeks time. It would be a shame to waste them."

Again Frank Palmer played for time, drawing slowly and deliberately on his cheroot.

"What's this equipment you want to order? You know I've already made arrangements for most of the supplies, don't you?"

"Crane spares, mostly, and a decent magnetic drill stand. We'll also be needing sandblasting gear at some stage And I have a whole load of electric hand tools at home that would come in really handy."

"There's a lot to be said for the idea," said Frank Palmer nodding slowly. "But let me sleep on it. I'll let you know in the morning."

* * * * *

"Tuesday, 23rd May

An eventful day! When I went down for breakfast Jack was jawing away with Frank Palmer as usual – I didn't think they'd noticed me. But as soon I sat down they both started grinning away at me like a pair of schoolboys. Then Frank said he had some good news for me – he was sending us home for a week! Which was something of a surprise – we are not due for home leave until October. It was really funny when I told the girls – they said they didn't want to go home! They really do love it here.

"We all went into Famagusta in the Moke (as Frank calls it) and went to have a look at the big house I've been asked to renovate. It must have been really beautiful when it was in use by the British, but now – what a mess! There is so much damage from the fighting – shell holes all over the place, and a really big hole in one side from some sort of bomb. Not a single unbroken window, and doors hanging off their hinges. Inside the house was just as bad – dust an inch thick everywhere, flaking paint, wallpaper hanging off in sheets. Floors littered with piles of old documents from the days when it was used as offices. Downstairs there are six rooms – three of them are enormous, with lovely parquet floors. The part with the bomb damage used to be the kitchen – again huge. Upstairs there must be ten bedrooms, all twice the size of our rooms at home. All the rooms have a balcony, but they looked rather unsafe and rickety, so we didn't go out on them. It's a shame such a magnificent house has been allowed to fall into such a dreadful state.

"Outside there is a big garden – or should I say jungle? There's a tennis court (with weeds as big as a hedge), and a vile, smelly pond with a broken statue of Venus in the middle. I can see what Frank means about the possibility of using it as a hostel, and I can't wait to start working on it, although you would think I'd have had enough of renovations. At least I don't have to live in it whilst it's being done.

"The other really good news today is that Frank has signed the lease on our new flat, so we can move in as soon as we like. We've decided to leave it until

we get back from the trip home – it's only three days time. Just think – we'll be home for the weekend."

Am I getting used to seeing damage caused by bombs and guns? I don't feel as bad as I did the first time I saw the bullet holes in the port walls and now I walk past that area quite often <u>and</u> don't even notice. Looking around this house hasn't had the effect on me I would have expected a couple of months ago. I suppose you get used to anything after a while. That's really awful!!!

Chapter Twelve

Turning off the main road, Jack piloted the old Wolseley through a claustrophobic modern housing estate, peering anxiously at the unfamiliar street names as they appeared, one by one.

"Fulmar Drive....Petrel Close....Curlew Way....Why do they have to use such ridiculous names? What does this ghetto have to do with wildlife?"

At his side, Mary was silently reading the same names from the A to Z.

"It's just up here on the left. Near to that telephone box. Number ten."

Jack edged the car into the only vacant parking spot and switched off the engine.

"Before we go in, Jack, are you quite sure about this? You've said so many times how difficult he is."

"He sounded fine when I spoke to him on the 'phone. Maybe he's mellowing a bit. Anyway, we're here now, so we might just as well see it through."

They were admitted into the small, neat, terraced house by a small, neat woman and shown into a small, neat living room. In a heavy Greenock accent she invited them to sit while she fetched his lairdship from the shed, and returned almost immediately with her husband.

Neil Geddes shook hands with Jack, and instructed his wife to make his guests some tea – using the best mugs, mind. Without his heavy leather welder's jacket he looked more emaciated than ever; he seemed to be much smaller than Jack remembered.

"I was surprised to get your call," said Neil, with the hint of a jeer in his harsh voice. "Efter the tribunal and all."

"Water under the bridge, Neil. I'm not a man to hold a grudge. You played your trump card and won. You'd have been out of a job soon in any case, when the yard went bust, but you weren't to know that. None of us did."

"I'll bet the gaffer knew, right enough."

"I don't think he did Neil. With the ferry job coming up he thought we would be able to hang on. But anyway, we're not here to talk about Marine and General. What do you think about this Cyprus job?"

"I've already got a job."

"What, welding on pipe flanges for eight hours a day at basic pay? Hardly the big time, is it?"

"I'm no complainin'. As long as I can feed ma bairns and put clothes on their backs."

"So I've had a wasted journey then?"

"I'm no sayin' that. I'm only sayin' I have a job. I'd mebbie move if it was wuth ma wail."

"So what are you getting now, forty – forty-five a week?"

"That's ma ain business."

Jack noticed the uneasy glance Neil gave Mary every time he spoke. The Scot was not comfortable discussing money with womenfolk present, and whereas he would have no compunction sending his own wife out of the room at such a time, he could hardly do the same with a guest.

"Mary runs the office out in Famagusta," said Jack by way of explanation. "She does the payroll, so she already knows what everybody gets. The top rate is a hundred a week. Half in Sterling, half in Turkish Lira, all found."

"All found, you say?"

"Yep! Bed, breakfast and evening meal. You'll be earning more than twice what you make here. And you'll be in at the start of something that is going to be huge."

Neil gazed steadily at Jack, stroking his little goatee beard while he thought. A cheap electric carriage clock perched on top of the television set ticked away the seconds.

"Why me?" he asked suddenly. "For that sort of money you'd have men queuing doon the road."

"We want the best, Neil. You might be an awkward bugger, but I'll bet there's no better man with steel this side of the border. We had our ups and downs at Marine and General, but I've never denied you're good at your job."

Again there was that searching look from under Neil's heavy brow.

"Aye, well, you can count me in," he said abruptly.

"Good man! When can you start?

"You'd best mak it four weeks. I'm a family man, and there's arrangements tae mak."

"Right. I'll get the boss to put a contract in the post as soon as he gets back to London."

As if responding to a cue, Neil's wife appeared with great mugs of strong tea, and a dinner plate piled high with mini chocolate Swiss rolls individually wrapped in foil.

"I'm goin' tae Cyprus, Hen," announced Neil as he dunked a Swiss roll in his tea.

"That'll be nice, love," she replied, her submissive smile betraying none of her intention to reprimand her husband when the guests were gone. Dunking his Swiss roll in front of company like that! Whatever must they be thinking?

Her guests' thoughts had, of course, nothing to do with Neil's lack of social grace. Mary had earlier voiced her reservations about the wisdom of employing a man who had a reputation for being difficult, but having now met him her instinct was finding in his favour. This was a happy and contented family; she could tell just by looking at the lovingly framed photographs gracing every polished shelf and cabinet. Similar thoughts were going through Jack's mind too. Seeing the man in the bosom of his family revealed a completely different person to the prickly, argumentative boilermaker of memory. Altogether, Jack was pleased with the result of the visit, even if the tea was undrinkable.

Another recruiting opportunity presented itself quite by chance later the same day. The girls had asked if they could be taken swimming at Mary's old workplace, and whilst he was in the changing room Jack bumped into a former colleague, a very good marine engineer who had just finished a contract in

Dubai. He was most interested in the Cyprus project, and gave Jack his new address so that he could be contacted when building reached the engine installation stage.

News of the project spread quickly through the local jungle telegraph, so there were telephone calls every evening from men eager for details. Very little work was coming out of the refinery, and with shipyards forever making redundancies after losing contracts to overseas competitors there was no shortage of skilled workers seeking gainful employment. In only two days Jack had a list of twenty names, mostly married men prepared to sacrifice the comforts of home life in order to keep the wolf from their doors. Unfortunately there was little opportunity to interview any of them because most of Jack's days were occupied tearing around in pursuit of various items that seemed to be available only from distant locations such as Birmingham or Bristol. The rest of his time was spent packing everything into plywood tea chests ready for shipping, including his own tools and a number of personal items which Mary wanted for the new flat.

As the end of their short visit home drew near, Mary found herself thinking wistfully that she really would like to stay for at least another week while her beloved little garden was looking so lovely. On one particularly beautiful evening Mary was dreamily watering the flowerbeds whilst waiting for Jack to return from one of his frantic buying trips. It was late, the children were in bed, and the tranquillity of the atmosphere was disturbed only by the mellifluous gurgling of a song thrush atop the dense white blossom of the hawthorn tree. She had reached the two dwarf Azaleas which had been struggling for survival ever since they were planted, and were now blooming with defiant vigour when her reverie was abruptly disturbed by the appearance of a little red plastic beach-bucket over the top of the garden fence, its bright yellow handle suspended by a piece of baling twine fastened to an old telegraph pole just the other side of the fence. For over a year this simple but ingenious device had been in use by Mary and the elderly lady who lived next door to facilitate the exchange of various neighbourly offerings almost on a daily basis. As the bucket was visible from the kitchen windows of both adherents to this delightful and friendly practice, all the donor had to do was place an item into the receptacle and pop it over the fence, there to dangle until noticed by the intended recipient.

Quickly setting down her watering can, Mary called to her neighbour, hearing the responding call with a sharp sense of nostalgia. Two neighbours chatting quietly over a country garden fence on a fragrant spring evening: what could be more delightful? In the bucket was a small bag of sweets: just a few barley sugars for the girls, whose bright laughter as they played in the garden had been sorely missed. In fact, she had missed them all; she felt so sad every time she looked out of her kitchen window and saw the bucket, hanging empty as a constant reminder. It just wasn't right, decent English folk having to go and work in foreign parts just because there were no jobs at home. She certainly would not be voting for this lot again; they had made a right mess of everything. These politicians were all as bad as each other, with their international this and their international that. It was all very well for them to talk about getting on bikes to find jobs, but how would they like it if it happened to them? Mary saw the tears of compassion welling up in the kind old eyes, and had considerable difficulty in holding back a like response. She regained control of her emotions by giving a lively account of their adventures abroad, extolling the virtues of the warm climate, the friendly people and the opportunity of advancing the family's fortune. When the conversation ended, however, Mary was left in a melancholy mood as she reflected on how easy it had been to slip back into their old life in these few short days, and how comfortably it fitted. Would they really be jetting off again in two days time to give up this gentle, tranquil existence for the heat and dust of a foreign land?

* * * * * * *

"Sunday 28th May

So here we are again, back into the world of sun, sea and the lovely Island that is Cyprus. It took us nearly fourteen hours from leaving home to arrival at Ercan. We went straight to the flat – I'm glad I made up the beds before we left for England. The girls were exhausted after all that travelling, but they were very good on our journey back. Jack was up this morning at the crack of dawn as usual, off to the yard and then on to the hotel to work on the pool. The trip to England is like a half forgotten dream already. I do believe I'm just a teensy bit homesick, seeing all the greenery at home is such a stark contrast to the brown sandy landscape surrounding us here.

"Frank Palmer went back to England while we were away, taking poor old Christopher back with him. Peter is still here, living in that awful flat all on his own. Jack is going to call in to make sure he's all right, but the poor chap must be missing his family. I do hope this hostel idea works out – I like the idea of doing something useful with my time here, and little old me might actually achieve something tangible. The trouble is, organising all the heavy repair work is bound to fall on Jack, and he has quite enough to worry about already, what with the yard to run and the swimming pool to fix.

Julia telephoned the office while we were away. It seems ages ago since our lunch – I think I'll ask her over to the flat for lunch next week."

Chapter Thirteen

Jack did indeed have plenty on his plate. Awaiting him at the yard was a great pile of paperwork, much of it left by Frank Palmer. Two invoices in particular drew his interest; one was from a well known steel stockist in Bristol listing the first consignment of steel for the tug, nearly a hundred tonnes in all; the other was printed on the impressive embossed stationery of a company declaring interests in Ships' chandlery, Marine Contracting, Steel Stockholding and Fabrication. The invoice was straightforward enough, specifying various items of lifting equipment and steel cutting gear to the value of £3,500, all consigned to Famagusta Navigation via Ipswich. What puzzled Jack was the address in the West End of London, which was most unusual for a firm dealing in heavy industrial goods. He also wondered why he had never heard of such a versatile and diverse company, having dealt with most of the major suppliers in his career, and why Frank Palmer was prepared to pay such hefty prices. In the end he passed the invoice for payment; the equipment was urgently needed, and he could always query the matter with Frank Palmer at a later date.

At the hotel, repair work on the swimming pool had progressed rather better than Jack had expected, as all the cracks had been sealed and much of the re-tiling had been done. Down in the pump room the situation was less encouraging. One new four inch valve had been fitted, but Jack saw straight away that it would have to be turned through ninety degrees for the stem to clear pipework yet to be fitted. Tools were scattered untidily on the dusty concrete floor as if the job had been abandoned because of some emergency. Donning his overalls, Jack steeled himself for another day of skinned knuckles and frustration, setting to with a dogged determination. There was no sign of Kaplan, and he learned later that the hotelier had returned to England and would not be back until the end of July.

Calling in to see Peter on the way home late that evening, Jack found the young man in surprisingly good spirits. He had transformed the flat from a hovel to a comfortable bachelor apartment; the air conditioning worked, the kitchen was immaculate, the chairs looked inviting, and the former stale reek of neglect was conspicuously absent. A neat stack of books graced the highly polished coffee table, and Jack studied the titles as Peter brewed him a cup of tea.

"So you're a Hornblower fan," he observed as Peter brought in the tea.

"This is the first time I've read anything like this," replied the young man enthusiastically. "I got the books from the library in the old city – your missus put me on to it. I'm going to read all of them. I think they're great."

"What have you been up to at the yard?"

"Not a lot, really. A bit of cleaning up in the welding shop. And I had a couple of goes with that acetylene contraption. What a work-up! Then when Chris went the boss gave me a couple of days off to settle in here. That's about it, really."

"So you like it out here then?"

"Well, I'm missing my family of course, but otherwise I'm happy enough. You've got to have a go, haven't you? Not like poor old Chris. He was really glad you sent him back home. I hope you haven't got the same thing in mind for me."

"No. I'm keeping you on. I think you'll make a good welder with the right guidance, and you'll get plenty of that once Neil Geddes arrives in about a month's time. He'll be leading the fabrication team, and he's really good. In the meantime you can work on the pool repair job out at the hotel. That'll really give you something to cut your teeth on!"

The transformation in the appearance of the flat had been enough to convince Jack that in Peter he had a man who took pride in what he did, and was plainly capable of working without supervision, so first thing next morning they drove out to the hotel where Jack carefully explained what was required to his eager and delighted young neophyte. He was about to leave for the yard when he was buttonholed by Sunara, the hotel receptionist, who told him that two English boys had turned up the previous evening quite out of the blue, and were waiting for him in the basement bar. Astounded by the news, he went off to meet them, wondering why no mention had been made of any new recruits, and hoping Sunara's reference to them as boys was not literal. On seeing them, however, his heart sank; boys they certainly were, both wearing Hawaiian shirts and knee-length Bermudan shorts. They were lounging as to the manner born on a great leather upholstered settee, drinking cold beer from tall glasses, their sandaled feet up on the coffee table.

"I'm Jack Durham," he announced testily. "Reception said you wanted to see me."

The two lads scrambled hastily to their feet smiling nervously.

"Mr. Palmer told us to ask for you when we arrived. We're here to work on the tug," explained the taller lad. He was very good looking, and sported a great mop of curly golden hair.

"What trade?"

"Sorry?"

"What is your trade? What work do you do?"

"I can do a bit of welding," declared goldilocks proudly. "I do all the welding on my dad's farm. I'm pretty good with machinery too. My name is David."

"Of course it is!" snapped Jack turning his baleful gaze on the other youth and causing him to visibly squirm. "And you?"

"My name's Ralph – er – I'm Chris's mate?" was the uncertain reply, sounding more like a question than a statement.

"Chris who went home a week ago, you mean?"

"He didn't tell me he was going home, did he?" whined the lad.

"And what do you do?"

"Sheet metal worker."

Jack could not stop himself from laughing out loud, much to the amazement of his audience.

"A farm mechanic and a sheet metal worker!" he cried. "What next? A cordwainer, perhaps, or even a milliner?"

The two youngsters had to endure an uncomfortable silence before Jack spoke again.

"I'm sorry, lads, but you're not quite what I was expecting. In fact I wasn't told to expect anyone at all. This is all a bit of a surprise. So bring me up to speed; what have you been told about our set up here in Cyprus?"

Encouraged by the conciliatory tone of Jack's enquiry, David spelled out the terms on which they had been offered employment by Frank Palmer. Hostel accommodation providing bed, breakfast and evening meal, a month's home leave twice a year, company transport for their own personal use, half their pay in Turkish lira and half in Sterling to be paid into their UK bank accounts on a weekly basis. They had also been told that Jack would reimburse them with their travelling expenses as soon as they arrived.

Jack felt sorry for the two youngsters as he disabused them. He would see what could be done about travel expenses, but he could offer them no transport. As for accommodation they could remain at the hotel, but they would have to work for their board and lodging by helping Peter with the pool repairs. Ralph said he was carrying a letter from Peter's wife, and was sent off to find him and deliver the document without delay. When he came back Peter was with him, looking distinctly worried as he asked Jack for a meeting in private. His wife's letter contained the disturbing news that no wages had yet been paid into their joint bank account and she was running short of money. Reassuring the young man that these inter-bank transactions sometimes took longer than intended, Jack promised to telephone Frank Palmer straight away to ascertain the reason for the delay in payment.

Back at the yard Jack battled all afternoon to obtain a connection with Frank Palmer's London office. It was nearly five o'clock before he eventually succeeded, and even then the line was very bad. He learned that David had been taken on primarily to work on a small cargo vessel that Medmarine would be operating out of Famagusta. The other lad had been signed up purely on the recommendation of Christopher, and had not been interviewed at all. He could be sent back home if he was unsuitable. As to Peter's missing salary payment, well, it was a complete mystery. The necessary mandate had been signed by Frank Palmer personally. These bloody banks were all the same; they wouldn't recognise efficiency if it had a ten-foot neon sign over it. Tell Peter he was not to worry; everything would be straightened out by the morning.

As the Mini-Moke took Jack on his homeward journey that evening it might have been on autopilot for all the attention he paid to the road. It was important to stay focussed, he told himself; he was a professional ship-builder here to build a tug. He really must not allow himself to become bogged down with all these inconsequential trivia, which ought really to be handled, by Famagusta Navigation, Osman Toprak or Frank Palmer himself. If this tug was ever to be built it was important to rid himself of unnecessary burdens and delegate responsibility wherever possible. There would have to be a serious meeting with Mehmet Boga, and it would have to be soon.

The opportunity for such a meeting presented itself the very next morning when a letter was delivered by hand from Famagusta Navigation concerning the proposed hostel. It read:

"Dear Mr Durham

Re: Joint Venture Agreement, Paragraph 4.

With regard to the above. I am glad to inform you that <u>the building under</u> <u>Plot No.86</u> has now been allocated to my Company, Famagusta Navigation Ltd. for the accommodation of your staff at a rental to be agreed on a later date. Therefore it would be advisable for you now to start making arrangements for carrying out the necessary repairs, and put it in a habitable condition at your own expenses, so as you could indeed move in the building as soon as possible.

Thanking you in anticipation of your kind co-operation in this matter. Please do not hesitate to contact me for anything that I'll only be pleased to assist you.

Yours faithfully
Mehmet Boga
Famagusta Navigation Ltd.
Acting Managing Director."

Jack was in the middle of some intricate calculations for the preparation of cutting lists, but he set the work aside and telephoned Mehmet Boga to find out if they could meet for a discussion right away. On reaching agreement he drove straight round to Famagusta Navigation's offices, only to be asked by a secretary to take a seat, as the Managing Director was engaged. By the time ten minutes had passed Jack was seething. He told the secretary he could not wait, and left a message for the great man to telephone the yard when he was free. As he stormed out of the building Mehmet Boga's window flew open.

"Jack! Where are you going? I thought we had a meeting."

"I can't afford to waste time sitting around in your secretary's office. You said you were available straight away."

"The stupid girl did not inform me that you were there. Come on up now. We have a great deal to discuss."

In Mehmet's office Jack declined the offer of coffee, determined to tackle the business in hand without wasting time on small talk. The Cypriot was not, however, to be denied his little diversion.

"Before we start to discuss the house, my friend, I have some very good news for you. The steel for the tug has just arrived in port."

Jack's expression did not change. Still angry at being kept waiting, and knowing that it was a favourite device of officials wishing to inspire awe in visitors, he had no intention of showing any of the joy he felt inwardly on hearing the news.

"When will it be discharged?"

"Tomorrow, we hope."

"And how will it be delivered to the yard?"

"By the usual method of trolleys which are owned by the Port Authority."

"So the steel will be loaded straight from the ship onto the trolleys?"

"Why do you ask, my friend?"

"Because I don't want to see a pile of steel rusting away on the dockside waiting for trolleys to become available. We don't want a repeat performance of the fiasco we had with the cement."

"I think you can leave the delivery of the steel to the Port Authorities, Jack. They are experienced in such matters. I will however mention your concerns to Selim Captain, just to put your mind at rest."

"While we're on the subject of steel, is there any news yet on that eight meter RSJ from The Government Store? It was supposed to be delivered to the yard while I was in England. We're going to need it for laying the keel, you know."

"I have written to the District Minister of Finance requesting him to intervene personally. Never fear, my friend, you will have your RSJ by the end of the week."

Jack took little reassurance from this statement, but aware of the futility of pressing the point any further, he took Mehmet's letter out of his pocket and unfolded it on the desk.

"So, on the subject of Medmarine House. Thank you for the letter. I'm surprised things have moved so quickly."

The great man closed his eyes and inclined his bullet head forward to acknowledge what he took to be a compliment.

"We aim to please. I am happy to have made my own small contribution."

Jack ignored the blatant arrogation, and settled back in his chair with a knowing grin.

"It makes you think the Government is desperate to get the place off their hands, doesn't it?"

"I cannot agree with you there, my friend. I happen to know that the Department has received a number of interesting proposals. It is a fine building."

"Which has been standing empty for the last four years," observed Jack, still grinning. He was beginning to enjoy the exchange.

"I consider the offer of a lease on this property to be most generous. It is a strong indication of Government support."

"So we'll have no trouble getting it rent free for five years then."

Mehmet Boga frowned as he reached forward to pick up the letter.

"At a rental to be agreed at a later date," he quoted. "I do not think we can expect them to agree a postponement of rent for five years."

"No, Mehmet, I'm not talking about a postponement. I'm talking about no rent at all for the first five years. I've done some rough calculations, and it's going to cost at least half a million Turkish lira to put that house in a habitable condition. It's rental value is no more than a hundred thousand per annum, so the rent free period will have to be at least five years just to cover the cost of renovations."

"If you will let me have your comments in writing, with a copy of your estimates, I shall be happy to take the matter back to the Department. But we must be careful not to ask for too much, or the offer may be withdrawn. I do not think Frank Palmer would be happy about that."

"He'll be even less happy if we take on some white elephant that will bleed us dry. Perhaps we'd better get Osman Toprak involved. He should know all about leases."

At the mention of the illustrious name there was an immediate change in Mehmet Boga's manner. His supercilious expression gave way to a conspiratorial smile, and he leaned forward in his seat, the leather creaking under his bulk.

"We must use every endeavour to get the best terms we can, of course. I shall write to the Minister personally as soon as I receive your own letter and the estimates. Are you sure you will not take some refreshment?"

"No, Mehmet. I'm going straight back to the yard and get that letter written. You'll have it within a couple of hours. That'll give you plenty of time to get your letter in the post today."

Suiting the action to his words, Jack worked feverishly on the fair copy of his rough estimates, and drafted a long letter raising every conceivable point, whilst expressing the hope that sight of the lease could be arranged within seven days. He smiled to himself as he rounded off with a pompous little paragraph of colonial officialese. With the ancient office typewriter on the floor of the Mini-moke he dashed back to the flat and dragooned Mary into typing up the finished article. Mehmet Boga found the correspondence waiting for him when he returned from a good lunch and a long siesta. He sighed, and tossed the papers, unread, into his in tray.

* * * * *

"Wednesday 31st May

We had our first home cooked meal today – lamb chops, boiled potatoes and spinach. Jack rigged up the television set and we all sat watching Poldark. The programme comes from the Greek side – dialogue in English, with Greek sub-titles. The adverts are all in Greek, of course. Most of them seemed to be about killing cockroaches, so we're not the only ones with that particular problem. The flat is already starting to feel like home – it will be even better when our bits and bobs arrive from England (if they ever do, that is).

"We managed to get through to Peter's wife on the office 'phone this evening. She's a lot happier now his money has been paid up to date. Peter is happier too, with a couple of English lads to keep him company. Jack is sending one of them back to England – apparently he is unsuitable. The other lad, David, is moving in with Peter. They do seem to get on very well together.

"Jack's in a better mood today. He was a bit grumpy when we first got back, but now the steel has arrived he has cheered up no end. Relaxing in front of the TV after some home cooking may have helped as well. I typed up a long letter to FNC for him this afternoon, re – the lease on the house. It all looks terribly complicated – but Jack seems to know what he's doing.

"My washing machine arrived this afternoon as well – one of the men from the yard plumbed it in. It's a German make, very well built and in excellent condition. Now I can do all the washing – YIPEE!"

Chapter Fourteen

A hundred tonnes of steel being unloaded from a British ship was a rare event in the Port of Famagusta, and the process was being watched with great interest, not just by the harbourmaster and customs officials, but also the various human flotsam that habituated the ancient dockside under the brooding mass of Othello's Tower. All day long the jib of Selim Captain's best crane slewed back and forth under the blazing sun, and casual onlookers admired the precision with which the huge slate-blue sheets were gently lowered onto sturdy dunnage, placed carefully over the time worn cobbles.

Blithely anticipating the arrival of his steel, Jack spent the morning preparing the area earmarked for its storage alongside the building pad. He was keen to ensure maximum efficiency in the construction process right from the start, and knew from experience the difference a little planning and foresight could make. By midday the space was all carefully marked out, with the various sizes displayed on wooden signposts driven into the hard, dusty ground, and lengths of old timber strategically placed as dunnage.

This done, he decided to start making full sized profile templates of the keel sections. With any luck they could be cutting steel tomorrow, or the next day at the latest. Emir and Halil, the two carpenters, eagerly assisted Jack to bend the long, thin fairing splines round the bold, hard sweep of the skeg, and the gentler curves of the stem and forefoot. By six o'clock the job was finished, with all five hardboard templates stacked neatly against the wall. Throughout the afternoon Jack had been working with a vague sense of expectation at the back of his mind, and not until this point did he realised that the convoy of steel laden trolleys from the port had not materialised.

As he drove along the quayside to investigate Jack could see no crane activity of any kind, and concluded that the discharge of his steel was complete. It would all be sitting on the trolleys waiting to be delivered down to the yard first thing in the morning. On approaching the berth, however, he let out a long groan of disappointment; the steel was sitting on the dockside, with not a trolley in sight. The area had been cordoned off with a makeshift wooden barrier, and an old night watchman in a tiny portable shelter mounted a somewhat ineffective guard over the site. Selim Captain's office was closed for the day, and the only occupant of the customs office spoke no English. He just pointed at his wristwatch and kept repeating the word 'yarin' which sadly Jack understood only too well. The Turkish word for 'tomorrow' was already burned deep into his soul.

Eight o'clock next morning found Jack sitting in the Mini-Moke outside the Harbourmaster's office, waiting for him to arrive. As the minutes ticked by, a steady fungal growth of frustration spread through him; his jaw was clenched, his brow furrowed, and his grip on the steering wheel was so tight that each knuckle had a little white peak. He had to wait for only ten minutes, but it seemed like an hour.

"Good morning, Jack. You are waiting for me?" said Selim Captain brightly. "You haven't been waiting long I hope."

"Oh, only ten minutes or so. I wanted to catch you early to find out what went wrong with the delivery of the steel yesterday."

"Wrong? Nothing went wrong. The discharge went very well. It was finished by four."

"Yes, but the steel is no good to me sitting on the dockside. I was hoping that you would load it straight onto the trolleys and bring it down to the yard. I discussed the matter with Mehmed Boga two days ago, he said he would mention it to you."

"He said nothing to me, Jack. But in any case he has nothing to do with running the port."

"Well, it was only a suggestion. I thought it would save time and money if you only had to handle the steel once. Now you've got to tie up a crane again to load the steel onto the trolleys."

"I understand what you say, Jack, but I cannot allow any outside interference with the running of the port. Your steel was not the only cargo being discharged yesterday you know. I did not have enough trolleys available to do as you suggest, and I did not have a crane available to offload in the yard. But don't worry. You will have your steel by the end of the week."

There was a note of finality in the Harbourmaster's tone that indicated further debate would be pointless. Again Jack had to consol himself with the thought that another two days would not really make a great deal of difference in the greater scheme of life, and he could always use the time to push on with the swimming pool job. Still feeling disappointed, and with a last wistful look at the heaps of steel already beginning to shimmer in the morning sun, he made his way off to the hotel and the delights of the pump room.

Walking into the hotel lobby as a contractor rather than a guest, Jack felt almost as if his identity had changed. This was confirmed by the attitude of Sunara at the reception desk whose tone was altogether more familiar than hitherto. She even asked him if he would drive out to her home when he had a moment to take a look at a generator that had been installed the year before and had never run properly. Making a vague promise to see what he could do, Jack escaped outside as soon as he could, and was both surprised and delighted at the progress on the swimming pool. The retiling was complete, and the grouting very nearly finished too. With a cheerful wave of his trowel, Ahmed beamed up at him from the vast, sweltering pit.

"Soon to swim!" he croaked through his parched lips.

"You will be the first one in," promised Jack.

Peter was in the pump room working with David. The heat down there even at ten o'clock had already compelled the lads to strip down to the waist, and sweat was dripping abundantly from the end of their noses. To Jack's delight they appeared to be fitting the very last section into the pipework puzzle.

"Mornin' boss," gasped Peter as he torqued up a nut. "Job'll be finished in about half an hour."

"I never thought I'd see the day. Well done! Well done!"

"The pump's working too, thanks to David. He's done this sort of work before."

"Hallelujah!" cried Jack. "We'll celebrate over lunch, and the drinks are on me."

Momentarily inclined to euphoria, Jack promptly returned to reception and offered to go and have a look at Sunara's reluctant generator straight away. She quickly found someone to cover the shift, and Jack followed her smart little car about halfway back along the Famagusta Road, then up a dry, bumpy track to an attractive newly built bungalow in the middle of an area of open scrubland. The generator was housed in a little lean-to shelter at the back, and Sunara left him to his initial inspection whilst she went inside the house to prepare some refreshments. When she returned with two glasses of beer, Jack saw that she had changed out of her work clothes and was now wearing shorts and a slinky top with a plunging neckline that left nothing to the imagination. Around her neck was a gold chain from which a heart shaped locket dangled just above a generous cleavage. With a sickening surge of panic Jack realised that he had completely misunderstood the intentions of this predatory female. The visit had absolutely nothing to do with the generator, which as far as he could see was in perfect working order. Sunara was apparently trying to seduce him!

Having gulped down his beer almost in one swallow, Jack proclaimed the generator to be fully functional, mumbled some excuses about being needed back at the hotel, beat a hasty retreat to the Mini-Moke, and drove back up the dusty track as fast as the uneven surface would permit. On reaching the main road his feeling of panic subsided, and he reflected that Sunara had shown no concern or even surprise at his headlong flight. He started to feel foolish; perhaps he had it all wrong. Either way, she must think his behaviour extremely odd, and he might have to face some embarrassment on his next visit to the hotel. And what about Mary? Should he tell her about the incident? No, he did not want her to know what a complete idiot he had been.

Back at the hotel Peter and David were in the sea, washing off the sweat and grime of the pump room. It was far too hot to eat, so they ordered a liquid lunch and sat in the shade of some palm trees by the side of the empty pool.

"So what's the next job, boss?" enquired Peter.

"All that length of four inch pipework from the back of the pool bar down to the sea has to be replaced."

"Christ almighty! There must be two hundred feet of the stuff!"

"Not quite, but it certainly is a fair old length. Our main concern is getting new steel pipe, and that may take some time. What I might do in the meantime is see if we can borrow some suction hose from the fire department. We'll need to beg, borrow or steal a suitable coupling as well. That might be a bit of a problem."

"There's an old derelict bowser parked across the road from our flat," said David. "That's got some couplings on it. I think they might even be four inch."

"Do you think one might be liberated without attracting too much attention?" asked Jack with deliberate casualness.

A slow smile of understanding spread across David's features, followed by a gentle nod.

"Good," continued Jack. "I'm going to leave you two rascals to enjoy a leisurely afternoon off. You've done enough for today. You can stay here if you like, but only on your best behaviour. No getting drunk, d'you hear? On second thoughts perhaps you'd better come back to Famagusta with me in the Moke."

"No, I'd rather stick around here for a while if that's okay," replied David. "I quite like the look of that Sunara in reception."

"You've got no chance there, mate," chaffed Peter. "She's way out of your league."

"You think? I'm not so sure." The slow smile returned. "Some of these posh birds like a bit of rough off the farm."

* * * * * * * *

Driving past Sunara's house on his way back to Famagusta, Jack looked across and smiled to himself. She was certainly going to have her hands full with David; that young man had hidden depths, and would be more than enough for the libidinous receptionist. Nevertheless, it had been a close shave this morning, and the possible consequences were too horrific to contemplate. His lack of experience with women had led to quite enough trouble in the past, and now that he had found a soul mate in Mary it behove him to be more circumspect in his dealings with the fair sex.

His mood, however, was still upbeat following the good news from the pump room, and he dearly wished to keep up the momentum. On reaching Famagusta he made straight for the derelict bowser mentioned by David, and was delighted to find the young man's information had been correct. His next port of call was Famagusta Navigation where he learned to his dismay that the bowser belonged to the Ministry of Finance. Going on past form it could take a month to negotiate the purchase of the coupling he needed. A relatively painless meeting with Mehmet Boga then followed, resulting in the loan of a lorry and the services of Onan for a visit to the fire department. Jack had the bit between his teeth and was now at full gallop.

At the fire station the pace soon slowed down to a canter. The officer of the watch listened to Onan's translation of Jack's proposal with no sign of interest on his heavy, sullen face. When the explanation was finished there was no need to translate the reply: a sharp upward tilt of the head accompanied by a single, irascible 'tut'. Onan tried again, and this time Jack heard the names Osman Toprak and Rauf Denktas mentioned. This approach met with far more success; they were directed to a store at the back of the station where they loaded several lengths of heavy-duty suction hose onto the lorry.

"What did you say to him?" yelled Jack over the screech of Onan's missed gear change on their way out

"I told him that Osman Toprak was entertaining President Denktas at the hotel this weekend. It is the fire department's duty to be helpful, in any case. They sometimes forget they are only public servants. We must return the hoses next Tuesday, in any case. Does that give you enough time?"

On regaining the hotel they found Peter and David back down in the pump room painting the new pipework. They seemed to be just as pleased as Jack when the hose was offloaded and found to be long enough for the job in hand. All they needed now was the coupling.

Before dawn next morning Jack left his sleeping household and made his way to the yard where he loaded up the Mini-Moke with pipefitting tools. From there he drove slowly round to the derelict bowser with theft in mind. He had been awake for a good deal of the night, his mind obsessed with the problem of how to obtain the precious coupling. If he followed the correct procedure and approached the Ministry, there were two possible outcomes. An agreement to remove one of the couplings would doubtless have to be ratified by other Departments, and written permission could take days, if not weeks, to obtain. On the other hand a refusal would probably lead to increased vigilance by the Ministry over their property, even if they did have no use for it, thus thwarting any future attempt at unauthorised removal.

Out on the north-eastern horizon of the sea, a brilliant shaft of light burst across Famagusta Bay as the sun's rim appeared, suffusing the massive old Venetian city walls with a soft golden glow. The air was fresh and almost sweet to the taste, with the gentlest of cool breezes wafting over the sleeping city. It was as if Mother Nature was aware of Jack's nefarious intentions and was doing her best to encourage him. He pulled up in front of the bowser and sauntered casually to the rear, trying to look as if it were his custom to go around inspecting abandoned vehicles at dawn. To his horror he found the coupling had already been removed, with recent traces of easing oil plainly in evidence.

Continuing the same show of nonchalance, Jack glanced up and down the wide, deserted boulevard to ensure his presence had not been noted, and walked back to the Mini-Moke. He put the uneasy sensation that he was being watched down to simple, justifiable guilt, until the realisation struck him that he was in full view of the FNC office building. Looking up at the front window of the flat he could see two faces grinning down at him, and David was triumphantly brandishing a familiar looking lump of metal above his blond curls.

* * * * *

"Saturday 3ʳᵈ June

Truly a day to celebrate. At last the swimming pool is full. Jack is absolutely over the moon – he's been swimming up and down it for the last hour, just to show it who's boss! A different man from yesterday – I've never seen him in such a foul mood – just because the steel hasn't moved from the dockside. He's become possessed by the job – up before dawn yesterday, and all last night working on the pool with Peter and David. Still, it's done now, and he's promised to take the day off tomorrow. We are all going to a boat auction – Jack's idea of relaxation!

I'm really glad Jack has decided to keep Peter and David on. They are really nice lads, and good workers too. I've started doing their washing too, as they don't have a washing machine. Our machine is really good – typical German efficiency. I'm having to get used to the mains water being switched off all day, we only have water supply after midnight, so that's when I start the washing machine! I do the ironing first thing in the morning before it gets too hot. The boys were so pleased when I gave them their laundry back all nicely ironed that they bought me a great bunch of flowers; what a lovely thought.

I have been teaching Wendy to swim today, what a fuss she made! She is in the sea most days with waves breaking over her head without a murmur, but in the pool she says it's more difficult – I don't know! She did swim a whole length on her back, and had everyone in stitches, protesting that she couldn't swim and telling me how cruel I was being. Then she promptly turned round and swam back again. What a madam! It did give everyone a good laugh though."

* * * * *

Between the shipyard gates and the long fuelling jetty that marked the southern end of the shipping berths was a wide area of weed-strewn concrete that had served as a lorry park in former times. Now it was considered unimportant, and through usage had become a depositary for various small craft, most of which were in an advanced state of neglect. It was here that the Sunday boat auction was to be held, and a number of additional small craft on road trailers had appeared for the occasion. Jack's little party of six was the only English presence, but a contingent of suntanned, fair-haired young Germans was also in evidence, their cachinnations prevailing over the general murmur of the large Cypriot crowd. There was a lively, even festive atmosphere to the occasion, enhanced by excited children darting about, dogs barking, gaily painted handcarts dispensing ice cream, and the ubiquitous mobile coffee stalls.

"Isn't that Selim over there?" asked Mary, standing on tiptoe to gain a better line of sight. "Perhaps we should go over and join him."

"That might not be such a good idea," muttered Jack. "We sort of had words on Friday."

"Oh Jack, you didn't!" she exclaimed in a horrified whisper. "Him of all people!"

"Well! He let me down on the steel. I don't know. Perhaps I did overreact a bit."

"Look, he's coming over," whispered Mary. "You are going to behave, aren't you?"

"Don't worry. It wasn't really that bad. Besides, it looks like he's prepared to make the first move. He knows he was in the wrong."

The Harbourmaster was plainly delighted to see Mary and the girls, whatever his feelings may have been toward Jack. He looked very handsome in his immaculate blue uniform, and took off his gold braided cap with a flourish to greet them.

"Good morning, Mary. Good morning Jack. Gunaydin Susan. Nasilsin bugun?"

"Iyim, tesekkurler," replied Susan shyly.

"Cok Guzel! Your daughter is speaking Turkish like a native, Mary. You must be very proud of her."

"We're very proud of them both. Wendy swam her first length of the pool yesterday."

"Well done, Vendy! Do you mean the pool at the Plâj Hotel? Is it in use again? After all these years! My congratulations to you Jack."

Smiling broadly, Jack grasped the offered hand with some relief; there were no hard feelings then. It was his own fault really. When the Harbourmaster had promised the steel by the end of the week he should have known he meant the end of the following week. This was Cyprus, not England; he really must try and embrace a more relaxed pace of life.

Commencement of the day's business was announced from a makeshift dais by a corpulent man whose stentorian voice filtered through an enormous black moustache. The first lot was a plywood speedboat with an outboard engine, both needing a great deal of attention. To open the bidding the auctioneer first declared the reserve price; he was obviously very experienced, and easily kept track as fierce competition sent the price rocketing to a figure Jack found impossible to believe. Mary had already taken the girls over to one of the ice cream vendors, and the two lads announced they were off to their favourite bar in the old city.

"Am I going mad," Jack asked Selim Captain, "or has that idiot just agreed to pay fifty thousand Turkish lira for that rig?"

"Yes. Fifty thousand. You think the price is too much?"

"It's outrageous. It's not worth half that amount."

"The price may be just a little high, but it is not surprising. Those little launches are very popular, especially in Girne. You cannot find such boats very easily these days on this side of Cyprus. Many were destroyed or went missing during the troubles. It's the engines that people want, and that's what makes the price so high."

"Are you bidding for anything here today?"

"No," said the Harbourmaster firmly. "How about you?"

"Not at these prices," replied Jack with a sardonic little chuckle. "Besides, I'm strictly a sail man. There aren't any sailing craft here."

"As I said before, Jack, you are welcome to use my little boat any time you wish."

"I am most grateful to you Selim. I shall probably take you up on the offer once we've made some real progress on the tug, but you know how it is. Business before pleasure."

"You have another saying in English, I believe. All work and no play..."

"Touché, Harbourmaster!" said Jack, smiling. "I have had it on good authority that I sometimes take life too seriously. Like last Friday, for instance."

"I know how difficult you must be finding it here. I was the same when I first started this job. When you see how well everything is run in England, Germany, the Baltic, even in Italy it is hard to accept the way things are done here. But in the end, all it really needs is a little more patience. We have been without a tug for all this time, so another couple of months will not make too much difference."

During this conversation another lot was sold for an exorbitant amount of money. Jack had hoped to see the bidding for some of the better craft that had appeared on trailers that morning, but it was obvious that the auctioneer wanted to shift all the junk first. According to Selim it was the Germans who owned the newer boats; they always carried very high reserves, and seldom sold. The same rigs appeared at every auction, and would sell only if the owner had fallen on hard times and had to raise some cash quickly. Even then it was usually a fellow German who made the successful bid.

By the time the third tatty heap of boxwood sold for a figure that left Jack gaping incredulously, he had lost all interest and looked around for Mary and the girls. He caught sight of them walking slowly out along the fuelling jetty eating their ice creams and his heart gave a leap of pride. This was his family. This beautiful woman and these two loving children were everything a man could want, and they had followed him without hesitation on this fraught quest to find their fortune. Mary, so elegantly English in her light summer dress and straw hat; Susan, slender as a wand, mind in the clouds; Wendy, her long blonde hair falling across her face as she gazed in silent reproach down at the ice cream she had just dropped into the oily water below.

Making his excuses to Selim Captain, Jack walked quickly over to the jetty and called to Mary. He would take them this very minute to see the Harbourmaster's yacht in which he would take them sailing on the blue waters of the Mediterranean Sea. It was moored alongside the ancient stone jetty near Othello's Tower. And he would also show them the steel with which the tug would be built! They would be in the presence of history.

"Well if the day job doesn't work out you could always make a living as a tour guide," said Mary with a wry smile. "You certainly have the spiel. I would not have thought it possible to wax lyrical over a heap of steel. But you're surely not intending to go sailing today, are you? I wouldn't have thought there was enough wind."

"Oh no, you're absolutely right. This weather's no good for sailing. I just wanted to take a look at the boat. You know, to see how she's rigged."

The four of them moved at a leisurely pace along the quay until they came to the place where the steel lay shimmering in the noonday sun. Curious as ever, Wendy reached out to touch the top sheet of the nearest pile before Jack could shout a warning, and she jerked her little hand back with a cry of pain as the heat seared into her fingertips. Susan spluttered in amusement, but immediately felt guilty at her schadenfreude and kissed the burnt fingers better.

There, tied up in what must have been one of the best yacht berths in the world, was Selim Captain's yacht 'Ceylan', a neat little sloop about seven meters in length built in fibreglass. As the deck was just about level with the flagstone surface of the jetty they all stepped aboard with complete ease and safety, and sat on the warm slatted wooden side benches of the cockpit. Susan wanted to look in the tiny cabin, and was thrilled to find the two berths and a little wash hand basin inside. Wendy soon joined her and within minutes their fertile imaginations had taken them off to that special place to which only children have a passport.

"So, what do you think? Not bad eh?" asked Jack.

"It's a bit small," replied Mary cautiously. "Can it really go out into the open sea?"

"Of course she can. This little ship could take you anywhere in the Med. I promise you, you'll love it, all of you. There's nothing like it for expanding the soul."

"I'm not sure that my soul needs expanding, but I'm willing to have a go as long as you're sure it's safe."

"We'll give her a try the first Sunday we get any wind. I'm telling you, you'll love it."

Mary was relieved to hear Jack talking about something other than the shipyard. She watched him carefully as he inspected the yacht's rigging and equipment and thought how youthful he could look when he was relaxed. For the rest of the day it was going to be just the four of them, she vowed to herself. A long, lazy *al fresco* lunch under the trellised vines of that little restaurant she had seen the other day; perhaps a visit to the Salamis ruins followed by a swim and some tea at the hotel; then back to the flat for a very, very early night, and definitely no midnight laundry sessions.

Luncheon was perfect. Succulent fillet steak, served up hot on a great sizzling platter, with generous bowls of tiny minted new potatoes and salad. Just under the canopy of vine leaves huge grasshoppers flitted across the crowded courtyard from one side to the other, keeping the girls endlessly amused. Wendy likened them to helicopters, but Susan preferred a more mystical analogy and identified them as the lost souls of wicked fairies. By the time lunch was over Mary felt it was too late to drive out to Salamis, and Jack was rather mellow, having drunk most of the wine. Instead, they wandered dreamily around the old city, ending up at the library bar where they all sat reading and chatting until twilight. Both children were tired out by the time they arrived home, and Mary had them bathed and tucked up in their beds within half an hour. Jack made no demur when she proposed an early night for themselves, and they ended the day in the best possible way.

They were both up at dawn the next morning, Mary to do some washing before the water was switched off, Jack to make an early start at the yard and catch up with his paperwork. At nine o'clock he went round to the FNC offices and waited for Mehmet Boga to arrive; he was determined to find out why more was not being done by the great man to ensure the steel was delivered to the yard. From the information provided by Selim Captain, the delay was due more to Famagusta Navigation than the Port Authority.

Mehmet Boga did not like Mondays; he relished being confronted with problems so early in the day even less. With a weary note to his booming voice, he explained to Jack that nothing had been done about moving the steel because the bills of lading were missing.

"Nonsense!" exclaimed Jack. "They were filed in the correct place in my office. Faruk knew exactly where they were. Why didn't you ask him?"

"We did not realise that the documents were missing until five o'clock. Faruk had already left for the day, and you were nowhere to be found."

"Oh come on, Mehmet. Everybody knows if I'm not at the yard then I'm down at that bloody pool. All you had to do was pick up a 'phone. In any case, why was it not until five o'clock on a Friday afternoon before anything was being done? Did you intend to ghost the job? I wish you had told me. I was on a ghoster too with Peter and David down at the pool."

"If you and your young friends choose to take on work outside the yard that is no concern of mine. I am here to facilitate the building of the tug using normal methods during regular business hours. The steel delivery is hardly a matter of life or death, is it?"

"No, I'm sorry Mehmet, that's just not good enough. We can't hope to succeed in building this tug unless we get more co-operation, both from you and the Ministry. Here are the bills of lading. I want the steel delivered to the yard within twenty-four hours, and I want that eight meter beam from The Government Store by Wednesday. And I want complete freedom to purchase whatever we need from The Government Store without having to fanny around with special licenses and endless pieces of paper. It's all turning into a bloody farce! If things don't start shaping up soon I'm going to pay a visit to the Prime Minister. We'll see if he can sort things out."

Mehmet Boga drew breath to thunder back with an equally impassioned reply, but thought better of it. He would not put it past this madman to carry out his threat, and there was Osman Toprak to consider as well. Perhaps a more conciliatory approach would bring the situation round in his advantage.

"Jack, my good friend, I understand your concerns, please believe me. I will go personally and speak to the District Commissioner of Finance this morning. I will pass on your request regarding The Government Stores with my full endorsement. As for the steel, well now we have the necessary documentation there is no reason why you should not expect delivery tomorrow."

"Again with that dreaded word tomorrow!" cried Jack. "What time tomorrow?"

"Please believe that everything will be done that is humanly possible, my friend. That is the best I can promise."

It came as no surprise to Jack that at five o'clock in the afternoon of the following day there was still no sign of the steel. He stood at the yard gates after the workforce had left and stared up the road towards the port, chuckling gently to himself. So this was the way it was going to be. Faruk came out of the office building, saw Jack, and came to stand beside him.

"Perhaps tomorrow, Jack bey," he murmured sympathetically.

"Well we shan't be here to receive it, Faruk. We shall be in Nicosia. First thing in the morning I want you to make an urgent appointment for me to see the Prime Minister. Make sure he knows it is urgent, Faruk. Tell him it is a matter of national importance."

* * * * * * * *

Mary was intrigued at breakfast next morning to see Jack in his best outfit, shoes gleaming and hair parted with unusual care.

"You're going through with it then? I thought you might change your mind once you'd slept on it."

"No, my love, this is it. Crunch time. Make or break."

"Should I start packing?"

"It won't come to that, don't worry. I might not even have to go."

"How come?"

"Before I left the yard last night I happened to mention my plan to Faruk. I should be very surprised if the old jungle telegraph wasn't in use last night."

"That's very sneaky. I like it."

"Whatever it takes, my love. Even if I do have to go native."

"So why are you suited and booted, if you don't expect to be going?"

"It's all part of the bluff. They have to believe that I am prepared to go through with it."

"You're right. You are going native."

Jack's prognosis was completely accurate. Faruk was anxiously awaiting his arrival at the yard, deliberately late.

"Good morning Faruk. So what time is our appointment with the Prime Minister?"

"I regret I was unable to get an appointment for today, Jack bey, but Onan has been in asking for you. He says it is most urgent. He is down at the customs office, and has asked if you would join him there as soon as you arrive."

"So if the Prime Minister cannot see me today, when can he see me?"

"I did not take it upon myself to make an alternative appointment."

"Well ring him up and try again. I definitely want to see him as soon as possible. Onan is at the customs office, you say."

"That is correct. He says it is most urgent."

Jack drove slowly to the customs office where he found Onan arguing with an official over the steel documentation.

"Mister Jack, this officer is saying that you will have to count each piece of steel before loading can start."

"Nonsense. The consignment can all be identified from the delivery note or the invoice. You can surely handle that, can't you?"

"We do not have a delivery note, and I am afraid I do not understand the invoice. I have no experience with steel in any case."

Jack considered the position before replying. There was no point in being too difficult at this delicate point of the proceedings, particularly as the wheels were finally turning in the right direction.

"I cannot possibly check the consignment personally. I am due in Nicosia for an appointment with the Prime Minister. Peter will have to do it. You stay here and I'll pop back to the yard and get him."

As bad luck would have it, a chain barrier had been erected across the entire dockside during the few minutes that Jack had been at the customs office, and his way back to the yard was now blocked. A surly port official sauntered arrogantly up to the Mini-Moke and ordered Jack to take the long way round, which meant driving into the old city and back out through the Cambulat Gate. Jack refused, so the official shrugged his shoulders, turned, and sauntered slowly back to his chair. In a cold fury, Jack left the vehicle where is was and marched off to fetch the Harbourmaster. Unfortunately, Selim Captain was not in his office, so Jack dragged out his assistant, telling him that he was going to use the dockside road, even if it meant involving Denktas himself. The assistant harbourmaster was an amiable young man, not used to dealing with large, irate

Englishmen, but luckily he had sufficient presence of mind to appreciate the implications of the situation in which he was becoming inescapably embroiled, and used his authority to have the chain lowered so that Jack could pass through.

Returning with Peter a half hour later, the way was again barred by the heavy chain, and the same despotic official refused to let them through. Despite the murderous feeling in his heart Jack was able to bare his teeth in an unconvincing smile, and he drove Peter back to the yard before going on to the offices of the Port Director himself. It was no surprise that the Director was engaged in an important meeting, so Jack returned to his own office and telephoned Osman Toprak.

By this time Jack was consumed with cold, hard anger, and it was with icy politeness that he told his tale of woe, following on with a long list of grievances. The steel delivery had been hopelessly botched; there had been no progress with the Susan's education; it was impossible to do business at The Government Stores; far from being co-operative, FNC were persistently obstructive; and now he was to suffer harassment from minor port officials. If the situation did not improve, he would be on the next available flight back to England. Convinced he was dealing with a man at the end of his tether, Osman Toprak promised to do what he could, starting with a call to the port authorities.

Whilst these events were taking place Onan had been waiting in the customs office for Jack's return with Peter, and wondering why it was taking them so long he decided to investigate. He appeared at the door of Jack's office and launched into a petulant reproach, which the beleaguered yard manager was in no mood to brook, and countered with an unkind comparison of Onan to his biblical namesake. When the outraged young Cypriot threatened to call a halt to the delivery of the steel, Jack coldly advised him to check with his master before embarking on such a foolish course, and stormed out of the office to seek sanctuary in the peace and quiet of the lofting shed.

Whether this display of histrionics made any difference Jack would never know. What he did know, however, was that within half an hour the first trolley load of steel lumbered through the yard gates followed by a mobile crane, and the whole delivery was completed by three in the afternoon with no further reference to paperwork on his part. The steel was at last in the yard, and now the real work could commence.

* * * * *

Wednesday 7ᵗʰ June

Julia came for lunch at the flat today – just the two of us. I cooked a beautiful fillet of beef with all the trimmings – including Yorkshire pudding that Julia had heard of but not eaten before. She thought it unusual, but said it was enjoyable – perhaps she was just being polite.

Buying the fillet of beef was a bit of a coup – I had a tussle at the butchers in the market when I asked for some fillet steak and was told that the fillet was kept by for the hotels and restaurants, after my insistence he suggested I could buy the whole fillet, smiling like he had the best of me, but I parried with agreement

– I <u>would</u> buy the whole fillet. Oh dear! That means we shall have to eat fillet steak for the rest of the week!!

Julia and I spent most of the afternoon chatting and laughing about practically everything under the sun (except our menfolk and their endless problems that is), but mostly about our children. Julia has taken to the girls, especially Susan with her quiet ways and sense of mystery. Her own children are much older, of course, and I think she's having a difficult time with her son at the moment. She expressed a strong preference for girls in general, which I can understand in a way – with a husband like hers!

We had such a good laugh together – we seem to have the same wicked sense of humour. She is one of those people you meet and there's an instant rapport – like you've know them all your life even though you have only just met.

She's flying back to England in a couple of days, but on her return we plan to meet up for lunch once a month- at least!

Chapter Fifteen

It was not until the end of June that Frank Palmer paid his next visit to Cyprus, this time accompanied by Neil Geddes. Jack and Mary were at Ercan to meet them off the Saturday flight just before midday. They drove straight to the Sands Hotel, a large, modern establishment on the southern outskirts of Famagusta, where Frank Palmer invited all three to lunch on a palm fringed terrace overlooking the sea. He directed their attention to the view southwards, where they could see many more substantial hotels, all standing cheek by jowl for nearly a mile along the seashore. Over the whole distance there was absolutely no sign of life. The beaches were all deserted, and the wide esplanade was devoid of both people and traffic.

"The forbidden city of Varosha," declared Frank Palmer dramatically. "Millions of dollars worth of prime real estate inhabited only by cockroaches, feral dogs, and UN patrols."

"Why is it deserted?" asked Mary, fascinated by the unnatural sight.

"It's the aftermath of the troubles. Varosha was developed by the Greek Cypriots in the late sixties to encourage tourism. When the Turkish army invaded in seventy-four they pushed into Varosha, and all the Greek Cypriots fled for their lives. The Turks thought they were onto a good thing, but they were forced to pull out and hand the area over to the UN. It's been uninhabited ever since. There was some looting, of course, but otherwise the whole place is exactly as it was left four years ago, frozen in time. A ghost town."

"It seems such a waste," said Mary. "Surely something could be done."

"You would think," replied Frank Palmer casually, "but knowing these people, they'll still be squabbling about it into the next millennium."

The Sands' terrace restaurant was a highly popular Saturday haunt both for young local professional people, and for the ubiquitous German tourists doggedly re-establishing their right to penetrate every corner of the globe. As they stood waiting for a table, Frank Palmer chatted away with his usual affability, keeping the conversation light and humorous. Once they were seated, however, he quickly switched to business.

"I've booked you in here, Neil, for a couple of reasons. Mainly, I think the Plâj Hotel is a bit too far out of the way, and this place is really handy for the yard. I'm going to move Peter and David in here too. It'll be much better for you all to be together, and I've managed to get quite a good deal on rooms for your families when they come out for holidays. I'm sure they'll love it out here, and I'm quite happy to help with the airfares as well. There's also another reason. Just round the corner, on the other side of the hotel there's a couple of big steel barges stuck up on the rocks, and I think there might be an opportunity for us in the salvage line. We can have a look at them some time during the week. I'd value your opinion on the possibility of repairing them, Jack. If there's anything in the idea there would be three of you on the spot; the opportunity seems too good to miss, don't you think?"

While he was talking, Frank Palmer had made a couple of attempts to call one of the waiters flitting energetically between the tables. With the terrace so full they were extremely busy, and paid him no heed. It was time to give more concentration to the job of gaining some attention, but waving, nodding, smiling, stretching his neck and raising his eyebrows still met with no success.

Neil Geddes, hungry and thirsty after his long journey from England, could tolerate the situation no longer.

"Hey, Jimmy!" he bellowed.

A waiter materialised instantly. His sudden appearance was so surreal that Mary was unable to hold back a little bubble of mirth that immediately spread first to Frank Palmer then on to Jack. Neil's face remained without expression as he placed his order for a well-done steak, but he was secretly gratified that his party piece had gone down so well. The others all ordered a light lunch, and Frank Palmer made sure there was no shortage of wine. Throughout the meal a flow of light, witty conversation was maintained, in which the dour Scot, stimulated by his initial success, played no small part. Every so often he would inject a laconic *bon mot* with such precise timing that Jack wondered if could be the same man as the prickly grouch he had known back in the cold reality of a British Shipyard. With coffee and brandies, the meal lasted well into the afternoon, and may well have continued even later had Mary not reminded Jack that Nihan would be taking the children back to the flat.

Leaving Neil to settle in and find his bearings, Jack and Frank Palmer dropped Mary off in Baykal before going on to the yard. It was a blisteringly hot afternoon, and both men were glad to be out of the sun in the comparative cool of Jack's office.

"Let's get straight down to business," said Frank Palmer. "You can start by bringing me up to date on progress."

"As I said in my telex, Frank, there hasn't been any progress. Well, not on the tug anyway. I've prepared a full report...."

"No, Jack. I've told you before, I don't want to know about reports. As far as I'm concerned reports are a complete waste of time. I just want you to tell me, as briefly as possible, what's been happening since I was here last."

"Well, if you're talking about the tug, absolutely nothing. We don't have a crane, we don't have any oxygen, and we don't have any acetylene. The only decent source of supply is The Government Store, and dealing with them is like trying to get blood out of a stone. All the commercial suppliers want silly money for substandard gear."

"You shouldn't be bothering with all this, Jack. This is all down to FNC. Get Mehmet Boga onto it. That's what he's paid for."

Jack laughed, and passed a file over to his boss.

"Have a look at that! Six letters confirming what we need, and I haven't even had an acknowledgement to one of them."

"You really do have a thing about going into writing, Jack. What's the matter with the telephone, or even a quick meeting?

Jack laughed again, but without any humour.

"If you have a look, you'll see that each letter confirms a verbal request, and then goes on to progress all the previous items that have not been sorted out. I always ask him in person, then chase up by telephone. Only if all that is ignored do I go into writing. It has to be done to protect our backsides. The first letter there deals with the eight meter RSJ we need when we lay the keel. I originally requested that back in May, and we still don't have it. I went over to The Government Store only two days ago to check the depth of the web – the moron in charge wouldn't even let me measure it!"

Frank Palmer read through the most recent letter, pursed his lips, raised his eyebrows and gave the file back to Jack.

"I had no idea things were this bad. I'll go and see Mehmet first thing on Monday. In the meantime I'll have a word with Osman Toprak."

"To be honest, Frank, I don't really see what either of them can do. The trouble is, they don't have any experience in the manufacturing process, and they have absolutely no concept as to the scale of this operation. It's impossible to draw up any sort of production schedule because you simply don't know when anything is actually going to happen. It's all so hit and miss. I can't even schedule laying the keel."

"Why ever not?"

"Well, apart from not knowing when we're going to get the RSJ, there's the problem of how we're going to cut the one inch plate. We've had a go with that Calcium Carbide contraption in the yard, but it won't go anywhere near the job. There is one guy in Nicosia who can supply acetylene in tubes, but the price he is asking is out of this world, and I'm by no means sure about the quality or the pressure. But even if we had acetylene, there's still the problem of oxygen. You wouldn't believe the song and dance to get a couple of bottles of oxygen! I don't want to sound like an old woman, Frank, but I really am getting a bit worried."

"You mentioned something about cranes. That can't be a problem. Provision of a five ton crane is written into the Joint Venture Agreement."

Yet again Jack had to laugh.

"It could be written in 22 carat gold lettering, but it wouldn't make any difference. There simply isn't a five-ton crane available. The harbourmaster has made it clear that turning ships round is his top priority, and we can only have a crane if it is not needed in the port. He also pointed out that the daily hire charge will be four or five times what you were led to believe by FNC. I'm still waiting for a decision from the Port Director about that old Jones machine, but he doesn't seem to be in any hurry to let us have it. These are really fundamental problems, Frank, and I haven't even started on the yard equipment or the pathetic electricity supply. There's hardly enough juice to run one pot, let alone six, and it's six we'll need if we're hoping to get her plated up this year."

Frank Palmer leaned forward in his seat confidentially.

"I can see you're very worried, Jack, and I appreciate your concern. But don't lose heart. I did tell you right from the beginning that it wouldn't be easy, but I'm looking at the bigger picture. I've got things going on outside the shipyard, and eventually they'll solve all these minor problems. All I need from you right now is to hang in there, and just do whatever you can. You're doing a great job, and I'm really glad I've got you on board. Just hang on. I promise things will get better soon. In the meantime, as I say, I'll have a word with Mehmet and Osman Toprak. FNC are definitely not living up to their side of the bargain, and I'm not having that. Not with everything I have at stake myself with this venture. Now, tell me Jack, is there anything happening with Medmarine House?"

"I'm afraid it's the same old story there as well," replied Jack, handing over another file. "Best thing is to take a look at the correspondence so far."

Frank Palmer quickly read the exchange of letters between his manager and Mehmet Boga, closed the file and slammed it down on the desk.

"The idiots!" he cried. "Do they think I was born yesterday?" He slumped back in his chair and added: "I suppose you're still waiting for a reply?"

"I've spoken to Mehmet about it at least half a dozen times since my letter, but he's now saying it's out of his hands. I think he's fed up with me chasing him all the time."

"I'm beginning to think we'd have been better off without FNC. Perhaps we should have gone straight to the Ministry ourselves. Do you think they'll go for the five years rent free?"

"We'd be mad to accept anything less," replied Jack firmly. "That figure of half a million for renovation is the least we can expect to spend."

"Right," said Frank Palmer, standing up, "that's enough doom and gloom for one day. If you'd be good enough to run me up to the Plâj Hotel so I can get cleaned up, we can all meet up for dinner later on. I think you've chosen a good man in Neil, by the way. He certainly seems to know his stuff. How are the other two shaping up?"

"Pretty good. Yes, good lads. Peter will come on well with Neil's guidance, and David is pretty good with machinery. I'm hoping to use him on fixing up the crane when we eventually do get our hands on it."

"Great stuff! Now, do you think you can round everyone up and have them at the Sands' restaurant for, say, seven thirty. We'll have a little celebration dinner to mark your success with the swimming pool. Kaplan sends his regards, by the way. He's asked me to thank you for all you've done out there. I know it wasn't easy, but it shows what can be done with some ingenuity and a little tenacity. Just stick with it, Jack. I promise you, we're really going to put this place on the map."

* * * * * * * *

As Famagusta's premier hotel, the Sands boasted a fine, modern, air-conditioned restaurant overlooking the sea. The view was, however, somewhat blighted by the presence of two huge steel barges perched on top of the rocks immediately in front of the wide plate glass picture windows. There they sat, in their rusting magnificence, a monument to man's impotence against the might of the sea. They had occupied this position of prominence for so long, that regular diners had grown used to the sight, almost as if the slowly decaying mass of battered steel were the work of some enterprising modern sculptor, and warranted no more attention than any other form of pop art. To Frank Palmer, however, they were covered in dollar signs, and represented yet another opportunity to extend the boundaries of his business activities. He was standing

143

at the window, gazing acquisitively at the barges as his dinner guests arrived, all in a body.

"Aha! The British contingent!" he gaily announced, turning to greet them. "Right on time I see. That's the ticket! Susan, that's a very pretty frock. And Wendy, you look very nice too."

Susan dropped him a graceful curtsey. She was reading 'Pride and Prejudice', so her imagination was running riot in this splendid great room with its sparkling chandeliers, luxurious drapes and ormolu furniture. Her host returned a polite bow, and led her with a great show of gallantry to the table he had reserved. David was quick to offer his arm to Mary, and Peter showed great presence of mind by taking Wendy's little hand, leaving Neil and Jack to bring up the rear, pretending to be disconsolate.

This charming little piece of theatre endowed the evening with a sense of special occasion. Again, there was no shortage of wine to complement the flow of conversation, and laughter predominated as the meal progressed. Frank Palmer had an endless supply of amusing anecdotes based on his extensive business travels; Neil had everyone in stitches with his wry description of an apprentice's life in a Clydeside shipyard; David's deliberately gruesome account of life on the farm, presented in graphic detail, had Susan and Wendy squirming in their seats, first calling for him to stop and then immediately asking him to go on. Mary laughed until her sides ached; not since the coffee bar gatherings in her teenage years could she remember such a lively gathering. It was all so spontaneous and unexpected; utterly delightful.

Frank Palmer, too, was gratified by the success of the evening. It had given him the opportunity of observing his little team together and assessing the compatibility of its members. He noticed that although Jack was relaxed, and joined in all the laughter, he remained just slightly aloof from the general badinage as if to guard against any undue familiarity. This showed a reassuring wisdom on the part of the manager; an appreciation of the fact that you could not be slapping a fellow's back in comradeship one minute and taking him to task in the next. Neil Geddes was an interesting man, too; despite his gaunt, almost cadaverous appearance he had the sort of presence that usually came only with success in life. He was obviously no lightweight, so why was he just a tradesman still working on his tools?

It was nearly midnight when the dinner party ended. Susan was still going strong, her eyes sparkling and colour high with the thrill of it all, but Wendy was fast asleep, curled up in a big leather armchair that had been carried over by two sympathetic waiters. As they all took their leave it was agreed that they would meet up again next day at the Pláj Hotel for a day of rest and recreation, once again as Frank Palmer's guests. Peter and David were told that their rooms were ready for them to occupy, so arrangements were made for them to drop Jack and his family off in Baykal and take the Mini Moke to move their belongings first thing in the morning. There was a great deal of hilarity as four adults plus two children all piled into the tiny jeep and drove off into the night. Frank Palmer signed the bill, gave the waiters a generous cash tip, and took a taxi back to the Pláj Hotel.

I could get used to this kind of life – a whole weekend of fun and frolic! We have just spent the day lounging about at the Plâj Hotel with Frank Palmer and the lads. We had a wonderful dinner last night, then Frank laid on a really good lunch again today. The waiters set up a table near the pool, and we all sat round in our swimming costumes – more decadence! There were great bowls of lovely fresh salad, heaps of prawns, grilled fish, kebabs – and of course no end of wine.

"In the afternoon everybody was down on the beach. We all went into the water – even Neil, after a great deal of persuasion. He said he couldn't swim, but Susan was having none of it. She practically dragged him down to the water, with Wendy pushing from behind – you could see he was loving it. It's obvious he's a good family man. As usual, Jack swam right out to sea – much too far for my liking. He must have been out there for more than an hour. When he finally came back in, Frank asked him what the weather was like over at Latakia! The two of them spent most of the afternoon talking shop – I imagine they are discussing the cargo ship that's aground on the rocks right up by Cape Andreas. I think Jack is going to drive up and have a look, in case it can be salvaged. It would be good to go with him and make a day of it."

Neil Geddes' very first job when he arrived at the yard was to try and make some sense of the calcium carbide acetylene pot. Jack wanted to know for once and for all if the process could be taken seriously, and knew the canny Scot would coax the best performance out of the equipment, if anyone could. The verdict came down much as expected, a resounding condemnation delivered with an impressive run of Clydeside invective that had Peter and David grinning like hyenas. On learning the difficulty of obtaining a reliable supply of acetylene at a reasonable price, Neil suggested using propane instead

Jack had already been offered propane by the gas dealer in Nicosia, but the price had been far too high. He decided to pay the dealer another visit, and take Neil with him. Together they carried out a number of tests, using both nozzles from the shipyard and some better equipment offered by the dealer. They finally reached a satisfactory combination, and Neil was able to execute one of his trademark precision cuts on a piece of scrap steel. As he was also happy with the quality of the oxygen, Jack decided to place an order on the spot for enough gas to cut out the keel profiles, despite the high cost.

Frank Palmer was at meetings for most of the week, so his appearances at the yard were both scarce and brief. On the last day, however, he called Jack to a council of war over lunch at the Plâj Hotel. It was far too hot to sit outside, so they had sandwiches served in the basement bar, much the coolest room in the hotel.

"You'll forgive me working off a list I hope," began Frank Palmer apologetically as he pulled a notepad out of his document case. "I try not to get bogged down with paper if I can avoid it, but there's been so much to do this week that I've been reduced to making lists. Normally I carry everything up here," he added, tapping his forehead."

"Putting things in writing?" chaffed Jack. "How have the mighty fallen!"

"It must be your bad influence. I've never done it in the past. Anyway – item one – the barges. Any joy?"

"They went aground in March during a freak storm. The firm that owned them has gone bust, so they have been taken over by the Cyprus Turkish Government, who now claim legal ownership. They are to be publicly auctioned on the eighth of July."

"Have you had time to go and look at them?"

"Yes. I went there with Neil, the day you were in Nicosia."

"And?"

"As you know, they are badly damaged, but they could be saved. We should be able to warp them off without too much trouble"

"Well, I think it might be worth having a punt. What do you think they're worth?"

"I wouldn't bid more than scrap value for them. There's a lot of work involved. And I do mean a lot. What would you do with them anyway?"

"There's a project coming up in Latakya. They will be crying out for barges when it goes ahead. I'd like you to let me have a cost estimate to get them back in the water with minimum repair, and towed round to the yard where we can do a proper job. You can send it by telex, and I'll let you know how much to bid. Do you have any experience bidding at auction?"

"Not really. I've bought a couple of cars at auction, and the odd stick of furniture."

"That's enough. I'm sure you'll do a grand job. Now – item two – the wreck up at Cape Andreas."

"I've checked with the Department, and access to the peninsular is still restricted. I've been told to apply to the Port Director for a special permit."

"Good. If you have any trouble speak to Osman Toprak. He says there shouldn't be any problem."

"Righty-ho. Item three?"

"Item three is oxygen supply. I'm not prepared to pay the price that shyster in Nicosia wants to charge us, so I'm looking into the possibility of setting up our own oxygen plant here in Cyprus. I happen to know of one going in Holland, so I'll be looking into it as soon as I get back to the UK. In the meantime we can import supplies direct from Antalya or Mersin in Turkey. I've got Mehmet working on it now, and he's to liase with you when he's sorted something out. I don't want you to get involved with any of the leg work – just tell him what you want and let him get on with it."

"If we wait for gas supplies to come over from Turkey it's going to delay laying the keel. The templates for the keel sections are all ready, and I was planning to start cutting as soon as we get the gas I've ordered from Nicosia."

"No, Jack. We have to start as we mean to go on. I'm not going to be held to ransom by local suppliers, not for a minute. The keel laying will have to wait until Mehmet has sorted out a proper supply line for gas and oxygen. You'd better cancel that order with what's his name in Nicosia."

"Okay, you're the boss What's next? That looks like a pretty long list you have there. Should I be taking notes?"

"No. The rest of this stuff is all for FNC to action. I know you'll be tickled at this – I've drafted a long letter that I'd like Mary to type out for me. It pretty much goes over the same ground you've already covered, but I think it might be better coming from me. I hope I'm not proved wrong. The thing is, there's to be a board meeting on the eighteenth of next month in Nicosia. I'll be back for that, of course. But if Mehmet doesn't get his finger out over the next two weeks we can bring everything up at the board meeting. Either way, we're going to get this all sorted. Here's the draft – I hope Mary can read my scrawl."

Jack accepted the document and briefly glanced at it.

"Yes, she won't have any trouble with that. Can we have a quick word about one or two domestic items, do you think."

"Of course we can," replied Frank Palmer, glancing involuntarily down at his wristwatch.

"Susan's schooling. Nothing seems to be happening. I wrote to the Consular Office at the address given to me by Osman Toprak back in April. I've heard nothing since."

Frank Palmer was angry and surprised.

"Osman Toprak told me this had all been sorted out," he cried. "I really am sorry, Jack. I hate it when people let me down on things like this. I'll speak to him before I leave. Don't worry, I'll get it sorted."

"The other thing is transport. I can get by with the Moke, but there's the other three men to consider, and FNC keep taking the old Toyota. I thought that was supposed to be for the sole use of our people."

"Yes, I've heard about that from Peter and David, and I'm very sorry. You'll find I've covered it in that letter, in the strongest terms. I don't think you'll be having any more problems. I've bought a couple of nice Range Rovers back in the UK, and I'll be shipping them out as soon as I can make suitable arrangements. Tell the lads just to be patient for a little while longer. You've got to expect some teething troubles with a venture like this."

* * * * *

"Tuesday 4th July

Today we made it all the way up the Karpaz peninsular to Cape Andreas. We had to have a special escort from the port director's office – a lovely little chap called Ali. Neil came with us, and Wendy. Susan didn't want to go so she stayed with Nihan and Suleyman for the day. There was just enough room in the Mini-Moke for all of us, with Wendy sitting on my lap. We were stopped at the same place as before, but Ali produced our passes and the soldiers let us through, all smiling and waving.

"It's deserted up there, and very eerie in the empty villages – ghostly almost. In the hills there are herds of wild donkeys scampering around. It seemed even hotter than it is in Famagusta – no wonder the donkeys have it all to themselves. Right up near the tip there is a monastery where we drank lovely cool water from a fountain in the wall.

We took loads of photographs, and Neil even managed to smile in some of them. He seems to be getting on very well with Jack – to think only six months ago they were on opposing sides in court, I'm glad they have resolved their differences – I like Neil.

"Jack and Neil spent a couple of hours poking around on the small cargo ship they were there to look at, but Jack said the only thing of any use was the deck winch. He said it would cost more to salvage than it was worth, so I suppose it will have to stay there forever. It's a shame that such an ugly great lump of rusting metal should be allowed to spoil such beautiful scenery. I wonder how many wrecks like that are scattered on various islands around the world?

"Before we left the office this morning I typed up a long letter from Frank Palmer to FNC which Jack had to sign in his absence. I hope it will have more effect than all the letters Jack has been sending over the past month."

* * * * *

The auction sale of the two barges at Sands was scheduled to start at 10 am on a Saturday, and it had attracted far more interest than Jack had anticipated. Mary attended with him, and after a leisurely, late breakfast with Neil Geddes in the hotel, they joined the large crowd thronging the car park where the auctioneer had set up his dais. It was the same man who had presided over the small boat auction in the port, and Jack recognised several other familiar faces, amongst them the Harbourmaster, Mehmet Boga, the port director and Kemal Aydin.

During the preceding week, Jack had gone to some lengths to survey the barges and draw up a really tight estimate for their repair. Telexes had been exchanged with Frank Palmer in London, a generous maximum bidding figure had been agreed, and Jack was feeling an intense excitement as the hour approached. The klaxon voice of the auctioneer called the assembly to order. He announced the reserve figure. It was more than Jack was authorised to bid.

"That can't be right," muttered Jack. "They're out of their tiny minds."

His opinion was evidently shared by all the hopeful bidders in the crowd, some of whom shouted angrily back at the auctioneer. A general murmur of disapproval quickly swelled to a torrent of protest as various animated discussions broke out all around the site. There was an earnest consultation between the auctioneer and an official-looking man in a pinstripe suit, followed by a defiant announcement bringing the proceedings to a close. This resulted in uproar, and the pinstripe suit was surrounded by angry protesters demanding a better deal. Only with the help of two large policemen was the poor man able to regain his official limousine and be driven away to safety. In the meantime the auctioneer had quite wisely slipped away.

Jack's own initial reaction was one of silent outrage at the thought of all the time he had wasted drawing up repair schedules and detailed estimates, but it soon subsided into a sense of philosophical amusement. Since Frank Palmer's last visit Jack had been far more relaxed in his dealings with both FNC and with government officials. If the reserve price had been set at a completely unrealistic figure why should he worry? The result of today's farce simply left one less item with which to concern himself. As matters now stood, he could spend the rest of the weekend at ease with his family instead of fretting over how to refloat and repair battered barges.

There was, however, a hidden dimension to this apparently fatalistic line of thought. In the back of his mind Jack was ever conscious of the impending joint venture board meeting, now only ten days away. There had been no more response from FNC to Frank Palmer's letter than there had been to his own. If Mehmet Boga was scurrying about finding a crane, sourcing gas supplies, or raiding the treasure chests of Government stores there had been precious little evidence that Jack could see. In only ten days time he would either have all the equipment he needed, or the crass incompetence of Mehmet Boga would be exposed for all to know.

In the meantime, Jack was content to concentrate on necessary re-organisation at the shipyard in preparation for laying the keel as soon as the gas was available and the elusive RSJ was delivered. A training programme for the welders was set up under Neil Geddes, who from the outset had commanded the respect not only of the local hands, but Peter and David as well. Under his tutelage skill levels increased rapidly, as did productivity. A long outstanding repair job on one of FNC's cargo vessels was successfully completed in record time, which resulted in further work coming into the yard as the good news quickly spread through the port.

One beneficial consequence of the delay in laying the keel was the opportunity to take some leisure time at the weekends, so Jack decided to take up the Harbourmaster's offer to use his little sailing boat. Mary was up a dawn on the appointed day, preparing sandwiches as she answered a string of questions from Wendy, whose excitement at the prospect of such an adventure was almost palpable. It was a particularly beautiful, peaceful Sunday morning, and by the time they reached the yacht's berth a gentle, offshore, south westerly breeze was raising small, sparkling ripples across the harbour.

"Absolutely perfect wind," declared Jack, gazing up at the burgee fluttering from the masthead. "Let's get aboard and make the most of it."

"Won't it blow us out to sea?" asked Mary cautiously. "I don't want to be out of sight of land."

"Fear not, my love. We shall be within a mile of land for the entire voyage. We'll sail up to Bogaz on a broad reach, have lunch, then sail back close hauled – if the wind stays in the south-west, that is."

Jack busied himself with the rigging, first bending on and hoisting the foresail, which he left flapping lazily in the gentle headwind. Before hoisting the mainsail he gave his novice crew the usual grave warning about the dangers of a swinging boom, followed by a quick briefing on the procedure he proposed to adopt once they had cast off.

"Up mains'l!" he roared, vigorously hauling away and cleating off the halyard.

"Let go forrard!" he yelled, springing onto the tiny foredeck.

"Let go aft!" he cried, and gently added: "You can do that one Susan. Just let go of the rope you're holding, let it slip through that big iron ring and pull it inboard."

They were off. Mary quickly took her bearings. The yacht was sailing smoothly in a wide sweep, gradually bringing her stern to wind. She was surprised how quiet it all was after the hectic flapping of the sails being raised, and Jack's zealous command calls to himself.

"Stand by to gybe!" bawled Jack, and then, more quietly: "Everybody duck!"

The boom swung easily across and Jack duly adjusted the trim of the sails.

"You can all stop ducking now," he said, laughing. "We'll be on this tack for the next couple of hours or so."

Mary raised her head and saw that they were now headed straight out to sea. Othello's tower quickly receded, and once they had left the shelter of the harbour she noticed their speed increase with the extra wind. Her only previous experience afloat had been a day trip down the Thames between Tower Bridge and Margate arranged by her school when she was eleven years old. It had been a defining moment in her young life, and the memories of that wonderful day came flooding back into her mind as she listened to the water now lapping at the yacht's hull less than a couple of feet from where she sat. How very different was this experience to that other voyage. The bustle and noise of a hundred or more excited children replaced by the periodic sound of Susan turning the page of her book. The insistent throbbing of engines replaced by the occasional slight creak from the tiller, or the single tap of a lazy block flopping over on the deck as the yacht heeled to the wind. The wharves, warehouses, factories, barges and tugs crowding London's waterway replaced by the sparse vegetation of a deserted coastline on one side, the distant blue horizon of the Mediterranean on the other, and not another vessel of any description within sight.

As she cast her mind back to that other voyage, more and more detail gradually came into focus. She remembered the clothes she wore, the plane trees on the embankment, the forbidding aspect of the White Tower, the thrill of boarding, the hard wooden seats, the exercise book she had filled with an account of all her feelings and impressions as the day progressed. Where was that exercise book now? How she would love to read it again!

"Look, Mum! The Plâj Hotel!" cried Susan in excitement. "Doesn't it look small!"

"Yes, it does," agreed her mother. "And I would say it's a lot more than a mile away," she added, giving Jack an old-fashioned look.

It might be as much as two," admitted Jack with a broad grin. "I'm just taking the most direct course from Famagusta to Bogaz, that's all. We can sail further inshore if you like, there's plenty of water. We're making really good time – we should reach Bogaz easily in time for lunch."

On they sailed, each with their own thoughts in the blissful silence. For Jack, too, this voyage was a new experience. His sailing had all previously taken place in the crowded tidal estuaries along the blustery Essex coast, frequently in pouring rain, with the ever present danger of going aground on shifting sand banks. Here, with eighty fathoms under his keel, no tide, a cloudless blue sky and a fine, steady, quartering breeze, it was easy to imagine he had sailed the little boat to heaven.

For Mary time seemed to be standing still. With absolutely nothing to do but lay back in total silence under the numinous sun, she was falling almost into a trance. The girls had both disappeared into the tiny cabin to find some shade, and Jack was obviously miles away in his thoughts. The boat's gentle, undulating movement gave her a sense of weightlessness. Closing her eyes, she abandoned herself to the mystic influence of the moment, and the sheer pleasure of this glorious day.

* * * * *

"Friday 14th July

A bombshell dropped today. Neil put through a telephone call from the hotel to his wife, and she informed him that no money has been paid into his account for the three weeks he's been working with Medmarine. Peter then telephoned his wife who told him a similar tale of woe. The same goes for David as well – his money hasn't been paid since he started, so he's owed six weeks' money. When I phoned our bank they said some money was paid three weeks ago, but altogether we are six weeks in arrears as well. That means we are owed six hundred pounds!

"Neil is absolutely furious, and has been trying to arrange his return flight home – without success so far because all the flights from Ercan to Istanbul are fully booked for the next two weeks. Peter is very upset, but as Frank Palmer is due back in Cyprus tomorrow he's prepared to wait and hear his explanation. David doesn't seem too worried, but he doesn't have any commitments, so it's not so bad for him.

"Jack has taken it very well, all things considered. He's sure that there will be some logical explanation, perhaps something to do with cash flow. But after all that business with Marine and General last Christmas I'm beginning to wonder if any of these so-called businessmen know what they're doing. One thing I do know – Frank Palmer is in for a pretty hot reception when he arrives tomorrow.

Chapter Sixteen

Jack and Mary drove to Ercan airport late on Saturday evening to meet Frank Palmer's flight, fully intending to tackle him about the missing wage payments on the drive back to Famagusta. Their plan was thwarted, however, by the presence of an English couple Frank Palmer had in tow, a man and a woman in their late thirties who were introduced as Harry, an experienced welder, and his girl friend Brenda. As there was insufficient room in the Mini-Moke for five adults, Frank Palmer called up a taxi and elected to stay with the newcomers for the journey to the Sands Hotel, leaving Jack and Mary to travel back on their own. All Jack could do with strangers present was arrange a meeting with Frank Palmer for the next day at the Plâj Hotel.

The meeting was held in the basement bar, and if Frank Palmer was surprised to see Neil and the lads he concealed it well. He listened first to Neil 's terse but forceful protest, apologised profusely, and launched into a diatribe against the inefficiencies of banks in general, and his own in particular. The Scot remained unmoved, and announced his intention of returning home as soon as he could obtain a flight, at which Frank Palmer merely became avuncular and pointed out the folly of allowing a hasty decision to ruin the opportunity of a lifetime, especially as the problem was neither serious nor permanent

Dealing with Peter's complaint was rather more difficult, as the incompetence of the bank had been blamed before, and could hardly be offered again as a credible excuse. Evincing great surprise, Frank Palmer could offer no explanation. As far as he was concerned, all the necessary arrangements for payment in the UK had been made, and should be running smoothly. First thing Monday morning he would put in a call to his accounts department in London, and find out what the devil was going on. Nobody was to worry. The last six months had been a period of extremely rapid growth for his group of companies, and the accounts department had been under a great deal of pressure. If mistakes had been made within his own organisation he could only apologise again, and promise that the situation would be rectified as soon as he returned to the UK.

Next to speak up was David, but by this time the mood of the meeting was much calmer, and his complaint was handled by Frank Palmer almost with ease. His assurance that there was absolutely nothing to worry about had steadily gained validity at each repetition, with the result that both Peter and David were feeling somewhat abashed. Even Neil's truculence was fading in the face of Frank Palmer's *sang-froid* as the meeting progressed

For his part, Jack had deliberately held back out of a sense that his management status demanded a more circumspect approach. It would be far more dignified to discuss the matter in camera, where he would surely have a better chance of being taken into his employer's confidence. There was certainly no point in prolonging the agony of this present gathering by adding his own complaint, only to hear the same old story for the fourth time.

Finally, as a gesture of goodwill, everybody was invited by Frank Palmer to stay for lunch as his guests, by way of apology for the inconvenience they had all suffered. This was a clever strategy, for he well knew how difficult it is to feel discontent after a good meal with plenty of wine, followed by an afternoon lounging by the pool, swimming in the clear blue Mediterranean, playing table tennis, or just chatting casually over a long cool drink.

And thus the crisis passed.

It was a tribute to British resilience when they all showed up for work at eight o'clock the next morning, each with his own motive. Jack's was perhaps the most powerful; he had already made a heavy investment of time, and had everything to gain by toughing it out. He had considerable experience concerning the difficulties a businessman faces from time to time, and had every reason to believe that the venture would eventually succeed. His own personal circumstances were not exactly a prime example of fiscal probity, and the Cyprus venture was still his best chance of dragging himself out of the mire. Peter's case was similar in that he had a family to support and a mortgage to pay, but he did not understand the vicissitudes of business life, so his reaction to unpaid wages was purely visceral. Even so, he was really enjoying the life and the work, and did not relish the prospect of returning empty handed to England. Why not wait and see, just for a week or so? As for David, he had no intention of going home, whatever the outcome. For him, Cyprus was the place to be, at least for the summer; after that, who knew?

Neil's attendance was the biggest surprise; his protest had been the most vociferous, and his attitude the most implacable. Frank Palmer had welched on him, which was unforgivable, but as there was no chance of getting off this bloody island for at least a fortnight, he might as well stand to and lend a hand. It was better than kicking his heels on his own in some bar, of that he was sure. In truth, having lain awake half the night, Neil had had convinced himself that he might have been too hasty. Like the others, he was unhappy with the thought going home with his tail between his legs, either to sign on or face another mindless factory welding job. He had already promised his daughter a holiday in Cyprus; he had even interested a couple of workmates in coming out to join him. What if your man Palmer was telling the truth, and it really was just a wee problem in the accounts department? No, it would be more canny to bide a while; he would give it two weeks, and see what happened.

* * * * * * * *

When Frank Palmer breezed into the yard to collect Jack on the morning of the Joint Venture board meeting he appeared to be in a very positive frame of mind. He was driving a hired Mercedes, and in his freshly laundered pale blue safari jacket looked every inch the successful, flamboyant wheeler-dealer. As they drove off in air conditioned splendour Jack did feel a little uneasy at first, but once they were on the road to Nicosia the smooth, reassuring motion of the car gradually dispelled the shadows from his mind, and he was ready for the business in hand.

They were the last to arrive at the meeting, which was convened in a room on the first floor of Osman Toprak's office building. It was an old but spacious chamber with a long, polished oak table down the middle, flanked by a dozen or so heavy wooden chairs. Overlooking Ataturk Square, a row of small sash windows ran the length of one wall, whilst a series of dusty old cartoon prints depicting bygone British dignitaries adorned the wall opposite. All the windows stood open in a vain attempt to relieve the stifling midday heat, and an electric fan in one corner did little to improve the fusty atmosphere. At the head of the table was a massive oak carver into which Osman Toprak had settled himself; down the table to his right sat Mehmet Boga and Muhan Timucin, the Port Director. Frank Palmer took his place opposite Mehmet Boga, and Jack sat across from the Port Director.

Osman Toprak opened the proceedings with a somewhat quaint air of formality, whereupon the minutes from the previous meeting in March were quickly read, adopted and signed. First item on the agenda concerned the building of a gatehouse, and a wrangling match immediately developed between Frank Palmer and Mehmet Boga as to how it was to be funded.

"With respect, Frank, we have never needed a gatehouse in the past. If you feel that it has now become necessary, then the cost will have to be charged to the tug project," boomed Mehmet Boga.

"With equal respect, Mehmet, I have to point out that allowing every man and his dog to wander willy nilly in and out of the yard just isn't on. Apart from the disruption to productivity, there is the question of security. Our agreement clearly states that the facilities of the shipyard will be upgraded where necessary, at the expense of FNC."

"But who is to decide what is necessary, my friend? If we cannot control our own costs we shall soon face ruin."

In this vein the two men haggled away for ten long minutes before Osman Toprak called for a vote. The Port Director voted with Frank Palmer; with a great sigh, Mehmet Boga conceded the point.

Item two related to the proposed hostel, now bravely named 'Medmarine House'. Jack listened incredulously to another protracted debate about whether it would be necessary for FNC to supervise the work, as they would hold the lease from the Government. With every show of deference, he pointed out that the actual terms of the lease were still unknown, and it would be most unwise to start work of any sort until those terms were agreed in writing. Completely ignoring this, Mehmet Boga and Frank Palmer continued to lock horns in a protracted argument that ended in stalemate when Osman Toprak asked for a motion 'to confirm that Medmarine can now start repair work and alterations.' Mehmet Boga so moved to unanimous agreement; Jack had no vote of course. After nearly an hour of fatuous waffle they were right back to where they had started, with not a word spoken about the administrative incompetence blighting the progress of the joint venture.

For another two hours the meeting progressed in much the same way. One trivial item after another was subjected to the minutest scrutiny and endless haggling over financial responsibility. Jack could not understand why Frank Palmer kept holding back when he had enough ammunition to blow Mehmet

Boga out of the water. So far, the meeting had been a complete waste of time; a curious ritual mating dance that never resulted in consummation. It appeared that nobody wanted to address the real issues, and Jack was beginning to seethe with frustration as the pointless charade dragged on through the enervating heat of midday.

His opportunity arose, however, when any other business was tabled. Having patiently held his tongue for three hours he was determined to have his say, regardless of protocol. If Frank Palmer was not prepared to speak up, there was no alternative. Jack was aware that his voice sounded harsh as he leaned forward to speak.

"I am surprised that the subject of building the tug is not included on the agenda. Perhaps we could discuss it now."

"I was not aware there was anything to discuss," replied Osman Toprak with a polite smile. "I understood that progress has been most satisfactory."

"In that case, I'm afraid you have been misinformed. Perhaps we could all take a look at the list...."

"Mister Chairman," thundered Mehmet Boga, "I do not think this is the time or place to discuss day to day matters concerning the shipyard. I can assure the Board that all the items on the manager's list are in hand."

"I'm sorry, Mehmet, but I beg to differ on two counts," persisted Jack. "In the first place many of the items on the list relate to fundamental policy issues, and in the second place I hardly consider items which have been outstanding for two months to be 'in hand', as you put it."

"Perhaps if you were to let Mehmet bey have a copy of your list," suggested the Chairman, "and make an appointment to go through it with him, this would be the best ......"

"Mehmet bey already has the list, which now contains forty-two outstanding items," returned Jack. "I have taken the liberty of preparing some copies."

He pushed a copy deliberately in front of each board member. Frank Palmer was smiling, as was Muhan Timucin, but the other two contemplated the document with an expression of distaste.

"Item one," continued Jack, firmly. "Steel RSJ. This is needed for laying the keel, and was ordered early in May, so..."

"Mister Chairman!" cried Mehmet Boga in protest. "Delays in the delivery of materials are not matters which should concern the Board. I can assure you...."

"I quite agree," shouted Jack above the resonant boom of his opponent's voice. "The Board should certainly not be troubled with delays in delivery. But that is not the issue here. The real issue is the persistent refusal of The Government Stores to sell us what we need. I don't want to keep running to Mehmet for every nut and bolt we need. Why on earth can't we be given a license to deal direct?"

At this, Mehmet Boga angrily brought his fist down on the table.

"I am Managing Director of the shipyard, Jack, not you. You are merely a technical adviser."

"Well in that case I'll jolly well give you some technical advice. If we don't start getting more co-operation from the Government and FNC on shifting some of the items on that list, you will never see a tug built in that yard."

"And perhaps I would have a better chance of dealing with your... your... 'list' if I did not have to spend half the day on the telephone listening to your endless demands."

At this point the Chairman wisely decided to intervene. He could see that Jack had the stronger case, besides which the exchange was showing every sign of becoming personal.

"Gentlemen! Gentlemen!" interjected Osman Toprak, "I believe I may have a solution to this little problem. You must understand, Jack, that Mehmet bey has many duties in addition to his involvement with the shipyard, and it is clear that with the best will in the world he simply does not have the time to give your list the attention it rightly deserves. I propose that FNC appoint a member of their staff, one who speaks good English, as an assistant manager dealing only with matters relating to the Shipyard. In this way all the outstanding items can be dealt with quickly and efficiently. What do you think, Mehmet bey? Do you have a suitable person on your staff?"

"I suppose I could appoint Onan."

"There we have it then. Let's take a vote on that."

Jack was so disappointed that Mehmet Boga had emerged unscathed from the exchange that he made no further contribution to the proceedings. Why had Frank Palmer not waded in with some support? His silence had enabled FNC to close ranks, and now Onan would provide an additional layer of protection for Mehmet Boga.

When the meeting was brought to a close, Frank Palmer went into a huddle with Osman Toprak and Mehmet Boga. Jack went over to the window where he looked out in brooding solitude at the teeming activity in the square below; before long he was joined by Muhan Timucin, the Port Director.

"So, Jack, did you find the meeting worthwhile?"

"Not really. I feel that very little has been achieved. We are still without oxygen, acetylene or a crane."

"But surely, the appointment of Onan as your assistant will help, will it not?"

"Very little, I'm afraid. Onan is a pleasant enough young chap, but he's a lightweight. He's no more effective at The Government Stores than I am."

"I may be able to help you myself on that one. The Minister of Finance is a distant cousin of mine. He also owes me one or two favours. I can arrange for you and Frank to see him this Friday, immediately after our monthly finance meeting. I'm sure he will be prepared to issue a license for you to trade with The Government Stores when I remind him how important the tug is for the port. You'll need to be there at about four o'clock, do you think you can make it?"

"Oh, we'll be there," replied Jack, hardly able to contain his elation, "you can be sure of that. And I can't tell you how grateful I am for your support in this."

"Well really, you have Kemal Aydin to thank. He has been keeping me informed regarding the difficulties you have been up against. I did not think it was my place to take any direct action myself, but after this meeting today I begin to see how much you struggle in your dealings with certain officials. Please remember, Jack, that my door is always open, and I am only too happy to help all I can. It is in everybody's interest that this project is a success."

As they shook hands, Jack felt a warm glow of satisfaction in the knowledge that he had made a powerful ally in this quiet, purposeful individual. Perhaps, in the end, the meeting had not been a complete waste of time.

Jack relayed his conversation with the Port Director to Frank Palmer as they drove back to Famagusta, and the news was very well received.

"What a stroke of luck, Jack! I was hoping to get an appointment with the minister myself and talk to him about those two barges. If we can get a permit to plunder The Government Stores at the same time so much the better."

"Well at least something constructive came out of the afternoon. That ridiculous board meeting! What a waste of time!"

"You think?" replied Frank Palmer, looking smug. "I'm not so sure."

"Three hours pussyfooting around with that pompous idiot. What good did it do?"

"Well it gave you a chance to bare your teeth. If Osman Toprak hadn't stepped in there could have been blood on the carpet."

"I just don't understand why they put up with him. The man is useless. Another thing I don't understand, Frank, is why you didn't have a go at him yourself? He's completely ignored your letter as well as all of mine."

"No, I think it's better if I leave the rough stuff to you. You know – the good cop bad cop routine. I don't want things to develop into a 'them and us' situation. I can use you as a sort of threat, if you know what I mean."

"Give me what I want or I'll set my Rotweiler on to you," suggested Jack.

"Yeah, that's the sort of thing. Osman Toprak reckons you've already put the fear of God into Mehmet. I gather you've savaged him a couple of times already."

"I've rattled his cage once or twice, but nothing serious."

"I think your idea of serious is a lot different to his. You have to remember he's used to having his own way all the time, with people running around after him. He's always going to find it difficult dealing with somebody like you."

"The trouble is, he's got Onan to shelter him from any blame now. We're out of the frying pan and into the fire."

"Not necessarily. Onan might not be the brightest pebble on the beach, but he is a protégé of Osman Toprak, as you may have gathered from that neat bit of footwork at the meeting. As far as attaching blame is concerned you'll find that Onan is the original Teflon man. Osman Toprak has made a very clever move. Now he can jerk Mehmet's chain using Onan as the choker."

Jack fell into a thoughtful silence; all this Machiavellian intrigue was the last thing he needed. So why not leave it to those that enjoyed it? If it meant the job would take two years rather than one, so what? There were far worse places than Cyprus in which to spend a couple of years. Work hard, save money, speak the truth, make friends: these maxims were relevant wherever you were. From now on he would steer clear of the politics and just take things as they came.

* * * * * * * *

Muhan Timucin quietly closed the door of the Finance Minister's air conditioned office behind him, bade farewell to the secretary and two clerks toiling in the sweltering atmosphere of the adjoining office, and stepped out into the wide corridor where Frank Palmer and Jack sat waiting on a long mahogany bench.

"The Minister will see you now," he announced softly. "You can go straight in. I'm happy to report that he is in a very good mood. He has already agreed that you can have the Jones crane for as long as you want it, free of charge in view of the fact that you will have to carry out the necessary repairs yourself. He has also agreed to issue you with a permit to buy from any of The Government Stores, and at the best prices. Furthermore, he is prepared to negotiate on the sale of the Sands barges. Between you and me," he added, tapping the side of his nose with his forefinger, "he is quite keen to get rid of them. Apparently the Prime Minister is insisting on their immediate removal. I wouldn't bother too much about that auction reserve price either; it was just a figure pulled out of the air by one of the clerks. Keep the meeting as short as you can; he likes to finish early on Friday and get down to his boat."

They were in the Finance Minister's office for barely twenty minutes, which is all the time it took to obtain The Government Store purchase permit, a broken crane and two dilapidated barges for a knock-down price. The documentation was all signed by the Minister himself.

"What a result!" whispered Frank Palmer as they walked down the long dark corridor towards the exit. "Let's get out of here before he changes his mind."

"It just goes to show how easy it can be if you know the right people," observed Jack. "Muhan Timucin has certainly done us proud this time."

"We'll have to find some way of showing our appreciation. Some sort of gift."

"I don't think he'd be expecting anything like that. I think he just wants his tug built as quickly as possible."

"Perhaps you're right. But anyway, let's get back and have a look at our barges."

On reaching the Sands Hotel they found Neil, Peter, and David on the terrace having a drink with Harry and Brenda. At Frank Palmer's suggestion they all made their way round to the rocks on the far side of the building to examine his new acquisition, and spent a good half hour discussing the best way to tackle the repair job. It was to be completely separate from the joint venture, using British personnel at weekends to complete the first phase of the operation, namely the preparation of the barges for re-flotation. Payment would be made in sterling by Frank Palmer, tax free, into their UK bank accounts, but at the basic rate only. Peter, David and Harry were quite ready to accept these terms; as far as they were concerned it would be far better to spend their weekends earning extra cash than frittering the time away in the bars of Famagusta. Neil was less responsive to the plan; as far as he was concerned, double time for work on Sunday was enshrined as a holy commandment, a matter of Christian principle not to be abandoned lightly, especially when you had the employer over a barrel.

It took the Scot less than ten minutes to convince Frank Palmer that double time for all was the only way forward, a victory that earned him the undying loyalty and admiration of his three colleagues.

That evening everybody was invited to another celebration dinner party, this time to mark the successful purchase of the barges. Again the wine flowed freely, the food was excellent, and everybody was in the best of spirits. Any lingering concerns about wages seemed to evaporate in the general sense of well being that spread throughout the company as the evening progressed. At about ten o'clock Frank Palmer made his excuses as he was leaving for England early in the morning, but before leaving the party he reassured them all that the wages problem would be sorted out first thing on Monday morning, and everyone would be paid up to date by the following day. He called for the bill and instructed the head waiter to provide anything his guests wanted for the rest of the evening, charged to his account. After he was gone, the conversation turned naturally to the subject of wage payment arrears; Neil voiced his intention of giving Frank Palmer until the end of the month. As for the barges, he could not see how they would ever be relaunched, but if your man was prepared to throw his money away it would be silly not to take it. The four men agreed that for the rest of month they would attend for work each day as usual, but nobody would be striving to break any productivity records. Jack grew uneasy listening to these somewhat seditious proposals, and suggested that they could use the time to tow their newly acquired crane round to the yard and start stripping it down, just to keep busy. All this talk of business dispelled what remained of their earlier conviviality, and the party broke up soon afterwards.

The following morning Jack, Mary and Wendy called at the Sands Hotel to pick up Peter and David for a day's sailing on the Harbourmaster's yacht. Susan had decided not to join them as she found being cooped up on a small boat for hours on end not to her liking; a day at the Plâj Hotel with Nihan's children was infinitely preferable. Neil had also declined the invitation, dismissing the activity as nothing more than a bourgeois pretension. It was, of course, Mary's idea to invite the two lads. Not only would it stop them wasting their money in bars, but it would make them realise they were part of a community that cared for their welfare. Less than a decade separated Mary's age from that of these two young men, yet she had assumed the role of den mother with her usual aplomb.

Favoured with a brisk offshore breeze they reached northwards along the coast towards Bogaz. Their exact destination was Bedi's bar and restaurant; a tiny, isolated ramshackle building situated right on the water's edge a mile or so south of the village. From their anchorage about fifty meters off the beach they all swam ashore, Wendy spluttering a continuous protest that she could not swim as Mary patiently coaxed her though the water. They feasted *al fresco* on grilled fish, salad, crusty bread soaked in olive oil and a great bowl of fresh fruit, all served up by Bedi's smiling wife and darkly attractive teenage daughter. As the only customers that day, the party was treated like visiting royalty, the glamour of the occasion being much enhanced by their unusual arrival under sail. After they had all eaten their fill, the afternoon was given over to a long siesta, followed by an hilarious impromptu game of rounders with Bedi and his family, using a twisted piece of driftwood as a bat. When Jack finally called for the bill it was presented shyly by Bedi's daughter, being the only member of the family who spoke any English. The total was so ridiculously low that he added a tip of fifty percent, which was gratefully accepted by Bedi only after a suitable show of reluctance. It was plain to see these gentle people were barely able to scratch a living in such a remote location, but money hardly seemed to matter in such idyllic surroundings. Bedi's daughter remained on the beach, holding the twisted driftwood bat to her chest as she watched the yacht sail away, and hoped it would not be long before the handsome young Englishman with the golden curls returned.

The return leg was completed almost on a single close-hauled tack, but as the yacht neared Famagusta the wind freshened and backed a little to the south, so Jack had to come about on the port tack for the final approach. With three men sitting out to windward and the sheets hauled in bar tight, 'Ceylan' stiffened bravely to the wind and creamed towards the harbour entrance with her lee rail under. Out of sheer exhilaration, Jack gleefully rendered 'Hearts of Oak' at the top of his lungs, much to the astonishment of his crew.

* * * * *

"Tuesday 25th July

I've 'phoned our bank twice this afternoon, and still the money has not been paid in. Jack has spent all afternoon trying to get in touch with Frank Palmer, but could only speak to his secretary every time. In the end he left a message, and asked the girl to pass it on as soon as possible.

Jack, Neil and the lads spent all morning dragging a beat-up old crane round into the yard with the tractor. They were like a bunch of schoolboys on a prank, all covered in rusty, greasy, dirt, delighting in their new toy – David has already started taking it apart to see if it can be repaired.

I went with Susan to the market this morning, and I'm really amazed at how well she is picking up the language. I know enough to buy everything we need, but Susan is capable of holding an actual conversation. Part of her time each day is spent with Suleyman learning Turkish and she certainly is doing very well. I spend a couple of hours each day on English and Maths with her, but I know that's no substitute for proper schooling. I hope we hear something of the ESB school soon."

* * * * *

It was just before midday when Jack received the telephone call from the bank in Famagusta asking him to collect an urgent telex addressed to him from England. Although he went straight away, the branch was closed for lunch by the time he arrived, and he pounded angrily on the wooden door. After a frustrating exchange with an unseen official on the other side of the door it was opened on the chain, a small brown envelope was handed to him, and the door slammed shut again. Standing there on the pavement he tore open the envelope and read the message.

"26.7.78
URGENT URGENT
PLEASE PASS TO MR JACK DURHAM MEDMARINE SHIPYARD FAMAGUSTA.
ALL MONIES PAID THROUGH BANK ON MONDAY 24TH HOLD RECEIPTS IN THIS OFFICE.
WILL NOT GO INTO DETAILS ON TELEX YOUR PHONE MESSAGE UNACCEPTABLE
CHECK AGAIN. PHONE ME IMMEDIATELY.
FRANK PALMER"

Jack sat in the Mini-Moke and reread the document twice more before its meaning sank in, but it was the manner in which it had been sent that puzzled him the most. Frank Palmer usually sent telexes addressed to Jack via FNC, and on one or two occasions had sent them via Osman Toprak if he wanted a greater degree of confidentiality. He had never used the bank as a post-box before, so why do so today? Only two possible explanations came to mind; either he had been unable to obtain an answerback from his usual connections, *or* he wanted to keep the message secret from Osman Toprak as well as FNC.

Back in his office, Jack tried to resume work, but the implications of the strange event played on his mind and ruined his concentration. When Mary arrived in the afternoon, he immediately showed her Frank Palmer's telex, which she, too, had to read several times before comprehension dawned.

"What does he mean about your 'phone message being unacceptable?" she asked quietly.

"I've no idea. Perhaps he didn't want his secretary to know about the problem. But what else could I do? If you can't get hold of someone, you have to leave a message, don't you?"

"Maybe he's right, and the money has been paid in. It wouldn't be the first time our bank has messed things up, would it?"

"We'll just have to keep ringing to find out what's happening. I know it can take a few days for cheques to clear, but he says in his telex that he is holding receipts, so you'd think that the money had been transferred by faster means. I just don't know what to make of it."

"Are you going to tell the others?"

"No, I don't see the point. It's bound to be the same story with them. I think it's best not to worry them until we know a bit more about what's happening."

"I wouldn't mind betting that Neil will be on to his bank today."

"Yes, but he doesn't know about this telex, so he won't be aware of the implications. Put in a call to the bank now. Let's see if there's any news."

It was nearly six in the evening before Mary was able to obtain a connection, and the news was much as they expected. The money had not been paid. In the meantime Jack put through a call to Frank Palmer only to be told by his secretary that he was in the Channel Islands and would not be back for two or three days.

Neil, Harry and the lads came into the office first thing next morning and confirmed they had all telephoned their banks to be told that they, too, had not been paid as promised. Jack showed them the telex message without mentioning the troubling implications, and tried to reassure them that the delay might well be something to do with clearing the funds. They all telephoned their banks again that afternoon only to receive the same discouraging news. On Friday the news was even worse. They had all been paid just one week's money, but the back pay was still outstanding. It appeared that Frank Palmer had been lying all the time. Two weeks had passed since their initial discovery of the problem; as only one week's money had been paid, the arrears had in fact increased. The position was steadily deteriorating.

For the remainder of the afternoon Jack kept trying to telephone Frank Palmer, but the lines to England were very busy, and he was unable to obtain a connection. Alone in his office after everyone had left, he continued trying well into the evening, but when he eventually succeeded there was no reply. The London office was closed for the weekend; there was nothing he could do except wait until Monday and try again. Being the last to leave the yard Jack walked round the sheds to check they were all secure, and with a heavy heart he locked the gates and drove off to meet Neil and the two lads at the Sands Hotel. They all sat round a table on the crowded terrace drinking beer as twilight fell. Each put on a brave face, but at heart they all felt the game was up. Peter confirmed that he had been able to book his flight home for the following Thursday; Neil's was booked for two days after that. David announced his intention of remaining at the Sands Hotel as Frank Palmer's guest for as long as possible and look for some sort of live-in job for the summer, perhaps at the Salamis Bay Hotel, or the Dome in Kyrenia. Everyone agreed to keep the whole business to themselves for the time being, as nothing would be gained by broadcasting their plight. It was also agreed they would keep their appointment next day at the house of Hasan Kirmizi, the welder. There was to be a party to celebrate the circumcision of Hasan's son, and all the British personnel had been invited to attend.

* * * * * * * *

On arrival at Hasan's house at around noon, Mary was presented by his wife with a beautiful, hand embroidered linen tray cloth to mark the occasion, and was ushered by her smiling host to what was plainly a seat of honour in the spacious living room. Susan and Wendy were given little upholstered stools, one on either side of their mother, but before long they were whisked off by Hasan's daughters to play outside in the garden. Neil and the lads had arrived some time before, and were sitting on a long, low studio couch drinking Cyprus brandy. They squeezed up to make room for Jack who promptly joined them in a glass of the coarse, fiery spirit. He choked as his throat closed in defence against the first swallow, whereupon David administered first aid in the finest tradition by thumping the victim enthusiastically on his back.

"Thank you David," said Jack in a hoarse whisper, wiping his eyes with a pocket-handkerchief, "but you can stop now while my spine is still intact."

"Cyprus brandy!" cried Hasan proudly. "Good, yes?"

"The very best paint stripper I have ever drunk," croaked Jack, holding up his glass in tribute. He recklessly tossed back the rest of his drink, and the whole process of choking and back thumping started again. "Don't worry, I'll do better with the next one," he gasped, blinking back his tears.

By the time the last of Hasan's guests had arrived the room was becoming quite crowded, resulting in a good deal of confusion as plates of food appeared and people tried to find places to sit. Mary offered her seat to a wizened old lady clad in black, and was rewarded with a torrent of toothless gratitude of which she understood not a word. The room was becoming very stuffy, so she made her way out into the garden and stood watching the children playing a complicated skipping game. She suddenly felt isolated and vulnerable. Susan and Wendy were with their new friends, bouncing about with not a care in the world. Jack was with Neil and the lads, seemingly hell bent on getting drunk, and who could blame them? She was in a strange land surrounded by people who spoke no English, and who were about to mutilate an innocent baby. The worst thought of all, however, was that her beloved bungalow with its beautiful little garden would again be at risk from seizure by grasping officials. When would the nightmare end?

Her thoughts were interrupted suddenly when she heard the cries of pain from Hasan's helpless infant son as the ritual knife sliced into his tiny member. Quite by chance she had been standing outside the window of the bedroom in which the ceremony was taking place. She hurriedly moved away and went back inside. Mercifully, it was all over in less than a minute, and as the screams gave way to whimpers in a gradual diminuendo, guests filed in to pay their respects to the brave little chap. When her turn came, Mary found herself looking into two huge, tear filled brown eyes staring back with indignation. A small bloodstain was slowly spreading from the centre of the baby's nappy, and her heart filled with compassion as she smiled down at him. Did she imagine it, or did he smile back?

When they arrived home later in the afternoon there was a handwritten envelope on the doormat addressed to Jack. It contained a brief message from Suleyman written out in a neat script by one of his daughters. The message read:

"Mr Stephen Clarkson arrived in Cyprus today, and is staying at the Plâj Hotel. Would you please telephone him as soon as you get this note?"

Chapter Seventeen

Rather than telephone, Jack decided to drive out to the Plâj Hotel and meet Stephen Clarkson face to face. As was now the custom for conducting informal business meetings, they gravitated towards the basement bar which they found conveniently empty.

"You're a sight for sore eyes," declared Jack as they settled with their drinks in the deep leather armchairs

"Why, is anything wrong?" asked Stephen, casually.

"Not with the tug, no. We are ready to profile the keel sections as soon as we get some gas. Is that why you're here? How long are you staying, by the way?"

"Only tomorrow. I'm going back on Monday. I need to check a couple of sections on the scrieve board. I think we may have a small problem with the lower chine in way of frames eighteen to twenty-four. I've been going over the offsets, and I've spotted a couple of anomalies. I know it's a Sunday, and I hate to be a pain, but do you think we can have a look at it tomorrow?"

Jack hesitated before making his reply, weighing the possibility that Stephen was here on reconnaissance for Frank Palmer; his appearance at this particular juncture really was highly coincidental. On the other hand, a professional naval architect would hardly make up a story about design errors. He decided the reason given for the visit had to be genuine.

"Of course we can. I'd only be wasting my time relaxing with my family if we didn't."

"Thanks, Jack. I really appreciate this."

"How's Frank, by the way? Have you seen anything of him lately? Is he back from the Channel Islands yet?"

"The Channel Islands?"

"Yes. I tried to contact him – when was it – Wednesday, and his girl told me he was in the Channel Islands. I thought you might know something about it, that's all."

"I know he's been negotiating a deal to sell one of his ships. Perhaps that was it. I don't really know. I haven't seen much of him lately."

"But as far as you know, everything's okay?"

"Yes, as far as I know. But why do you ask? There *is* something wrong, isn't there?"

"The truth is, I don't really know," replied Jack, hesitating again before adding:

"Tell me, Stephen, does Frank Palmer owe you any money?"

Stephen Clarkson was obviously disturbed by the question, and cleared his throat nervously before replying.

"Oh, come on, Jack. What sort of question is that? What would you think if I asked it of you?"

"I'd tell you."

"Okay. So does he owe you money?"

"I asked first," countered Jack, with a grin.

"Frank is my client. You know I can't talk to anyone about our financial dealings without his express consent."

"Which he's hardly likely to give."

"Quite."

"So we both remain none the wiser," concluded Jack, standing up. "I'm going to have another drink. What can I get you?"

"I'll just have a beer. And some peanuts, if they have them."

When Jack returned with the drinks he apologised for the absence of peanuts, sank back into the depths of his armchair and stared hard at his colleague as if trying to read his mind. Stephen fumbled for his pocket-handkerchief and started to polish his spectacles. There had been time for both men to think

"So, where were we?" asked Jack.

"Being none the wiser, I believe."

"Well we can't have that, can we?" said Jack impatiently. "So let me fill you in with some rather disturbing news. Frank Palmer is seven weeks behind with our wages. Not just me, all the lads as well."

"There must be some simple explanation. Have you spoken to him about it?"

"Of course we have. We all tackled him about it when he was over last week."

"And what did he say?"

"He blamed his accounts department. He didn't seem the least bit worried about it, and promised to put everything right when he got back to the UK."

"And?"

"There is no 'and'. The money still hasn't been paid, and now I can't get hold of him. I've stopped all work on the tug, and won't be starting again until we're paid. We've all got families to support and mortgages to pay."

"Does Osman Toprak know about any of this?"

"No. We're keeping it to ourselves for the time being. We haven't told anyone at FNC either."

"But they must have noticed that you're not working on the tug."

Jack gave a hollow laugh and replied:

"Mehmet Boga isn't interested enough to notice! None of them has a clue what's going on. We had a joint venture board meeting at Osman Toprak's offices when Frank was over last week. What a fiasco! I'll show you a copy of the minutes tomorrow, if you fancy a really good laugh. It was like something out of Fred Karno's circus. I was all set to take Mehmet apart, but Frank wouldn't back me up and they closed ranks to save his skin. Mehmet Boga is a complete waste of time. Ever since I've been out here he's done nothing but stand in the way of progress. No, Stephen, as far as FNC is concerned they think it's the lack of acetylene, propane and oxygen that's holding things up. I've made it quite clear that we cannot make any progress until a proper supply line is established. I've also made it clear that we can't build a ship without a crane, and there's no sign of a solution to that problem either."

Stephen stared silently down at his beer for several moments before his next enquiry.

"Does all this effect our session on the scrieve board tomorrow?"

"Of course not. I'm not going to let you come all this way for nothing, am I? In any case, Mary and I haven't actually stopped working. I'd want to know a lot more about what's going on before I'd down tools myself. Your visit couldn't have come at a better time. Come on, Stephen, you must be able to tell me something."

"Honestly, Jack, I can't. This has all come as a complete surprise to me. I haven't really had much to do with Frank since you became involved, and recently I've been really busy with projects for other clients. I had no idea things were as bad as this."

"You say as bad as this," said Jack, pouncing at the phrase like a terrier on a rat. "That implies that you *are* aware of some problem."

Again Stephen found something interesting at the bottom of his glass to help him collect his thoughts.

"I can only say that he's selling 'Baltic Surveyor'. If Medmarine does have any short term cash flow problems – and I have to stress that I am not actually aware of any – then they will certainly be solved when that deal goes through."

"Thank you, Stephen," said Jack, smiling with relief. "That's all I needed to know. Though why he couldn't have told me this himself I just don't know."

"I'm sorry Jack, but I have to make it clear that I've told you nothing. As far as I'm aware all Frank's companies are trading successfully and making good profits."

"Enough said," returned Jack, still smiling. "You have indeed made your position perfectly clear. As far as I'm concerned this conversation never took place."

Working together on the scrieve board the following morning the two men put all thoughts of Frank Palmer, Medmarine and the Famagusta Navigation Company from their minds. Here, in the lofting shed, there was no room for surmise or conjecture. There were no political minefields to negotiate, or diplomatic eggshells to avoid crushing underfoot. Indisputable, exact measurement was the order of the day, and they welcomed the discipline imposed upon them by their endeavours as they crawled about the board on their hands and knees. Columns of co-ordinates were checked, and checked again; splines were bent to fair curves with infinite care and precision; perpendiculars were struck with devout reverence; finally the small error was found and eradicated. Mission accomplished.

The day ended with an invitation for Jack, Mary and the girls to dine at the Plâj Hotel as Stephen's guests. Care was taken to exclude from their conversation any reference to work or money, and the evening was passed pleasantly enough, with a late swim in the pool just before twilight. A somewhat boisterous game of handball soon developed, and the evening air rang to the delighted cries of the children as they all floundered and splashed about. Who could guess, witnessing this sublime scene, at the troubles which blighted the lives of this innocent family?

As he said his farewells to Jack and Mary at Ercan airport the next day, Stephen made a final attempt to reassure them that they had no cause for concern regarding the future of the tug project. He undertook to meet with Frank Palmer as soon as possible, and keep them informed about any significant developments. On the now familiar journey back to Famagusta, however, they both had the same topic on their minds, and Mary was on the telephone to the bank as soon as they arrived at the office. The money had still not been paid.

Tuesday afternoon's call to the bank produced no better news, and it was the same on Wednesday. Jack put in yet another call to Frank Palmer, only to be told by an indifferent female that he was away from the office. As he was trying to impress upon the girl the urgency of his need to speak with her boss he was discourteously transferred, with no warning, to a junior employee who was even more apathetic than her predecessor. The situation seemed hopeless, but Jack had the bit between his teeth, so he kept trying, despite the indignities he was obliged to suffer.

Thursday morning found Jack and Mary yet again on the airport run taking Peter to catch the midday flight out of Ercan. During their short time together they had all become really good friends, and spirits were very low as they exchanged farewells. Jack promised to do everything he could to secure Peter's back pay, and advised him to act as if he were simply taking some leave if Frank Palmer should contact him at home. Watching the aircraft take off, Mary felt such a surge of compassion for Peter and his family that she could have wept but for her determination to maintain a stiff upper lip in the face of adversity. Jack sensed her sorrow and suggested going into Nicosia to see if they could obtain passes to visit the English Sovereign Base at Dekelya. After a good deal of traipsing about from one Government office to another they were eventually directed to the right building, where they optimistically submitted themselves to the lengthy application procedure only to be told the passes would not be issued for another two days.

Immediately on their return to the office Mary made her routine telephone call to the bank in England. She was hardly able to believe her ears on being told that eight hundred pounds had been received by telegraphic transfer from Jersey. Arrangements had already been made for her to telephone the bank branches used by the British team, so she was able to confirm that they too had all been paid up to date.

* * * * *

"Saturday 5th August

Up betimes to take Neil to the airport. Jack has told him to contact Frank Palmer first thing on Monday to make sure all the equipment needed at the yard is on order. Neil says he's coming back now all the money problems have been sorted out, but I'm not so sure he really means it. We'll just have to wait and see.

"Harry and Brenda are also going back to England, and won't be coming back. Harry says he's not prepared to be messed about with his money, and

Brenda is already feeling homesick. She says she doesn't like the heat out here, and is missing all her favourite television programmes. Jack says he's not at all sorry to lose Harry. And so another two bite the dust!

"We picked up our passes for the ESB today, and decided to try them out straight away. The check-point at Ayios Nikolaos is only just over a mile from the flat, so we decided to walk in case there was any problem taking the Mini-Moke through with Northern Cyprus number plates. It felt strange – the four of us trekking along that hot dusty road on foot – almost like we were refugees, but it was lovely seeing the Union Flag flying high over the buildings. We passed through easily enough, and spent the rest of the afternoon wandering around the camp. It really was amazing – just as if a little piece of England had been plonked down in the middle of nowhere – a vision of gleaming white paint and beautifully kept grass. 'If it moves, salute it! If it doesn't move, paint it!' as my old dad used to say. There were grass tennis courts, a superb open air swimming pool, lovely wooden pavilions with wide verandas – it was more like a holiday camp than an army base. And everywhere was spotless.*

"We went in the NAAFI stores, and that really did make us feel we were back home. All those familiar brands we just take for granted – pork sausages, Wiltshire bacon, cornflakes, our favourite tea, – and all of it dated recently, not like the stuff from our local shop in Baykal which is dated before 1974! It didn't take long to fill our shopping basket – and everything was so reasonably priced. I bought the girls a pack of coloured felt-tip pens each and two sketch pads. We did have a bit of a problem at the checkout because we didn't have any Cyprus Pounds – the manager was most indignant when Jack offered him Turkish lira. Luckily they were quite happy to exchange some Sterling I had with me, so we were able to hang on to our booty. It certainly is a wonderful place to buy food, but I don't think we shall be able to use it very much because they won't take Turkish Lira. It's practically impossible to get hold of Cyprus Pounds at the official exchange rate, and if we use the black market we lose half the value of our money, and I'm certainly not having that!"*

* * * * *

Putting the recent dark days of uncertainty behind them, Jack and David threw themselves back into the fray with renewed purpose and vigour. The RSJ strongback for the keel arrived at last, and was set up on the building pad the same day, with all the support struts welded in position by David and Hasan Kirmizi. They started trying to cut out the keel sections, but again the inch plate proved too much for the equipment they had. Jack trod his familiar path round to the FNC offices to remind Onan that the problem of gas was now in his province, and was amazed when the young Cypriot came up with a short term solution. His cousin, Avkuran, was a steelworker who ran a little workshop of his own just outside Famagusta, and had built up a very good reputation in the port. Why not give him a try?

The experiment was a complete success. Avkuran arrived in a smart, clean pick-up truck and proceeded to unload his gear, which was up to date and well maintained. Jack could see straight away from the way Avkuran set up his equipment that he knew what he was doing, an impression that was soon confirmed by the steady progress of his cutting flame along the chalk line. So impressive was the result that Jack told Onan to enquire if a permanent job on the tug would interest this able man, so after some hard bargaining over remuneration, Avkuran was duly taken on as leading hand. Keel cutting was at last in progress.

It was on a particularly hot, oppressive Friday afternoon whilst checking keel section templates in the lofting shed that Jack noticed out of the corner of his eye a figure standing silently in the open doorway. He looked up to find a slight, stooping man of European appearance, wearing a baggy tropical suit and a brand new Panama hat. With every show of courtesy, the stranger removed the hat, stepped with great deference across the threshold, and introduced himself as Kenneth Huson, from the Island of Jersey.

"I am looking for Mr. Frank Palmer," he continued in a quiet but assertive manner. "I believe he has something to do with this establishment."

"Mr. Palmer is our Managing Director, yes. But I am afraid he is in the UK at the present time. Perhaps I can be of assistance. My name is Jack Durham."

The visitor walked across to Jack and they shook hands.

"Mr Durham, would it be possible to enquire in what capacity you are engaged here?"

"I'm the yard manager."

"And do you think I could trouble you a little further by asking when Mr Palmer might be available, that is to say, when is he due back?"

"I don't know about that, but I do think it would be a good idea to let me know what this is all about."

"Ah, I am afraid I am not at liberty to divulge the purpose of my visit, other than to say it is a matter of the utmost delicacy which I must discuss with Mr. Palmer in person."

The impression in Jack's mind that he was speaking with some sort of genteel bailiff was growing stronger by the minute. He decided to try and find out a little more and said:

"I'd hate to think that you've had a wasted journey all the way from the Channel Islands. Let's pop along to my office and see if there's a date for his return in the diary."

As they walked up the yard Jack humoured the mysterious visitor with just a little general information, enough to break the ice and appear co-operative. They seated themselves in the two comfortable chairs in his office and chatted harmlessly about the comparative climates of Cyprus and Jersey. Gradually each became less guarded, and more interested in learning about the other man's dealings with Frank Palmer. To shift the conversation onto a more confidential level, Jack gave a brief explanation for his own presence on the island.

"So really," said the visitor, "you are just here on a fixed contract to build the tug. How very interesting. Might I venture to ask if you have any of your own money invested in the project?"

"A small amount," lied Jack, thinking the visitor might open up more readily to an investor than he would to someone that was just an employee.

"So you are satisfied that adequate funding is in place to complete the project?"

"The Turkish Cypriot Government is responsible for funding the project. Our involvement is mainly technical."

"But you do hope to make a profit."

"There's no taste in nothing," replied Jack. "But now I really do think you should tell me why you wish to see Mr. Palmer. You mentioned funding a moment ago, is that why you're here? To offer funding?"

The visitor shook his head and gave a dry little chuckle

"Please excuse my mirth, Jack – I may call you Jack? But nothing could be further from the truth. I see many similarities between the situation you have described here in Cyprus, and that of my own company in Jersey. I fear you may find Mr Frank Palmer is not all he appears to be. You see, he owes my company many, many thousands of pounds. But that is a mere bagatelle in comparison with the money he owes other companies in the aviation industry. Shall I tell you more?"

"Please do," replied Jack, not without a certain degree of apprehension.

"My company is in the aircraft repair business. We were approached at the beginning of the year by Mr Frank Palmer with a proposal to modify a passenger plane he had purchased in the United States. He intended to operate out of a UK airport, so the modifications were necessary to comply with the regulations laid down by the British Aviation Authority. We undertook to complete the work, and did so well within the time frame he had specified. When we came to bill him– in excess of twenty thousand pounds – Mr Palmer was nowhere to be found. His office address in St Peter Port was deserted, and all our efforts to trace the wretched man came to nought. The plot then thickened. The American company from whom Mr Palmer purchased the aircraft sent a representative to Guernsey for the purpose of obtaining the balance he owed. That, of course, ran to a great deal of money. They, too, were anxious to have their account settled, but had been unable to locate him. Because their aircraft no longer conformed to American aviation specifications they were reluctant to take it back in its altered state, but as the story unfolded it became even more bizarre. Even if they were prepared to repossess their property they could not, because it emerged that Mr Palmer had sold the aircraft on. A small charter company in Sussex now claims ownership and the matter is consequently subject to litigation. My only interest in this sordid business is to get the money owed to my company. We cannot afford to write off such a large sum. Hence my unscheduled appearance at your door."

Jack remained silent; he simply did not know what to say. Could this extraordinary tale possibly have any basis in truth? If so, the implications would be endless. He needed time to think. Say nothing. Play for time.

"From your stunned silence, Jack," continued the visitor; "I gather this has all taken you by surprise. Might I further surmise that you yourself have found dealings with Mr Palmer in matters relating to money somewhat – how shall I put it – unorthodox?"

Again, Jack had nothing to say, and simply sat shaking his head. He must have time to think.

"Come on, old chap," persisted the visitor, "can you help me, or not?"

"I don't see how I can," replied Jack at last. "I'm sure you can understand that I'm not at liberty to discuss Mr Palmer's affairs with a complete stranger. I mean, we've only just met – I don't really know you from Adam, do I?"

"I appreciate what you say, old chap. All I'm asking for is a UK address, or even just a telephone number. I'm right in assuming that Medmarine Limited is based in the UK, am I not?"

"As far as I'm aware it's incorporated here in Cyprus."

"But you did mention earlier that our mutual friend is presently in the UK. You must know his telephone number at least."

"And you must know that I cannot let you have it."

It was the visitor's turn to remain silent. He sat staring at Jack with an expectant smile on his patrician features. At length he stood up slowly and offered his hand.

"I commend your loyalty, Jack," he declared, still smiling, "and I fully understand your position. I should naturally do exactly the same in such a situation. I only hope you find Mr Palmer deserves your trust in him. Just in case you change your mind, here is my card. I shall be staying at the Saray in Nicosia for a day or so. You can always contact me there if you so choose. Could I trouble you for one of your cards, do you think?"

"I'm afraid I don't have any. It's just one of the things we haven't got round to yet. I'm sorry."

"Think nothing of it. The absence of anything so definite as a business card does not surprise me in the least. But I do so hope you will be in touch."

With these words, Mr Kenneth Huson walked out of the yard to his waiting taxi and disappeared, leaving Jack in a state of bewilderment. At least he had time to think, now that his mind was no longer besieged by a clever and persistent adversary. Was the story true? Jack had an uncomfortable feeling it was. What should he do? He had no idea. Perhaps consult Osman Toprak? No, talk to Mary first. Nothing must be done in haste.

He parked the Mini-Moke in its usual place outside the flat, and sat for a moment or two watching the children at play in the dusty street. They no longer took any notice of the jeep, or his homecoming at the end of the day. There was Susan, playing tag with her friends at a breathlessly energetic pace. There, too, was Wendy, pouring imaginary cups of tea for her own little chums in a neighbour's front garden. As usual the ever vigilant Grannies sat on their wooden chairs outside nearly every front door. But although everything was so familiar, Jack suddenly felt alienated from it all, as if he were watching a scene from a film. It was not until Mary emerged from the front door of their apartment that the strange spell was broken.

"What are you doing, sitting out here? Is everything alright?" she enquired.

"I'm not really sure. I had this weird visit today from an English guy looking for Frank Palmer. I'll tell you all about it indoors – it's far too hot out here. God! What I wouldn't give for a decent pint of ale right now!"

In the relative coolness of the kitchen he related the details of Kenneth Huson's visit as Mary prepared their evening meal. She listened quietly to his account, but made no comment when he had finished.

"So, what do you make of it?" asked Jack after a long silence.

"Do you think the story is true?"

"I've no way of knowing, but my gut feeling is to believe him. You couldn't really make up something like that. What would be the point? Perhaps we should go and see Osman Toprak."

"I'm not so sure about that Jack. Surely you should speak to Frank first. If it's not true, telling Osman Toprak might cause trouble. If it is true that certainly would mean trouble."

"No, I should definitely give Osman Toprak a visit, he will know what to do. He and Frank are quite chummy and I'm sure he'll know what's going on."

Jack tried to telephone Osman Toprak from Suleyman's flat upstairs, but there was no reply from his office number; he had obviously gone home for the weekend. On reflection, Jack decided to leave the matter until Monday, and treat it not as an emergency but as something that had occurred in the normal run of business. In any case, they already had plenty to occupy them over the coming weekend, as Neil Geddes was due back on the following day, accompanied by his daughter and two steelworkers he had managed to recruit. Arrangements had already been made to meet at the Sands Hotel for lunch, followed by a visit to the yard in the afternoon.

When Jack, Mary and the two girls arrived at the Sands at the appointed time, the terrace bar was even more crowded than usual. David was the first to notice their arrival, and he waved them over to a table on the far side. Terry and Greg, the two steelworkers, were brothers, both in their thirties; they had cheerful, open countenances, firm handshakes, confident voices, and were dressed in the ubiquitous psychedelic Bermudan shorts under loosely fitting Hawaiian shirts of outrageously lurid design. Neil's daughter, Sandie, was a demure young woman of twenty or so years, with a strong, pleasant face and short-cropped hair. She readily accepted Susan's invitation to a guided tour of the hotel facilities, and they made their escape down to the beach with Wendy, all quite relaxed in each other's company.

"So, Terry," said Jack, addressing the elder brother, "I'm told you and Neil go way back. I suppose he's already told you about the set-up over here."

"You mean all the trouble you've had getting paid?" retorted Terry with a mischievous grin.

"Well, not that specifically, but I'm glad he's put you in the picture. At least you know what you're both letting yourselves in for."

"The way we see it," explained Terry impassively, "is nothing ventured, nothing gained. We'll give it a month and see what happens. If it all goes pear-shaped again, it's offski on the next flight home. At worst we'll have a month in the sun at Frank Palmer's expense. But if it does work out, we'll be onto a bloody good earner. Either way we're not going to lose, are we?"

"As long as you remember you're here to work," cautioned Jack, "and not just on an extended jolly."

"Jawohl, mein Fuhrer!" cried Terry exuberantly, startling a party of Germans at a nearby table. "Arbeit macht frei!"

"Steady on, Tel," murmured his brother, anxiously. "You'll get us thrown out before we've even started."

"You'll get your money's worth out of us, Jack," declared Terry. "Don't you worry about that. Me, my little bruv' and Neil, we're like the holy trinity of steel fabrication. You've heard of The Iron Ring? You're looking at the guys who made it. We are work animals."

"Well, if you can weld as good as you can talk I shan't have any complaints," returned Jack. "Now it's my round, I think. If I can get a waiter, that is. Over to you, Neil."

"Hey, Jimmie!" bellowed the Scot.

Chapter Eighteen

Terry had made no idle boast concerning the impact he and his brother were to have on productivity at the yard, together with Neil. Avkuran, the new addition to the local team was promptly admitted into 'the iron ring' on the strength of the work he had already done, and reciprocated just as promptly by bringing in more of his own cutting gear, and two tubes of precious acetylene gas. In just three days all the keel sections had been cut out and ground to a finish. All the basic labouring jobs such as lifting, grinding and tacking were carried out by the local men, who responded readily to the sudden change in pace. A couple of the keenest even adopted the practise of the British team to work through the long, traditional midday break, and as each day passed, one or two more left the shade of the sycamore fig tree to brave the intense heat of the afternoon sun.

On the fourth day a crane became available, so they were able to lay the keel. Jack felt an immense surge of pride as the tug's broad, curved stem piece was swayed up, stayed with steel braces, and welded onto the long straight run of the keel. Up went the massive skeg followed quickly by the elegant counter section, with willing, grinning local workers handing up the braces almost before the heavy segments were in place. When it came to tacking on the braces the younger, more agile hands clambered like monkeys up rickety wooden ladders precariously supported by long wooden props held in place by the older men, all oblivious to the safety hazards. Several times Jack was so horrified by the risks being taken that he was tempted to stop work until proper staging could be erected, but knowing the scarcity of scaffolding materials he just crossed his fingers and trusted to luck. Throughout the day Neil and Terry kept up a relentless pace, to which the local hands responded with a zeal that astounded Faruk Kurnaz, who had never before witnessed such enthusiasm. It was well past the usual time for going home when the last brace was welded in position, but nobody seemed to be in any hurry to go home. Small groups had formed around the building pad as they all stood gazing at the strange steel sculpture that rose up incongruously out of the ground and there was a general swell of laughter when a battered old crow alighted on the very top of the stem-head to mark the historic occasion with a squirt of birdlime.

Driving home with Mary at the end of the day Jack seemed unaccountably tense.

"You're very quiet this evening," she remarked. "I thought you'd be over the moon now that the keel is laid."

"Oh, I'm chuffed to nuts about the keel," he replied, steering well clear of a cyclist wobbling along the road with a long piece of glass under his arm and a child on his crossbar.

"In that case, why am I expecting your next word to be 'but'?" asked Mary.

"Well, you know. I can't get that visit from Ken Huson out of my mind."

"Well why don't you ask Frank about it?"

"I'm still not sure that would be best. Did you 'phone the bank this afternoon?"

"Of course, and this week's money has already been paid in."

"And the lads?"

"Neil and David have been paid. I don't know about Terry and Greg because I haven't had their bank details yet. I didn't 'phone Peter's bank either, because he's probably in touch with them himself."

"I don't know whether to go and see Osman Toprak or not He might even know about the situation already. I'd look a right idiot if he did."

"Why don't we go and see him about something else, and just drop it into the conversation. We could go and see him about Susan's schooling, seeing as he's done nothing about it."

"Good idea. That's just what we'll do. I'll see if he can see us tomorrow."

After tossing and turning in the sweltering heat of a long, airless night bedevilled by strange dreams, Jack rose just after dawn and started writing some notes in preparation for the forthcoming meeting. He had a strong presentiment about the whole affair and wanted to make sure his thinking was straight. When he telephoned to make the appointment his voice betrayed a degree of tension that was quickly noticed by Osman Toprak, who was sufficiently curious to suggest a meeting later that day. There was none of the usual waiting ritual when they arrived; the clerk had been given strict instructions to show them in straight away. Completely ignoring Mary's suggestion to generate an indirect approach, Jack launched straight into his account of Kenneth Huson's visit.

"Have you spoken to Frank about any of this?" asked Osman Toprak, trying to hide his disquiet.

"No. The whole business has put me in a bit of a difficult position. It's a bit tricky going to your boss and saying you've been told he's up to no good, don't you think? We really could do with some advice. That's why we've come to you."

"I'm not sure I can help, Jack. This all comes as a complete surprise to me. I knew Frank was hoping to organise some direct flights from the UK to bypass Istanbul, but I know nothing about the details. You say this man Huson left his card – do you have it with you?"

Jack took the card out of his wallet and handed it over to Osman Toprak who studied the details carefully.

"You say he came to the yard last Friday. That's a week ago. Why didn't you come to see me sooner?"

"I wasn't sure what I should do. The last thing I want is to be disloyal to Frank. I didn't even know if I should believe any of it. It's all so bizarre. But the more I thought about it all, the more likely it seemed that there must be some truth in the story. I mean, you could hardly make something like this up, could you?"

"After so many years in business I am never surprised at what people will make up, especially where money is concerned. And you have to remember, there are two sides to every story."

"I realise that," returned Jack. "Normally I wouldn't have taken any notice, but there has been something else."

"What do you mean?"

Jack now had the uncomfortable feeling that he might be saying too much. It had been gradually dawning on his ever anxious mind that he could be digging his own grave. If Frank Palmer really was in financial difficulties, further exposures could damage his credibility, resulting in jeopardy for the whole tug project. What then? Back to England to join the dole queue?

"Well, there have been problems with the Sterling wages."

"What sort of problems?"

"Arrears in payments. You might as well know, I suppose. Frank fell eight weeks behind with our Sterling wage payments."

"That's not really any of my business. I'm not sure you should be telling me about any of your private financial arrangements with Frank."

"It's hardly a private matter," replied Jack angrily. "It wasn't just us – the whole British team was affected. Work on the tug was brought to a standstill for two weeks."

"So how much does he owe you?"

"He doesn't owe anything now. He paid up all the arrears last week."

"Ah, there you have it then," exclaimed Osman Toprak, plainly much relieved. "There must have been some passing cash flow problem. As you must know, most businesses suffer from that sort of thing from time to time."

"I'm well aware of that," replied Jack impatiently, "but I've never known it to affect the payment of wages. Two months without any pay is a serious matter for a wage earner, and I include myself in that category. We have a mortgage to pay on our home in England, and I for one cannot afford to work for nothing. I had no idea that this job would be so insecure. This business with Ken Huson has got me really worried. I'm beginning to wonder if I did the right thing dragging my family out here."

Osman Toprak considered his response to this statement with care; he could see his attempt to gloss over these troubling events was not going to succeed. Moreover, he was well aware that Jack's input had become crucial to the success of the whole tug project. Perhaps it was time to offer the Englishman a little reassurance.

"What I'm going to say now is in the strictest confidence, and must not be discussed outside this office," said Osman Toprak gravely. "Can I rely on your complete discretion?"

"Absolutely," replied Jack

"And yours too, Mary?"

"Of course."

"First, let me say that I have no reason to believe that Frank Palmer has any financial worries of any kind. I have known him for over five years, both as a friend and a business colleague, and have always found him to be completely straightforward. We would never have considered going into the joint venture with Medmarine unless we were sure the business was sound. Having said that, I am now going to make you a promise, mainly to put your mind at ease, but also to show how much we appreciate your efforts so far."

After pausing a moment for effect, he continued in a quiet, confidential tone.

"If, for any reason whatsoever, Frank does have to withdraw from the tug project before it is complete, you will be offered a contract of employment by Famagusta Navigation with terms at the very least equal to those of your current contract with Medmarine. I say this only because we want you and your family to feel happy and secure in Cyprus, and from what you have just told me I realise that the past two weeks have been extremely difficult for you both. We are all aware of the technical problems you face every day, Jack, and all I can promise is more of the same. But things will gradually improve, and if you stick with us, the rewards in the long term for both Medmarine and you personally will be considerable."

There was another carefully timed pause, this time to allow opportunity for a reply. As both Jack and Mary remained silent, Osman Toprak was obliged to continue.

"Do you find what I have just said reassuring?"

Jack looked across at Mary, who decided it was now her turn to speak.

"It's alright as far as it goes, I suppose. But I for one would be a lot happier if Susan's schooling was being sorted out. We are no further forward than we were four months ago. And that's one of the things you said you would see to yourself."

Osman Toprak responded with an unctuous smile to disguise his irritation at being proved wanting. Why did Jack always have to bring this difficult woman to his office?

"My dear Mary, you know the difficulties we face with communications to the other side, but I will try and find out if there has been any progress. Now, if we could just return to the other matter, am I correct in assuming that you have told no one else about Mr Huson's visit?"

"You're the only person we've told," replied Jack

"I suggest we keep it that way for the time being. Least said, soonest mended. Leave it all with me. I would also advise you to say nothing to Frank about the matter. It would be embarrassing for him to learn you came to me first – in fact it would be embarrassing for you as well."

Osman Toprak glanced conspicuously up at his wall clock before adding:

"Now, is there anything else I can do for you?"

"Not unless you've got twenty tubes of oxygen in the back office," replied Jack with a grin.

* * * * * * * *

A week after the meeting at Osman Toprak's office, a letter from BFPO 58 was delivered to the flat. It was from a Captain Robert Holt of the Signals Regiment at Larnaca explaining how to go about enrolling Susan with the Army Education Service. As she read the brief contents, written in a crisp, breezy, military style of address, Mary took great comfort in the wise providence of her motherland. Here was the benign, comforting presence of Britannia, ready to guide and protect them in their hour of need, as she had done for so many in generations past. For her own part, Susan was thrilled at the news that at last there was the possibility of returning to a conventional seat of learning. She had found the rigour of her Mother's improvised classroom somewhat demanding after the easy going pace she had known at school in England.

One aspect of this positive outcome which did, however, give Mary some cause for concern was the payment of school fees. According to Jack's contract of employment this would be the responsibility of Medmarine, but recent events had not exactly been encouraging in this respect. On the other hand they now had Osman Toprak's promise of continued support if Frank Palmer was out of the equation. Was Osman Toprak aware of the commitment to pay school fees? Mary cast her mind back to the first occasion when the whole question of education was discussed with him on his boat in Kyrenia. She remembered his exact words very clearly; he had given his personal guarantee. That was all very well, as far as it went, but none of Osman Toprak's guarantees could be invoked whilst Frank Palmer was still responsible for their welfare. It would be so important to secure payment in advance for at least a year, and Mary resolved to tackle Frank Palmer on the matter at the very first opportunity.

The chance came rather unexpectedly during the following week when Frank Palmer paid an unscheduled visit, accompanied by Peter, who had decided to return now that the money situation was under control, and had even brought his wife and son for a short holiday. The whole British contingent was invited for a buffet Sunday lunch at the Plâj Hotel, which turned out to be a very lively affair indeed. Frank Palmer took the position of honour at the head of the long table set up by the pool; to his right sat Jack, and to his left Mary. Next to Jack sat Wendy, then Neil, Sandie, Greg and Terry; David claimed the seat next to Mary, then came Peter's wife and son, Susan and Peter on the end opposite Terry. As usual the food was superb, and of course there was no shortage of wine to free the minds and the tongues of all who partook. Among the foremost of these were Jack and Terry, between whom a certain degree of good-natured rivalry had developed. Terry was of a flamboyant, outgoing personality, and he took a delight in teasing Jack, whose far more serious nature and slower wit left him virtually defenceless against the lightning attacks from his assailant.

"Look at this!" cried Terry, looking at Mary and unbuttoning his Hawaiian shirt to reveal a bronzed, hairless chest. "The body of Adonis, all beautiful and brown in just two weeks. I don't know how you can keep your hands off me!"

Jack's reply came back quickly enough, but the delivery was somewhat laboured.

"Why would she want to handle a bag of bones like that when she's already got a *real* man?"

"Ooooooh!" chorused the assembly, delighted by the gathering momentum of the exchange.

"Okay then," returned Terry, "let's have a look at *your* chest. Go on, let's see how brown *you* are after months of this beautiful sun."

Jack smiled confidently as he replied to the taunt by slowly standing up and ripping open his shirtfront, sending buttons flying in all directions.

"Ecco l'uomo!" he declared.

With a theatrical flourish, Terry put up his hand to shield his eyes and turned his face away in mock horror.

"Oh no – put it away! I didn't know human flesh could *be* that white. And all that hair! Poor Mary! What's it like sleeping with a Yeti?"

More in this vein followed at intervals throughout the afternoon, and every time the two adversaries locked horns there was an appreciative audience, including the hotel staff who were taking turns to come out and witness the fun. Sunara, the hotel receptionist on duty that afternoon spent most of her time hovering around the table, wishing fervently to be included. She had enjoyed a brief encounter for a week or so with David, but this had finished as soon as he learned she was married, so she was now on the lookout for a new victim. Who better than Jack, sitting there with his shirt gaping open for want of buttons. Sensing his disquiet at her presence, she guessed correctly that he had not told Mary about his visit to her house. Maybe he was interested after all, thought Sunara. Perhaps Mary did not have such a tight hold on him after all. Mary, with her lovely fair English rose complexion and her two beautiful children, and her quiet, ladylike manners. Why should she have it all her own way?

Coming up behind Jack, Sunara laid her hand on his shoulder. The gesture was made with such overt intimacy that it was noticed by just about everyone round the table, and conversation quickly drained away to a trickle as they all looked across to where she stood.

"Jack, my generator is playing up again at home," said Sunara, loud enough for everyone to hear. "Do you think you could come out and have another look at it when you have a bit of time?"

She then looked straight at Mary as a stunned silence fell over the company.

Terry was the first to recover, letting out a hoot of delight.

"Well I must say, Jack, I've heard it called many things before, but I don't think I've ever heard it called – what was it – her *Generator*? I can see you've got hidden depths!"

To cover their sense of embarrassment, everyone started to laugh, even the children who had little understanding of the situation. Under cover of the general hubbub Jack mumbled a promise to send out a yard mechanic, and Sunara swaggered off with a final triumphant glance at Mary.

"Don't worry love," Terry called after the retreating figure, "if Jack can't fix you up I'm always available – day or night."

Once again, the steelworker's wit was rewarded with general laughter; even Jack and Mary joined in to disguise their own confusion. It was Frank Palmer who came to their rescue by proposing a general adjournment to the beach. His suggestion met with unanimous approval, and in a noisy straggle they all made their way down to the comfort of sun-loungers and beach umbrellas. Jack and Mary managed to position themselves away from the rest of the company to ensure a little privacy for the inevitable discussion to follow.

"Can I get you a drink, my love?" asked Jack, solicitously

"I'm not your love," returned Mary sharply. "How could you?"

"How could I what?"

"Embarrass me like that. So you've been to her house, have you?"

"That was ages ago. She said there was something wrong with the generator, and asked me to take a look at it, that was all."

"And what was wrong with it?"

"Nothing. It was working fine."

"Perhaps her *husband* had already fixed it."

"I suppose so, yes."

"So what did he say when you showed up in your suit of shining armour?"

"Well, he wasn't actually there at the time."

"I can't believe I'm hearing this," whispered Mary furiously. "It just gets worse and worse."

"I don't know why you're getting your knickers in such a twist. I drove out there, checked the bloody generator, couldn't see anything wrong, so I came away again. I couldn't have been there more than five minutes."

"So you say," retorted Mary, struggling to suppress the violence of her emotions. "You're either a liar or an idiot."

"Oh I can't talk to you when you're like this," declared Jack standing up. "I'm going for a swim."

He stripped off down to his trunks and ran full pelt over the burning sand, flinging himself angrily at the oncoming waves. Mary watched him pull away from the shallows with long, easy strokes and hoped he would not swim out too far this time. He really was such an idiot.

So intent was she on Jack's progress out to sea that she did not notice the approach of Frank Palmer, and it was only on hearing the adjacent sunbed creak under his weight that she realised she was not alone.

"He swims very well, your old man," observed Frank Palmer.

"Yes. He was a competitive swimmer in his youth. But I wish he wouldn't go out so far. I'm always worried he won't be able to get back."

"So you do want him to get back then," he quipped with a sly grin. "I couldn't help noticing you two love birds were having words just now. Nothing serious, I hope."

"No, nothing serious."

"I wouldn't worry too much about that business with Sunara back there. There's something not quite right about that girl. I've tried to warn Kaplan, but he won't hear a word said against her."

Mary was fully aware that Frank Palmer was on a fishing expedition, but she ignored the clumsy cast of his lure and mounted her own counter attack.

"Oh, I'm not bothered by all that rubbish. It's just that I'm a bit worried about the money situation."

"You've absolutely no reason to worry on that score, Mary. Everything is now fully under control."

"I really do hope so. I really don't want to go through all that again. We very nearly lost Neil, you know, and Peter. As for Terry, well, you've seen what he's like. He'd be off like a shot if he wasn't paid on time, and his brother with him."

Frank Palmer eased himself up on the sunlounger to a more upright position in an attempt to regain his air of authority. He always found Mary's gentle, persistent style of discourse difficult to handle.

"No really, Mary, you must believe me when I tell you that last month's troubles are well and truly behind us. Our cash position is extremely robust."

"In that case, this is probably a good time to discuss the payment of Susan's school fees. We are hoping to get her started at King Richard's School in about three week's time, and the fee has to be paid annually in advance."

"How much are we talking about?"

"Eight hundred and eighty eight Cyprus pounds. I'm afraid I don't know what that comes to in Sterling."

"Leave it to me, Mary. If you let me have the full name and address of the school before I go back to the UK I'll have my secretary make all the necessary arrangements. What about her travel arrangements? Will you need any more money for that?"

"We can take her as far as Ayios Nikolaos, but from there she has to take the school bus into Dekelya. I don't know how much that will be yet, but I shouldn't think it will come to much."

"Whatever it is, just let me know. I don't want you worrying about money. Do you have everything else you need?"

"I think so. Everything else is fine – on the home front that is."

"In that case how about making a start on the house? Just on a part time basis to begin with. I thought we could start you off at, say, forty pound a week?"

"That sounds about right."

"Do you want it paid in Turkish Lira or in Sterling?"

"Oh, Sterling. Definitely Sterling."

"Into the same account as Jack's wages? It's just in your name anyway, isn't it?"

"That's right. When do you want me to start?"

"Right away, if that's convenient. I want to keep the house completely separate from the yard operation, so you'll need to recruit a reliable local to make a start on clearing up round the outside."

"Wouldn't it be better to start on the house itself? There's such a lot to do on the inside."

"No, not for the moment. I don't want to start on the building work until I've sorted out one or two things on the lease I'm not too happy about. But I do want to show that we're making a start, even if it's only clearing that jungle of weeds."

"How will he be paid? Will he go on the FNC payroll?"

"No, no. The less they have to do with the house the better it will be. I'll leave a month's wages with you in cash, and then you can pay him weekly out of that. Is that okay?"

"Yes, that's fine. I'm quite looking forward to it."

"Then it's my pleasant duty to welcome you officially into Medmarine," announced Frank Palmer, standing up to depart. "I know you've been helping Jack out unofficially, and I really appreciate your efforts, but I'm a lot happier now you're actually on the payroll."

"No more than I," admitted Mary with a wry little smile. "We could certainly do with the extra money."

Frank Palmer smiled in return, somewhat uncertainly, and glanced out to sea.

"It looks like Jack is on his way back to port," he observed. "I'd better leave you in peace." He gave a final chuckle before adding: "I hope you'll go easy on him."

With Frank Palmer gone, Mary sat watching Jack's steady progress back to the shallows and smiled to herself. He really was an idiot, she thought. But he was her idiot, and she was stuck with him. Whatever the future held, she wanted to spend it with him and no other

Jack staggered slowly back up the beach trying not to appear exhausted, the hot sand burning the soles of his sea-wrinkled feet. He flopped down on the recently vacated sunlounger and looked enquiringly across at Mary.

"So, what did *he* want?"

"I'm not talking to you," she replied, feigning a sulk. "If you want to talk, go and find that trollop Sunara, or whatever she's called."

"Oh, you're surely not still on about that," groaned Jack. "Why don't you give it a rest?"

Mary took him at his word, and did indeed give it a rest. The rest lasted for the remainder of the afternoon and throughout the evening; on their return to the flat they undressed, showered, and climbed into bed, all in complete silence. As it was their shared custom to sleep naked, Mary placed a long bolster between them. Before long, Jack's hand stole surreptitiously across the divider to Mary's side of the bed until it met her buttocks.

"Get *off* me, you third rate Casanova!" she whispered.

He flounced back over to his own half of the bed, and lay away from her on his side, brooding in silence. The noise from the cicadas did not usually bother him, but tonight it seemed intolerably loud and persistent. Despite every window in the house being open, there was not a breath of movement in the air, and the stifling heat banished all hope of sleep. For an hour or so they both lay tossing and turning to such an extent that the single coverlet ended up in a crumpled heap on the floor at the end of the bed.

By two o'clock they were both racked with thirst. Jack crept out the kitchen and came back with two glasses of water. As he padded round to Mary's side of the bed and placed her water on the nightstand she could see the outline of his body, and shut her eyes quickly in a vain attempt to stop her resolve melting away. When he had emptied his own glass, Jack lay on his back staring moodily up at the ceiling. Mary took a long draught of her water and said:

"That's better. Now there's something else I need you to do for me."

"And what's that?" asked Jack, feeling his sap rise.

"I want you to take a look at my generator," she whispered, and flung herself across his body. "I think it might need a really good service."

Chapter Nineteen

The day before Frank Palmer's return to England another joint venture board meeting was convened, this time at Osman Toprak's residence just outside Kyrenia. They all sat round the large mahogany table in the centre of an elegant and spacious dining room, and Mary was in attendance to take the minutes. She was especially pleased to be there because it gave her the opportunity of seeing Julia again, and when the meeting finished the two women took tea out on the terrace overlooking the sea. The men remained in the dining room to drink their tea, putting the world in general to rights. Jack listened with only half his attention; the other half was taken with watching Mary through the open French windows. He could see how much she was enjoying the pleasure of some sophisticated female companionship, observing with admiration the graceful gesture of her hands as she spoke, and smiling unconsciously whenever he saw her laugh.

Jack and Mary were the first to leave; they had to be back in time to collect the children from Nihan. As the Mini-Moke bounced down the long drive leading to the highway both were thoughtfully silent.

"You seem to get on very well with Osman's missus," said Jack as soon as the road surface was good enough to permit conversation.

"Yes, I really do like her."

"What were you talking about so intently?"

"Oh, all sorts of things. Mostly about our families. She's been having trouble with her son. He's a bit older than Susan, and she says he hates it here after living in England."

"Do they have any other children?"

"They have a daughter, but she's at London University."

"What's she studying, do you know?"

"Law. It's what her father wanted."

Driving through the Beshparmak pass they both fell silent; when the road straightened out on the other side Jack spoke up again.

"What did you think of the so called board meeting? I suppose you were bored out of your mind."

"No, not really. I thought it was quite interesting."

"I can't think why. They kept going round in circles. I'm surprised it didn't make you dizzy."

"Well at least you got Medmarine house sorted out. And the gas supply problem."

"Two out of ten items," scoffed Jack. "But I suppose that's pretty good for Cyprus."

"I don't know why you're being so negative," replied Mary quietly. "Things have been going quite well for the last couple of weeks, haven't they?"

"Yeah, I suppose you're right. It's just that I can't stand wasting my time with these stupid meetings. I'll be okay once we get some bloody gas and make some progress with the tug."

The solution to the oxygen and acetylene supply problem agreed at the meeting was quite ingenious. The island would be scoured by Onan to locate fifty gas bottles. He would then accompany the bottles aboard one of the Famagusta Navigation Company vessels to Mersin in Turkey, and stay with them while they were cleaned and filled with the appropriate gases. A contract would be negotiated to refill the bottles on a regular basis at a fixed price to be agreed at the outset. In the meantime gas would have to be obtained from the one reliable source in Nicosia, irrespective of the exorbitant price, in a bid to catch up with the time already lost. There had been the usual wrangling over who should foot the bill for all this, with Frank Palmer trying his best to distance himself from the extra cost, but the vote came down squarely against him and he accepted the decision in his usual philosophical manner.

With the establishment of a gas supply, such as it was, came a renewed sense of purpose at the yard. Under Neil Geddes' general supervision two teams were organised; Terry headed up one of them with his brother and Peter to assist, plus one local welder and two labourers; Avkuran led the other team consisting entirely of local men. Terry's team was assigned to fabricating the steel frames, taking their pattern from wooden templates made up by Jack and the two local carpenters in the lofting shed. The job of Avkuran's team was to fit the completed frames onto the keel once they had been craned into position.

This set-up promised to be highly effective, but progress was still blighted by the lack of a permanent crane. Repairs to the old Jones crane were at a standstill awaiting replacement spare parts from England, and availability of machines from the port was still erratic. It was the port authority's best crane, the huge twenty-five ton capacity Italgru that finally did lumber into the yard to hoist the first frame into position. The driver was worried that the ground would be too soft to bear the weight, but Avkuran managed to persuade him to take the chance. A great sense of anxiety prevailed throughout the yard as the driver inched the great machine off the road to the position required, and an even greater sense of relief when the ground held. Frame N° 20 was located at the point of maximum beam, approximately half way along the length of the tug, and once in position gave the nascent structure its third dimension. Jack and Neil checked the position again and again to ensure accuracy at this most critical juncture; the markings on this frame would provide the datum line for every subsequent section to be added, and an error in any dimension or plane would spell disaster.

Because it was impossible to rely on the availability of a crane every day, Jack suggested to Neil that both teams should work on frame fabrication on those days when a machine could not be spared. Under the Scot's tutelage, Avkuran quickly picked up the necessary tricks of the trade, responding proudly to the increased responsibility. Another advantage in this division of labour was the ability to stockpile several completed frames to be fitted in quick succession on those days when a crane did arrive. As the job progressed from these tentative first steps, confidence among the local welders increased rapidly, and a spirit of friendly competition soon developed between the two teams. Quite apart from the pride they all took in their work, national honour was also at stake.

Not content with competing only with Avkuran, the irrepressible Terry managed to take Jack on as well. His team was working so well that the time soon came when they had finished fabricating all the frames for which lofting templates were available, so Jack had to crank up his own production rate to keep pace with the demand. Nothing loath, he pitched in with a will, determined to reach a point where he was so far ahead that he would be safe from Terry's persistent mocking banter. By rising early and starting work just after dawn each day he would soon have the situation under control. The two local carpenters were quick to notice that their boss was coming in two hours before anyone else, and volunteered to do the same. Within a week the stack of numbered frame templates had grown sufficiently to enable Jack to saunter out on to the fabrication site and tease Terry about his lack of progress. It was all just good, clean fun, but it had a remarkably favourable influence on the rate at which the tug was taking shape. This in turn gave rise to a further welcome benefit, as it enabled Jack to demand higher priority on cranage, to the extent that a machine was now left permanently at the yard.

Another great success at this time was Onan's gas purchasing trip, from which he returned triumphant with thirty tubes of oxygen and twenty of high-grade acetylene. Their delivery by lorry to the yard was a source of great wonder to the local yard hands, none of whom had ever seen such a quantity all in one place. The price of this gas was little more than half the amount demanded by the dealer in Nicosia, and FNC had agreed on a nominal charge for shipping and handling. Terry was the first to use the new supply, cutting out large circular access holes in a bulkhead plate for the chain locker, and gave high praise for the quality. Having an established gas supply also enabled work to be started on the wrecked barges at the Sands Hotel. Every Sunday the five British men worked a nine-hour shift at double time pay rate under the private arrangement with Frank Palmer. As the work involved cutting out a great deal of damaged plating, the extra demand on gas led to the rapid depletion of Jack's precious stock, and as soon as he had enough empty bottles, they were on their way back to Mersin aboard an FNC freighter to be refilled.

By the time the ship returned a week later the yard's gas stock was perilously low, and Jack breathed a sigh of relief when he saw the vessel docking. An unpleasant shock awaited him, however, when the newly arrived bottles were impounded by customs for want of an import license. He learned to his horror that every time a new supply was sent from Turkey, a separate import license would have to be obtained from the relevant ministry. Off to the government offices in Nicosia he rushed, only to cool his heels for two hours sitting in a hot, stuffy corridor awaiting the pleasure of a senior customs official. When he was shown into a spacious, air conditioned office Jack took an instant dislike to the fat, balding incumbent, right down to his wobbling jowls and his small effeminate hands.

With a bored, sullen expression the official glanced briefly at the bill of lading Jack had just placed before him and let out a heavy sigh.

"Your application for import license should have been made ten days ago."

"Yes, I'm sorry about that," replied Jack, forcing the apology past his lips. "An oversight on the part of FNC."

"Most regrettable oversight."

"Indeed," agreed Jack, as he glanced longingly at the large carousel of rubber stamps on the side of the desk. "But do you think you could frank the bill straight away for me please?"

The official's thick, black eyebrows shot up in horror at the suggestion as he replied:

"You surely do not expect me to grant import license just like that. And for such large quantity."

"Well I was rather hoping you could see your way to helping us out, just on this occasion. We'll know better on the next consignment."

"Next consignment? I do not understand. You had fifty bottles of gas only last month. Here is bill for another thirty bottles, and you say you want even more bottles! What can you possibly want with all this bottles?"

"No, no. You don't understand. These aren't additional bottles. They are the same bottles as we had before. They've just been to Mersin for refilling. It's the gas inside the bottles we use, not the bottles themselves."

The word 'bottles' had been repeated so many times that it was beginning to sound ridiculous and seemed to be ringing in Jack's ears. He could feel his temper rising steadily as his dislike for the official increased with every passing minute

"I'm sorry, Mr. Dur-ham, but I shall have to refer this matter to my superiors. It does not appear to be in order. We have to be very careful with importation of chemical substances."

"But surely your department has already been informed why we need the gas. We're building a tug for the Port Authority, for Christ's sake! We'll be needing thirty bottles every week when we really get going. You've got to be able to do something. We're practically out of gas as it is. If we don't get these bottles tomorrow the whole job will grind to a halt. There will be more than twenty men standing idle."

"I regret the matter is outside my authority. Perhaps if you call back tomorrow..."

Jack leapt to his feet in anger, but managed to control himself with an immense effort of will. He simply stood glowering down at the official in silent, impotent rage.

"Is there something else you wish to say to me, Mr Dur-ham?" he enquired with a smirk.

But Jack merely smirked in return and said:

"No. I shall come back tomorrow, as requested."

When he returned at eight o'clock next morning the vital import license was handed to him on arrival by one of the clerks in the outer office. The document bore the previous day's date stamp, confirming Jack's suspicion that the matter could easily have been finalised on his first visit. He was convinced the delay had been deliberately engineered, probably just to give him a lesson in humility. But whatever the reason for the delay it did not affect the satisfying outcome of his endeavours; he now had access to his gas which meant production would not be held up after all. And before he left the office he filed two more applications to cover the importation of a further one hundred bottles. Let them take the bones out of that!

So rapid did the fabrication work advance, in fact, that a new problem was starting to emerge; they were running short of scaffolding. The reluctant Onan was pressed yet again into service for a visit to The Government Store, but despite being armed with a note of authority signed by the Minister of Finance himself they immediately ran into the usual brick wall. With a great deal of satisfaction the storekeeper explained to Onan that there was a general shortage of scaffolding in Northern Cyprus, and the great stacks that had been languishing for the past four years in the weed infested dust outside The Government Store were already earmarked for important building repair jobs. No scaffolding could be released without the written authority of the Minister for Public Works. Jack wasted the rest of the morning trying in vain to deal with the problem on the telephone, followed by yet another abortive trip to Nicosia where he wasted many hours hanging about in various corridors of power in the misplaced hope that a personal appearance would swing the case in his favour, all to no avail.

Jack reacted to this frustrating situation with his customary arrogance. The scaffolding would simply have to be stolen from The Government Store. At dawn the next morning FNC's large flatbed, driven by Jack and bearing a half dozen volunteer Cypriot yard hands, pulled up between the piles of rusty tubing and worn out boards. One furtive, sweaty and backbreaking hour later the lorry was clattering its way back to the yard, with the mission accomplished. They had carefully excluded anything that bore marks of identification, and Jack was confident that the raid had escaped observation. In any case, his crime could scarcely be considered serious, especially if the circumstances were taken into consideration.

Fortunately there were no repercussions, and work continued to advance at a vigorous pace. The delivery of a large consignment of cutting and welding equipment that Neil had ordered when he was in England meant the two steelwork teams could now work at maximum efficiency, and moral was at the highest level it had ever been. They were now fabricating and fitting frames at the rate of two a day, and the actual shape of the hull was becoming plainly recognisable. Every day a small group of spectators formed outside the gates to observe progress, and various government officials frequently turned up with foreign delegations to show off the technical prowess of their young nation.

One small problem that did persist was communication with England by telephone, about which Jack could do absolutely nothing. When they had first arrived on the island, telephone contact had not been possible at all, but the situation had gradually improved for a while up to the beginning of August. Since then the service had again deteriorated rapidly to the point that it was again impossible to obtain a connection, which meant that nobody was able to check on their bank account to ascertain if the Sterling wage payments were still being made on time. This did give rise to some concern among the British lads, but Mary kept trouble at bay by promising to make the necessary enquiries in person, as the family was due to fly home for some leave in less than two weeks time.

* * * * *

"Saturday 30th September

Wendy's birthday today, and the lads are organising a party for her this evening at the Sands Hotel – the perfect ending to a really great month. Even better still, we picked up our flight tickets today. Just to think, this time next week we'll be home in England for two whole glorious weeks! My cup runneth over!

"My old gardener at Medmarine House is starting his holidays today. He has done such a good job in his first month that I've given him an extra week's money out of our own kitty. It wasn't a lot really, but he was so grateful. I hope I don't still have to work when I'm as old as he is.

"Come to think of it, this day is thrice blessed! We finally received our proper full time ESBA passes in the post this morning, which means Susan can start at King Richard's as soon as we get back from leave. It has been a bit of a slog, but we seem to have got there in the end. Susan is really excited about it all – I think she has been missing the social life at school. She has made no end of friends with children in the neighbourhood here, but it can't have been easy for her. I think she's really looking forward to seeing all her old friends back in England too. I know I am."

* * * * *

It was an all male gathering that greeted Jack, Mary and the two girls when they arrived at the Sands Hotel for the birthday celebrations; Sandie Geddes had gone back to England along with Frank Palmer and Peter's family. As they made their way over to the large table in the middle of the open terrace the lads welcomed them with a great deal of cheering and a noisy rendering of "Happy Birthday". Wendy, not used to being the centre of attention, peeped out shyly from the folds of her mother's skirt, newly bought specially for the occasion. Mary's whole outfit was the object of much admiration, especially when the men discerned that she wore nothing under the flimsy white shawl draped daringly around her shoulders, with only a small jewelled brooch holding it in position.

As it was Saturday there was a band playing that curious East meets West style of popular music indigenous to the Eastern Mediterranean. Mary and Susan were much in demand as dancing partners, and Wendy too was whisked off by each of the lads in turn, to be whirled around high above the dance floor while she laughed with delight. David was a very good dancer, but he had never learned to jive so he persuaded Mary to show him the moves. The band obliged with the strangest version of Bill Hailey's 'Rock around the clock' that had ever been heard, but the compelling beat was still there and the couple put up a very creditable performance to the lively encouragement of their fellow dancers, some of whom even tried to emulate their gyrations. Mary abandoned herself to the relentless rhythm, and only a miracle prevented the shawl from escaping on more than one occasion.

All this activity resulted in a great deal of thirst, which in turn lead to a great deal of toping. The only drink that Mary really liked was brandy, and as she did not want her throat cauterised by the local spirit, Cognac was ordered. Her companions all followed her lead, and as the evening progressed everyone became extremely merry. Just before midnight, David suggested they all go skinny dipping in the moonlight, and to Jack's horror Mary welcomed the idea. Announcing sternly that it was well past her bedtime he piloted her off in the direction of the exit to a chorus of protests, herding Susan and Wendy along in front of him.

Jack returned alone to the Sands Hotel the following morning to check if there would be any work done on the barges that day. He found a crapulous group of five dissolute souls sitting idly on the terrace, painfully sipping bottled water. Even Terry could not summon up the spirit to engage in any repartee when Jack humorously enquired what time they would be making a start. It emerged that the price they had to pay for the previous night's debauch was not just a hangover; they had been presented at breakfast with a drinks bill of breathtaking proportions. The importation of French brandy was subject to a really savage rate of duty in order to protect sales of the domestic product, so even at a wholesale wine and spirit merchants the cost of a bottle was prohibitive. With the addition of two hundred percent corkage charge, each double they had drunk with so much abandon had cost the equivalent of a full hour's work.

At Jack's suggestion they all trooped off to beard the hotel manager in his office. The poor man, surrounded by five large Englishmen and one murderous looking Scot, tried to play the situation at arm's length, pointing out that he had not been on duty at the time in question. The deputation was not prepared to be fobbed off in this way, and dug in for some serious negotiations. Jack pointed out that they were all in Cyprus on work of national importance, and it was incumbent upon local traders to lend all the support they could. These were working men, not millionaires; they had wives and families to house, clothe and feed. It was understandable that they should wish to let their hair down once in a while, being away from their loved ones for so long. Would it not be possible to let them have a special rate in view of the fact that they were almost permanent residents at the hotel? Fortunately, the manager was a good man at heart, and yielded at length to the persuasiveness of Jack's argument. He agreed to waive the corkage on this one occasion, and bill them at cost. The men all filed out, thanked Jack for his intervention, and went off to put on their work clothes.

* * * * * * * *

The postman arrived to deliver two letters just as Mary was leaving the flat to take her usual walk in to work; it was the last day before their holiday and she was in the best of spirits. She put the letters unopened into her bag before waving goodbye to the girls at the window of Nihan's flat upstairs and set off at a leisurely pace thinking about the tasks before her that morning. All she really had to do was write up the day book, collect the wages cheque from FNC and make up the pay packets for the five British workers. She could be back home by three, and finish off the packing.

Walking through the familiar narrow streets of the old city she stopped to look in two or three shops, still on the lookout for unusual souvenirs. She resisted the temptation to have a last coffee in the main square, and made her way past Lala Mustafa Camii, along Cambulat Yolu and through the massive gate in the city wall. As she approached the yard her pace slowed even more as she took in the imposing sight of the tug framework rising from a confused mass of scaffolding. It was rather moving to reflect that tomorrow they would be leaving this life they had built in these most unlikely surroundings for the peace and tranquillity of England. Equally compelling was the thought that in two short weeks they would be back to do it all over again. Would the tug look different when they returned, she wondered. Would Neil be able to hold the whole thing together in Jack's absence?

Once inside the office she shared with Jack, Mary sat at her desk and looked around at the room's comfortably familiar contents. Through the window she could see Jack out in the yard talking to Terry; they seemed to have developed a new bond since the party last Saturday. Faruk came in to wish her good morning in his polite, detached way, and left the office post on Jack's desk. Would she like a coffee, or perhaps a cold drink? What time would she be going to the bank this morning? Was she looking forward to going home tomorrow? No doubt there would be plenty to do after all this time away.

It was only when she looked in her bag for a tissue that Mary realised she had not yet opened her two letters. One was from the telephone company, confirming that a telephone line for their flat had become available. The other was from England, and she recognised the handwriting; it was from Morris, at the bungalow. Strange to think that she would be seeing him in person tomorrow night. She frowned a little as she endeavoured to decipher the thin, spidery scrawl.

"Dear Jack and Mary,

Trust you are still enjoying the sun etc. I am sorry to have to remind you of the clouds gathering in England. We have been given notice to quit the bungalow by your benevolent trustee in bankruptcy and really I am asking for your directions as to what you would like doing with your furniture and effects.
If you don't take the view to hell with it and let the vultures gorge on everything, we could try to arrange storage for the furniture and I can try to sell the car – except I don't have the logbook & presumably if that is in your name it can't be sold anyway.
Trust that you are now so settled that this episode is a mere pinprick. I must admit I find it all a little disturbing over such a trifling sum.
Anyway look forward to hearing from you

All the best
Morris"

Mary found the reference to a trustee most puzzling; she had always thought he was called a receiver. She was also puzzled by Morris's use of the word bankruptcy, and not knowing what to make of it all went out in search of Jack; he was back in the lofting shed and looked up with a smile as she entered.

"Good morning again, my love. Are we all packed and ready?"

"Jack, this letter arrived from England this morning – it's from Morris."

"How about that! We'll be seeing him tomorrow night."

"I think you'd better have a look at it right away."

As Jack read the letter Mary could tell from his furrowed brow that he, too, was puzzled by the contents.

"What's all this about trustees and bankruptcies?" he cried. "Morris has got it all wrong."

"Do you think so? He is an accountant, after all. I should have thought he'd know all about that sort of thing."

As realisation dawned, Jack's mind raced, with one catastrophic thought crowding in after another.

"My God!" he gasped. "If he is right and I've been declared bankrupt *in absentia*, you know what that means."

"Yes," replied Mary calmly. "It means that Frank Palmer has been welching on us again. It means we're going to lose our home."

"After all we've been through, and now this," said Jack, his voice quavering with emotion. "At least we're going to be back in England for next week. I'll get in touch with the receiver first thing on Monday. I'm sure it can't be as bad as it looks. There must be something we can do to save the situation. In any case, we don't actually know yet that he hasn't been paying us, do we? It might all just be a mistake. Maybe it's the bank. Maybe they've cocked up the payments to the receiver."

"Oh do shut up, Jack," cried Mary. "Listen to yourself. You're beginning to sound just like *him*." She vented a long sigh before adding darkly. "I had a feeling something was wrong, ever since we've been unable to get through on the 'phone. Well this just about does it. I'm really going to give him a piece of my mind."

"I know how you feel, Mary, but we've got to put a brave face on it for today, just in case there is something we can do about it all. We can't let on to the others yet. There would be hell to pay."

"I realise that," replied Mary angrily. "But they've all been working flat out six days a week, probably for nothing. It just isn't fair."

"We don't have the full story yet," said Jack. "Just carry on as normal for a Friday. Get the wages cheque from FNC, make up the lads money and the petty cash as usual. We have to tough it out, just until we get back to England."

Back in the office, Mary telephoned the accounts clerk at FNC to see if the wages cheque was ready for collection. It was usually late, and today was no exception, but the clerk did tell her that Mehmet Boga wanted Jack to call round to the offices to discuss an urgent matter that had just arisen. As she had nothing of any importance to do until the wages cheque was ready she decided to go with Jack to see Mehmet Boga, and ask him why she was kept hanging about for the British worker's money every single Friday. She was just in the right mood to tell that pompous ass his fortune.

For once in his life, Mehmet Boga came straight to the point as soon as they were shown into his office.

"I regret we have some rather bad news for you today, Jack," he announced. "We are unable to issue a cheque for the wages of British personnel at this time."

"I don't understand. Why not?"

"I am not at liberty to provide you with full details. It is a matter of the utmost delicacy. I can only suggest you get in touch with Osman Toprak. Only he has the authority to explain our reasons for withholding payment."

"Has Famagusta Navigation gone bust?" asked Jack suspiciously.

"The financial standing of this company is beyond reproach. It is ridiculous to suggest such a thing."

"Then what the hell is going on? We've done the work, now we have to be paid."

"I repeat, you will have to get in touch with Osman Toprak. I am very sorry, Jack, but that is all I can say on the matter."

In troubled silence Jack and Mary returned to the yard. Osman Toprak was not prepared to discuss the situation over the telephone so they had to drive into Nicosia for a meeting. Here again there was none of the usual preamble, and the Cypriot came straight to the point.

"Mehmet's actions are perfectly in order," he said dispassionately. "I cannot give you the whole picture because we are not in possession of all the relevant information ourselves. What I can tell you is that certain financial irregularities have come to light, and we cannot proceed further until the matter is cleared up. Frank Palmer has been recalled, and will be here on Monday."

"But we're all booked to go on leave tomorrow," protested Jack.

"My advice is to postpone your leave until you have spoken to Frank," replied Osman Toprak. "I am very sorry, Mary. I know how much you must be looking forward to going home, but there is nothing more I can do in the matter."

"I understand," said Mary calmly, "but I would like to know how you managed to contact Frank Palmer."

"How do you mean?"

"Was it by telephone or by telex?"

"By telex, of course. It is not possible to get a telephone connection to the UK at the present time, as you probably know. Even the telex is unreliable at times."

"And you're sure he'll be here on Monday?" persisted Mary.

"Of course. Here is his telex confirming arrival time," replied Osman Toprak, handing the document across the desk to Mary. "He has to come. He has no alternative."

On the drive back to Famagusta Mary stared at the road ahead trying to arrange her thoughts, but it was impossible. No matter which way she viewed the situation it was a disaster. She fought back the rising sense of anger only to face the disappointment that loomed in its place. Was it really only this morning when she strolled happily through the old city looking at souvenirs? How could this all have happened so suddenly, and caught them so much off guard? Had they missed any vital clues that could have given them some sort of warning? Had they just been deceiving themselves all this time?

As soon as they arrived back at the yard, Jack called his five British colleagues into the office and told them the bad news. They took it remarkably well, almost as if they had been expecting something of the sort. Even when he referred to the news received from England indicating the possibility of further arrears in their Sterling payments, they all showed remarkable solidarity. If Frank Palmer had run out of steam, they all agreed, what was to stop them finishing the job without him?

"But I can tell you one thing for certain," added Terry with a demoniac chuckle. "We're going to have a bloody good weekend at the bastard's expense."

* * * * * * * *

Frank Palmer duly arrived on Monday, was met at the airport by Osman Toprak and escorted off to an emergency meeting of the joint venture board in Nicosia lasting for the rest of the afternoon. It was not until late evening that he reached the Sands Hotel to face his disgruntled employees in the residents' lounge, and the strain of recent events showed plainly in his appearance. The blue safari jacket was crumpled and out of shape; the desert boots were scuffed and needed brushing; purple bags hung below his bloodshot eyes. Incredibly, for all these visual signs, none of his troubles could be detected in his manner of speaking, which was upbeat and optimistic.

"Sorry to keep you guys hanging about all day," he began, with breezy confidence. "Bit of a heavy session at the JV meeting. One or two little problems that needed sorting out. I can't turn my back for five minutes before something new crops up. Still – the burden of high office, eh? I gather you had a bit of a problem of your own over here on Friday."

"Excuse me, Frank," said Terry, showing his impatience, "but you do *know* we didn't get our Turkish lira for last week, do you? I don't call that a bit of a problem – I call that a total bloody disaster."

"I can only apologise on their behalf, lads. But it's all straightened out now. Your money will be ready first thing in the morning. The whole thing was a complete misunderstanding."

"What about our gelt in the UK?" asked Terry.

"What do you mean?"

"I mean are we getting any."

"Oh, there's no problem in the UK," replied Frank Palmer with a dismissive laugh. "My problems are all out here, mainly due to FNC and their kack-handed way of doing things. Haven't you been checking up with your bank branches? After the last little set to I did tell you to check every week and let me know if you found anything wrong. I can't be expected to keep tabs on every little transaction. We have literally thousands of pounds going through our accounts every day."

Mary noticed the beads of perspiration on Frank Palmers brow, and the deadness in his eyes when he smiled. She could tell he was lying.

"We haven't been able to get through to England on the telephone for some time," explained Jack. "It's been getting steadily worse since the middle of August. There's no other way of checking. None of our bank branches have telex."

"Well I'm sure when you do check you'll find everything is as it should be. If you do find anything amiss let me know straight away. Now if you'd all like to go through to the bar, I've opened a tab for you, just to show my appreciation for all the good work you've been doing. Order what you like, and I'll be through in a minute. I just need to have a quick chat with you, Jack, and you too, Mary, before we join the others."

The men all seemed reluctant to leave the matter where it stood, but Frank Palmer was already indicating that the discussion was at an end by rummaging in his briefcase for some papers. Slowly they all rose to their feet and drifted off in the direction of the bar.

"So, Jack," he continued after the men were all out of earshot, "Osman Toprak tells me you've been making great progress. What stage are we at now?"

"There's a full progress report waiting for you at the yard," replied Jack, somewhat uncomfortably. He was finding this breezy, expansive manner of speech almost insulting. How could the man possibly keep up this pretence of being in control? There had been no real explanation for last Friday's fiasco with the money, but in the absence of any hard facts it was difficult to find a way of steering the conversation back to the subject.

"Always with the reports," chaffed Frank Palmer. "All I want is a quick run down."

"The framing is about eighty percent complete. The main bulkhead is in place, so is the foam tank. We'll shortly be in a position to start on the chine bars."

"Excellent! What will they be doing while you're away?"

"They'll be finishing off the framing, fitting two more bulkheads, and then starting to run through with the upper chine bars."

"Who have you left in charge? Neil, I suppose."

"Yes. He's fully conversant with what's required."

"And you're quite sure he's up to the job? We don't want any slip ups at this stage of the game. I've got a lot riding on this project."

"I'm quite sure," replied Jack evenly. "He's fully reliable."

"As long as he gets paid on time," added Mary sharply. She too was finding the interview irritating.

Frank Palmer blanched visibly at this comment, but he recovered in an instant.

"Ouch!" he quipped. "But I quite understand your frustration after last Friday's little episode." He handed her a cheque, adding: "Perhaps this will bring back that lovely smile of yours. There's two week's holiday pay for you and Jack, plus an extra week as a well-earned bonus. I hope you have a really good time on leave, and come back hot to trot. When's your flight, by the way?"

"Wednesday, if we can get seats," she replied, putting the cheque in her handbag.

But she made no attempt to smile.

Chapter Twenty

In the taxi taking them from the railway station to the bungalow Mary had a heightened sense of anticipation, even though she had no idea what awaited them when they arrived. The mention of vultures in Morris's letter had conjured up images in her mind of an empty shell with no light fittings and a garden overgrown with weeds, just like the abandoned houses they had seen at Bogaz. She looked anxiously out of the window as the vehicle pulled up in the road outside, but everything looked exactly the way they had left it over four months ago. As she stepped out of the car, the damp October chill in the night air cut right through to her bones, and another worrying thought rose in her mind. What if they could not even get in?

The key slid into the lock easily enough, and Mary closed her eyes in silent prayer at the moment of truth. It turned. They were home. Relief flooded into every fibre of her being. She tried the light switch. It worked. Now the kitchen. Praise be! The gas was still on. She lit the front two burners on the stove, and went through to the living room. Bless you Morris! The fireplace was set ready for lighting, and the basket was full of dry logs. They would be cosy in less than an hour.

Susan and Wendy sat wrapped in blankets as close to the incipient fire as their mother would allow, while Jack brought in the suitcases and set about lighting the hot water boiler. There was no food in the house, and all the local shops had long since closed. Mary considered the possibility of fish and chips, or even the local pub, but decided against it. At least they had hot water for a bath, and going without just one meal would not harm anyone. Tomorrow they would go into the village and stock up to their hearts' content; they would also pay that all important visit to the bank.

After their best night's sleep for several weeks, Jack and Mary were up at six, unpacking and setting the house to rights. With the help of jump leads and a neighbour's car the old Wolseley was coaxed miraculously into life, and by eight o'clock they were all ready to sally forth down to the village. Their first port of call was the little high street café where they all did justice to bacon and eggs for the first time since Kaplan had served it to them in that other life that now seemed like a dream. Shopping at the new supermarket took best part of an hour, so by the time it was all loaded into the boot of the car the bank was open. Yes, the manager would see them straight away.

The situation was as bad as it could be. No payments had been made for the last six weeks. Including the money Frank Palmer had agreed to pay Mary for working on Medmarine House, they were once again owed nearly a thousand pounds. With genuine reluctance the manager confirmed Jack's worst nightmare had indeed become a reality. In the absence of the agreed monthly payments, the Official Receiver had instituted bankruptcy proceedings; a major accountancy firm had been appointed as trustee of his estate and would be putting the bungalow on the market.

Mary handed the cheque Frank Palmer had given her in Cyprus over to the manager and asked him to use express clearance. Surely nobody in their right mind would hand over a dud cheque knowing it would be presented within two days, she thought. Four hundred and fifty pounds was not a fortune, but it might just be enough to keep the wolves from their door for the time being. They would have to arrange a meeting with this trustee as soon as possible. She wasn't going to give up her bungalow without a fight.

When Jack telephoned the trustee he was encouraged by the helpful tone of the young female appointed to the case who was only too happy to grant an appointment the same day. Having left the girls in the welcoming care of their elderly neighbours, Jack and Mary drove up to London and arrived at the trustee's opulent office building with a strong feeling of foreboding. Their case officer did her best to put them at their ease, and the new situation was explained to them in simple terms. As Jack was now officially bankrupt, the whole burden of insolvency had been lifted from his shoulders. The bungalow would be sold to pay off his debts, and the trustee's fee would be taken out of any remaining proceeds. As it was most unlikely that the property would fetch enough to cover all the debts as well as the expenses, he would have to remain undischarged for a further five years.

"Isn't there any alternative?" asked Mary, having listened carefully to all that had been said. "I hate the thought of losing our home after all the hard work we've put into it."

"You could try for an annulment," replied the trustee. "But it could be a long hard struggle."

"Can you explain it to us please?"

"Well, an annulment puts you back to where you were before everything went wrong, but you do have to pay back every penny you owe, and pay our expenses into the bargain. The biggest debt is your mortgage, and you would have to obtain the consent of your building society. But I must say they have been most accommodating so far, so I can't see any reason why they wouldn't agree."

"How long would all this take?" asked Jack.

"It could take years. It depends on how quickly you can pay off the debts, which of course depends on how much money you earn. But you have to bear in mind that the longer it takes, the more you will have to pay us in fees."

"How much do you charge?" enquired Mary.

"My time is charged at forty pounds an hour, but if one of the partners is involved it is quite a bit more. We only charge for the time we spend on the file, which could be as little as two or three hours a month on a simple case like yours. Say between a thousand and fifteen hundred a year."

"Plus the money to pay off the debts," added Jack. "I don't see how we can afford it."

"But I think we should try," insisted Mary quietly.

"The trusteeship does confer complete protection," continued the trustee, glancing at Mary with sympathy. "The one thing it does give you is time. I'm working on one case that is now in its third year."

"Can we at least have a try?" asked Mary, turning to Jack.

"If you think it's worth the effort, we can give it a go," was his non-committal reply

"So what do we have to do now?" said Mary, smiling with relief.

"The first thing I need to do is take down a few employment details. I believe you're working overseas, is that right?"

"Yes. We're working in Cyprus."

"Oh how lovely. All that sun. I do envy you. And what is your income."

"Jack is paid a hundred pounds a week in Sterling and another hundred a week in Turkish currency. I get fifty pounds a week paid in Sterling, working part time."

"So you're in the Turkish sector," declared the trustee in surprise. "That's very brave. Wasn't there a war in that part not so long ago?"

"That was four years ago," replied Mary. "Things have settled down quite a bit since then."

"So how much do you think you could afford to pay each month?"

"Well we can easily manage to live on the money we're paid out there, so the rest can all be paid over to you."

"Six hundred a month. Are you sure you can manage that much? It's best to leave a margin for error."

"Say five hundred a month then."

"Let's make it four hundred, then you won't feel under so much pressure. You can always pay in the odd lump sum if you feel you can afford it. At this rate you'll be clear in no time. Now, we need to set up a meeting with someone from your building society. When do you have to be back in Cyprus?"

"We're not sure yet, but it will probably be in a couple of weeks' time."

"Then let's set a date for the end of next week. Shall we say here at eleven o'clock on the nineteenth?"

"Yes, that's fine."

"That just leaves the matter of our fee. We're up to just over three hundred at the moment, and there's quite a bit for me to do before the meeting. Five hundred should cover it. Is that okay?"

Mary anticipated Jack's reaction and was quick enough to silence him with a kick under the table.

"That will be fine," she replied, "but we'll need a couple of days to get the money together."

"Of course. You can let me have it when we meet next Thursday," said the young woman with a smile.

"And thank you for all your help. We really do appreciate it," returned Mary in conclusion.

Walking back to the car park in silence Mary could sense Jack's brooding hostility, and was prepared for his outburst as soon as they were inside the car.

"What the hell did you agree to that for? We haven't got five hundred pounds."

"I've got two hundred in my savings account, and we've just paid another four hundred and fifty into my bank account."

"Oh, and of course there's no chance that'll bounce, is there?"

"Well if it does you'll just have to pay Frank Palmer a visit and beat it out of him!" she cried angrily.

"And all that nonsense about paying four hundred a month. Where's that coming from?"

"Frank Palmer. Look, are we going to sit in this car park all day, or are you going to start the car and get us home?"

They drove in silence until they were out of the city traffic; Jack was the first to speak.

"We don't have to go back to Cyprus if you don't really want to. I can always get a job on my tools."

"No, I don't want you doing that. We're going back to Cyprus and we're going to finish the job. You remember what Osman Toprak told us. If Frank Palmer drops out of the picture, the job will go to you. We just have to wait for the right moment, and we need to be in Cyprus when it comes."

"What about Susan's schooling?"

"Well pay for it ourselves, if we have to. And if we're still out there in a year's time we'll do the same thing for Wendy."

"You *have* been giving this a lot of thought, haven't you?"

"I thought of nothing else on the flight back. We've built a good life out in Cyprus, and I'm not giving it up just because of that toad Palmer. And we're not giving up on the bungalow either. It's not as if we were penniless anyway. We've got over a hundred thousand Turkish lira sitting in the Cyprus account. That ought to be worth something."

"Christ, I'd forgotten about that with everything that's been going on. It's worth two thousand Sterling at the official rate. The trouble is, we can't get at it until we go back."

"Perhaps Kaplan would be interested in doing a deal. He's probably making far more than he needs over here, and not enough over there. The Plâj Hotel can't be making any money – it's never more than half full."

This mood of optimism sustained them for the rest of the day and into the next morning. It came to an abrupt end, however, when they called in to the bank to learn that the cheque had not cleared due to insufficient funds. Jack telephoned Frank Palmer's London office only to be told that he was still in Cyprus and was not due back until the weekend; Mary telephoned Sandie Geddes who confirmed that nothing had been paid into her father's account for six weeks, and her mother had been obliged to take a temporary cleaning job to make ends meet. Peter's wife told a similar tale of woe; she had been forced to borrow from her elder sister, and was also looking for a job. She had written to her husband several times but there had been no response, either by telephone or by letter. For all she knew the poor man could be dead.

"He can't be allowed to get away with this," declared Mary when she had finished telephoning round the other banks. "All this aggravation! There must be something we can do."

Jack decided to pay a visit to Stephen Clarkson; maybe he would be prepared to open up a little more this time. Surely he was as keen as anybody for the tug to be a success. In the event, very little came out of the meeting. Frank Palmer did owe him a hundred or so for last month's work, but that was nothing out of the ordinary. He did know there had been another cash flow problem, but as far as he was aware it had been resolved two or three weeks ago. Convinced that the designer was covering up for his client, Jack pressed him almost to the point of rudeness, but met with no success. There was nothing for it but to await Frank Palmer's return to the UK and tackle him direct.

Despite the chaos surrounding their financial affairs, Jack and Mary thoroughly enjoyed the weekend. Long walks over the forest with the children in the gentle October sunshine seemed to renew their courage and determination. After a splendid lunch of roast beef on Sunday they made for their favourite place where the pony track crossed a wide, shallow stream. It was a particularly beautiful afternoon with almost no wind and a perfect temperature for loitering about. The girls went paddling, while Jack and Mary sat on the bridge with their feet dangling just above the water, at perfect ease in the soft warmth of the early autumn sun.

"You know what we should do?" asked Jack, breaking a long contented silence.

"No," replied Mary, keeping her eyes closed, "but I'm sure you're about to tell me."

"We should get married."

"Very funny," she murmured, still without opening her eyes.

"I'm serious, Mary. I want to get married."

Now her eyes were open, searching his face for the truth.

"Where has this come from? You've always said you'd never marry again."

"Yes, I know. But things are different now. We've both got our divorces through, and – well – it just seems to make sense."

"I get it," she said, closing her eyes again. "You're just worried about having different surnames on all the documentation."

"Oh, for heaven's sake," he snapped. "Of course it isn't"

"If this really is a proposal of marriage, you might do better if you stopped barking at me."

"It's because I love you," he said softly.

She turned her head slowly towards him once more and opened her eyes to look into his. Could she see the light of true love in those moist, brown orbs? There was certainly emotion, and it was probably as close to love as anything within his capability. But she was absolutely sure of her own feelings, and knew she could love for both if need be. Smiling, she turned her head away and closed her eyes again.

"In that case I agree. We should get married."

* * * * * * * *

The day after Frank Palmer arrived back in the UK Jack drove up to London for a meeting. He parked in Hanover Square and walked the two hundred yards or so to Medmarine's offices, pausing on the way to peer through the window of an expensive looking restaurant across the narrow street that he guessed would be Kaplan's. On reaching his destination he was surprised to find no nameplate outside, but the street door was unlocked so he entered and climbed the steep, narrow staircase to the first floor, feeling more apprehensive with each step. Could this really be the London headquarters of a thriving international shipping company?

Opening onto the wide landing were a number of wooden doors, all finished in the old fashioned stain, grain and varnish style which added a ghostly air of faded gentility to the grubby decor. One of these doors had an upper panel of frosted glass bearing the company name in chipped black lacquer. Jack could hear the busy clatter of a manual typewriter on the other side; he tapped politely on the glass panel and entered. It was a typical outer office with three desks all occupied by young women in their early twenties. The room gave a general impression of clutter, with ledgers and lever arch files piled on top of the cabinets that lined one of the walls. Fluorescent lighting supplemented the vain attempts of the sun to penetrate the grime on a large sash window, barred for security. Glazed partitions separated two adjoining rooms; one was fitted out as a waiting room with the usual easy chairs and a coffee table covered with back numbers of 'Ships Monthly'; in the other Jack could see Frank Palmer seated at a wide desk, talking earnestly on the telephone. He beckoned Jack straight in with a smile and a wave of his hand.

"So, Jack, enjoying your holiday?"

"I'm amazed you can even ask."

"I beg your pardon?"

"You must have known that last cheque you gave Mary would bounce. How could you do this to us? We're both worried sick."

"Ah, yes, I remember now. You're quite right, there was a bit of a mix up on that account last week. It's all cleared up now – just get your bank to put the cheque through again, it will clear this time, no problem."

"Oh come off it, Frank. You know you haven't paid any of us a penny in the last six weeks. You owe us over thirteen hundred pounds, and god only knows what you owe the lads with all the overtime they've been putting in on the barges. Why don't you just come clean and tell us what the hell is going on?"

Anger flashed into Frank Palmer's eyes and his nostrils flared as he fought to control the rising emotion. The look of fury vanished as quickly as it came.

"As you know, Jack, I always encourage an easy, informal working relationship with my employees. It makes life so much easier if we all work together in a relaxed atmosphere. But there are limits, and I'm here to tell you that I will not be spoken to such an impertinent manner. Kindly moderate your tone."

Jack was struck dumb; this was something he could never have expected. The sheer, cold-blooded nerve of this man was almost beyond belief. What a performer!

"Don't you think I've got good cause to be impertinent, as you call it? You must know what you're doing isn't right. We're just working men, not millionaires. We rely on our wages to pay the mortgage and feed our families. Some of us are even in danger of losing our homes."

"I hear what you say, Jack, but it doesn't excuse rudeness. If there are problems then we need to sit down quietly and work them out together, calmly and logically. Now I've told you that the problem at the bank has been sorted out, so you'll just have to instruct your bank to re-present the cheque. I give you my word it will be alright this time."

"Well I've got a better idea," replied Jack, taking the returned cheque out of his pocket. "I will tear up this cheque, and then you can write me out another for thirteen hundred and fifty pounds, made out to cash, and come with me to the bank and authorise a cash withdrawal. It'll only take ten minutes, I noticed your branch when I parked in Hanover Square."

Again the quick anger returned, and again was instantly suppressed.

"I just told you, Jack, I'm not having this. Either you show proper respect or we'll have to end this conversation here and now."

A very good move, thought Jack. His opponent was obviously quite adept at dealing with confrontation. A new tactic would have to employed. If they did fall out there would be no chance of receiving any payment at all.

"I don't intend any disrespect, Frank. I just want you to understand that we really need this money. I mean we really do need it."

Frank Palmer leaned back in his chair and looked thoughtfully at Jack for a few moments as though weighing his next response.

"You've been a model employee so far, Jack, and there's no denying what you've achieved out there in the past few months. I'm really glad I've got you onside. Perhaps it is best if you know the full details of the situation we are facing in Cyprus, but what I'm going to tell you now can't go any further. Do you understand what I'm saying?"

"Of course," replied Jack earnestly. "I can be a lot more use to you if I'm in the picture."

"I mean not a soul outside this office. Not Mehmet Boga, not Neil or any of the men, and especially not Osman Toprak."

"I understand."

Taking a deep sigh, and leaning forward again, Frank Palmer began his explanation.

"I've no need to tell you of all people how difficult it has been to get this operation off the ground in Cyprus. When I was setting up the deal I was promised all sorts of co-operation and assistance by Famagusta Navigation and by the Government. As you know, they have failed to live up to their end of the bargain, which means we've practically had to deal with the whole situation ourselves. Right from the beginning there have been sceptics saying it would never work – that it would be impossible to build the tug in that yard. But you've proved them wrong, and I'm grateful for that. If you hadn't been out there I'm quite sure the project would not have progressed beyond the planning stage. The trouble is, because of all the delays and all the supply problems, the cash flow forecast has gone completely by the board. We're supposed to be getting stage payments in hard currency as the tug progresses, but there have been niggles and quibbles from FNC at every turn. We were supposed to get a twenty percent stage payment when the keel was laid, but it's been held up because of a query on the steel certificates."

He walked over to a water cooler and came back with two plastic cups of water.

"I'd offer you some coffee, but the girl forgot to get any milk this morning. You just can't get the staff," he quipped, draining his cup.

"Anyway," he continued, "to cut a long story short, I'm in the process of selling one of my ships to subsidise the tug project until I can prise some money out of the Turkish Cypriot government. I'm reluctant to sell her, because I did have plans to base her in Famagusta as a sort of sin ship for the Arabs – I think I already told you about her. Well the sale is agreed and I'm expecting payment literally any day. As soon as the money is in the bank I'll square everybody off."

"Why didn't you tell me all this sooner? It could have made such a difference if I'd known."

"It's not your job to worry about money, Jack. That's what I'm here for."

"But all those missed wage payments and bouncing cheques. You must have known it would catch up with you sooner or later."

"I know it doesn't look good, Jack, but it's FNC to blame really. That stage payment has been promised time and time again, *ad nauseam*, but it never materialises. I'm owed tens of thousands of pounds, and believe you me I'm doing everything I possibly can to collect."

Jack took a few moments to reflect on all this new information. It had the ring of truth, and he was no stranger to the problems faced by businesses from time to time. The fall of Marine and General Engineering which had marked the beginning of all his own financial problems was still relatively fresh in his mind. Nevertheless, he must know where he now stood; the meeting with his trustee in three days' time loomed large.

"So when can I present this cheque again with any chance of it going through?"

"The sale of 'Surveyor' is due to complete on the twentieth – this Friday in fact. You'll be okay after that."

The interview was over; there was nothing more to be said. The two men exchanged a few bland pleasantries and Jack left the office with mixed feelings. He now had a better picture of the circumstances surrounding all the past irregularities, but he was still coming away empty-handed, which would hardly impress the trustee. There was one last possibility, of course: Mary's idea of approaching Kaplan with the currency exchange proposition.

As it was past midday Kaplan's restaurant was beginning to fill up with suited businessmen eager to push their expense accounts and their waistlines to new limits. As soon as Jack was inside the door a Cypriot waiter bustled up to him, bristling with energetic efficiency. A far cry from poor old Ishmael at the Plâj Hotel, he thought. No, Mr Kaplan was not at the restaurant today, but he would be in tomorrow. With a wretched sense of his own failure, Jack trudged back to the car, wondering what on earth he would tell the trustee.

Mary listened to his account of the interview with Frank Palmer as she prepared the evening meal. It was a comfortable, familiar custom that had been with them since their first days together, and their quiet, intimate conversation greatly relieved Jack's troubled mind. He had telephoned the trustee to postpone their meeting as soon as he arrived home, and could not help but notice the edge in her voice as she pressed him for a definite appointment. Having managed to wriggle out of actually naming a particular day, Jack had at least gained a little more precious time, and that was all that could be done for the moment.

On Friday he drove back up to London for another session with Frank Palmer, but the sale of the passenger ship had still not completed, so he came away empty-handed again. He did, however, have a brief meeting with Kaplan, who laughed out loud at the suggestion that he might like to buy some Turkish lira. The currency was a joke as far as the Cypriot was concerned, and as much as he liked Jack, business was business; when it came down to hard cash there was no room for sentiment. Jack also thought he detected a certain reserve in Kaplan's manner of speaking that had not been present during any of the time they had spent together in Cyprus, but the impression could well have stemmed from his vulnerable state of mind.

The following week Jack made the trek up to Hanover square every other day, coming away with nothing more than excuses and new promises on each occasion. When he crept home with his tail between his legs after the fourth abortive visit, Mary noticed how drawn he was looking, and decided that he needed a pep talk.

"You're doing your best, Jack. We mustn't give up hope. Cyprus is still our best bet for getting out of this mess. We just have to be patient. I've got a good feeling that everything's going to work out fine in the end."

"I'm not so sure, my love. I'm beginning to wonder if he's just stringing us along."

"Why would he bother to do that? It wouldn't make sense. No, he needs you back out in Cyprus, and he jolly well knows it. You're his only hope now all the others have quit the job."

"But we don't even know if this ship he's supposed to be selling actually exists. I'm beginning to wonder if it wouldn't be best to cut our losses and try to sort something out back here."

"And just let him get away with it? You must be joking. We're going to keep pestering him until he pays us what he owes. In any case, there's all that money sitting in our account at Isbank. We're certainly not walking away from that."

"According to Kaplan it's just about enough to buy a Mars bar. The official exchange rate is nothing but a load of propaganda. We'd be lucky to get a grand for it on the open market."

"A thousand pounds is not to be sneezed at. How long would it take you to earn that sort of money on your tools?"

"I know what you mean, my love. But I'm really fed up with trolling up to London and coming back with nothing to show for it."

"Then maybe we should all come up with you. See how he likes having a family camping on his doorstep. We'll buy the girls a load of toffee apples, and get nasty little sticky finger marks all over his precious international headquarters. See how he likes that!"

In spite of his gloom Jack burst out laughing at the notion.

"Do you know, that might not be such a bad idea. We could make a day of it."

"Even better," she replied, "we could make two days of it. I've been meaning to take the girls to the Natural History Museum for some time now. We'll go up by train, and get a family room for the night in one of those grotty little hotels in Cromwell Road. It'll be fun."

Jack leapt to his feet, beaming from ear to ear, and took her in his arms. She had worked her magic, and he was a man again. Squeezing first his shoulders and then his waist she added:

"I can see we're going to have to start feeding you up as well. You're nothing but skin and bone. I don't want to be standing next to a skeleton when we get married next Saturday."

Chapter Twenty-one

"Sunday, 5th November

Well the deed is done. We were married yesterday at the registry office, and I am now officially Mrs Durham. Morris and Pat acted as witnesses, and Morris's sister Joan was there too. It was a bit cold, so I wore my brown two-piece suit and cream blouse with the frilly front. My two little bridesmaids took it all very seriously. We had a lovely reception, put on by Joan at her house in Brockenhurst. There were just the seven of us, but we had such a good time and took loads of pictures.

"So here I sit on this beautiful morning in these gorgeous surroundings, a respectable married woman writing up my diary – (I didn't get a chance to do it yesterday – Jack kept me rather busy all last night). This house is really lovely – it's brand new with four bedrooms and a lovely garden backing on to the New Forest. I'm really looking forward to our bungalow being finished, so we can feel secure and comfortable with no money worries, though when that will be heaven only knows!

* * * * *

Their troubles were, however, still very much in front of them. It was now nearly four weeks since they had returned to England, and their perilous situation had not improved at all. Only Mary's dogged determination and calm persistence kept them going; Jack had really wanted to give up right from the beginning. Nevertheless he kept going up to London three times a week, all at his wife's insistence; it was pointless telephoning, because Frank Palmer was not accepting calls, particularly from people to whom he owed money. Neil, Terry and the lads had all returned home in October; they had tried telephoning Frank Palmer, but their calls were never put through, and they soon gave it up as a bad job.

With all this time on her hands, Mary decided to decorate the two bedrooms, assisted by Jack on the days he was not travelling up to London. They always worked very well together, with Mary's steady sense of purpose mitigating Jack's mood swings. He tended to fly into a rage at the least sign of any difficulty, but Mary put this down to the frustration he must be feeling at his dealings with Frank Palmer. One particularly frightening tantrum occurred after Jack had made his first ever attempt at plastering. When they were scraping off the old wallpaper in the girl's bedroom, a great lump of the old lime plaster came away, leaving the brickwork gaping out at them. Jack cheerfully mixed up a tub of new plaster undercoat and set to with a will, making a really good job of the repair, and a great deal of mess, of course. As it was setting, the plaster started to peel away from the top where there was no adhesion to the brickwork. Frantically wielding his new steel float and dashing copious amounts of water in all directions, Jack tried in vain to postpone the inevitable. When the top section obstinately insisted on falling to the floor Jack completely lost his temper and started to pound it with a claw hammer, shrieking obscenities at the top of his voice. It was a terrifying spectacle that showed a dark side of his nature that Mary had not seen before. When he had calmed down, Jack apologized profusely to Mary and the girls; they forgave him at once, but the incident left behind a tiny splinter of unease that would be a long time in growing out. Fortunately, their elderly neighbour possessed some skill with a plasterer's float and came to their rescue, watched with admiration by Mary, and with relief by Jack.

At the end of their sixth week of enforced home leave Jack drove up to London for his routine Friday visit. The situation seemed hopeless to him, but Mary was in charge of their finances now, so as long as she was prepared to keep giving him money for the petrol, the least he could do was keep up the siege on Frank Palmer's office. This time, however, seemed different; the girls greeted him with smiles instead of the sullen scowls to which he had grown accustomed, and he was even offered a cup of tea when he entered. Frank Palmer, too, was in an upbeat mood.

"Things are on the move, Jack, my old buddy. I've got some very good news for you."

"The passenger ship. You've finally closed the deal?"

"No, that's still ongoing. But I have managed to raise some finance on one of my other ships at very good terms. We're not quite out of the woods yet, but at least I can get you back out to Cyprus. Can you let me have an account of what I owe you to date?"

"Certainly," replied Jack, taking a notebook out of his pocket. "As of today it comes to just under two and a half thousand, including this week's money."

"That can't be right. It can't possibly be more than fifteen hundred."

"No, it's definitely two and a half. Mary has been keeping a careful record. Take a look for yourself."

Frank Palmer scanned down the column of neat figures and checked them against a typed list.

"I can see a couple of places where you've gone wrong, Jack. You've included six weeks' pay in Turkish lira. That's due to be paid by FNC. Then you've got over a hundred for expenses, what's that for?"

"Coming up to London three times a week."

"That's fair enough, I suppose. So if we knock off the six hundred you'll be getting from FNC in Turkish lira, it leaves nineteen hundred. As you've been messed around a bit I'm prepared to round it up to two grand. Is that okay?"

"I'm happy with that."

Frank Palmer opened his desk drawer, took out two bundles of twenty pound notes and placed them on the desk in front of him.

"I'm prepared to settle up with you here and now," he said in a confidential tone, "but I need you to do something for me in return. Kaplan happened to mention that you have a hundred thousand Turkish lira in your account at Isbank. I want you to let me have that money in return for this two thousand in

Sterling. I'm offering you the official exchange rate, which as you know is twice what you'd be able to get on the open market"

"But that would mean you still owed us two thousand. No, I'm sorry Frank, that's just not on."

"You haven't heard me out yet. I'll deposit another two thousand Sterling in your bank account by the end of the month. Think about it carefully, Jack."

Jack did think. Two thousand pounds would make a world of difference to their financial situation, now at crisis point. Another two thousand, if Frank Palmer honoured his pledge, would go a long way to paying off the trustee. If the offer was refused they would receive absolutely nothing, and their savings in Cyprus would simply sit in their bank account, doing them no good whatsoever. The choice was perfectly straightforward.

"Okay, Frank. I agree."

"Good man. This means we can make a fresh start, and really go for it. I've drawn up this little agreement for us both to sign. It's only a formality, but I always like to get things like this down in writing. It avoids any misunderstanding."

Reading through the brief wording Jack smiled as he came to the last paragraph, which read:

"In the event of Mr Durham not returning to Cyprus for any reason whatsoever, this agreement shall be his irrevocable authority for Isbank to pay from his account the sum of 100,000 Turkish Lire (One Hundred Thousand) to Mr Frank Palmer on demand."

They both signed the agreement, Jack pocketed the money, and they shook hands on the deal.

"Now, how soon can you get back to Cyprus?" asked Frank Palmer. "I want to start making up for lost time straight away."

"Just as soon as you send us the tickets."

"You'll have them within the week"

Jack telephoned the trustee for an appointment as soon as he arrived home. Mary heard the excitement in his voice and guessed there had been a favourable development at last. She listened to his account of the meeting, slowly counting the money as he spoke.

"We'll give the trustee fifteen hundred on Monday, and keep five hundred in the current account just in case there are any hiccups in the future," she said firmly. "I can't understand why he wants Turkish lira, though."

"I don't care why he wants them," returned Jack, "but he's not going to get any of ours."

"But you've signed that agreement. You'll have to give them to him, won't you?"

"After all he's put us through? I don't think so. The boot is on the other foot now. We'll see how *he* likes being messed about for a change."

Mary gave a little chuckle as she relished the idea. Why not? Why not indeed?

"I'd like to be a fly on the wall when you tell him."

"Never fear, my love. I shall make sure you have a ringside seat."

There was much to do if they were going in only a week's time as the bungalow would have to be prepared for what could be an absence of anything up to six months. On Monday they attended the meeting with the trustee and an official from the building society. The trustee seemed well satisfied with the money, showing no sign of surprise that it was paid in cash, and the building society representative was most understanding, readily agreeing to the trustee's repayment plan. He explained it was the society's policy to co-operate fully in cases of genuine hardship such as this; the society was really like a very large family, always ready to look after its members. Nobody wanted to see them thrown out onto the street.

Four flight tickets arrived in the post that same day. Frank Palmer had certainly wasted no time in arranging them. Mary gasped when she read the time and date of departure; they would be leaving in just two day's time. The pace of preparation became almost frantic over the next twenty-four hours, with very little sleep for either of them, but the die was now cast. Once again they would be leaving the sanctuary of hearth and home for a fragile promise of salvation and a very uncertain future.

* * * * * * * *

It was a tired foursome that arrived at the Baykal flat at one in the morning, so within half an hour they were all tucked up in bed. Jack was asleep as soon as his head touched the pillow, but Mary lay awake for some time planning what had to be done the next morning. They would have to sort out some heating because the rooms had felt quite cold when they came in. She would also have to find some way of dealing with the cockroaches that had been multiplying steadily in the kitchen during her absence, despite the care she had taken to ensure no means of sustenance had been left for them. The kitchen was always kept spotlessly clean, but try as she might Mary had never quite succeeded in banishing the loathsome creatures. Perhaps there is still a brand of insecticide I haven't used, she thought. One that actually works. There must be a better way than battering them to death with the dustpan.

When the Famagusta branch of Isbank opened their doors next morning Jack was among the little group waiting outside. He withdrew all but a couple of hundred lira from the account, took the money back to the flat and asked Mary to hide it in a place of safety. His next port of call was FNC to ascertain the position regarding six week's back pay, amounting to thirty thousand lira. Much to his surprise, Mehmet Boga seemed very pleased to see him, and the two men chatted amiably enough about how to revive the tug's flagging production schedule. There had been virtually no progress during Jack's long period of enforced absence. The crane had disappeared back into the port, Avkuran had left to work on his own again, and moral was at its nadir. When Jack brought up the subject of money he was again surprised and delighted when Mehmet picked up the telephone and instructed the accountant to draw up a cheque for the full amount. It was obvious that the directors of FNC were prepared to welcome him back with open arms, and Jack began to wonder if they were at last tiring of Frank Palmer.

The next item on the agenda was transport, as the Mini-Moke had long since been taken back by the hire company. In this Mehmet Boga regretted he could be of no assistance. The old Toyota that had originally been assigned to the yard for use by British personnel had finally given up the ghost, and there were no plans to replace it. Using the extension in Onan's office on the ground floor Jack telephoned Alaydin at the car hire company who simply laughed at the request to provide another vehicle. When Medmarine paid the money already owed for the Mini-Moke the matter could be given consideration, he politely suggested.

This setback left Jack on the horns of a dilemma. If he was correct in his reading of Mehmet Boga's conciliatory attitude at their meeting this morning, he was sure Frank Palmer's days in Cyprus were numbered. But was this the right time to bring matters to a head by refusing to pay Frank Palmer the Turkish currency as agreed? There could be little doubt regarding the outcome of such a refusal; the gloves would be off. Without personal transport, however, he would be severely restricted. Perhaps it would be better to wait until Frank Palmer had fulfilled his contractual obligation to provide a company vehicle before making his move.

Turning these weighty considerations over in his mind, Jack walked slowly back to the bank and asked them to clear the FNC cheque with all possible speed. Fortunately it was also the branch used by the company, so Jack had to wait only ten minutes until the money was in his own account. He decided to withdraw the whole amount in cash, and as he watched the notes being counted an idea began to form in his head. If he used the money to pay what was owed to Alaydin on Frank Palmer's behalf he would actually be acting in the best interests of Medmarine, and solve his transport problem into the bargain. Furthermore, it would provide added justification if he did refuse to hand over any cash, and enable him to take the high moral ground. Using a public call box Jack telephoned the car hire company once more. At the mention of cash settlement and a month's hire paid in advance Alaydin could not be more helpful. He would have a Ford Escort delivered to the shipyard within the hour.

The welcome Jack received when he walked through the yard gates moved him deeply. As news of his return spread through the various sheds and workshops the men all came to shake his hand; Adem Usta the yard foreman was particularly joyful, and Jack noticed the tears welling up in the good man's smiling eyes. They all asked after Mary, and expressed their joy on learning that she too had returned, and would probably be back at the yard before the end of the week. The only man to show no emotion was Faruk, who merely enquired in his usual polite, detached manner if the family had enjoyed their extended leave in England. Jack looked quickly through the pile of correspondence on his desk, and started to sort it into urgent and non-urgent piles, but it was not long before he abandoned the task to go out and inspect the tug.

It was obvious at first glance that nothing had been done in the six weeks he had been away. There was a great deal more rust following a recent fall of rain; it might even prove necessary to sand blast the structure before plating commenced, resulting in more expense and delay. Much of the scaffolding was missing, and Jack noticed it had been spirited over to the dilapidated old trawler still sitting on the slipway. A half finished frame lay on the ground, the weeds already starting to obscure its form. With a wry smile Jack recognised the precision of a long run of welding; Neil's work, without a doubt. Finding a team as good as the one he had just lost was not going to be easy, but perhaps he could make a start with Avkuran, and there was always the possibility of importing Turkish welders from Izmir.

By the time he finished this depressing little tour of the structure, Alaydin arrived with his replacement car. Their deal was quickly concluded and Jack gave his young friend a lift to the Itimat taxi point before driving home to see Mary. True to form she had competed all the unpacking, thoroughly bottomed the kitchen, laundered all the bed linen and with the help of Susan and Wendy, amassed an impressive pile of dead cockroaches. She was delighted with the replacement car and they all set off to Nicosia in search of means to heat the flat.

Early in the following week Jack was surprised to receive a telephone call from Frank Palmer, back in Cyprus a little ahead of schedule. He was speaking from Mehmet Boga's office and asked Jack to pop round for a brief council of war. Mary needed to use the photocopying machine at FNC so she went with him. They had just reached the top of the broad marble staircase leading up to the first floor offices when Frank Palmer emerged from the great man's room.

"Ah, Jack," he said brusquely, completely ignoring the presence of Mary, "I see you've arrived safe and sound. We'll have to have our meeting a bit later on – I'll be tied up with Mehmet for a while yet. In the meantime perhaps you could just pop down to the bank and take care of that other matter we discussed in London. I've decided it might as well be in cash."

Up to that very minute Jack had been uncertain if he would actually refuse to hand over the money in the event of demand, but Frank Palmer's arrogant, offhand tone had made him see red. The man was back to his old high-handed ways, pretending that nothing had happened. What was more he had completely ignored Mary, which was unsupportable; they were being addressed as if they were a couple of lackeys.

"Yes, about that money, Frank. I think I'll just hang on to it until you've paid the other two thousand Sterling into our bank account at home. It's only a couple of days away, so it won't make a lot of difference will it?"

Eyes ablaze with fury Frank Palmer walked menacingly up to Jack until they were standing practically nose to nose. He was by far the heavier man, but Jack had the advantage of height, and was much fitter.

"That was not our agreement," he snarled. "I need that money *now*."

Jack stood glaring back at his adversary with matching fury, fuelled by a frustration that had had been building up for months. He was now a pressure vessel waiting to explode.

"You can't seriously expect me to hand over that sort of money after the run around you've been giving us for the past six months. What sort of an idiot do you think I am?"

"I've told you before, Jack, I'm not prepared to tolerate disrespect from my employees. You need to think carefully about what you're doing. I give you fair warning: either you hand over the money as agreed, or you'll have to face the consequences."

"I'm sorry Frank, but the money stays where it is until the two grand is in our account and cleared."

"So be it. But don't say you haven't been warned."

With these words Frank Palmer turned and disappeared back into Mehmet Boga's office, slamming the door behind him. For his part Jack turned, smiled at Mary, and shrugged his shoulders. There was nothing for it, they both agreed, but to carry on as normal and await Frank Palmer's next move

They had both been working for a couple of hours back in their own office, when Onan turned up with an envelope addressed to Jack in Frank Palmer's handwriting. It contained notice that his contract of employment was terminated forthwith, and threatened 'action' if a hundred thousand Turkish lira was not paid into Frank Palmer's personal account within the next two days.

"So, what happens now?" asked Mary.

"First we go home to collect the money. Then we pay Suleyman a visit – he should be at the Plâj Hotel about now. Then we go to see Osman Toprak. It's a good job we've got some wheels."

"Why do we need to see Suleyman?"

"A pound to a penny he's owed rent. We're going to settle up with him."

Jack was absolutely right, of course. Suleyman had not received any payment for rent since the day he had signed the agreement with Frank Palmer, and was overjoyed when Mary settled the account to the end of the year. He had been promised payment in Sterling to fund a family holiday in London, but having chased Frank Palmer countless times without success he was now living in hope rather than conviction, and only his sympathy for the plight of the English family had prevented him from exercising his legal right to re-possession.

In Nicosia, Osman Toprak was most alarmed on hearing Jack's account of the confrontation with Frank Palmer.

"You see, Jack, this makes things very difficult for me. I understand your position, and the reasons for your actions, but I have certain business obligations to Frank and…."

"But you are also Chairman of Famagusta Navigation, and a director of the joint venture. Surely your obligations to the tug project are more important."

Osman Toprak sat thinking deeply for several moments before making his reply.

"I cannot be seen to take sides, but I do believe it would be the best thing all round if we can find a way of settling this dispute amicably, and get you back to work on the tug. I do not think either of you has acted wisely, but in the heat of the moment mistakes can be made. Now before I say any more, there is one thing I have to know for certain. Do you really want to continue working on the tug?"

"Of course we do, but only as long as we're paid properly and all this messing about with money stops for good."

"So assuming Frank was indeed just overcome with the heat of the moment, I am prepared to act as mediator between you both. Would this be acceptable?"

"Absolutely."

"Then here is my suggestion. You will deposit the money with me, to be held in trust, until you and Frank have had a chance to meet and discuss your differences in a calm and proper manner. I should be happy to be a party to such a meeting. If the dispute is not settled to your complete satisfaction, the money will be returned to you in full. Do you agree?"

"Well not altogether, Osman. I like the idea of you acting as mediator, but I'm not happy at handing over a hundred thousand lira. We are actually owed forty thousand at this moment, quite apart from the two grand he owes us in Sterling"

"But Frank led me to believe he paid you up to date in London. How can he owe you that much already?"

"Two weeks wages is twenty thousand lira, and another twenty thousand for petty cash."

"You can't possibly have spent twenty thousand in petty cash."

"Fifteen thousand to Suleyman for rent arrears on the Baykal flat, and another five to settle the account for car hire. We've had to pay it all out of our own funds."

"Fifteen thousand sounds rather a lot for the flat. How many months were owing?"

"Suleyman hasn't received a penny from Frank Palmer since we moved in last May."

Osman Toprak frowned. He genuinely did not know how bad the situation had become. Jack seized the opportunity to press home his advantage.

"You see it's not just us and the lads he's been messing about. He probably owes money all over the island. I can't understand why you are all putting up with it."

"I don't think that sort of remark has any place in this discussion, Jack, so I will ignore it. If you really wish to continue working for us at the shipyard, some way out of this dispute will have to be found. I understand why you do not wish to deposit the full amount, so I suggest we make it sixty thousand instead. So how about it?"

Jack looked across at Mary, who nodded without hesitation.

"I think it's the best way," she agreed, taking the money out of her bag.

Osman Toprak quickly scribbled a receipt outlining the conditions under which the money was being paid, and handed it to Mary.

"I will contact Frank and set up a meeting for the earliest opportunity. I take it you will be available at short notice."

"Well we haven't really got much else to do," replied Jack, "considering we're out of a job."

* * * * * * * *

The meeting was arranged for two days later at noon. Jack and Mary arrived to find a tired-looking Frank Palmer already ensconced in Osman Toprak's office.

"So, who wants to go first?" asked Osman Toprak once the polite but guarded greetings had been exchanged.

"I think that had better be me," replied Frank Palmer, anxious to take the initiative. "Look Jack, Osman has persuaded me that I may have acted in haste by dismissing you as I did, and perhaps he is right. I don't really know. What I do know is that your attitude towards me has not been right for some time. If there's one thing I can't tolerate it is insubordination. There has to be discipline in any organisation. Without it no business can function properly."

"My attitude, as you call it, is caused by only one thing Frank. The fact that you don't pay my wages in accordance with my contract. Like any other working man, I need to have my money every week on the dot. It's not like I'm on a percentage or anything like that. I'm just a hired hand in all this."

"That doesn't justify welching on a firm deal. You know my situation, and you know I really needed that money."

"Tell me, Frank, is the two grand you promised me in our account in England yet?"

"That's beside the point. You signed an agreement to pay me a hundred thousand lira on your return to Cyprus."

"I'd be pretty stupid to do that when you already owe me sixty thousand."

"Don't be ridiculous. I paid you up to date in London."

"That was two weeks ago. According to my figures we are owed just over sixty thousand. It's all down here, take a look.

Frank Palmer accepted the neatly typed sheet of figures, his hand shaking as he scanned down the columns.

"This item for air tickets – twenty-three thousand. I've already paid for those."

"The return half is only valid for six weeks. We discussed this already if you remember. You agreed to deposit twenty-three thousand in our account so that we always had means of getting the family home if necessary. As for the money for Susan's school fees, where's that supposed to be coming from? It's due this week."

At this point Osman Toprak saw that he would have to come to Frank Palmer's rescue.

"Gentlemen, I think we're getting a bit off the track here. This meeting was not meant to include detailed financial negotiations. We are here simply to establish if you both wish to continue working together."

Jack's response was firm and measured.

"I've already told you, Osman. I am one hundred percent committed to the tug project. My dearest wish is to stay here and finish the job."

"And you, Frank?" enquired Osman Toprak.

"You know better than anyone how much the success of the yard means to me, Osman," replied Frank Palmer wearily. "I'm happy to let bygones be bygones and make a fresh start."

"That settles it then," declared Osman Toprak, visibly relieved by the outcome. "It simply remains to agree the disposal of the sixty thousand I am holding in trust, and we can put the whole unfortunate business behind us."

"I'm prepared to accept Jack's figures," returned Frank Palmer. "A balance of forty thousand, I think you said."

"What about the money for Susan's school fees?" asked Mary

"I'll take care of that as soon as I get back to London."

"And the two thousand in Sterling?" demanded Jack.

"That'll be down to eighteen hundred now," replied Frank Palmer quickly. "You've already deducted the equivalent of two weeks Sterling wages in the account you've just given me."

"But I still need to know when I'm going to get it."

"I'll settle up as soon as the sale for 'Surveyor' goes through. I can't say better than that."

"So are we all agreed, then?" asked Osman Toprak, fearing that the haggling might go on for ever.

Jack held out his hand to Frank Palmer in reply. The two men shook on the deal, and shared out the money as agreed.

As they left Osman Toprak's offices, Frank Palmer invited Jack and Mary to join him for lunch at the Saray Hotel to celebrate their truce. They took a table near the window overlooking the square, and Frank Palmer proposed a toast as soon as their drinks arrived.

"I'm glad we have this opportunity to have a proper chat away from all the pressures of the working day. I think we successfully cleared the air this morning, and I really do feel this marks a new beginning to our relationship. Now that we've reached a better understanding I think it's time to bring you up to date on developments within my group of companies. From now on I want you to be fully in the picture regarding everything that goes on, good or bad."

"That's all I've ever asked, Frank. If you'd done it right from the start, none of this trouble would have happened."

"No, I didn't really know you well enough to take you into my confidence. But it's different now. I've seen you under pressure and know you can handle it. What I want to do now is lay down a plan for the next six months so we both know where we are going. I think the three of us are going to make a great team. If we all pull together, well the sky is the limit."

"Here's to teamwork," said Jack raising his glass. They clinked glasses and drank the toast.

"So here's the plan," continued Frank Palmer, leaning urgently forward in his chair. "I've decided to make Cyprus the base for my entire operation, for two very good reasons. The first one is to take advantage of the tax breaks that are available to companies out here. The second reason, even more important perhaps, is to run more efficiently. I'm wasting so much time dashing backwards and forwards, but if I'm based here permanently I can lift a huge weight off your shoulders, Jack, and leave you to concentrate on getting the tug finished."

"I'll drink to that," replied Jack, raising his glass again.

"The first thing I need to do is get a decent flat sorted out. Efkav have recently finished a new block overlooking the sea round by the Sands Hotel, and I've agreed terms on a two bedroom unit on the fourth floor. The trouble is I haven't got enough in my account over here to pay the deposit. I thought I was going to have a hundred thousand lira by today, which I was going to use getting everything set up, but of course you weren't to know that. It's my own fault for not keeping you in the picture, I suppose. But this is my proposal now: If you will pay the deposit of twenty-five thousand lira to Efkav for the flat, I'll put the sterling equivalent of five hundred pounds into your UK bank account."

"How can we be sure that you really will pay the money in?" asked Mary, who instantly saw the possibility of paying another lump sum to the trustee if Frank Palmer was genuine in his proposal. Even now, after all the disappointments and broken promises, she felt it was worth taking the gamble to convert their savings into hard currency.

"I can only give you my word," replied Frank Palmer. "I know there have been a few hiccoughs over money in the last few weeks, but once the deal on 'Surveyor' goes through there will be enough cash to finish building the tug with plenty to spare. Then when 'Seahorse' arrives we can put her to work on the Tripoli run and start earning some real money over here."

"When is she due to arrive?" asked Jack

"Next week sometime. She's had to put in to Gibraltar with engine trouble, otherwise she'd be here already. It never rains but it pours. It means I have to call in at Gib on my way back to the UK, and I could do without the extra hassle right now. Look, you two, why don't you take a minute to talk it over while I go for a pee?"

"So, what do you think, my love?" asked Jack as the pale blue safari jacket disappeared through the swing doors.

"I just don't know what to think. We've no way of knowing if he's telling the truth about either of these ships. What sort of ship is 'Seahorse' anyway?"

"It's a roll-on roll-off vehicle ferry. An ex naval supply vessel with a ramp at the bow so cars or lorries can drive on and off. I put in a tender for her refit when I was still at Marine and General, but we lost the job to another yard."

"So you've actually seen it. It does really exist."

"Oh yes. It's where I first met Frank. It was Stephen that first introduced us. He was the consultant naval architect on the job. I must have told you all this before, surely."

"I expect so. I just can't remember."

"The point is, do we give this exchange idea a go?"

"Well it's only Turkish lira we'd be risking. It's not as if we were gambling with real money, is it? And we could certainly do with the sterling, which he'd have to pay sooner or later."

"I agree. I'll tell him we're happy to go ahead then."

As they all left the Saray Hotel Jack offered Frank Palmer a lift to the airport, where he was catching the afternoon flight to Istanbul and then on to Gibraltar. A genuine cordiality seemed to have sprung up between them born of relief on both sides. Jack felt they were more on equal terms now that he had been taken into his employer's confidence. For his part, Frank Palmer appeared perfectly at ease with the new relationship, and spoke enthusiastically about his plans for 'Seahorse' all the way to the airport. He shook Jack's hand with sincere warmth at the departure gate, and even went so far as to bestow a light kiss on Mary's cheek

"I'm out of my mind," said Jack as they drove back to Famagusta. "I should have gone in for the kill instead of offering to help him out."

"No. We've done the right thing," returned Mary. "I'm quite sure about that. Now that you're both working together it will make all the difference."

"You don't think he's finished then?"

"Of course he's not finished. People like Frank always bounce back. Everybody gets a bad run of luck now and then, it's just the way life goes. I really do think we're doing the right thing by easing his burden – it might make just the difference we need to succeed."

"Putting it that way, I suppose you're right. We'll go straight to Efkav when we get back and have a look at these flats."

The smart new apartment block looked most impressive from the outside, with an attractive pink marble clad finish and neat tiers of balconies overlooking the upper harbour. They quickly found the letting agent's office on the ground floor and produced the letter of authority and documentation Frank Palmer had given them. A tiny lift still smelling of newness whisked them up to the fourth floor, and they let themselves in to the empty flat. It was spacious and finished to a very high standard, with composite marble floors and beautifully plastered walls painted the usual light magnolia. Pulling up the metal blinds Mary looked out over the harbour and to the wide blue Mediterranean beyond. Lovely views and just right for a bachelor flat she thought, but I prefer our apartment in Baykal.

Jack paid the deposit to the agent, handed the receipt to Mary for safekeeping, and pocketed the two sets of bright new keys.

"Well he certainly knows how to look after himself," observed Jack as they drove away.

"Yes, it's alright for someone like Frank, I suppose, but I like ours much better."

"So do I, as it happens. All the same, it might be a good idea for us to keep a spare set of keys. He doesn't have to know about it, and you never know when they might come in handy."

* * * * * * *

Sunday, 3rd December

"Phew! What a few weeks these have been! When we met Frank at the FNC offices I was very worried boiling point had been reached, and blows would ensue, but now those problems have melted away. What next, I ask myself.

I cannot fathom Frank at all. I know nothing about business but to me he seems to be chasing moonbeams, and has too many irons in the fire. Does he know what he's doing?

A strange call yesterday – I was supposed to be meeting Julia for lunch next week, but she telephoned to cancel – giving no reason – and her voice sounded strained. We didn't make any other arrangements to meet soon either – I wonder if it has anything to do with our visit to see Osman – we shall see!

It seems a long time ago since my first entry into this diary and what my expectations were. In fact I suppose I don't really know what my expectations were. As far as Cyprus is concerned that certainly has lived up to them. It's beautiful here and the people are lovely – well mostly – and actually our lives have been pretty good – well again mine has. I think Jack has found life very difficult in the shipyard and his dealings with officialdom. I do miss the lads from Blighty; it really is a shame they had to leave.

Susan still isn't in school, which is a bit of a worry. I hope when she does eventually start she'll not find it too difficult to catch up. I was thinking of trying out the local school for Wendy. I'm not too sure how she would manage with the language and everything, but I think it's worth a try. Back in England she'd be going into a nursery school soon anyway.

Chapter Twenty-two

With peace declared between Jack and Frank Palmer the future prospects of the Famagusta Shipyard looked set to improve, but storm clouds had started to gather in another direction. Support from FNC had been gradually ebbing away ever since the British steelworkers had deserted the project *en masse*, and Mehmet Boga had stopped trying even to appear helpful. When Jack asked him for some assistance at The Government Store to acquire some furniture for Frank Palmer's new flat, the great man was quick to remind him that housing British personnel was not part of his job. Neither was he interested in the shipyard's transport problems; Medmarine was running the yard, so any vehicles needed would have to be provided by Frank Palmer. FNC would continue to honour its contractual obligations under the joint venture agreement, which meant wages for all shipyard workers would be paid, but that was all. Jack was now virtually on his own.

The real reason for Mehmet Boga's disenchantment came to light quite by accident when Jack was asked to organise a repair job on one of the small coasters based in the port. She had sustained some plating damage just above the waterline when docking in Antalya, and had to be back in commission within three days for an important cargo run back to mainland Turkey. Jack calculated that with the labour at his disposal the deadline could be met only by working round the clock for seventy-two hours, so he divided the men into two shifts on the basis of eight hours on, eight hours off. One shift was headed up by Hasan, whose work had improved considerably under Neil Geddes; the other was lead by Avkuran, who had already been persuaded to return to the fold. Kemal Aydin was representing the ship's owners, and he agreed with Jack that the repairs would be carried out alongside the vessel's usual berth in the port.

Fortunately, the gauge of the ship's plating was the same as that of the tug, so all the necessary materials were to hand. The job went like a dream without the slightest hitch, and the steelwork was completed well in time to allow several coats of paint to be applied. Jack stayed with the men for almost the whole seventy-two hours, during which time he came to know and respect Hasan far more, not just because of his work but also for his personal qualities. During one of their severely short meal breaks together Jack learned from Hasan that Frank Palmer was said to owe FNC in excess of two million Turkish lira, and this information came from no lesser person than Mehmet Boga himself. Rumours of the English businessman's lack of probity had been circulating in the port for some time, and sympathy for Jack and his family was running high in every quarter.

By the time the job had reached the painting stage Jack was completely exhausted. He left Hasan in charge while he went home for some sleep, but returned after only six hours to ensure the shipyard's repair bill was paid in full before the vessel sailed again in the evening. The account was settled in cash, and the skipper added a generous bonus, which Jack distributed among the delighted men. He deposited the money in Medmarine's account at Isbank and returned to the yard where Faruk gave him the message that his presence was urgently required round at the FNC offices.

Jack sensed trouble was in store as soon as he set foot in Mehmet Boga's office.

"Sit down Jack," ordered the great man, adding 'please' only after seeing his visitor made no move to comply. Having made his point, Jack took his place in the seat he had used so many times before.

"I understand the job on 'Dalga' has been completed," said Mehmet Boga, "and payment has already been made in cash."

"Yes, it has."

"Have you handed the money in to our accounts department for banking yet?"

"No. I've already paid it in to the Medmarine account at Isbank."

"Then you have acted incorrectly. That money belongs to FNC."

"I beg to differ, Mehmet. My understanding is that Medmarine runs the shipyard now. It was agreed at the last joint venture board meeting if you care to remember."

"You know full well that the situation has changed completely since then. You cannot expect FNC to continue paying the men's wages and leave Medmarine to keep all the proceeds from their work. It is out of the question."

"The money paid by FNC is just for work on the tug project."

"But there has been no work on the tug for the last two months!" cried Mehmet Boga in frustration. "Your men have all deserted the job."

"You can't expect skilled tradesmen to work for nothing, Mehmet. They went home because they weren't getting paid."

"And whose fault is that? It's certainly not mine."

"According to Frank, it is your company that has caused all the problems by not meeting the stage payments according to the contract."

"That is preposterous!" bellowed Mehmet Boga. "The stage payment for the keel was made in full. The next one is not due until all the steel has been delivered from the UK, and will be paid as soon as we receive the correct BV certification. We do not owe Medmarine one cent. In fact it is the other way round. At the last count Frank Palmer owes my company over two million Turkish lira."

Jack was stunned by this revelation. It was one thing to hear the figure as a rumour from the lips of Hasan the welder, but confirmation from Mehmet Boga, the Managing Director of a duly incorporated Cypriot company was quite another. Through the maelstrom of thoughts racing around in his mind Jack was aware of Mehmet Boga's voice booming out again.

"I do not understand why you came back to Cyprus, Jack. You should have realised the position was hopeless when you were still in England. You have dragged your wife and family back here for what? To work for a man who obviously has no personal integrity, and no regard for any of his countrymen?"

"We came back because we *do* have integrity, and because we have the highest regard for the people who depend on our skill and technical knowledge. We came back to finish the job, with or without Frank Palmer."

"In the name of Allah! What can you possibly mean?"

"I mean there is no reason why FNC or even the Government couldn't finish building the tug without Medmarine. It has already been discussed with Osman Toprak, and he has given his undertaking that if Frank Palmer withdraws from the joint venture, I shall be offered the job of project engineer."

Mehmet Boga was rendered momentarily speechless by this news. He glared across the massive desk at Jack in stark amazement. Did these English madmen never give up, even when the situation was hopeless?

"Osman bey has said nothing to me of this," he replied at length. "It is a ridiculous idea. It could not possibly work."

"Of course it could," insisted Jack. "I have nearly twenty years experience in this type of work. All it takes is some proper organisation."

"I refuse to discuss the matter further. I called you here to hand over the money for the 'Dalga' job, not to listen to your childish dreams."

"And I must respectfully decline. I can take instruction only from Frank, or from Osman Toprak as his personal representative. I'm sorry Mehmet."

"Then I suggest you contact one of them for instructions very soon, before my patience runs out."

Jack did telephone Osman Toprak as soon as he returned to the yard. He felt exhausted after his long vigil on the 'Dalga' and the subsequent battle with Mehmet Boga, but he was aware that both Medmarine and himself were hanging on by the finest of threads. Osman Toprak listened patiently to Jack's account of the meeting, advised him to leave the money in the Medmarine account, and promised to let Mehmet Boga know what was happening. The matter would have to await Frank Palmer's return to Cyprus.

On returning to the flat Jack flopped wearily back into an armchair and stared vacantly at the adverts on the television screen, hardly conscious of the high-pitched, insistent torrent of Greek pouring from the loud speakers.

"Well?" enquired Mary as she handed him his tea.

"Well what?" returned Jack.

"You mean to say you haven't noticed?"

He looked first at her shoes, then her skirt and finally her hair.

"Not that," she said, laughing. "On the table. Next to the TV. The telephone!"

"My God! When did that arrive?"

"Shortly after you left this morning. I've been trying to 'phone you at the office. Where have you been all day?"

"I'll tell you about it later. So it actually works, then. It's a pity we can't get through to England."

"We could try. Maybe things have improved while we've been away."

"You're right. Let's try the bank. They should still be open. Give them a call now."

To their astonishment, the connection came through in just under ten minutes. Jack could tell from the look on his wife's face that the news was not good; not a penny had been received from Frank Palmer. Would this nightmare never end?

For the next four days they checked twice a day with their bank, and tried constantly to reach Frank Palmer. All was to no avail; the telephone at Medmarine's London office rang and rang, but was never even answered. FNC produced the wages cheque on Friday without any problems, indicating that Osman Toprak had used his powers of persuasion with the FNC board members. Production on the tug was still in limbo, and once again moral in the yard slid inexorably into decline. There was also neither hide nor hair of Frank Palmer. Rumours began to circulate around the port that he was gone for good, and would never dare to show his face in Cyprus again. Jokes were made about 'Seahorse', a phantom ship that had been lured to destruction by mysterious Sirens. Even the unshakable Osman Toprak was beginning to doubt his own wisdom in promoting the joint venture.

The silence was finally broken by telex. The message was received on the machine at FNC with instructions to forward it on to Jack. It read:

"FOR THE ATTENTION OF JACK DURHAM
IT HAS COME TO MY ATTENTION THAT YOU HAVE CONTACTED THE FAMAGUSTA NAVIGATION COMPANY WITH THE DELIBERATE INTENTION OF TRYING TO CARRY ON THE CONSTRUCTION OF THE TUG ON A DIRECT BASIS AND HAVE ACTED IN A WAY THAT WOULD ONLY DISCREDIT MYSELF AND YOUR EMPLOYERS.

AFTER CONSIDERATION OF THE PROBLEMS THAT HAVE EXISTED ON BOTH SIDES AND IN VIEW OF THE ASSISTANCE I GAVE YOU IN LONDON AND YOUR ASSURANCE THAT YOU WOULD ACT IN THE BEST INTERESTS OF THE COMPANY, YOU HAVE NOW LEFT ME WITH NO ALTERNATIVE BUT TO TERMINATE YOUR EMPLOYMENT AS FROM LAST FRIDAY. I WILL BE IN CYPRUS NEXT WEEK TO FINALISE MATTERS WITH YOU.

FRANK PALMER
MEDMARINE LIMITED"

Jack sent back an immediate reply refusing to accept the dismissal and denying the accusation. He went into considerable detail regarding the money he was owed, knowing it would be read by everybody at FNC. The moment had come, he thought; time to finish the bastard off.

Muhan Timucin was his next port of call. The Director of Ports had always given Jack his full support, and could prove a valuable ally in the battle to come. Frank Palmer had failed in his first attempt to dismiss Jack; if he were made to fail in his second attempt he would look completely ridiculous and would lose any remaining credibility on the island. It was obvious that this latest desperate move was merely to disguise his inability to pay Jack what was owed.

On to Nicosia with Mary to consult Osman Toprak, who was by now a very worried man. His dream of glory in the eyes of his fellow countrymen as the man responsible for opening the port of Famagusta to international shipping was slipping away, to be replaced by a nightmare in which two crazed English gladiators were locked in a fight to the death. He cursed the day he had met Frank Palmer, and gave up a silent prayer to Almighty Allah to light his way through the dark and difficult terrain ahead. In the event he managed to remain sitting precariously on the fence, and promised Jack that an early meeting of the FNC board would be convened to decide the best way forward. Until Frank Palmer returned, Jack would still manage the shipyard on behalf of FNC, from whom he would continue to receive the local currency portion of his wages.

This bridgehead established, Jack returned to work with a will. It was of vital importance to restore morale as quickly as possible, so another thorough clean up of the yard was organised to ensure the men were kept fully occupied. They responded very well, and the old sense of urgency soon started to return. The plight of their British colleagues was general knowledge; Neil and Terry had made sure of that before they left. Now this valiant Englishman had returned, prepared to battle on by himself if need be, his family by his side. Showing him some solidarity was the very least they could do.

Jack divided his own time between physically helping with the clean up and preparing a full appraisal of the tug structure, complete with a revised production schedule through to final completion. He was assisted in this by Mary, who came in to the yard every day to type up his notes, attend to the daily correspondence, and provide support and encouragement. Twice each day she telephoned the bank in England, and twice each day she called Frank Palmer's office number only to hear an unanswered ringing tone at the other end. It was not until half way through December that she realised that Christmas would soon be upon them, and for the first time in her life she had made no preparations for the occasion. She looked across the office to Jack, busily scribbling away at his notes.

"What are we going to do about Christmas?" she enquired softly.

"I think we can assume Christmas is cancelled this year, my love," he replied without looking up from his work.

"Not in my house it isn't!" she declared, in a tone just loud enough to command the full attention of her spouse.

"Don't you think we've got enough to worry about without adding Christmas to the list? Besides, we're in a Muslim country. They don't celebrate Christmas over here."

"More's the pity, I think they would enjoy it if they did. Anyway, I'm a Christian mother with two young children, and we are jolly well going to celebrate Christmas in the usual way."

"Mary, we just can't afford it. We have to conserve every penny we've got. There's no telling how long it'll take to get rid of Frank Palmer. We could well be in for the long haul."

"I know all that, but it's beside the point. We're having a proper Christmas, and that's that."

"And I suppose I don't get a say in the matter."

"Not when you talk like that, no. I can't believe you're actually prepared to ignore Christmas. You're nothing but an old skin-flint!"

"I'm only saying…."

"I don't want to hear it, Jack!" said Mary, "Anyway, I think it would do us good and cheer us up a bit too."

Jack felt a lump rise in his throat, and a wave of shame swept over him. What sort of a creature had he become? He moved swiftly over to Mary's desk and knelt beside her.

"You're absolutely right, my love. I'm so sorry. I just wasn't thinking straight. All this business with Frank Palmer has addled my brain."

She forgave him instantly and completely, and took one of his great paws in her own small hands.

"It doesn't have to cost a fortune," she explained. "Look at last Christmas. We didn't have any money then either, but it was lovely all the same. I know we're in a bit of a fix, but we still have to think about the girls."

"We'll go down to the NAAFI shop as soon as we finish here today. I really am so sorry, my love."

"You'd better get up off your knees," she replied with a smile. "Someone might come in."

* * * * * * * *

Three days later Mary and the girls were happily engaged in decorating the flat for Christmas when they heard the front door being opened. It was Jack, and he was in a high state of excitement.

"This you'll never believe!" he cried, bursting into the room.

"Are we going to like this?" asked Mary.

"It's 'Seahorse'. She's just arrived. She's tied up at the top end of the port, near the yard."

"Good God! Does that mean Frank Palmer is here too?"

"No, no, he's not aboard. But I'll tell you who is."

"The Christmas Fairy?"

"Better than that. Her skipper is Ron Woods."

"Should that mean anything to me?"

"You remember surely. It was only a couple of years ago. He's the guy who came to tow that old minesweeper away from Marine & General. He had that little tug you liked."

"What, Timmy the Tug you mean?"

"That's the one."

"And you're telling me he's just turned up here, in Famagusta?"

"Yes. He's Frank Palmer's skipper, and you should hear what he's got to say about that! There's Ron, and three or four young English lads with him. Come on, they're waiting for us down at the harbour. He says he's dying to meet you again."

Although she would never dream of confessing to it openly, Mary did harbour a strong belief in fate, so the unexpected appearance on this far flung island of someone they actually knew was to her a highly favourable omen. As they drove down to the harbour she tried to summon a mental picture of Ron Woods, but with no success. Their previous meeting had been all too brief; nothing more than a quick look round a smelly, oily tug boat, and breakfast in a dockside greasy spoon at some ungodly hour of the morning. Her first impression when the car pulled up alongside 'Seahorse' was one of horror and dismay as she viewed the battered rusty hulk that loomed before her. She made her way up the rickety gangplank clutching Wendy's hand. Ron Woods was obviously pleased to see her again, but in reality it was like meeting a stranger. He was not a large man, but his frame was strong and wiry, with lean, muscular arms. The red of his full beard was so dark as to be almost black, and his features were lined and coloured by countless hours of exposure to sun, wind and weather. From this rough, almost forbidding countenance shone a pair of blue eyes that never ceased smiling. Ron Woods was an incurably happy man.

Down in the main saloon Ron introduced his crew, consisting of three powerful looking youngsters in their early twenties who cheerfully made room for everyone to sit around the long, narrow mess table. Although a great deal of money had been spent on her refit for civilian use, 'Seahorse' was still essentially a military ship, and the accommodation was sparse and cramped. Dripping with condensation, exposed pipework ran in all directions, and long, open gaps in every run of cable trunking testified to hurried repairs with scant resources. Worn seat cushions and peeling paint added to the general atmosphere of neglect, along with the chipped crockery and bent teaspoons.

Not to appear inhospitable, Ron opened a five-litre can of olives and poured some into a battered but spotlessly clean aluminium saucepan to hand round. They were the best olives Mary had ever tasted; huge, succulent fruits that melted in the mouth. She passed up on the offer of cheap Spanish wine, accepted a glass of bottled water, and settled down to hear the skipper's account of the voyage from England to Cyprus.

"We were buggered right from the start," he began. "Sorry, Mary, I'll just rephrase that. We were at a disadvantage right from leaving Pompy. Frank would insist on setting off before all the work was completed. We didn't know why at the time, but you know what he's like. It was the middle of the night when we cast off, and we had a good run down the channel, but just after we passed Ushant the port engine gave up the ghost. He'd told us on no account were we to put in anywhere on the way – straight through to Cyprus he said. It was alright for him, sitting in his comfortable office up in London, but we were the poor sods – sorry Mary – the poor souls who faced crossing the bay on one engine. It was absolute bloody murder, wasn't it lads?

"Well, the old girl took it like a good'un, and we made it right down to St Vincent when bugger me – sorry Mary – but the starboard engine started playing up. We didn't really have any choice. We had to put into Gib. But as soon as we tied up, the Admiralty Marshall's office slapped a writ on the mast. Then we learned why Frank had been so anxious for us to get out of Pompey. He still owed for a big chunk of the refit, and he'd got us to do a moonlight so he didn't have to pay up. What a caper! We were lucky they didn't lock us up and throw away the key.

"Anyway, we managed to get the starboard engine sorted out, but not the other bugger – sorry Mary. First thing we have to do now we're here is strip the port engine right down and get to the bottom of the trouble. By the way, Jack, have you got anyone at the yard who knows anything about marine engines?"

"I'm afraid not," confessed Jack reluctantly. "One of those things still on the to do list."

"Not to worry. We'll muddle through somehow. So Frank Palmer then turns up with a proposition. If I sneak 'Seahorse' out of Gib, he'll bump my quarter share up to a half."

"So you're part owner. I didn't realise that," said Jack with great interest.

"You don't imagine I'd have gone through all this just for wages, do you?" returned Ron, grinning through his beard. "But stuck down there in Gibraltar with no money and bugger all food – sorry Mary – I didn't really have much of a choice. Bearing in mind that my house was already mortgaged up to the hilt to get the money to buy my corner in the first place, that is. Don't ask me how we got away with it, but we actually managed to sneak out of Gib under the cover of darkness again. I think Frank did some sort of fancy footwork ashore. Don't ask me what, but I don't think we'd have got out otherwise.

"The rest of it is pretty ordinary, really, apart from getting shelled as we passed Benghazi. I thought we'd better steer well clear of Malta, just in case, so we kept pretty close to the African coastline past Libya. Suddenly there's this bloody shore battery taking pot shots at us. We retaliated, of course, in the true Nelson spirit. We pointed our little crane at them, and the shelling stopped. So there you have it. A tale of theft and deception on the high seas."

"I suppose he owes you money," said Mary.

"Not a penny have we been paid since we left Pompey. He threw us a few crumbs when he came to Gib, but that was barely enough for food and drink. We're all skint, so I bloody well hope you've got some money."

"We're in exactly the same position as you are, Ron. He owes us as well. We're just scratching along in the shipyard waiting for him to show up. He's even tried to sack me, twice, just to get out of paying what he owes."

"Yeah. He's a slippery one right enough. But what's your story, Jack? How come you're here?"

Jack gave him a quick rundown of events to date, at the end of which Ron vented a long, low whistle.

"Bugger me – sorry Mary – is there no end to that man's depravity? I thought my situation was bad enough, but at least I've got the chance of making some serious dough once we lick this old tub into shape. But if the natives don't take you up on your offer to finish the tug yourself you're buggered, aren't you? I am so sorry Mary. Force of habit I'm afraid."

Mary just smiled and asked:

"Have you any idea at all when Frank Palmer is coming back to Cyprus?"

"I wouldn't think it'll be till after Christmas. We're all flying back to Blighty in a couple days time for the holidays. He's supposed to be taking me and the lads out to dinner on Christmas Eve. Some posh gaff up the West End. You're not staying here for Christmas, are you?"

"We have to," replied Jack. "There isn't any choice. We have to be here when he shows up, and we don't know when that'll be. It would be just our luck to miss him if we went home."

* * * * * * * *

Christmas was a desolate affair for Jack and Mary, starting from the moment Ron and his crew departed for England. Losing the company of this easy going, cheerful little band of pirates heightened their sense of isolation and reminded them yet again how vulnerable they were. The total indifference of Famagusta to the cherished festival of Christmas compelled them to spend much of their time in the English Sovereign Base Area at Ayios Nikolaos. On Christmas morning they had a bad argument arising from Jack's miserly and indifferent attitude; he had not even bothered to buy his bride of six weeks a card. They called a truce over lunch, which Mary had taken great pains to make as festive as circumstances permitted, but even that was overshadowed by Wendy being unwell with Cyprus blister. It looked so bad that Mary decided it should be seen by a doctor, so they spent two hours or more at the hospital. Here again, there was no sign of Christmas in the vast, cold, impassive building, and the doctor examined Wendy with a cigarette dangling from his lips. Mary fumed inwardly at the man's slovenly, offhand attitude, but held her tongue knowing how ineffective any protest would be.

On Boxing Day Frank Palmer arrived, and Jack was invited to an emergency meeting of the joint venture board, this time at the office of Muhan Timucin. As usual, accusations flew in all directions, but with the Port Director in his corner Jack won the day, resulting in full reinstatement as shipyard manager. Both Osman Toprak and Mehmet Boga kept their heads well below the parapet in case a stray shot came their way, but it was the blood of Frank Palmer that stained the boardroom carpet at the end of the day. In any other circumstances his injuries would have proved fatal, but yet again he emerged from the fray bloody but unbowed. The man appeared to have more lives than a cat.

Back at the yard office Frank Palmer and Jack had their own private meeting. Once again they reached an agreement as to the amount of money that was owing, and once again Frank Palmer promised to settle up as soon as he returned to the UK. Jack knew that it was all a waste of time, but he also knew that due process had to be followed if his takeover plan was ultimately to succeed. He handed over the keys to the Efkav flat, and the deposit slip for the cash paid into the Medmarine account. There was an air of finality about their handshake as Frank Palmer took his leave; both men understood it would be a fight to the finish, with no quarter given.

One bright spot on an otherwise bleak horizon was the New Year's Eve party Kaplan had arranged at the Plâj Hotel. It was to be a full dinner-dance affair with a top band from Nicosia, and Mary was looking forward to it immensely. A family room had been reserved for them, which meant they would be able to make a day of it. They arrived shortly after midday, and were met in the lobby by Kaplan, who was delighted to see them.

"You'll need to book in, of course," he said, "but we needn't bother with passports, seeing as you're practically locals now."

"Is Sunara not on duty today?" asked Mary casually.

"No. I'm afraid I had to let her go. Caught her with her fingers in the till. If there's one thing I can't stand it's sticky fingers. You expect the odd bottle of beer or bar of soap to go missing, but when it comes to handfuls of cash, that's a different matter. They'd been at it for months, her and her husband – it must have cost me a fortune."

They all made their way into the bar, where a magnificent log fire crackled out its warm welcome. Kaplan ordered sandwiches for them before hurrying off to supervise preparations for the evening's event; there was an air of bustle and anticipation throughout the whole hotel which contrasted vividly in Mary's mind with the sluggish depressing atmosphere of limbo at the shipyard. She would have loved to help in the preparations, to be part of the activity which surrounded her, but had to content herself with the thought that at least they would not be spending New Year's Eve on their own in the flat, watching television programmes in Greek.

In the afternoon the family went for a walk along the beach to the Roman ruins. The weather was perfect for the occasion with the wintry sun, suspended low in a pale, nacreous sky, shedding an almost holy light over the deserted amphitheatre. Mary thought wistfully back to the day when her steps had first brought her to this beautiful place. She watched the children as they renewed their acquaintance with the ancient stones, remembering how Wendy had grazed her knee and Susan had kissed it better. Even Jack's thoughts rose above his dark, brooding obsession with Frank Palmer as he sat next to his wife, savouring the sacred atmosphere with her. They walked back arm in arm, remembering those glorious sun drenched days of summer when the year held so much promise, and they had basked in the warmth of Dame Fortune's smile.

As the family entered the hotel ballroom for dinner that evening Mary was delighted by the festive atmosphere. Balloons, banners and bunting covered the entire ceiling; gleaming gold-painted cardboard decorations festooned every window; spotlights blazed all over the room. A large mirrored ball turned slowly over the dance floor, scattering darts of light in every direction to bounce yet again off gleaming cutlery and sparkling glassware. Brightly coloured crackers and shiny party hats adorned all the tables, to which splendidly dressed ladies with their penguin suited escorts were being led by keenly attentive waiters.

Jack and his ladies were shown to their own table by young Ishmael, his face beaming with pleasure at being recognised by Mary. She settled into her seat and looked round at all the smiling faces for anyone she might recognise. Selim Captain was there with his pretty young wife; so too was Muhan Timucin, with his stout, jolly wife and two children in their late teens. At a table over on the far side of the room sat Kemal Aydin, who happened to look up and wave as their gazes met. There was no sign of Osman Toprak or Mehmet Boga, so Mary assumed they would be at another function, probably at the Dome in Kyrenia.

By time the band started to tune up the room was packed to capacity. In came the first course, delivered with a military precision that was a tribute to Kaplan's draconian training methods. The quality of both the food and the wine was superb, inspiring Jack to ask Mary for a dance well before the dessert was served. Being the first couple onto the floor their daring was rewarded with a light ripple of applause, punctuated by a cry of encouragement from Kemal Aydin. Jack did surprisingly well, considering he danced so rarely; his steps seemed to be guided by the magical influence of the evening, so powerful was its effect. To Mary's everlasting wonder they returned to the floor again and again, Jack's confidence increasing with each visit.

Not long before midnight Kaplan came over and asked Mary to dance. As they moved slowly across the floor he opened the conversation with his usual demand.

"When are you going to come and work for me, Mary?"

"You'd better be careful. I might even have to take you up on that if things don't improve,"

"Frank still messing you about with money?"

"Yes, he is. But I'd rather not talk about that just now. I just want to enjoy the evening. I really didn't expect anything like this."

"New Year is a big thing over here. I suppose it's stayed with us from the days of British Rule. You'll notice most of the people here are old enough to remember those times. I think they probably miss all the excitement of Christmas as much as you. How was your Christmas, by the way?"

"That's another thing I don't want to talk about. But this evening makes up for everything. Thank you once again for inviting us."

"The best is yet to come. Things get really lively after midnight. You wait till you see all these fat ladies doing a Scottish jig."

"I love Scottish dancing!" cried Mary in delight. "I learned to do it in school. We had a Scottish teacher one year, and she taught us all the steps. She says I was quite good at it."

"Now why doesn't that surprise me?" said Kaplan with a chuckle

After a deafening climax at midnight, the band struck up a Scottish reel. Mary could vaguely remember what she had learned, but it had certainly been nothing like the wild paroxysm into which Jack flung himself in response to the music. She tried to keep up with him as he performed his version of a highland fling, but under the influence of far too much wine he whirled her round with such violence that her head started spinning. Ultimately the band switched to a wild Eastern dervish tune, whereupon all the ladies hurried back to their tables while their dignity was still intact, leaving their men to compete with each other in a primitive excess of testosterone. In the thick of this mayhem was Jack, his perspiring face lit up with a manic expression of defiance as he cavorted absurdly through the can-can into the fortieth new year of his life.

* * * * *

"Monday 1ˢᵗ January 1979

What new horizons are promised us in this year of 1979-I wonder? A jolly good start, last night at the party – or I should say end to 1978. Jack really let his hair down – was it an explosion of pent up emotion following the frustration of the last few months – mayhap?

Kaplan made me another offer of a job at the hotel – I was wondering whether to take it, particularly if he were to pay me in sterling – that would bolster our finances somewhat. Although I don't think Jack would approve. Can't think why!

I still haven't heard from Julia – perhaps she's been away to London. I think I'll give her a ring next week and wish her 'A Happy New Year', to get the ball rolling; it would be good to know if there <u>is</u> anything wrong. Also I have missed our little get togethers – I do enjoy our lunch and a chat.

Chapter Twenty-three

With the New Year came a complete change in Jack's outlook, despite the fact that nothing had been paid into the bank account in England. He sat down with Mary to plan their strategy, and the first thing they decided was to enrol both Susan and Wendy with the local schools in Famagusta. It was a drastic step, but they were both convinced that it would be for the best. Immigrant children in England often started their school life without the advantage of speaking the language; why should it not work the other way round? Susan had already picked up enough Turkish as a result of Suleyman's tuition to enable her to make friends, and Wendy would soon catch up with similar help. The schools were clean and well run, and the teachers spoke English to varying degrees, so it was well worth a try. If the idea failed to work out they could always go back to morning lessons with Mary, which had been quite successful in the past.

Mary was confident that Susan would thrive in the somewhat unusual environment, whatever the language difficulty at first. She was not so sure about Wendy, however, who had no previous experience of school life. A child's first day at school was a big enough step in itself, but having to cope with a foreign language at the same time could well prove to be a major stumbling block. But Wendy marched off confidently hand in hand with her new teacher with never a backward glance at her mother, standing at the edge of the playground. When Mary arrived to collect her child at the end of the school day, she had to prise her away from a crowd of eager little admirers, all anxious to be her best friend. The teacher could not praise her new pupil highly enough; she said Wendy's presence had inspired the whole class, which had behaved better and worked more diligently than at any time in the past.

Not to be outdone in the academic stakes, Jack settled down seriously to the task of learning Turkish himself, and found the language to be reassuringly straightforward and logical. For two hours each evening he poured over his grammar book and preliminary reader, scribbling page after page of exercises in an old notebook. Every day saw an improvement in his spoken Turkish, which gradually made him more effective in the yard. His time would come, and when it did he would not be lacking in communication skills.

When Ron Woods and the crew of 'Seahorse' returned after nearly a month in England, social life also took a turn for the better. Most days they all met up for an hour or so after Mary had collected the children from school, sometimes at the café in the main square, or more often on board the ship in what was jokingly referred to as the stateroom. They usually played cards, or sometimes backgammon, a game at which Susan mercilessly trounced all comers. The rest of the time Ron and the lads worked on stripping down and rebuilding the engines, chipping away at the rust, or slapping on gallons of navy surplus battleship grey paint, turning 'Seahorse' from a slow, wallowing rust-bucket into the fine ro-ro ship that would make them all rich.

Work started picking up at the yard, consisting mainly of small fabrication jobs and some occasional light engineering projects for the machine shop. Jack also agreed a special rate for the carpenters to tackle the planking on the old trawler still sitting on the slipway. It was important to him that this crumbling eyesore should be removed as soon as possible, and he now did all he could to co-operate with the owners. No effort was spared in preparation for the day when work on the tug would be resumed, which Jack truly believed would be soon.

* * * * *

"Tuesday 23rd January

Susan and Wendy have settled well into their new schools, and enjoying themselves into the bargain, which is such a relief.

Also it was good to welcome the chaps from 'Seahorse' back, they are a friendly bunch of guys, and Jack now has someone to tell his troubles to – apart from me that is. Talking to another man in the same 'boat' – so to speak – Ron has a better understanding of what Jack is going through.

I was on the point of 'phoning Julie last week when she called me. It was really good to hear from her, and she sounded like her old self. We are meeting up in February for lunch. Looking forward to that very much.

* * * * *

By the end of January life had again settled into a routine; the situation was not ideal, but Mary resolutely made the best of it. Each school day she walked with the girls into the old city before going on to the yard. She enjoyed this time of the day, with the crisp winter air colouring their cheeks as they strolled through the narrow streets chatting casually about nothing in particular. Most of the tiny stone built terraced houses along their route had front doors opening straight onto the cobbled pavements. Was it just coincidence that so many Cypriot matrons happened to be shaking their mats or cleaning the outside of their parlour windows as Mary and the girls passed by? It was not long before the exchange of friendly smiles blossomed into words, sometimes about the weather, other times praising the girls' appearance. Most charming of all was the daily reception for Wendy by her fellow pupils as they lined themselves along the playground perimeter, calling her name and thrusting their arms through the boundary railings to touch her blond hair as she passed.

Less charming was the occasion on which Wendy went missing. Mary arrived at the school to collect her at the normal time, but the child was nowhere to be seen. The usual crowd of mothers waiting at the gate soon sensed Mary's distress and started grilling their own offspring with sufficient severity to render them speechless with fright. Mary was sick with worry, but maintained an outward appearance of calm as she walked over to the school building in search of a teacher who could speak English. A thorough search of the entire premises yielded never a clue; Wendy had simply been spirited away. The head teacher was just about to telephone the police when a commotion in the corridor outside his study indicated that some news might have broken. A small boy was frogmarched into the room by his mother, who proceeded to smack the back of his head until he repeated what he had told her outside in the playground. He had seen Wendy going off up the street with another little girl.

Once the abductress had been identified, her address was soon found, and an anxious, but now hopeful Mary accompanied Wendy's own teacher to a small block of flats at no large distance from the school. Heart pounding, she entered the shabby building with her guide and climbed a steep concrete stairway to a landing with two nondescript doors. There was no response to her urgent knocking at the first door, but the other door was opened impatiently by a stout, elderly woman wanting to know the cause of all the noise. Yes, the little English girl was here. She had been invited for tea. Why, was there anything wrong?

* * * * * * *

It was on a cold, windy afternoon early in February that Frank Palmer eventually showed up at the yard, accompanied by two men in their middle twenties. Incredulously, Jack found himself shaking hands with two newly recruited English steelworkers who were to form the nucleus of his fabrication team; more would follow as soon as they were needed, once work on the tug had been resumed. Never, in all the hours spent plotting and planning, had Jack even so much as considered such a move; once more he had underestimated the cunning and tenacity of his adversary. He had been outmanoeuvred yet again. If he accepted the situation he would be forced to resume work on the tug as Frank Palmer's creature; if he refused to co-operate he would be forced to walk the plank for mutiny. To make matters worse, Frank Palmer still appeared to have the support of FNC. The men would be housed in the flat over the offices, and would go on the shipyard payroll for the local currency portion of their wages.

Mary's reaction to this turn of events was typically philosophical.

"I don't see what you're worried about," she said after listening to Jack's mournful account of the event over afternoon tea. "Those two won't hang around for long once they hear about all the trouble Frank Palmer's in, and all the misery he's put everyone through. He didn't mention anything about our money, I suppose?"

"As a matter of fact, he did," replied Jack with a guffaw. "I've been saving the best bit 'till last. He has sent our bank a cheque for six thousand Dutch guilders!"

She burst into laughter and said:

"My God! You just could not make this up! You did say Dutch guilders? Why not Indian rupees or South American escudos? How does he come up with this stuff?"

"Apparently he's moved all his money into an account with the Amsterdam-Rotterdam Bank as part of the big plan to go offshore. It all sounds a bit far-fetched, but with Frank Palmer you just never know."

"I suppose the first step is to 'phone the bank and find out," suggested Mary, reaching for the receiver. "Dutch guilders! Whatever will that man come up with next?"

The bank manager was most relieved to receive her call. Yes, they had received the cheque and presented it for clearance, which would take about three weeks and involve quite high charges. And when would they be returning to England? He had received a call that very day from Jack's trustee asking for the January payment, which had not been made due to insufficient funds. Mary replaced the handset thoughtfully; a stratagem was forming in her mind that could turn the situation a little more to their advantage.

"How about taking a spot of home leave?" she said slowly. "On medical grounds."

"What medical grounds? We're all as fit as fleas."

"Stress. You're suffering from stress and need to consult your own doctor. You have lost a lot of weight – that's a sure sign of stress."

A smile slowly started to spread over Jack's face as he began to understand.

"Think about it," she continued. "It will give us the chance of explaining the situation to the trustee. She'll understand when she knows what's been happening. We can also keep tabs on that cheque, just on the off chance that it's genuine. But best of all, you won't be here for Frank Palmer and his little chums to pick your brain. Without you they're bound to make a mess of it."

"God, I'm glad you're on my side," declared Jack, taking her in his arms. "Lucretia Borgia has nothing on you."

"It's just common sense, that's all," she replied, reaching up to kiss him. "Now put me down and I'll go and start packing. We might even be able to get a flight tomorrow."

* * * * *

"Thursday 8th February

Arrived home in the wee small hours after the most horrendous journey yet – the flight between Ercan and Istanbul was bad enough, but when we were airborne from Istanbul to London two swarthy looking types jumped up from their seats – one ran down to the back of the plane while the other grabbed the microphone from the stewardess and rattled away excitedly in Turkish. Jack and I looked at each other both thinking the same – hi-jack. When the man finished talking the Turkish passengers erupted in cheers and clapping. Jack asked the chap across the aisle what was it was all about and learned there had been some change in their government. What a relief!

"We were up early to make sure we got down to the bank as soon as it opened. No money, of course, and no news yet from Holland about FP's latest bit of nonsense. We did manage to exchange just enough Turkish lira to make January's payment to the trustee. God only knows what we'll do at the end of this month if no money comes through.

"We saw the trustee in the afternoon, and she was very helpful again. When we explained the whole situation she told us not to worry. She even offered to go

after FP on our behalf, but Jack said no. He said it would only make things difficult in Cyprus if word got round about his bankruptcy.

"It's lovely to be home, but the weather is bitterly cold after Cyprus. Thank heavens for our lovely log fire! I'd completely forgotten how cold our bedrooms are in the winter – there was ice on the inside of all the windows when we got up this morning.

"We're going up to London tomorrow to see if there's anything going on at FP's office. We'll have to go up by train because the poor old Wolseley seems to have given up the ghost."

* * * * *

As the day was fine it was decided to walk the mile or so from Waterloo station up to the Medmarine offices. They went via Trafalgar Square so that Susan and Wendy could feed the pigeons, and strolled at a leisurely pace along Regent Street for Jack to admire the architecture. On reaching their destination they found the street door of the office building was open so they entered, with quite unnecessary stealth, and made their way softly up the creaking wooden staircase, as if they were hoping to catch Frank Palmer in some undefined act of malfeasance as long as they made no sound.

The outer office door was locked; Jack peered through the keyhole and whispered that he could see the desks and what appeared to be a divan bed, but no people. He tried the other doors on the landing to find them all locked shut, and continued on up another flight of stairs to the second floor. Daylight filtered feebly through a grimy skylight, but there was no sign of life and all the doors were locked. A damp, desolate air of neglect hung over the entire building, and Mary was relieved when they were back outside again.

Across the street Kaplan was looking out of his restaurant window wondering, as he did at this same time every year, if trade was ever going to pick up again. He let out an involuntary cry of surprise and delight when he spotted Mary's red bobble hat and recognised the wearer. In a trice he was at the door, calling them in out of the February chill. They were ushered into a cosy booth at the back of the restaurant, and were joined by Kaplan who pulled up a chair at the end of the table.

"You've been over the road, I suppose," he said solicitously. "You will not find much joy there, I'm afraid. I haven't seen him for weeks."

"He's in Cyprus. He arrived a week or so ago," returned Jack.

"The nerve of that man! And what about you? Are you back for good?"

"No, no. We're just home for a spot of leave, and to sort out some stuff at the bank."

"He's still messing you about for money, then. I can't understand why you put up with it."

"It's all part of the master plan," explained Mary. "We're just playing the waiting game."

"I suppose it might pay you to hang on for a while. I can't see that he'll last much longer in Cyprus. Osman Toprak's just about had enough of it all, and without his support Frank has no chance."

"What is it with those two?" asked Jack. "It's almost as if Frank has some sort of hold on Osman."

"Well, I suppose you could say that," replied Kaplan hesitantly. "They go way back – before the troubles. I never did know the full details, but Osman owned a little passenger ship that used to do the run across to Crete. When the war started, the ship happened to be in Iraklion, so he was worried that it might be grabbed by the Greeks. To make sure that didn't happen Osman transferred ownership over to one of Frank's companies in exchange for shares. For some reason or other the ship has stayed in Crete ever since."

"I knew there had to be something," said Jack. "Poor old Osman Toprak!"

* * * * * * * *

When the Rotterdam cheque was returned unpaid due to lack of funds it was not exactly unexpected. As far as Jack was concerned it was a further indication that Frank Palmer was struggling to survive against ever mounting odds, and was rapidly running out of room to manoeuvre. The situation had developed into a war of attrition, so it was important to maintain a cool head and steady nerves, but from now on nothing short of Frank Palmer's total annihilation was going to satisfy Jack's longing for revenge. It truly was an obsession, a compulsion to win at all costs, regardless of the financial consequences should he lose. He was convinced that right was on his side and that he would ultimately prevail.

So back to Cyprus they all trekked to join battle once again, only to find that the enemy had decamped and was nowhere near the field of combat. On the day before their return 'Seahorse' had left for Tripoli, her cargo deck crammed to capacity with lorries conveying boxes of oranges. Frank Palmer had sailed with them, and was not expected back for at least a week. The bearer of these tidings was Mehmet Boga, who was looking far from well as he stared abjectly across the expanse of his desk at Jack. Since his promotion to the exalted heights of senior management he had always been so skilful in avoiding trouble, taking great care to ensure there was always a scapegoat in case of need. Now trouble was arriving from so many different directions and at such a relentless pace that he had been overwhelmed. As far as he was concerned, the problems with the joint venture had spiralled out of control, and he found himself right in the middle of a disaster zone with no bolthole and not a scapegoat in sight.

On his return to the yard Jack was treated to another really warm welcome from the Cypriot workers. The two British newcomers had already gone home with the inevitable result that production on the tug was once again at a complete standstill. A brief inspection of the work that had been carried out in his absence revealed a number of problems that would require extensive rectification. It was abundantly clear that Frank Palmer had again taken on a couple of random, semi-skilled steel fabrication workers at face value in a desperate attempt to keep the tug project alive.

As he walked home on that sullen February afternoon Jack took thoughtful stock of the new situation. With the two British steelworkers out of the way his first impulse was to seize the initiative by starting rectification work on the tug structure. He was sure he could count on the support of Kemal Aydin for corroboration as to the necessity. On further consideration, however, he decided against the idea; any work on the tug at this stage of the game could only redound to the credit of Frank Palmer. Better to continue in the present state of limbo until 'Seahorse' returned from Tripoli.

To occupy his time as profitably as the circumstances would permit, Jack started work on yet another technical appraisal of the tug project, for which he enlisted the support of Kemal Aydin. They spent several hours inspecting the structure, taking careful measurements as they progressed from one frame to the next, and produced a detailed report that would represent the basis for resumption of work. It did not make pleasant reading; eight frames at the stern would have to be removed for rectification, and the recently fitted chine bars would have to be replaced entirely. Ten tonnes of steel plate had disappeared from the stockpile, as had many precious gas bottles and a large quantity of other consumables, presumably all sold off by Frank Palmer at some point to raise cash. In short, the position was now critical.

When the job was finished, Kemal Aydin took Jack and Mary round to the Famagusta office of Navko, the port's main shipping agents, and introduced them to the principal, Ozer Dastan. The firm had always been agents for FNC, and had also been appointed to act for Frank Palmer since the arrival of *Seahorse*. Ozer wanted to meet Jack in the hope that he could learn more about his new client and gauge the truth of various rumours that had been circulating ever since *Seahorse* sailed for Tripoli. He was the third generation of the Dastan dynasty, and had grown up with the business that he now ran with a restless energy combined with an urbane and courteous manner acquired from a first class education in England. The agency's success under his leadership had enabled him to branch out into other activities very early in his career, making him one of the most successful businessmen in Northern Cyprus.

Sitting in his tastefully furnished office they all made the usual small talk for a few minutes, but it did not take Ozer long to bring the conversation round to the subject of Frank Palmer.

"Usually I take no notice of port gossip," said Ozer, "but I've got an angry Kurdish sea captain who comes in two or three times a day demanding to see Frank Palmer, and he's starting to frighten the girls. He says he paid Frank in advance for a VHF set, and has heard nothing since. Now he's saying if he doesn't get either the radio or his money back he wants Palmer's head on a stick. The trouble is, I think he really means it. You never know with a Kurd. They shoot first and ask questions later. Then there's all this business about owing money to FNC and the trouble with the tug. Now I'm even hearing stories about some Gibraltar tobacco barons who are looking for him. Apparently they made a considerable payment up front for a high-speed launch he sold them for moving contraband across the Straits, and they're still waiting for their boat. I just don't know what to make of it all, and Kemal thought it might be a good idea for us to compare notes. Is Frank Palmer really some sort of international crook, or what?"

"I don't know anything about tobacco barons," replied Jack, "but I can confirm the tug project is in deep financial trouble. Apart from the money Frank Palmer owes FNC, he owes quite a bit to me personally, and I'm aware of other debts in England and the Channel Islands, and possibly the authorities in Gibraltar. The man just spreads financial chaos like a virus. He should have been thrown out of Cyprus months ago, but he does have one very strong ally, and that's how he manages to keep going."

"You mean Osman Toprak?"

Jack said nothing, but shrugged his shoulders in resignation. There was a long silence before Ozer spoke again.

"Kemal tells me that you could easily finish the tug without Frank Palmer. What's stopping you from doing it?"

"I can't take the job over until Frank Palmer is completely out of the picture. Officially, the joint venture agreement is still in force, so I have to wait until it is formally cancelled. But it seems as long as there's a chance he'll pull through, the support is still there."

"But what chance has he got of pulling through now? None at all, by the sound of it."

"I think his plan is to subsidise the tug project with earnings from *Seahorse*. She's his one and only chance as far as I know."

Both Ozer and Kemal burst out laughing together.

"In that case he really is finished," declared Ozer. "He'll be lucky to cover his fuel bill on this Tripoli run. *Seahorse* is nothing but a glorified tank landing craft. There's no place for a ship like that in Famagusta. I only took on the agency as a favour to Osman Toprak. That's the last favour he'll ever get from me, the crafty old dog!"

"Well at least you won't wind up out of pocket like the rest of us," returned Jack.

"Don't you believe it. I let him charge his fuel bill to our account!"

Now it was the turn of Jack and Mary to laugh. How on earth did the man do it?

"Coming back to the tug," continued Ozer, "do you really think you could run the job on your own?"

"Of course. There's no doubt about it."

"What about the financial side. Have you got anything in mind?"

"The money would either have to come from FNC or from the Government."

"Have you ever considered private funding?"

"It has never crossed my mind," replied Jack. "Why, do you think there would be any interest?"

"There could well be. I think you'd find quite a lot of support within the business community here in Famagusta. We've all been following your progress ever since you arrived on the Island, and I can tell you there's a lot of sympathy for your situation. What we can't understand is why you've put up with Frank Palmer for so long."

"We always thought he would pull through, with the help of the ally I mentioned."

"Osman Toprak doesn't run the whole bloody island, despite what he might think. If I were you I wouldn't rule out the possibility of building the tug without

Osman Toprak, or FNC, or for that matter the bloody Government. Just think about it, is all I'm saying."

Jack did think about it. He thought of little else for days, turning every possible detail over and over again in his mind. But his thinking was still clouded by his visceral need for victory over Frank Palmer. There had to be one final, conclusive battle, with the winner taking all.

* * * * *

"Tuesday 27th February

At last Julia and I have found time for that long overdue lunch date. She drove over to Famagusta this morning and we went to the Sands Hotel. We were both very well received there, and the manager asked after Osman – Julia said they were distant cousins – everyone here seems to be related to everyone else! Anyway we had a lovely lunch of fillet steak with salad. We chatted away about our children and she asked after Jack – if he was well etc. I asked after Osman and she said he was not himself lately, not sleeping and very moody – personally he strikes me as being the 'moody' type! She apologised for cancelling our last lunch date but things had become rather difficult between her and Osman. I had the feeling she wanted to say more but held back.

Walking back to her car she asked if I would like to spend a couple of days with her in Kyrenia next month – with the children of course – but she didn't mention anything about Jack. I was a bit stumped for a reply, but I did agree if Jack was OK with it.

* * * * *

Seahorse did not return to Famagusta on her due date, nor was there any explanation for the delay either by telephone, telex or radio. There was no way of communicating with the vessel, so there was nothing to do but wait. Days passed by without any news, and into their usual routine Jack and Mary incorporated a daily visit to Navko, where they frequently stayed for an hour or so chatting with Ozer and drinking tea. He always had time to spend with his two new friends; Mary's quick mind delighted him, as did her throaty chuckle, bright smile and shapely figure. Her knowledge of shipbuilding amused him immensely, and he thought Jack a very lucky man. As he came to know them better, Ozer grew more and more convinced that the idea of funding the tug project with private money would work. But first he must find a way to rid Cyprus of that charlatan Palmer

When *Seahorse* finally did arrive she slipped unannounced into port shortly after midnight on Sunday morning, and tied up at her usual berth. Jack did not learn about the event until several hours later when he received a telephone call at home from Ozer Dastan just after dawn. Within ten minutes Jack was on his way by taxi down to the quayside. There she was, sure enough, with the crew busily occupied hosing and sweeping down the empty deck. Ron Woods was standing on the dockside talking to a customs official. He saw Jack and gave him a cheery wave.

"Is Frank still aboard?" asked Jack.

"I'm afraid not, old chap. He's gone back to his flat to get some sleep."

"How was the trip?"

"Bad to start with, but then it got worse. What say we meet up at the coffee shop in half an hour, and I'll tell you all about it?"

Over breakfast in a dingy little harbour snack bar, Ron Woods gave his account of the voyage to Tripoli. After a smooth crossing they dropped anchor outside the harbour to await berthing instructions, but after three days they still did not have permission to enter. Frank Palmer took the ship's launch into Tripoli to tackle the problem, but returned after four frustrating days without success. By this time the mood amongst the thirty or so lorry drivers was turning ugly. Cooped up on a small ship with no recreation facilities and nothing to do but play backgammon or cards, they had long since lost the sense of camaraderie that had marked the beginning of their voyage. Conflicts of personality were breaking out all over the vessel, and on two occasions violence very nearly flared up over the outcome of a card game. To make matters worse, the galley was running short of food, and the drivers had taken to eating oranges all day long to stave off the hunger. The resultant overload on the heads had added to the ship's misery, with desperate men resorting to the use of buckets.

Worst of all was the fact that the cargo of oranges had started to spoil. There had been a period of particularly fine weather in the eastern Mediterranean, and the fruit had been exposed to the blazing sun every day for a week. Orange juice had started to seep out of the crates, eventually dripping down onto the steel deck below where it congealed into sticky blobs with the adhesive power of super-glue. As each day passed the rate of dripping increased, to the extent that the deck had to be pressure hosed down with seawater at least once in every four-hour watch.

Again Frank Palmer went ashore in a last desperate attempt to make the authorities see reason, but rather unwisely he spoke sharply to a customs official. He was promptly relieved of his passport and spent two days in a detention cell before being released with a strong warning that he was not to return. Whilst all this was happening, Ron Woods was facing a mutinous band of starving lorry drivers who threatened to throw him and his crew over the side if he did not weigh anchor and return immediately to Famagusta, preferably without Frank Palmer. With his decks coated in congealed, orange juice, his newly painted bulwarks streaked with human excrement, and hardly a morsel of food aboard, even Ron's relentless optimism was in danger of giving way, but he did manage to hold out long enough for the launch to be spotted leaving the harbour entrance. He had already given the order to start engines and go to single anchor when a badly shaken Frank Palmer clambered aboard at the eleventh hour.

Radio silence on the approach to Famagusta had been Frank Palmer's idea, as was the carefully timed arrival in the small hours of Sunday morning. As soon as *Seahorse* had berthed, the drivers more or less took over. Completely ignoring all the usual formalities they simply drove their lorries off the ship and disappeared hungrily into the Cypriot hinterland.

"So, what happens now?" asked Jack when Ron had finished his extraordinary tale.

"I've absolutely no idea, old bean. Your guess is every bit as good as mine. I own half a ship but haven't got any money. I can't even feed the crew, let alone pay them any wages. The other half is owned by a con artist who also happens to be as mad as a hatter. My home is mortgaged up to the hilt, I've bugger all income, and I'm stranded thousands of miles from home on a God forsaken island that the rest of the world doesn't want to know. So as you can see, my cup fucking well runneth over!"

* * * * * * * *

Frank Palmer was already at the yard when Jack arrived for work just before eight on the following morning. He appeared to be well rested, in a surprisingly good mood, and greeted Jack like a long lost brother.

"I suppose you've heard all about the fiasco in Tripoli from Ron," he said with a chuckle.

"Yes. I'm really sorry it didn't work out. Better luck next time, perhaps."

"Well, you know how it is. These things happen from time to time. What doesn't kill you makes you stronger, I always say. But it has left me a bit short of funds, so you might have to wait a couple of days for last month's money."

"I'm sorry Frank, but you owe a lot more than a month. It's actually three months. That cheque for six thousand guilders bounced I'm afraid."

"Oh, that's not possible. I'm sure I left enough in to cover that. Did you try re-presenting it?"

"Of course not. I wasn't going to pay another lot of charges just to be told again that there were no funds."

"Well I don't know what's gone wrong, but I promise I'll get it sorted straight away. I'm flying back to the UK today, so let me have a note of what I owe you and I'll have the money in your account by the end of the week."

Jack smiled, but said nothing. He had heard it all before.

"No, I mean it Jack," insisted Frank Palmer. "I'm completing the sale of *Surveyor* in two days' time, and the money will be in your account by Friday. I'll probably be away for a couple of weeks, so I'd like you to keep an eye on the flat for me. Here are the keys. You can help yourself to booze and what's in the fridge. I'll be out and about for most of the time so there won't be a lot of point trying to contact me at the office. You can always leave a message and I'll get back to you. Anyway, you know the ropes by now, so you should be alright holding the fort until I get back."

Again, Jack could find nothing to say, but his smile had disappeared. He was listening to a man who had apparently lost all touch with reality. There was absolutely no point arguing with him. It was a positive relief when Frank Palmer's taxi arrived to take him off to the airport, and as the two men shook hands Jack offered up a silent prayer that it would be for the last time. For some time afterwards he sat in his office deep in thought before picking up the telephone to call Mary, just to hear the reassuring sound of her voice.

In the afternoon Jack had a visit from Ron Woods, looking tired and drawn; he had just been served with a writ against *Seahorse* on behalf of the authorities in Gibraltar. With Frank Palmer gone, Ron faced full responsibility on his own, and he had no way of finding anything like the money being demanded. Jack offered to take him on at the yard as general foreman, but even at the maximum pay rate available it would take months to free the ship. Unless Navko could come up with a shipping contract that would pay a substantial sum in advance Ron would have no option but to return home and face destitution.

The following day three more writs were served on *Seahorse*, and the police arrived with a warrant for the arrest of Frank Palmer on charges of fraud. Not only had the same half share in the ship been sold three times to three different people, but it had also been used to secure substantial loans with two branches of the same bank. It would take forever to sort out the mess, and Ron knew there would be precious little left once the vultures had taken their share. His one consolation lay in the fact that Frank Palmer would not be able to set foot on the island ever again.

Chapter Twenty-four

Following Frank Palmer's ignominious departure, an emergency meeting of the Famagusta Navigation Company's board was convened at Osman Toprak's headquarters in Nicosia. Jack was asked along as the only surviving representative of Medmarine Limited, and Mary was also invited to attend because she always made such a good job of taking down the minutes. With no transport of their own they had to take the Itimat taxi, which as usual was full to capacity. Mary ended up on the back seat squeezed uncomfortably between Jack and a fat, perspiring businessman, whilst a trio of murderous looking uniformed Turkish soldiers in the centre row of seats chain smoked throughout the whole journey. By the time they arrived in Nicosia Mary's throat was raw from the coarse, mephitic fumes.

As they entered the boardroom, Jack and Mary could see straight away that a prior conference had already taken place. Osman Toprak was in his usual place at the head of the table, with Mehmed Boga on his right and Muhan Timucin to his left. Jack took the seat next to Muhan Timucin, and Mary sat next to him on the end. This arrangement was not to Osman Toprak's liking, so he abandoned his chairman's throne of splendour and moved his papers down the table to sit next to Mehmet Boga, bringing him opposite to Jack.

"Shall we proceed straight to the relevant item on the agenda?" began Osman Toprak. "I think we're all familiar with the background on this, and the reason we have asked Jack and Mary to attend this meeting. I'm afraid that it is my painful duty to inform you that it will not be possible for Famagusta Navigation to fund the building of the tug. The whole project is to be postponed indefinitely until…."

"But last August you promised…" protested Jack.

"Please hear me out Jack," insisted Osman Toprak. "I know exactly what I said in August, but the whole situation has changed completely since then. We have discovered that the scale of Mr. Frank Palmer's fraudulent activities has been far worse than we thought. Not only does he owe this company more than two and a half million Turkish lira, but he has also managed to take every penny of the Sterling which was set aside for the later stage payments for the tug."

"How the hell could he have done that without actually robbing the bank?" demanded Jack.

"Through a company called Skegmar, which provided false shipping documentation that fooled not only us, but our London bankers as well. It was not until the money was all gone that we found out Frank Palmer controlled Skegmar Limited, and by then it was too late. We are as much a victim in this disaster as you yourselves."

"Except you're not three thousand miles from home with no money and no job and the bailiff trying to take your house!" cried Jack.

"We fully sympathise with you, Jack, and we're prepared to keep you on the payroll while we try to sort out the financial chaos left by Frank. But it would only be the local currency part of your salary. We do not have the means to pay you anything in Sterling."

"That's no good to me. I've got a mortgage to pay. I really do feel you're letting us down, Osman."

Mehmet Boga shot a baleful look across the table at Jack and barked:

"Rubbish! What about the way Medmarine has let *us* down? Millions and millions of Lira all vanished into thin air. It will take us years to recover from this disaster, but we are still offering to help you out. How can you say we are letting you down?"

"I exposed Frank Palmer's crooked ways to you months ago," shouted Jack. "If you'd acted then, the tug would be nearly finished by now. Yet again in November things came to a head, and you let him get away with it that time as well. The disappearance of all that money is entirely your own fault. Now the situation is a complete shambles and all you can do is offer us a few crumbs. It's too little, too late. I want the same terms as my original contract."

Incapable any longer of concealing the personal antipathy he felt towards Jack, Mehmet Boga spoke again, even more vociferously:

"If the generous offer we have made you is not to your liking, the solution is obvious. You should return to the UK without further delay."

At this suggestion Mary stood up so quickly that her chair toppled backwards. Her eyes were ablaze with fury as she spoke out:

"This decent, honest man has worked himself into a state of exhaustion for you people, and all you can offer him in return is a choice between a pittance and the door. You're pathetic, all of you! All you can do is sit around and talk, or shuffle silly bits of paper around. What happened to all the support you promised, Osman? It's not as if we asked for much is it? Just a decent place to live and a proper education for our children. We've had no support at the yard either – nothing but words and excuses. And as for that…that…dreadful man Frank Palmer, we've asked for help time and time again, and just ended up with more words, more excuses, more lies. When are you going to start acting like men, and do something about making this thing work?"

In the pregnant silence that followed Jack retrieved Mary's chair and gently eased her back into it. She sat glaring defiantly first at Mehmet Boga then at Osman Toprak; neither of them could meet her gaze as they sat mumchance. Below the table Jack took her hand and squeezed it gently. It was Osman Toprak who finally decided to brave a few words, but he spoke very quietly.

"It isn't that we don't want to help, Mary. We *do*. But the truth is we simply do not have the means. It is not just FNC that has suffered at the hands of Frank Palmer, we have all taken very substantial personal losses, and our reputations within the community have been damaged as well. We too have families to support, and our first responsibility is to them."

He glanced quickly across the table at Muhan Timucin who gave an almost imperceptible nod.

"There is just one other possibility which Muhan bey has mentioned to me," continued Osman Toprak. "I understand there is quite a lot of support for you in the port, and it may be possible for you to obtain the necessary funding through a consortium. If that were the case, we might be able to consider leasing the yard facilities to you, at least until the tug is built."

This did not please Mehmet Boga, who was fully prepared to make his feelings known to all.

"I am completely against the idea," he thundered. "Surely we've all had enough of this nonsense by now. It is just like throwing money into a fire."

"FNC would not be taking any more risk," returned Muhan Timucin, "and the port still needs a tug. We have nothing to lose by trying again."

Yet another long silence ensued. Mehmet Boga wore a petulant expression as he contemplated the horrors of leasing the yard to a consortium of hard-headed businessmen like Ozer Dastan. He had hoped to see the last of Jack Durham at this meeting, but it seemed his torture at the hands of this English madman would never be at an end.

"So there you have it, Jack," said Osman Toprak. "If you can arrange alternative private funding we can explore this one last possibility. Without it there is nothing we can do except postpone the whole project indefinitely."

"I think it's a great idea," declared Jack, triumphantly. His moment had finally come.

"We would have to make one condition," warned Osman Toprak. "You would have to resume work on the tug straight away. By that I mean tomorrow. It has been weeks since anyone has been near the job, and this makes us look really bad."

"Nothing would please me more. We'll start work on the rectifications first thing in the morning."

"Are you happy about all this, Mary?" asked Muhan Timucin.

"If my husband is happy, then so am I," was her simple answer.

The ride back to Famagusta in the Itimat taxi was just as cramped as before, this time with a large family of mainland Turks who ate non-stop throughout the whole journey. One foul smelling package after another was unwrapped and devoured in quick succession, but not until it had first been thrust under Mary's nose in a mute but hospitable attempt to involve her in the feast. As the very sight of all these unidentifiable delicacies turned her stomach, Mary had no difficulty in politely refusing. She did, however, find herself struggling with an impulse to burst into laughter at the sheer absurdity of the life she was leading.

Jack was first into the yard the following morning, and set a pace that surprised the men, who by now had practically given up all hope The arrival of a mobile crane shortly after nine o'clock soon galvanised them into action with the result that by midday work was again in full swing. By the end of the week all the gloom and despondency of those long winter months was behind them, each man eager to play his part in the miraculous resurrection. Weeds disappeared, workshops were tidied up, litter was removed, even the office windows were cleaned, all on the instructions of Adem Usta, intent on making the most of this second chance. Spring was in the air, and in the heart of every member of that willing and contented band of men as they strove to justify Jack's trust in their abilities. Petty differences and internecine quarrels were forgotten as a sense of unity and comradeship returned to daily life. Allah be praised for his love and mercy!

* * * * *

"Monday 19th March

Arrived home – home? – back to Baykal this morning after a lovely, relaxing – if odd in some respects – weekend in Kyrenia. Julia certainly knows how to spoil a person and the girls too.

She picked us up from the Itimat stand Saturday morning and whisked us off – just the four of us – to a cosy little restaurant for lunch in Kyrenia. What a lovely atmosphere the place had! After lunch we went shopping – Julia's idea – she had asked if we had brought our swimming costumes, I said no as it was March and thought the weather wouldn't be warm enough, but she said she has an indoor pool – so we bought new ones.

Back to her house – what a beautiful place, right on top of a cliff with lovely views and the sun making the sea sparkle. We spent the afternoon lazing by the pool, swimming and reading – Susan and Wendy had a great time – Wendy not moaning any more about being unable to swim – she has in fact become quite a good little swimmer. Susan is a very good swimmer too, with excellent style which Julia commented on.

After a light supper Susan and Wendy were shown up to their rooms – one each – which Susan was over the moon about. Beautiful bedrooms and so comfortable. It didn't take long for them to adjust to this new lifestyle and settle in as to the manor born!

Julia opened a bottle of wine and we sat together on her luxurious sofa, chatting while sipping wine, eating the most delicious olives, with cheese and biscuits – I was born for that sort of life. The evening passed so very quickly and before we realised it was gone midnight. Julia showed me to my room, where, as I went in she gave me a kiss on the cheek. Is that a Turkish custom?

On Sunday she asked if I would like to go out or relax for the day by the pool. I opted for the pool much to the delight of Susan and Wendy. The day went by in a flash – again swimming, chatting and reading. I did ask where her husband was this weekend, and she rather casually said he was doing something boaty. I had to smile, knowing what she meant.

After the girls had gone to bed Julia suggested a swim, I agreed but my costume was still rather wet so she said we should go in without costumes. I was rather taken aback by this, but thought – Oh what the ...! – so that's what we did. It actually felt lovely with nothing on, so free. But Julia! Well, I have not seen her in this light before. She was like a young girl. We swam, and I suppose you could call it frolicked around for a while before I became quite chilled. We dressed, resumed our places on the sofa and sipped our wine etc as the night before. At eleven I said I should call it a day so Julia saw me to my room and kissed me on the cheek again before I went to bed. She asked if there was anything I wanted and I said I didn't think so before she shut my door. I lay awake for a while thinking about the day and I felt sort of strange about it!

* * * * * * * *

Rectification work on the tug was well into its second week when Jack received a telephone call from Frank Palmer. There were the usual spurious reassurances about Sterling payments to which Jack listened patiently before steering the conversation back to reality.

"Frank, Ron has been trying to get in touch with you ever since you left. He's been 'phoning your office but there's no reply. Is it all closed down there now?"

"No, of course it isn't. But as I've already told everybody, I'm out of the office most of the time. At the moment I'm down in Yarmouth sorting out the sale of *Surveyor*, and I'll be here for at least another week."

"Well, I'd better tell you the bad news myself, then. I'm afraid *Seahorse* has been seized. She's got about half a dozen writs nailed to the mast."

Frank Palmer made no reply

"Are you still there, Frank?"

"Yes, I'm still here. Go on."

"There's also a warrant out for your arrest."

"That's ridiculous!" cried Frank Palmer. "On what charge?"

"Fraud, I think."

Again there was no reply.

"Frank?"

"Yes, I'm still here. I can't imagine what's gone wrong out there, but I can't possibly get away from the UK at the moment. Tell Ron to sit tight until I can get out there to sort this mess out. He can use my flat if he needs somewhere to stay. What's your situation?"

"How do you mean?" asked Jack, cautiously.

"I mean what's happening at the yard?" He sounded impatient. "Are FNC still paying you?"

"Yes, but only on condition that I start work on the tug again. We've been going through all the rectification work."

"What rectification work?"

"The work carried out by those last two guys you sent out. It was all wrong."

Silence.

"Frank, are you still there?"

"Yes. Look, Jack, here's what I want you to do. Carry on with the tug for the time being. I'm relying on you to keep FNC happy until I can get back out to Cyprus, which won't be until after sale of *Surveyor* has completed. Tell Ron I'll be out as soon as I can, but in the meantime I don't want him contacting Osman Toprak. Have you got all that?"

Feeling there was nothing to be gained by telling Frank Palmer about the cancellation of the Joint Venture agreement, Jack simply said 'yes'.

"I'll call you again on Saturday morning, at about midday your time, so make sure you're at the yard when I call. Just hang in there, Jack. It all depends on you now."

* * * * * * *

It was not just work on the tug that occupied Jack's time. Once again the port was providing a steady flow of minor repair work, some from FNC, others from Ozer Dastan who was eager to promote the yard's reputation under Jack's management. One such job came up when Ozer telephoned late on Monday afternoon asking Jack to go and see Captain Metcalfe of the Motor Vessel *Bracadale*. She was a British ship making an unscheduled call at Famagusta to find out if the port had any repair facilities to help with some boiler trouble. There had been a good deal of excitement when she arrived, for she was by far the largest vessel the harbour had admitted since the troubles, and it was only because she was in ballast that she had managed to squeeze in.

When he received the call Jack set off on foot for the *Bracadale* immediately. She was at the far end berth just inside the harbour entrance, dominating the entire port with her sheer size. Her arrival had been watched by a number of admiring locals who continued to loiter expectantly along the quayside, waiting for the next stage of the entertainment. Amongst all the grubby little coasters with their rusting steelwork and cluttered decks, the *Bracadale* looked immaculate in her newly painted livery and gleaming white superstructure. As he covered the last two hundred meters, Jack had plenty of time to wonder what the yard could possibly have to offer such a magnificent, well maintained ship.

After climbing the long flight of boarding stairs, Jack was met by a smartly dressed deck hand and escorted up to the bridge where Captain Metcalfe and his chief engineer were poring over some blueprints laid out on the chart table. They welcomed their visitor warmly and told him the nature of their problem. It was nothing serious, they explained, but some of the tubes in the domestic hot water boiler had started to leak at an unacceptable rate, and would have to be blanked off. The chief drew a rough sketch of his requirements, and Jack was able to assure him that the devices could be fabricated in the machine shop within twenty-four hours. If the chief used this time to shut down the boiler and make the necessary preparations the whole operation could be wrapped up in two or three days.

By noon next day the blanking devices were ready, and Jack took them down to the *Bracadale* in a pickup truck borrowed from FNC. Whilst they were being fitted Jack was invited to the officers' mess where he sat at a well stocked little bar with Captain Metcalfe and the First Officer drinking American beer. Later on they were joined by the Chief, still in his boiler suit, who declared the job a complete success. Captain Metcalfe produced a large cash box and counted out ten crisp new ten-dollar bills, silently gratified that he was being asked to pay so little. With business out of the way the conversation turned to more sociable matters when the Captain invited Jack and his family to join them for dinner in the officers' mess that evening. It was an invitation that was eagerly accepted.

Mary took immense delight in the occasion from the moment the taxi pulled up alongside the *Bracadale*. A beautiful early spring twilight served to enhance her sense of wonder as she stepped out onto the cobbled quayside and gazed up at the towering mass of the ship's hull. She was even more enchanted on entering the officers' dining saloon to find the table laid fit for a king's banquet and six uniformed Merchant Navy officers all eager to welcome her. Her expectations had been informed by her visits to the *Seahorse*, with hirsute seamen guzzling beer straight from the bottle, all crammed cheek by jowl round a small table, flickering light bulbs and a constant odour of diesel fuel. Now all she could smell was the wax polish on the elegant light oak panelling from which sprouted discreet uplighters. Wine was breathing on the sideboard, and there was not a beard in sight. Captain Metcalfe was the biggest surprise, with his quiet, refined manner putting Mary more in mind of a public school headmaster than the commander of a great ocean going cargo ship.

In the relaxed atmosphere of the mess bar they all sat swapping yarns, but it was definitely Mary who was the centre of attention. Perched up on a bar stool, looking stunning in her best party frock, she was having the time of her life. Jack was seated across the saloon at a corner table talking to the captain, but was watching Mary the whole time out of the corner of his eye. He could see that the younger officers were beginning to compete for her favours, each following time honoured rules of naval hospitality whilst deploying his own particular weapon of charm. The very youthful looking second officer claimed a special ability which would enable him to identify Mary's place of origin just by listening to her speak. His rivals all confirmed that these powers were indeed remarkable, so Mary agreed to go along with the game. After several unsuccessful attempts the experiment was aborted and amidst a great deal of laughter the reason for the young man's failure was subjected to the most rigorous analysis.

Far more assured was the First Officer's offensive. He offered to give Mary a personal guided tour of the ship, taking care to show Jack the courtesy of requesting his permission. Watching his wife leave the saloon with this tall, personable young man in his smart uniform, Jack immediately started to doubt the wisdom of his liberality, but realised how ridiculous a refusal would have been. His disquiet grew steadily with each passing minute, reaching a state bordering on panic before the absconders returned after an absence of half an hour, with the First Officer's uniform jacket draped over Mary's shoulders.

Dinner was a splendid affair, with a succulent joint of roast beef for the main course complemented by steaming tureens of fresh vegetables and good vintage wine, all dispensed by two young stewards with unobtrusive finesse. So good was the apple pie served for dessert that everybody had two helpings, even Mary for whom such indulgence was without precedence. She avowed it was the best meal she had ever eaten, whereupon the captain's cook was summoned to receive her compliments in person. Again Jack was watching her from across the table, marvelling to himself at the way she carried it all off. Seeing her now, who would have thought she was tied to a penniless bankrupt, virtually banished from his homeland to scratch a living on some hostile foreign shore? Tonight she was the belle of the ball; tomorrow she would be back in the daily grind of domestic drudgery facing the ever-present threat of homelessness. She was just as capable in either situation; what a truly amazing woman!

There could be no doubt that Mary was enjoying this enchanted evening in a way that Jack's pedestrian spirit could never truly appreciate. Her bright, quick mind thrived on the speed at which the conversation flashed to and fro across the table. She always appeared to be ahead of the game, with a lambent wit that singed any who approached too close. This was by far the liveliest dinner the mess had enjoyed for many a long sea mile, and the First Officer went so far as to suggest that Mary should be signed up on the spot as entertainments officer. Susan promptly volunteered to join the ship's company as cabin boy, much to the delight of the two young stewards, and Wendy was rated bosun's mate, in charge of floggings. This left only Jack without a job, but as nobody could think of any use for him, it was decided to leave him behind to finish building his tug.

To round off the evening Captain Metcalfe invited his guests to stay and watch a film. The projector and screen were soon set up and seating arranged so that everybody had a good view. It was no co-incidence that of all the films in the ship's library the Captain chose a recently released tongue-in-cheek version of Robin Hood starring Sean Connery. Nothing could have suited the mood of the evening better than this traditionally English tale with all its irreverence for authority and defiant attitude to life's eternal struggle. Mary laughed until the tears rolled down her cheek, and even Jack forgot his troubles long enough to manage the occasional chuckle.

It was nearly midnight by the time they left the ship and took a taxi home, all four silent with their own thoughts of England and home. Wendy asked if they could pay another visit the following day, and was most upset when Mary explained that the ship was sailing early in the morning, and they would never see Captain Metcalfe or his officers again. They all resolved to rise early and watch the departure from the quayside.

"So," said Jack as Mary snuggled up to him in bed, "did he try anything on?"

"It would serve you right if he did," she chided. "Why on earth did you agree to it in the first place?"

"I'd have looked pretty pathetic if I'd refused, wouldn't I?"

"So you let your wife walk off with a complete stranger just to show what a big man you are. You didn't seem the least bit bothered."

"Well I bloody-well was bothered. Especially when you came back wearing his jacket."

"It was chilly on deck and I left my shawl in the bar."

After two or three minutes silence Jack spoke again.

"Anyway, you didn't answer my question."

"What question?"

"You know full well what question. Did he try anything on?"

Mary sat up, switched on her bedside lamp and turned to face him.

"Well if you must know, I'm not really sure. He took me first to the engine room, then to this games room and asked me if I wanted to play table tennis. When I said no he took me to his cabin…"

"His cabin!" exclaimed Jack.

"He didn't actually try anything, but I got the distinct impression that he was sounding me out…"

"The bastard!"

"We just had a drink and a bit of a chat, that's all. I don't really know if he was expecting anything more, but when he got up and closed the cabin door I told him we ought to be getting back. He insisted on visiting the bridge, which was quite interesting, but I started to feel the cold as we were coming back down again, and that's when he gave me his jacket."

She took a sip of water from the glass on her nightstand before adding:

"He had a beautiful cabin. It was huge, with soft lighting and a great big double bed…"

"Come here, you hussy!" growled Jack, pulling her towards him.

* * * * * * * *

Bracadale's departure left the whole family with a strong feeling of homesickness, but life had to go on. Mary started spring-cleaning, redoubling her efforts to rid the kitchen of cockroaches for once and for all. The girls had school to occupy their minds, and were looking forward to the forthcoming children's festival celebrations. Work on the tug made heavy demands on Jack's time; he was at the yard from dawn to dusk every day except Sunday, determined to make up the lost ground as quickly as possible. He kept in close contact with Ozer Dastan who was promoting the tug project assiduously to the business community of Famagusta, with enthusiastic support from Kemal Aydin.

On the other hand, Ron Woods' situation had deteriorated completely. Even more writs against *Seahorse* had arrived, forcing him to the realisation that his investment was now worthless. But if his ship was about to go down, he was determined that it would do so with all guns blazing, accompanied by a fanfare of publicity that would ensure Frank Palmer would never operate another ship as long as he lived. He had already turned down an approach from a political journalist following the disastrous trip to the Lebanon, but now he wanted the full story of Frank Palmer's iniquity to be exposed, including all the details of how the Joint Venture agreement had collapsed with the loss of so much money. Jack was reluctant at first, but eventually yielded to Ron's persuasive argument that it was time the international shipping community was rid of this irresponsible charlatan. How many more lives would be ruined if this insidious cancer were allowed to go unchecked?

Closeted in the untidy, smelly saloon of *Seahorse*, Jack and Ron worked through all the evidence with an eager young journalist. He was ruthlessly competent, with a sharp, percipient mind that homed in on every significant item with unerring accuracy. He had already amassed a huge file of his own by following up all the writs that had been issued, but the manner in which Jack and his family had been treated added a compelling element of human interest to the story. Reports, letters, dishonoured cheques, diary entries, all provided irrefutable proof of Frank Palmer's guilt. The date for publication was fixed for 9th April, a year to the day from Jack's arrival to take up his duties at the yard.

Chapter Twenty-five

Sitting alone in his elegantly appointed office, Ozer Dastan stared down at the front cover of the magazine on the desk before him. A grainy picture of the tug's gaunt steel skeleton took up the whole page, with the single word 'SKANDAL!' emblazoned across the bottom. He sighed as he turned to the article inside, but was interrupted by the insistent jangle of the telephone, a private line that bypassed the switchboard. It was yet another call asking him what he thought about this business down at the shipyard. He knew the two Englishmen concerned, didn't he? Was it true about all the writs? Had the police caught up with this Frank Palmer character yet?

For the eighth time that morning Ozer found himself being pumped for information that he simply did not have. He had tried several times to call Osman Toprak and Mehmet Boga, but their direct lines were constantly engaged, suggesting they were suffering a similar bombardment themselves. Having read the article several times Ozer was still at a complete loss to understand why Jack had gone to the press. The damage inflicted by all this adverse publicity could well prove fatal to the delicate negotiations currently being undertaken with certain wealthy businessmen. Two of them had already called to express their concern; the others had probably not yet had a chance to read the piece.

The six pages of well documented fact indicting both the Government and the Famagusta Navigation Company left no stone unturned. Despite an extra large print run, the magazine was sold out within two days, such was the public interest. Neither Osman Toprak nor Mehmet Boga were actually named in the article, but their association with FNC was sufficiently well known in all the most important circles to ensure their telephones rang non-stop from early morning until well into the evening. In Nicosia, Famagusta and Kyrenia the scandal soon became the main topic of gossip at parties and business lunches, growing a little more lurid with each telling. By the end of the week Frank Palmer's notoriety had spread from Cape Andreas to the enclave of Erenkoy, and the humiliation of the Famagusta Navigation Company was known to all.

It took Jack some time to realise he had made a terrible mistake in joining Ron Woods' quest for revenge. The first to point this out to him was Mary, who knew nothing about the whole affair until he presented her triumphantly with a copy of the magazine. Had she known about the article in advance she would have moved heaven and earth to prevent its publication.

"But it's all in Turkish," she protested, leafing through the pages.

"Well of course it is," returned Jack. "Turkish is the official language in Northern Cyprus," he added, with laboured sarcasm.

"So how do you know what's being said? I know you do speak a bit of Turkish around the yard, but you're not going to tell me that it's good enough to read a magazine article."

"There's all the documentary evidence they've used. That's all in English. I got Faruk to give me the gist of the rest."

"Oh Jack, you idiot!" she cried. "You can't trust Faruk. Don't you understand? Mehmet Boga is his boss! He'll only tell you what he thinks you need to know."

"So what difference does that make?" snarled Jack, his expression hardening to a glare.

"Oh, I give up!" she exclaimed in frustration. "If you can't see the difference then…well I just give up."

"No, come on. I really want to know. You just called me an idiot."

Mary was so angry that she knew she had to remain silent. How on earth could a man who had brains enough to tackle the intricacies of shipbuilding be so lacking in foresight when it came to everyday matters?

"Come on, woman! Why am I an idiot?"

Again she held her tongue. A serious argument was the last thing they needed at that moment.

"Well I shall assume from your silence that you know you're talking rubbish. I'm off for a meeting with Ozer. We'll probably go for something to eat, so you needn't bother about any dinner for me. I might be late getting back, so don't wait up!"

* * * * * * * *

Ozer Dastan was on his own at the Navko offices when Jack arrived, just after six. The agent appeared tense and nervous as he invited Jack to sit down. He pointed at the magazine on the desk before him and said:

"This was not a good idea, Jack. Why did you do such a thing?"

"I should have thought that was obvious," was Jack's prickly reply. "To get Palmer out of the way for once and for all."

"But he has already gone. It was quite unnecessary to do anything more."

"We wanted to make sure."

"Well you've certainly made sure of one thing. You won't be building any tugs in the near future. Not in Cyprus anyway."

Completely taken aback, Jack felt his throat tighten as he croaked his response.

"Why? What's happened now?"

"You've frightened off all the backers. Every one of them has pulled out. And I have to say I feel the same way too."

"But that's absurd. Why should a magazine article make any difference? It's all true, isn't it?"

"If it is true or not doesn't matter. You should never give this sort of information to the press. If you have done it once, you could do it again. You have put me in a very difficult position. I can no longer support you in this matter."

Jack remained silent, rooted where he sat as the realisation of his own stupidity finally penetrated his confused brain. For the sake of some petty vendetta against a completely worthless man, his one chance of redeeming the

253

situation had been ruined. A feeling of panic rose inexorably through his body. He heard the beat of his heart in his ears and a cold sweat broke out across his brow. They would be returning to England not in triumph, but in disgrace. The bungalow would be lost, he would be deep in debt and without a job.

Ozer saw the look of horror that had spread across Jack's face, and wondered what was going through the poor man's mind. Genuine compassion was in the agent's tone as he spoke again.

"Don't take it too hard, Jack. Perhaps it was just one of those things that was never meant to be. The will of Allah affects us all. I may not agree with some of your actions, but I still value your friendship, and Mary's too."

"Thank you, Ozer," replied Jack with a wan smile. "I'm sorry if I've caused you any embarrassment I really am grateful for all you've done."

"What will you do now?"

"Back to England, I suppose."

* * * * * * *

In a daze Jack made his way out of the old city, through the gate, past an emaciated old beggar woman crouched on her haunches and along the dusty road towards Baykal. The panic attack he had suffered in Ozer's office had settled down to a dull, enervating despair that deepened with the advance of twilight. By the time he reached home he was in two minds whether he could face Mary, so he stood for several minutes outside the front door in a stupor of hesitation, fumbling with his latchkey.

When he finally summoned the courage to enter, Mary was in the unlit hallway waiting for him.

"Mary, I'm so sorry," he whispered, eyes brimming. "I really am such a fool."

"I know," she replied simply.

"Can you ever forgive me?"

In the semi-darkness of the hallway Mary heard the pain in his voice and stepped into his waiting arms. He clung to her so desperately that she could feel the rapid pounding of his heart. With some difficulty she pulled away from the embrace and switched on the light.

"Jack, whatever is the matter? You look awful. Has there been an accident?"

"I've ruined everything," he wailed. "The backers have all pulled out."

"Is that all? Thank God for that! I thought for a moment that something serious had happened. Come and sit down in the kitchen. You can tell me all about it while I get you something to eat."

Taking his hand, she led him into the kitchen like a great, imbecilic child; never had she seen him so downcast. His account of the meeting with Ozer Dastan held no surprises; she had expected such an outcome ever since she saw the magazine article. In the short time Jack had been away from the flat that evening, Mary's restless mind had considered at least a dozen likely scenarios, but had always returned to the one they were now facing. It was so simple really. If there was nothing for them in Cyprus they would go back to England, find jobs, pay off the trustee and win back their bungalow.

Fortified by Mary's strength, Jack soon started to recover his spirits as they considered the limited options available to them. One remote possibility persisted in Jack's febrile thinking that might just lead to a last minute salvation. He would write to the Prime Minister offering his services as a consultant direct to the Government. Mary listened patiently to the proposal with a growing sense of its absurdity; the idea was patently impractical, but if it helped to restore her husband's self-esteem it was worth considering for that reason alone. As she watched him writing out the letter on the kitchen table, intent and full of purpose, Mary was struck by how much the man resembled a child.

Baykal, 12th April 1979

Dear Mr Prime Minister

Construction of 24 metre Tug at Famagusta

Following the recent developments concerning the affairs of Mr Frank Palmer's company, Medmarine Ltd I understand from the Famagusta Navigation Co. Ltd that both the Tug building contract and the Joint Venture Agreement are to be cancelled.

As the Engineer in charge of the Tug construction so far I should like to offer my services to your Government in appraising the present situation and for the future completion of the Tug through to launching.

In the meantime the failure of Medmarine Ltd has left me and my family stranded here without money either to buy our passage home to England, or to live on. It is necessary, therefore, to apply to your Government for financial assistance either in the form of passage home for the family and our belongings, or a living allowance whilst we await the outcome of your Government's deliberations on the future of the Tug project and the Famagusta Shipyard.

An early reply would be very much appreciated.

Yours sincerely

Jack Durham"

At Jack's insistence they delivered the letter by hand to the Prime Minister's office in Nicosia, travelling both ways by bus to save money. With their local currency reserve at such a perilously low level, Mary would not listen to talk of taxis.

* * * * * * * *

It was not long before the news that Jack had written direct to the Prime Minister reached the ears of Osman Toprak. The information came straight from the Premier's personal private secretary who telephoned the beleaguered businessman to complain about the four telephone calls the office was receiving each day from Jack, trying desperately to urge a response. The secretary hoped Osman Toprak would appreciate that the Prime Minister could not possibly become embroiled in such a contentious issue, especially after the damning magazine article that had appeared only a few days ago. After apologising profusely, Osman Toprak was obliged to promise that he would deal with the matter immediately. Being rebuked by a civil servant rankled deeply, particularly as he had been unable to defend his position, so he was in no mood for debate when he telephoned Jack with an ultimatum. Either he stopped pestering people for money, or he would be dismissed.

Jack found the threat of dismissal deeply offensive, but it brought him to the realisation that his own position was growing weaker by the day. In a thoroughly despondent mood he sought solace aboard *Seahorse*, where he knew he could find a stiff drink and a sympathetic hearing from Ron Wood. They sat in the wheelhouse drinking cheap Cyprus wine whilst commiserating with each other. It was Ron who came up with the idea of taking revenge.

"Have you still got the key to Palmer's flat?" he asked Jack

"Yes. Why do you ask?"

"And is all that gear still in it? The fridge and the washing machine and the telly I mean."

"As far as I know. Why?"

"I'll tell you for why shipmate. We're going to have it all away."

"What on earth for? You're flying back to England tomorrow, and I don't suppose we'll be far behind you. It wouldn't make any sense."

"We can ship it all back to England."

"How?"

"I've already arranged to ship some stuff back by lorry. There's plenty of room for a bit more. But we'll have to be quick, because the truck's already booked on the ferry. We'll have to do it tonight."

"But what about documentation? We haven't even got any invoices."

"Oh for Christ's sake Jack, you sound just like an old woman. The truck driver is a mate of mine. He's one of the poor bastards that sailed with us to Tripoli. All he needs is a bung, and he's as happy as Larry. Are you up for it or not?"

The idea would have seemed ridiculous to a sober man, but Jack had been matching Ron glass for glass and had drunk far more than he should. As the idea took root in his befuddled brain it seemed to promise not only revenge, but adventure and profit too. It also appealed to a vague, sentimental belief in loyalty to a comrade in adversity. He would just be helping out a friend in need.

"Go on then. Let's do it."

The raid was planned for midnight, a suitably adventurous hour at which most of the other residents in the Efkav block would be in bed asleep. Ron arranged to borrow a small pickup truck to transport their loot from the apartment block to the bonded warehouse where the transport to England was being loaded overnight. Rather than use the stairs they decided to use the tiny lift, despite the fact that it could accommodate only one item at a time. Being slightly the worse for drink they made far more noise than intended, breaking into fits of laughter several times as they shoehorned various bulky items into the narrow lift compartment. It took them nearly two hours to complete the task and drive away with their ill-gotten gains. The haul consisted of a fridge-freezer, a washing machine, a dishwasher, a huge television set, and sundry small items of electrical merchandise. At the warehouse it was all loaded into a container and carefully concealed by the transport's legitimate cargo. All this physical activity had a sobering effect on Jack, who was beginning to doubt the wisdom of their nocturnal foray, so he was most relieved when the container doors were closed and the seal applied. They returned to *Seahorse* with their appetites sharp set, so Ron used the last of the ship's provisions to rustle up two splendidly eclectic omelettes that they ate in the wheelhouse, watching dawn stealing across the silent harbour.

Ron was flying back to England later that same morning. The losses he had sustained as a result of his ill-fated partnership with Frank Palmer would probably take him the rest of his life to recoup, but his irrepressible spirit enabled him to face his disastrous situation with an equanimity possessed by very few men. Throughout the taxi ride to Ercan airport he spoke enthusiastically to Jack about his plans for the future as if the mayhem that had befallen him over the previous six months had been a mere prank. He now appeared to hold no grudge against Frank Palmer whatsoever, taking the view that the man had just been unlucky, and giving him all due respect for making the attempt.

The two men sat drinking beer while they waited for the flight to be announced. Even when Ron disappeared through the departure gate Jack was in no hurry to leave. Through the observation window he watched the passengers straggle out to the waiting aircraft and he was still there to witness the miracle of take off. Not until the plane disappeared into the blue haze did he emerge from his crapulent state of trance and think about going home to Mary.

He found her in the tiny back garden tackling an ants' nest.

"You've seen him off safely then?" she said, looking up with a smile.

"Yep. We're on our own now, my love," replied Jack with a dramatic sigh.

"Quite a send off, eh?" she remarked, sniffing the mixture of stale sweat and alcohol fumes wafting across from her husband as he lowered himself onto a sun lounger.

"Had to be done," he grunted, and fell into a deep sleep of exhaustion.

* * * * * * * *

Mary awoke with a shiver, knowing instinctively that something was wrong. She heard the distinctive squeak of the metal gate in the front garden, and switched on her bedside lamp. The alarm clock showed just past four o'clock.

Now somebody was pounding heavily on the front door.

"What the hell was that?" croaked Jack, sitting up bleary eyed.

The blows on the solid wooden door were renewed with such force that it rattled on its hinges. With an oath, Jack leapt out of bed and pulled on his trousers. Susan and Wendy appeared in the doorway, their bewildered faces pale in the darkness.

"It's alright," said Jack. "Go back to bed. It's probably only Suleyman."

Another thunderous summons stopped short as Jack opened the door and swung it back to reveal two heavily built uniformed police officers.

"Mister Jack Dar-hem?"

"Yes. What's wrong? What is happening?"

"You come with us. Please to get dressed."

"Don't be ridiculous. It's the middle of the night. I'm not going anywhere."

The speed at which the two policemen moved in and seized Jack's arms effectively ended any further protest. They were highly trained, immensely strong, and quite prepared to use whatever degree of force necessary to do the job. Completely lacking any experience in situations of such a physical nature, Jack was as helpless as a child.

"Alright, Alright! I'll go with you. Just give me five minutes to get dressed."

"Two minutes," returned the policeman, letting go of Jack's arm.

In the bedroom Jack talked as he dressed.

"This is probably something to do with *Seahorse*. It's all I can think of."

"Maybe it's something to do with that magazine article," whispered Mary.

"See if you can get hold of Osman Toprak. He'll know what to do," said Jack, speaking loudly enough for the two policemen in the hall to hear.

"I'll try, but it is Sunday. He'll probably be down on his boat."

A gibbous moon, low in the western sky, provided Mary and the two girls with just enough light to watch from the porch as Jack was escorted off and bundled into the back seat of a waiting police car. Wendy even went so far as to wave goodbye as the car sped off into the night. The innocence of this gesture gave Mary a sense of reassurance; she knew Jack well enough to be sure that he would not commit a criminal offence. In all probability the incident would be connected in some way with Frank Palmer's nefarious activities. She would wait until nine o'clock before trying to contact Osman Toprak; Jack would surely have everything straightened out by then.

Back in their snug little beds the girls were both asleep again within five minutes; Mary searched in vain for something to occupy her mind while she waited for Jack's return. The washing and ironing was all done, and she had already cleaned right through the flat on the previous day while Jack was with Ron Wood. She looked in on the sleeping children, and sat for a while looking alternately at their beautiful, innocent faces lit by the dim glow filtering through the glass panel above the door. But despite the peace and tranquillity of the atmosphere her mind was racing through every possible explanation for the events of that morning, trying urgently to find a way of helping Jack in his hour of need. Anger started to encroach on her thoughts as she realised there was nothing she could do but wait in a sort of bovine acquiescence for the outcome. How had they ever come to such a pass?

In a sudden fit of restlessness, Mary opened the French doors and stepped out onto the veranda. She threw back her head and breathed deeply of the morning air to drive away the darkness in her mind. In the distance a cock crowed; another answered with an asthmatic rattle that brought a smile to her lips. The monotonous yapping of a neighbourhood dog was growing more insistent at the approach of dawn, whose pale light now silhouetted the roofline of adjacent houses. In the stillness, Mary's whole being gradually became suffused with a mystical sensation of total self consciousness; it was as if she could actually feel the earth beneath her revolving round its axis, carrying her with it through time and space. The moment passed on as suddenly as it had arrived, leaving Mary shivering in the cold. She started to laugh; a soft, low chuckle of self-deprecation. What in heaven's name was she doing, standing there alone, thousands of miles from home, catching her death of cold as she waited for another day of madness to dawn?

Back inside the flat Mary drew a bath and lay luxuriating in the welcome, comforting warmth, sipping tea. She was calm now, surrounded by her natural watery element, fully in control of her thoughts as she considered the implications of the morning's events. One single fact was emerging with crystal clarity; they were fighting a losing battle to stay in Cyprus. They had simply outstayed their welcome. It was time to go home.

When she had dressed, Mary brought out her small enamelled ditty box from its hiding place in the wardrobe, took out the bundle of Turkish lira notes inside and carefully counted the money. There was sufficient to purchase four flights back to England with enough left over for a week's provisions and the taxi fare to Ercan airport. All that remained was to convince Jack to abandon his foolish belief that any help would be forthcoming from the Government, if indeed he would need much convincing after being carted off by the police in the middle of the night.

At nine o'clock there was still no sign of Jack, so Mary called Osman Toprak's home number. There was no reply. She telephoned the office in Nicosia with the same negative result. Her third call was to the operator to ascertain the number for the Famagusta Police; not until then did she realise that she had no idea where the police station was, or even if Jack had actually been taken there. For all she knew he could even have been taken to police headquarters in Nicosia, there to remain incarcerated until she could summon help.

Mary was in the middle of a fraught conversation with the duty desk sergeant at the Famagusta Police station when she heard a car pull up outside, followed by the slamming of doors. She rushed over to the window and saw Jack shaking hands with a plain-clothes officer and the uniformed police driver; her relief was so intense that she was shaking from head to toe.

When Jack walked into the room he was wearing a sheepish grin, but made no move to embrace her.

"Well, that was interesting," he remarked flippantly.

Mary found his nonchalance irritating, and thought it best to remain silent. She now had a strong sense of foreboding.

"Any chance of a cuppa?" he asked casually.

"Of course," she said, rising to her feet. Her body was no longer shaking, but she longed to be taken into his arms. The longing was in vain. Even though she passed him with deliberate slowness on her way to the kitchen, he made no attempt at any embrace. As the kettle came to the boil Jack came in and sat at the small table, fiddling with his keys.

"I suppose you want me to tell you what it was all about," said Jack, addressing the back of Mary's head.

"It might be a good idea," she replied, turning to face him. "But only if you want to."

"The whole thing was a misunderstanding really. All that electrical equipment in Frank Palmer's flat had been supplied on credit, and the shopkeeper wanted to know when he was going to get paid."

"I don't see what that has to do with you."

"They thought I was still working for Palmer."

"So how come the police were involved?"

"Well, the shopkeeper got wind that the stuff was being shipped back to England in a container, and assumed the worst. He brought the police in to stop the container lorry before it was loaded onto the ferry."

"And did the police find anything in the container?"

"Yes. It was all there."

"And do I want to know how it got there?" asked Mary, handing Jack his cup of tea.

He tried to delay his answer by taking a sip of tea, but succeeded only in burning his mouth.

"It was Ron's idea. He just wanted to get his own back on Palmer and perhaps make a bob or two. How were we to know that the bastard hadn't paid for any of it?"

"I don't think I want to hear any more of this," declared Mary. "You're just unreal!"

So saying, she marched out of the kitchen into the bedroom, slamming the door behind her. Jack rose to follow her, but thought better of it. Within half a minute she was back in the kitchen doorway, beside herself with anger and frustration.

"So what happens next?" she demanded. "Are you going to be charged or anything?"

"No of course not," replied Jack with a nervous laugh. "I explained we were just taking goods in lieu of the money Palmer owed us and they were most sympathetic. Once they knew the full story they were okay about the whole thing, even the guy who supplied the stuff."

"In that case, the sooner we get out of here the better. First thing tomorrow we're going into Famagusta to buy our tickets home."

"But what about the letter to the Prime Minister? We have to wait for his reply."

"For God's sake Jack, when are you going to wake up to reality? Don't you understand? They don't want us here. It's time to go home."

Jack fell silent, his brain searching feverishly for a suggestion that would enable them to play for time. He simply could not accept that they had reached the end of the line. In desperation he seized on the only idea he believed Mary might consider.

"We should try and get FNC to pay for our passage home. We'll go and see Osman Toprak. We'll do it first thing tomorrow."

"It's time to go home Jack. It's over!" she stated firmly.

* * * * * * * *

Osman Toprak met Jack's request for financial assistance almost with derision. News of the Englishman's run in with the police had reached him by telephone first thing in the morning, so he felt fully justified in taking a hard line.

"We have done everything we can, Jack. You cannot expect us to suffer such a large expense in addition to all the money we have already lost in this business. I'm sorry Mary, but that's the way it is. I can only suggest that you apply to the British High Commission for help. They are responsible for repatriating you and your family, not us. "

"And how are we going to do that when they're on the other side of a bloody great wall?" protested Jack.

Osman Toprak scribbled an address on his notepad and handed it to Jack saying:

"Go and see this man. He's in the ministry office just up the road. Use the entrance off Girne Avenue. He can connect you straight through to the British High Commissioner's office. Tell him I sent you and he will do everything he can to help. Come back here when you've finished to let me know how you get on."

The office was easy enough to find; a small annexe smelling of dust and old ledgers, in which a weedy looking clerk in a grubby Fair Isle tank top sat behind a table piled high with bulging manila folders. He listened attentively to Jack's explanation, dialled a number and wordlessly handed over the receiver. Jack found himself speaking to an attaché with a cut glass accent who did not even let him finish making his request before coming back with a refusal.

"Can't be done, old chap. You're on the wrong side of the jolly old green line. You have no legal status in Cyprus because actually you are classed as illegal immigrants. Awfully sorry, but we just can't help. Only thing I can suggest is to try the so called Prime Minister over that side, or even Denktas, if you can get hold of him."

It seemed to come as no surprise to Osman Toprak that the mission failed, but it made no difference to his refusal to offer any assistance from FNC. He handed Jack a typewritten notice of dismissal giving him twenty-four hours to clear his office of any personal belongings. Despite the awkwardness of the situation, the parting handshake was congenial enough, with Osman Toprak even bestowing his usual kiss on Mary's cheek.

On returning to Famagusta they went straight to the travel agent's office to book the flights back to England, using nearly all the cash Mary had saved. Handing over the money provided the necessary catharsis for both of them, releasing an overwhelming sense of relief. They strolled hand in hand across the sun drenched main square in front of the old cathedral to their favourite cafe, and sat outside chatting quietly over their drinks until it was time to collect

Susan and Wendy from school. The girls' excitement on learning that they would soon be going home for good showed clearly enough to confirm Mary's suspicion that they too had recently found life difficult. There had been no complaint from either child; secure in the deep, constant love of their Mother, they had both taken the difficulties they encountered with complete equanimity.

With less than a week to go before their final departure there was much to be done. All the personal belongings which had been shipped out from England were once again packed into tea chests provided by Ozer Dastan, who offered to store them free of charge until he could find a ship's captain willing to take them back to England at no charge. Mary accompanied Jack on their last visit to the Navko offices with the tea chests piled into the back of Avkuran's little pick up. As they entered the reception area, a big, dark, menacing looking seaman emerged from Ozer's office, and brushed rudely past Jack on his way out to the street. Ozer, beckoned them in, and Jack quipped:

"I certainly wouldn't like to bump into him in a dark alley at night! He looked as if he was about to murder somebody."

"You're not far wrong Jack," replied Ozer. "That was the brother of that Kurdish sea captain I told you about – you know – the ship to shore radio? Apparently Frank Palmer was found yesterday floating in the harbour at Antalya with his throat cut. His sins have finally caught up with him."

Mary looked horrified and bit her bottom lip. "Oh, surely not!" she whispered, "who would do such a thing?"

"There would have been a queue," rasped Jack bitterly. "How did they identify the body?"

"Apparently it wasn't easy. He'd been in the water for some time, and had been badly beaten, but his passport was still in his jacket pocket."

"I'm surprised they left that on him," remarked Jack.

"Oh, I don't know," replied Ozer. "I would think it was an execution rather than a robbery. That silly gold medallion he wore was still on the body as well. They obviously wanted to make an example of him."

"I know he was a bit of a rogue," observed Mary, "but he didn't deserve such a dreadful end."

"Well, that's that then," said Jack after a prolonged silence, each with their own thoughts. "I guess it's time to say goodbye."

As a parting gift Ozer presented Mary with a small brooch beautifully worked in tiny, brilliantly coloured mosaic, and made her promise always to remember him with kindness.

Taking leave of everyone at the shipyard was also marked by emotion. Jack and Mary went round together, making sure they missed nobody. Faruk had been instructed to remain with Jack the whole time if he did visit the yard, but when he saw the affection in which the men held the English couple he had the grace to disappear back to his office and leave them all to it. Adem Usta, the yard foreman, seemed to be the most affected; again there were tears in his eyes as he shook Jack's hand for the last time. Hasan Kirmizi, the recalcitrant welder, had prepared a little speech in his capacity as spokesman for the workers. It was his own way of expressing gratitude for all he had learned during the past year, a period of comparative peace in his unrelenting struggle against capitalist exploitation. The two carpenters, with whom Jack had worked so closely in the lofting shed, hid their sadness behind broad, genial smiles and much bobbing of heads. They gave Jack two exquisitely carved wooden dolls, one for each of the girls, finely painted in the bold colours of Cypriot national costume. Only Faruk showed no particular concern, confining his own expression of emotion to a minute, slow nod at the final farewell handshake.

* * * * *

"Monday, 23rd April

Today was National Children's day, which I think is a really lovely idea. The people of Famagusta certainly take it seriously, and the main event is held in the football stadium, with all the local schools involved. Susan and Wendy were there in the thick of it, taking part in a display of marching and movement. Hundreds of Mums and Dads turned up in their Sunday best – there seemed to be more adults watching than children performing. We saw everyone we knew, Kemal, Muhan, Selim, Ozer – each with his wife. They all came over to have a chat and say how sorry they were we are leaving. Lovely, lovely people.

"The weather was perfect for the event – clear blue sky and a gentle sea breeze to keep the temperature just right. I took loads of pictures – I do want my last photographs of Cyprus to be happy ones. We've been through the mill a bit in the last six months, but it has all been such an amazing adventure so I'm glad we did it. How else could we have spent a year on this beautiful island and made so many interesting friends? I know our time here hasn't exactly been a runaway success from a financial point of view, but we're not actually any worse off than we were when we first came out. Not like poor old Ron, and all those other people that have been ruined by Frank Palmer. At least when we get back to England we can both get jobs and start rebuilding our lives again.

Jack has taken it all pretty hard, I'm afraid. He was so utterly convinced that if we hung on for long enough he would get the tug contract. But I'm not sure that the magazine article and getting arrested was the right way to go about impressing the local bigwigs as to his management style! He's still obsessing about Frank Palmer, even after learning of that poor man's death. I'll have to try and persuade him to forget all about it and write the whole thing off to experience. It's the only practical thing to do.

I telephoned Julia – she did sound very upset we were leaving – I invited her to come for a visit when next she is in England, and said I would write to her when we are settled. That cheered her somewhat. She said she'd been on the verge of 'phoning me several times, but thought if she didn't I wouldn't be going – some illogical thought there I suppose, but I understand her meaning. I shall miss her very much, our lunches and chats. Such a warm-hearted, generous friend.

"So there it is! Our last day in Cyprus has been a truly happy one. We're off first thing in the morning, so I had better just go and make sure that all the last minute packing has been done.

"Oh to be in England, now that April's there."

* * * * *

A lowering sky frowned over London's Heathrow airport as the four weary travellers emerged from the terminal building, shivering in the cold, damp air. Leaving Mary and the girls huddled together, Jack went over to the long row of black cabs, approached the vehicle at the head of the rank and tapped on the driver's window.

"Good afternoon, driver. We need to get down to Southampton. How much would that be?"

"Sorry guv. No can do. Too far for me."

Moving on to the next cab, Jack repeated the enquiry with undiminished optimism.

"Good afternoon. We need to get down to Southampton. How much would that be?"

"No chance, mate. I finish in an hour's time."

The driver of the next cab was standing alongside the one behind, talking to his colleague. They both declared their lack of interest in Jack's proposition. By the time he reached cab number six he was asking 'any chance?' rather than 'how much?' The eighth driver did show some interest, but laughed out loud when Jack explained that he had only sixty-six dollars to pay the fare.

It was indeed the truth of the matter. To buy their flight tickets they had used all their Turkish lira plus thirty-four dollars from the *Bracadale* job. Mary's modest reserve of Stirling had been used to pay the excess baggage surcharge at the check-in. They had landed at Heathrow with just sixty-six U.S. Dollars between them.

Jack made for the last cab in the line watched anxiously by Mary and the girls who were now feeling the cold quite severely His progress along the rank had also been watched by the cab's young driver, curious to know what was happening.

"Having trouble, boss?" enquired the driver politely.

"Just a bit," replied Jack, trying to sound unconcerned. "I need to get myself and my family down to Southampton, but none of your colleagues seem to fancy the trip."

"How many of you?"

"Only four, including two kids. There's quite a lot of luggage though."

"Southampton, you say?"

"Yes, just outside. But there is something else. I've only got sixty-six U.S. dollars to pay the fare. Can you do it for that?"

There was a hint of desperation in the tone of Jack's enquiry that further piqued the young cabby's curiosity. A man lands at Heathrow airport with a wife, two children, a load of baggage, and only sixty-six dollars to his name. If it was the truth there must be some story behind it. Anyway, he'd be needing dollars for his trip to New York next month, and Southampton was not really all that far away. With another look at Mary and the two girls pitifully shivering away at the roadside, the cabby made a quick mental calculation and nodded.

"Okay. I'll do it for sixty-six dollars, paid up front. Get in quick before I change my mind!"

By the time they reached the county boundary sign for Hampshire the two children were asleep, both snuggled up to their mother on the back seat. Jack was still bending the cabby's ear with a graphic account of their trials and tribulations. He had just finished recounting the Rotterdam Bank episode, which drew a long, low whistle of wonder from the young driver. But in his own mind he was now convinced that Jack was stark, raving mad. How did this fine looking woman ever get mixed up with such a loser? It could only be love.

"Oh, you ain't heard nothin' yet," Jack was boasting. "Wait till you hear about the trip to Lebanon..."

Mary had been listening up to this point with half her attention, but was growing increasingly troubled by this public airing of their private business. She had tried several times to catch Jack's attention in the hope that an imploring look would induce more caution in what he was saying, but he was oblivious to her silent entreaty. For her own peace of mind she must allow her thoughts to drift off to a more peaceful and agreeable place. As the sound of Jack's voice mercifully receded from her conscious mind Mary looked out of the window at the lush green scenery rolling past, and smiled contentedly.

"I'm glad to be in England, now that April's here," she murmured softly to herself and kissed the forehead of each sleeping child.